WOMAN OF THE YEAR

WOMAN OF THE YEAR

T.B. MARKINSON

Copyright © 2024 T. B. Markinson

Edited by Kelly Hathaway

Cover Design by Miranda MacLeod

This book is copyrighted and licensed for your personal enjoyment only. All rights reserved. No part of this publication may be reproduced, stored in a retrieval system, or transmitted in any forms or by any means without the prior permission of the copyright owner. The moral rights of the authors have been asserted.

This book is a work of fiction. Names, characters, businesses, places, events, and incidents are the product of the authors' imagination or are used fictitiously. Any resemblance to actual persons, living or dead, events, or locales is entirely coincidental.

NOVEMBER

CHAPTER ONE

Mist clung to the grass in a dense blanket of fog as we waited for the small window in the stadium's red brick ticket kiosk to open. Though the sun was barely up, we were far from the only people in line.

"It's freezing out." I tucked my gloveless hands into my pits, shuffling my feet to increase the circulation. I shot an accusing look at my wife. "Why are we here?"

"Yeah. Why are we here?" Our daughter Olivia shared my accusatory look, but her gaze was fixed squarely on me, as if somehow it was my fault we were all here on Thanksgiving morning instead of in bed where we belonged.

"You always set such a great example for the children," Sarah hurled at me before softening her expression as she turned to our oldest. "We're here to cheer for my school's football team."

"On Thanksgiving?" I whined. "What does football have to do with Thanksgiving, anyway?"

"Careful," Sarah cautioned. "There are parts of this country where saying that out loud might be a hanging offense."

"I've never understood it. I mean, what are we grateful for? Head injuries?"

"I think it's more about spending time with family," Sarah said.

"But we could spend time with family without freezing our butts off in a stadium parking lot," I grumbled. Just then, the window in the kiosk slid open with a metallic screech, and the line inched forward. "We're finally moving. Thank God."

"See? I knew you'd get into the spirit of the holiday if you tried," Sarah teased.

As we ordered the tickets, Calvin pretended to throw an invisible football to Fred, who feigned catching it before raising his hands up touchdown style.

"That will be $30," the woman in the booth announced.

"For a high school football game?" My jaw dropped at the exorbitant figure. "Don't we get a discount for you working there?"

"It's the big rivalry game," Sarah explained. "The tickets cost more."

I opened my mouth to object, but a low, warning growl emanated from my wife's throat as she whipped out two twenties and slipped them through the opening. I knew better than to say anything else, even when Sarah told the woman to keep the change.

"I would like it noted," I said through clenched teeth, "that even though I'm also a teacher, I've never dragged any of you to a football game at my school."

Sarah raised an eyebrow. "You teach at an all-women's liberal arts college. They don't have a football team."

"Beside the point," I huffed, annoyed that Sarah had called me out on this technicality so quickly. "It's nine o'clock in the morning on a holiday. We have people coming over today. Shouldn't we be home getting ready?"

"The turkey's already in the oven." Sarah held out the

tickets to the volunteer at the gate as she ushered the children into the stadium ahead of us. "And I'm the one who was up at four to get everything ready."

"That's what I mean," I argued. "I should be at home right now, doing my part to watch the turkey."

"Oh, no." Sarah shook her head so hard her hair whipped around her face. "You're not allowed anywhere near the oven when it's on. Or have you forgotten last time?"

"How was I supposed to know the handle on that pan would melt?"

"It was plastic, Lizzie!" Sarah's exasperation was palpable. "Plastic. In an oven."

Ignoring Sarah's barb, I followed her and the kids into the stadium, my sour mood deepening with every step. I was not a fan of crowds, and high school football games were the epitome of crowded. The bleachers were packed with people, all wearing either blue or red and strictly segregated by team color.

"I don't think I care for how this is set up," I muttered, dodging an overzealous fan waving a foam finger in my face. "It feels as partisan as a political convention."

"It's just a friendly rivalry." Sarah shot me a warning look, clearly tired of my complaining. "You need to relax."

Easy for her to say, I thought. Sarah was always so composed, so in control. I, on the other hand, was a bundle of nerves everywhere I went. But I wasn't going to get any more sympathy, so I sighed and resigned myself to at least try to enjoy the experience.

"Snacks!" Olivia exclaimed, pointing her slender finger toward a concession stand with lines of people three deep.

"Thank God." I smiled as I realized this was the second expression of gratitude I'd made already today. No one could accuse me of not getting into the spirit of the holiday now. "I'll take the kids. You get us seats."

"Don't forget to buy some fifty-fifty raffle tickets," Sarah instructed, looking relieved to be rid of all of us for a few minutes. "I heard the pot last time was four hundred and fifty dollars, and the winner takes half."

"What's half of that?" I wondered aloud. "Two seventy-five?"

"Two twenty-five, and thank you for the reminder that you should never be put in charge of our finances." Sarah waved toodle-oo fingers as she darted into the crowd with two stadium chairs clanging against her back.

"Come on, kids," I said. "Let's get snacks to make this experience bearable."

"Does my school have a football team?" Calvin held up a parka-covered arm and attempted to flex his muscles in a classic body builder pose.

"I don't think so," I answered quickly, pretty sure I knew where this was heading based on the sparkle in his eyes as he watched a group of kids at the edge of the field throwing a football back and forth. "Besides, it's not good for you."

"Why?" Demi reached for my hand, the only one who still liked to do that in a crowd.

"It causes brain damage," I explained. The group ahead of us cleared out, and we made it to the front of the line, where a big picture menu was propped up on an easel. I pointed to the options. "Look, they have hot dogs. Who wants one?"

Ollie, Fred, and Demi each raised one finger, while Calvin held two in the air. I ordered seven. After that, the kids rattled off other items they wanted, including popcorn, M&Ms, donuts, and a bag of potato chips for each.

"We're going to need to win the raffle to pay for the booty," I said with a laugh.

"Booty," Fred shouted through megaphone hands, causing a few heads to turn.

"What do you want to drink?" I asked the group.

"Hot chocolate," they chorused.

At this point, I realized I was in a jam. We'd ordered a lot of food and piping hot drinks. How would we get it all to the seats without spillage? I went into planning mode with the determination of a four-star general plotting a battle.

"Freddie and Calvin, you two carry the popcorn, candy, and donuts to Mommy and then come back here in a jiff to help with the rest. Okay?"

They nodded, zipping off on their mission.

"Here you go. Each of you can carry two hot dogs. Remember they're not both yours." I dispersed these items to Ollie and Demi. "Please take them to the seats and then come back for your drinks."

I then ordered hot tea for me and coffee for Sarah.

"Oh, and some raffle tickets," I added to the woman behind the counter who was adding up our total on a portable calculator.

"Three or ten?" she asked.

"How much are they?" I asked, wondering why one wasn't an option.

"Three for five or ten for ten," she replied.

Now, I was no math genius, but even I recognized this blatant attempt to swindle the people who purchased only three tickets.

"I'll take ten."

"Your total comes to $56," the woman said with a smile.

I choked back a cry of pain as I reached into my wallet and pulled out three twenties. This family excursion had just cost us nearly a hundred bucks. The woman counted out four-dollar bills, very slowly, and gave me a questioning look as she held out my change, casting a hinting glance at a jar labeled Music Booster Donations.

"Keep the change," I muttered, feeling like they'd still managed to swindle me despite my best attempts to outsmart them.

I found Sarah in the front row and sat down next to her, positioning the snacks in my lap after handing her the coffee. "High school football games are a total racket. This morning cost us a hundred bucks."

Sarah said nothing but was glaring at me with her arms crossed.

"What?" I bit into one of my hot dogs. "It was your idea to come. Did you want a hot dog?"

"You have two on your lap."

"They're—" I was going to say mine but corrected to, "Yes. One's yours, obviously. Like you said; I can't be trusted with numbers." Not that it was all that hard to count to two, but my brain spluttered, and that was what I came up with instead of confessing I'd forgotten to get Sarah a hot dog in the first place.

"Or with taking the kids to the concession stand. What were you thinking?" Sarah demanded. "We're having a massive dinner in a few hours. You won't have any room left."

"Have you met me?" I laughed. "I can eat an entire Thanksgiving meal any day of the week and still have room for hot dogs."

"Lizzie." There was warning in Sarah's tone.

"I mean, not the disgusting veggies, of course," I continued on. "Those are a hard no. Everything else, though, I'm your gal. Thyroid problem, remember?" I tapped my neck in the general location of the gland.

"You've been in remission for years. You don't need to eat this much all the time anymore. Your body's getting plenty of nutrition." She wrinkled her nose as she motioned to the hot dog. "Not from that."

"Does that mean you don't want the second one?" I put a protective hand over it and hoped for the best.

"Of course, I don't want one. I just had breakfast, and I'm saving my appetite for dinner." Sarah expelled a gust of warm air from her lungs, forming a cloud between us.

"Suit yourself." I took another bite, devouring it in a single swallow. "I guarantee I will eat every single bite on my plate today."

"I'll hold you to that. In the meantime, you might want to use all that brain food you're eating to start thinking of ways to discourage Calvin from playing football." Sarah pointed to the grass off to the side from where we sat, where Calvin and Fred had joined the group of kids in tossing around the football and making tackles.

"Me? I'm not sure I'm the right woman for the job," I insisted. "You're more persuasive, and I don't want any of our children to suffer brain damage."

"Good point," Sarah said. "Being around you is enough of a bad influence on them."

"Exact—hey!" I nudged her side with an elbow. "I'm going to remember that one."

She laughed, and the anger that had been swimming in her eyes dispersed.

"Calvin!" Demi stood up, her jeans soaked in hot chocolate. The football rocked back and forth on the ground in front of her.

"Uh, sorry." Calvin wore a sheepish expression as he retrieved the ball and handed it back to one of the kids.

"Calvin! Freddie! Both of you sit back down with the family," I instructed with a stern tone. "No more football."

There. I'd laid down the law. Sarah couldn't say I hadn't.

Sarah sighed. "I'll hold your hot dog while you take Demi to change into a clean pair of pants. Remind me when we get home to restock our emergency stash in the car."

"Anyone else get hit?" I looked around Sarah to survey the damage.

"I need the bathroom." Freddie hopped back up from the bench, wiggling in the telltale way that suggested he was serious.

"Me too!" Ollie was on her feet in a flash.

"Calvin?" I asked, but his eyes were glued to the action on the field. Just what the family was missing. A football player.

Hours later, after the game ended in victory, we were pulling into the driveway.

Sarah held onto the headrest, her neck stretched to eyeball all the children in the back of the SUV. "I need all of you to change your clothes and wash your hands and faces before our guests start arriving."

"Which is any minute now," I couldn't help but add.

As if the universe was on my side, my dad and Helen pulled into the driveway behind us.

"How was the game?" Dad asked when he got out of the car.

"Cold," I answered.

"Amazing!" Calvin wore the largest starry-eyed grin I'd ever seen on my son.

I tossed shade at Sarah. If Calvin ended up brain damaged, it was definitely her fault.

"Lizzie, I hope you have an appetite. I brought your favorite. Mac and cheese." Helen grasped a casserole dish between two oven mitts.

"Gimme all the mac and cheese." I patted my belly, suddenly aware that the hot dogs were sitting heavily. That was odd. I could usually polish off a couple of dogs without blinking an eye.

Helen smiled. Sarah rolled her eyes. My belly gurgled, and I found myself wondering how I was going to get through a full meal in just a few minutes time. There was a teensy-weensy chance I'd overdone it at the game.

Inside the house, the smell of turkey overtook my senses. I

wasn't a huge fan of poultry these days, but I'd be able to choke down a slice of dark meat. Right?

My belly gurgled again, letting out a whining noise I wasn't sure I'd ever heard before.

Maddie and Willow were in the kitchen, prepping all the food for serving.

The countertop was heaped with enough side dishes to feed half the state. I remembered my boast about being able to eat everything on my plate, and that wicked glint in my wife's eyes when she'd said she would hold me to it.

The doorbell rang, and I rushed to answer, greeting a group of my students I'd invited to join us because they weren't traveling home for the holiday. "I'm so glad you could make it."

"We made sweet potatoes." Brittany held a glass dish.

"And rolls," Chase proudly proclaimed.

My heart sank just a little as I saw all the food. "Let's get everything into the kitchen. Follow me."

Rose and Troy rocked up before I had a chance to close the door.

"Who wants stuffing?" Troy cradled two containers in his arms. "And pecan pie?"

"I love you." I grinned foolishly, while trying to dig my waistband away from my gut. If I could loosen it a little, surely the weird, uncomfortable feeling would go away just like that. Maybe I needed a different pair of pants.

"Sure looks like a lot of food," Sarah commented as she walked past the counter. I could've sworn there was a hidden message in her words.

It was a lot of food, and not a single thing I didn't happily chow down on when presented with the opportunity. I knew one thing. If Allen and Gabe brought a side dish I liked, I was going to be in some serious trouble.

"Knock, knock." There stood Leonard, Sarah's boss, in the open doorway. "A little birdie told me you love parsnips. It's not a veggie I normally eat, but this seemed like the day to try something new."

"Leonard, you rock." I put my hand up for a fist bump, even as my fighting spirit died a little bit inside me. I was going to have to come clean and admit I had been wrong. There was no way I was going to be able to eat everything our guests had brought.

In the kitchen, I surveyed all the dishes once more. Sarah came in and stood beside me.

"Not one person brought Brussels sprouts," she commented with a pointed look.

"Or glazed carrots, or green bean casserole," I said, my voice trembling slightly. "What's wrong with these people?"

"You hate all that stuff."

"I do, but you love it." My lips twitched into a smile at my quick recovery.

"Hey, Sis, happy Thanksgiving!" Allen set a dish on the counter.

"What is that?" I asked, praying for him to say some obnoxious veggie.

"Mashed potatoes. Gabe hates them, so he brought potato wedges."

"Lizzie loves both of those," Sarah informed him with obvious, cruel glee. "She's looking forward to trying absolutely everything today."

If I'd been hoping she'd forgotten my boast, I was in for serious disappointment.

"Wonderful," I trilled in the fakest voice I could muster even as my hand went to my belly. I'd never experienced being pregnant, but I was pretty sure I could be mistaken for about fourteen weeks along right now. What had I done to myself?

"I think everyone's here," Sarah trilled. "Why don't you rally the adults to get their plates. I'll make yours if you help the kids."

I nodded.

"Why aren't there hot dogs?" Calvin grumbled when I put the smallest piece of turkey on his plate. I pressed my lips together, the thought of hot dogs making me want to puke my guts up.

"We had those earlier," I reminded him. I was amazed he could have forgotten, considering mine were still sitting in my stomach like a lump.

"I want more."

"At the next game," I said without thinking.

He perked right up, ending his complaints. Instantly, I realized my blunder. I wanted to dissuade him from the sport, and instead, I'd just promised he could go again. Sarah was going to kill me, assuming my own reckless concession stand misadventure didn't finish me off first.

Finally, I took my seat, and Sarah slid a plate in front of me. I stared at it in confusion, searching for a serving spoon. "Is this for everyone? I need a plate to put it on."

"No, darling. It's all yours." I knew from the way she said *darling* that her intention was to murder me. "You said you wanted all the foods. I hope you've saved your appetite."

"Thanks, honey." I tucked a napkin into my shirt, determined to meet my fate with dignity. "You're the best."

CHAPTER TWO

"Psssst!" Willow followed up her whispered greeting by stealthily moving into the library. At least that was what I assumed she was trying to do given her hunched shoulders and repeated glances around the room like she expected an assassin to drop from the ceiling and hack her to pieces.

Okay. Maybe she didn't look that scared.

For quite some time now, Sarah has been trying to ween me off letting my mind go to the absolute worst-case scenario. It's an uphill battle, but if Thanksgiving dinner taught me anything, it was that sometimes my wife might be right when it comes to her observations about me. So perhaps it would be better for me to say that Willow was being unusually cautious.

"What's up?" I scooted my laptop to the side to rip my eyes off the essay I was grading. That was another change Sarah had been working on with me, getting me to be more present. Or some woo-woo term like that.

Willow shushed me with a finger to her lips, her eyes bouncing around the room. Willow's serious as a heart attack expression was not her normal look, and frankly, it was freaking me out a little. She was the loosey-goosey type, and I was the *world is ending* one. This played well on the history podcast we recorded together.

We weren't recording, though. Which led me to start wondering if I should be worried about assassins.

"I need your help," she said out of the side of her mouth. Now she was sounding more like a mafia wise-guy than a spy, and I was even more confused than before. Who exactly was the bad guy I should be watching out for?

I reached for a mechanical pencil. It wasn't much, but could I use it to stab someone's eyeball in a pinch? Would it be best to extend the lead? It wasn't *lead, lead* anymore, was it? Had it ever been? Making a product out of pure lead didn't sound wise, but then again, when have corporations ever done the right thing when they could get away with the cheapest?

"I have something only you can see." She tapped the box pressed to her chest.

Now I really had no idea what was going on. But I seriously doubted I would need to stab the box with my pencil, so I set it to the side.

"You know we're the only ones home, right?" I leaned back into my chair, threading my fingers behind my head.

Willow frowned, putting a hand on her hip. "Why didn't you tell me?"

"You didn't give me a chance. What's all this secrecy about?" Again, this wasn't like Willow at all. She was always lecturing me about not being open enough or whatnot.

Huh. It struck me that both Sarah and Willow liked to lecture me about how to be a better person. What did that mean?

"Maddie's Christmas gift arrived." Maddie was a good friend who had moved from Colorado with us, and she was also Willow's girlfriend. The two of them rented the apartment in our basement, which meant I knew a lot more about the ins and outs of their lives than I probably wanted to. Actually, there was no probably about it.

"It's not Christmas yet, is it? I mean... is it close enough to be in trouble?" My body went cold as I closed my eyes, trying to remember today's date. Was this why everyone was instructing me about simple things? Because I was bad at life?

"No, you're safe. It's only the twenty-fourth."

"Of December?" My heart did this thing where it sped up to about quadruple the normal rate and then started flipping in circles inside my chest.

"Of November, silly." Willow tilted her head like she wasn't sure what to make of me. "Yesterday was Thanksgiving, remember?"

"Oh, right." I put my hand on by waistband, which still seemed abnormally tight from gorging myself the day before.

"Look, I had to buy this because I got a good deal, but Maddie is the worst snoop on the planet." Willow cradled the box against her chest like at any moment Maddie would propel from the ceiling and rip it from her grasp.

This was a tidbit I didn't know about Maddie, but I was more focused on how many days I had left to shop for my own gifts. A month? It didn't feel like enough.

"How does this involve me?" I asked when it seemed clear Willow had no intention of making her point any time soon.

"Can you hide Maddie's gift for me in a place she won't look?" This was said with an absurd degree of reverence, like I'd been asked to hide the actual holy grail.

I narrowed my eyes at the plain box. "What is it?"

"It's a stupid smart scale." She blew out a raspberry as she glared at the box.

"Wait, which is it? Stupid or smart?" I scratched my head, trying to puzzle this out. "Are scales supposed to be smart? Like watches and phones?"

"This one is, which is what makes it so stupid. It has a lot of bells and whistles." Willow laughed, seeming more like herself. "I mean, I'm not into scales. People should just be themselves and not worry about their weight. You know what I mean?"

I nodded sagely but couldn't help noticing the bulge of my stomach when I leaned forward in my chair. It didn't used to do that. Now I was curious. How much did I weigh? And what would a smart scale tell me that a dumb scale couldn't? I was dying to know.

Not wanting to be considered vain, I did the only logical thing. I pretended not to care about scales, too.

"Our scale collects dust," I told her. I was 99.67% sure the main reason for that was because neither of us had bothered to change the dead batteries.

"I hope this one gets put away and forgotten, too. It gives way too much information, including a BMI reading, which I object to on principal. Do you know a Belgian mathematician, not a doctor"—she waved an angry finger in the air—"came up with the BMI concept in the early nineteenth century? It doesn't take other factors into consideration, aside from someone's height and weight. How stupid is that? It really is a stupid smart scale." Willow tittered over her joke.

Meanwhile, I was still laser-focused on the abnormally prominent feel of my stomach pressing against my pants. "Uh-huh. What other factors should be considered?"

"Bone density and muscles. A really fit person can technically be obese based on their BMI score. It's idiotic, if you ask me." Willow's face turned scarlet, like it did when we discussed the unfairness of history on our podcast.

"If you feel this passionately about it, why'd you get Maddie the gift?"

"It's what she wanted. I asked five times, and her answer never changed." Willow gave a *what can you do* shrug. "Most women would find it insulting if they got a scale for Christmas. I feel like I'm being set up."

"Sarah would kill me if I got her one." I tried imagining the fire coming from her eyes but had to shut it down to avoid suffering from nightmares the rest of my life. I already had problems sleeping. I didn't need to add more kerosene.

"I would as well." Willow rushed to add, "Not you. I meant I would kill the person who gave it to me."

I nodded, focusing my thoughts on the task at hand. "When you say Maddie is a master snoop, just what am I dealing with? Do I need to take this to Rose's place?"

"Now, there's an idea. We can both go." Willow seemed ready to leave right on the spot.

"We can't right now. That's where everyone is." I tapped my fingers on the desk, still not enjoying the feel of my stomach resting on my waistband. For the majority of my life, I never had to worry about my weight, but things had definitely shifted in the wrong direction in recent years. I couldn't put my finger on when it had tipped into the uh-oh zone, but something told me that line had definitely been breached.

"Why aren't you at Rose's?"

"I sneezed." That didn't have any connection to weight gain, did it?

Willow nodded knowingly. "Rose is still worried about COVID I take it?"

"I don't think she'll ever not be worried about it. Although, I have a lot of essays to grade, so it worked out to my benefit." I remembered the conversation at hand. "I can tuck that scale away under my bed until I get the all clear to go to Rose's. My dad's house is too far away for Christmas morning if you want to keep it hidden until then."

"Rose's place works, but can I ask for one more favor?" Her facial expression could only be described as pained.

"S-shoot," I stuttered, worried what she might come up with next.

Willow made finger guns, adding laser-like sound effects,

making me laugh. Considering the stink I caused when Maddie moved Willow in without consulting either Sarah or me, I couldn't imagine not having Willow around now. In Maddie's defense, it was when the world was shutting down for COVID, and she didn't want to be away from Willow. Willow's always made me laugh, and it all worked out in the end.

"Can you test out the scale?" Willow asked. "I can't bear to stand on it myself, but there's nothing worse than opening a gift on Christmas morning only to discover it's broken."

If I had to be a hundred percent honest, I would admit I had planned to test the scale out once I was alone. I wasn't jazzed about hopping on the scale with a witness, knowing I wasn't exactly in the best shape of my life. But given Willow had serious objections to the scale and a valid reason for someone to try it out, I didn't see a way to say no.

What was the worst that could happen? Confirmation I need to lose weight? I already suspected that much.

Willow added, "You've got a good head on your shoulders and won't let all the stupid numbers weigh on you. Weigh." She broke out into a fit of giggles. "See what I did there?"

"I'll be fine. I'm terrible at numbers. I can't even tell you what BMI stands for."

"Body Mass Index."

"You learn something every day." I could have done without that fact, but too late. It was locked in my head now. Mass. As in massive. I didn't like the sound of it.

"I need scissors to open this," Willow said. "I'll be right back."

I went back to grading, sighing when I came across the use of the word pubic when the student clearly meant public. I highlighted the word on my computer screen, missing the old days when students turned things in on paper. There'd been a satisfactory feeling that came from circling something in red ink. Now I had to squint at the screen, giving myself a headache.

"I'm back!" Willow announced.

"This student wrote pubic instead of public." My eyes scanned the page. "It's here again." I hit control F to do a search. "Eleven times!"

"Sounds like they did a search and replace. That can be dangerous." Willow eased a Styrofoam piece out of the box. "I need to remember how this goes back in. I'll take a photo. That'll help. No way do I want Maddie to think I stepped on this devil machine, giving it tacit approval in any way."

"Didn't they read it before hitting the submit button? Unbelievable." I muttered, still reeling over the typo, missing my red-pen days all the more.

"Aha. We're in business now. You r-ready?" Willow's voice cracked.

I stood. "Yes. I need a distraction before I fail this student for being a moron. Pubic. The paper is littered with pubics. It's not the first time a student has done something like this, but does it hurt to be extra cautious?"

"I just need to enter your height and age into this app on my phone so it can make the calculations."

After giving Willow the necessary details, I kicked off my slippers and pressed my foot on the scale, bringing it to life. As I stepped onto the glass surface, both Willow and I looked down to see the numbers.

Several numbers flickered, and the number 30 appeared in red for a split second before settling on 29.8, the digits now yellow.

"Why did it flash red?" I got off the scale and back on. "It did it again!"

"It doesn't mean anything. That's what I was telling you earlier."

"30 isn't my weight. I know that much. What does it mean?

And why yellow? Caution?" I got back on, the same thing happening. "Look at my heart rate. It's high, isn't it?" I had to narrow my eyes to make out the digits. "What does it say?"

"120," Willow said quietly. "Maybe the scale isn't working. I think the box was dented."

"As much as I hate to admit this, the weight seems in the ballpark." I continued to stare at the numbers on the scale, distress washing over me.

"It doesn't mean anything, Lizzie. Remember, it's a manufactured number by a mathematician. Having a BMI of thirty doesn't mean you're obese."

"Obese?" I screeched. "Thirty means I'm obese? That's why it flashed red?"

"No," Willow insisted. "It's only 29.8."

"Oh great. Point 2 decimals from obese. Hence the yellow, I guess." I pictured myself in five years, having to be wheeled onto a post office scale to get an accurate measurement. "This isn't good. Not good at all."

"It's this scale. I'm sure of it. I got an early Black Friday deal. Now I see why it was on sale." She kicked it with her foot. Not hard enough to cause any damage to either the scale or her foot. "I'm going to return it. Maddie's just going to have to buy her own. I can't contribute to this patriarchal bullshit." Willow put a hand on my shoulder. "I'm so sorry I put you through that. It means nothing. Absolutely nothing. Let it go."

"Yeah, of course." I swallowed. "I better get back to grading."

"Me too. The life of professors." Her laughter was forced.

So was mine.

Once she was out of the office, I couldn't focus on grading.

For one second—no, more like three seconds—I had been obese. A technicality, maybe. But who really knew? Add in the worrisome heart rate, and one thought plagued my mind.

Was I going to die? What if I was about to make Sarah a widow with four young kids before either of us turned forty?

CHAPTER THREE

I couldn't get the smart scale, or my possible impending and tragically premature death, out of my mind. I wished Willow hadn't taken the scale with her because I wanted another chance to prove it had been wrong. Several days later, while preparing to record our podcast, I tried to ask Willow in a breezy way, "Hey. What'd you end up doing with that scale?"

"I wish I could report I hacked it to a million pieces before burning it, but I simply returned the fucker." Willow avoided my eyes.

Was she embarrassed for the f-bomb?

I highly doubted it.

Did she suspect I was still reeling from my weigh-in experience? I was without a doubt. Not that I would share that morsel with her or anyone. No, this struggle was between me and the scale. Human versus machine.

"What are you getting Maddie now?" I didn't really care, but I thought maybe Willow had a good idea I could steal for Sarah's gift. No matter how I tried, I kept coming up empty-handed.

"She's been hinting about a weekend away at a spa. It's something we can do together." Willow plugged her headphones into her mic.

"Those are the best gifts." My mind raced. Time away with Sarah would be a fantastic gift, but I had a hard time kicking another thought out of my head. If Willow got rid of the scale she'd bought, I'd have to buy a new one. I needed to see if the original scale had truly been defective or if I was on the doorstep of obesity, which I knew from several late-night Google sessions would lead to diabetes, heart problems, and liver failure.

Wait. Was that last one caused by alcohol?

Willow's shoulders hunched and worry lines surrounded her eyes.

"Ready to history?" I put my headphones on.

There was relief in Willow's eyes, before holding up her index and pinky finger, rocker style. "History on."

It was our usual way to switch from idle chitchat to recording, to get our heads in the game.

After the recording was done, I stood in the kitchen, waiting for my tea water to heat up, while pursuing scale options on Amazon. I refused to be lured by a cheap deal like Willow had been. I wanted quality and accuracy. If I was going to do it, I wasn't holding back. The one I was leaning toward was almost five hundred dollars. I had to admit it was a ridiculous amount of money to spend on something that in all likelihood was going to piss me off. But, if I'd learned one thing in the past thirty-eight years, it was that I had to be me.

Besides, I really didn't want to wreck Sarah's life by dying young just because I wanted to be miserly.

I added the scale to the cart. Amazon suggested some healthy eating books, and I added those as well. Before I could finalize the purchase, Sarah burst into the kitchen. "There you are. I need you."

"Just in time for a cup of tea." I poured hot water into my mug. "Herbal or black?"

"I don't have time for tea." She rubbed her fingers into her temples.

"What kind of world do we live in when you can't have a cup of tea?" *Keep it lighthearted, Lizzie.* Something about Sarah's mood screamed my evening was about to be ruined.

"The one where I'm the mom of four kids. Are you going to help me or not?" She slung the words at me.

"With what?" I retrieved a mug for Sarah. The woman seriously needed to take a chill pill. Would it be wrong to add a sedative to it?

"The Christmas tree."

"That's your emergency? Decorating the tree is a festive holiday tradition." I bobbed the tea bag in my mug. "There's nothing to stress about. We can have tea while we decorate. Look at me, multitasking."

"You're a true inspiration for modern womanhood."

"I'm sensing sarcasm. Does that mean you don't want a cup?" I started to put the extra mug back into the cupboard.

"Will it hurry you along if I say yes? I want to get this bitch of a project done. I'm late doing it. I'm behind on everything. I hate this time of year."

"At least you have Christmas spirit. That's what really matters." If Sarah was now sensing some sarcasm, she wouldn't be wrong. I poured a second cup of tea, eyeballing the Baileys with longing. "Let's get the tree done."

"You should know by now that parents don't have the luxury of Christmas spirit. We do everything we can to survive. Get with the program." She clapped her hands in a put a step in it motion.

I did a mock salute, feeling lighter on my feet. Maybe I didn't need that fancy scale after all. Witty banter with Sarah was all I needed to power me through life.

The chaos in the living room smashed all the lightness out of me, and I sat in one of the chairs, gaping at the destruction. There were boxes everywhere, heaped with piles of twisted electrical cords that looked like spaghetti noodles gone amuck. "This is going to take all night."

"Just to get the lights on, yes. I need you to untangle this bundle." She dropped a huge tangled mess onto my lap.

"What happened to our organizer thing you raved about a few years ago?" I slanted my head, trying to determine where I should even begin with the jumbled wad she'd given me. If it wouldn't destroy the planet, my first impulse would be to throw them in the trash and buy new ones. Sometimes feeling responsibility for the future of the human race could be such a curse.

"I couldn't find it last year, so this happened."

"At least you accomplished your job. You sucked all the Christmas joy out of me."

"Yes, it's all my fault. Less complaining. More doing." Sarah got to work on sorting out a different wad of lights.

"Will this be a fire hazard?" I tried undoing one of the strings, only resulting with it becoming more entwined. "It can't be good for the wires."

Sarah didn't respond, too focused on the task at hand, and when she was in this mood, it was best to do as told. Even if that meant I wouldn't sleep the rest of the year, too worried about the kinked wires sparking a fire. Of course, we never left them on overnight. Could lights that weren't on still spark?

I was about to ask this question aloud but thought better of it. "Hey, I got some movement here. How are you getting on?"

"Fine."

I looked at her disaster, which miraculously wasn't a disaster anymore. "How'd you do that so fast?"

"Magic. I'm going to start on the outdoor lights."

Now I was getting annoyed, and took an angry slurp of tea.

Sarah wore a knowing smile.

By the time we got the lights on the tree, I was a verifiable Grinch. "Who invented Christmas lights anyway?" I paused for a moment so I could google it on my phone. "Edward Johnson. I have a new enemy, and I hope he suffered a painful death." I feigned spitting on the floor.

"That seems harsh." She wrapped an arm around my shoulders. "It'll look so pretty once the decorating is done. Besides, it makes the kids happy."

"How are you so perky all of a sudden? I'm exhausted."

"Because this has been weighing on me. I usually put the tree up the day after Thanksgiving. I'm behind. Now I won't be after tonight. At least on this front. One step at a time. And I have you to thank for that." She kissed my cheek.

"Now you're flat out lying. I haven't done anything." I hoisted the tangled mess as proof.

"Not true. You're here with me, helping, while the kids are staying at your parent's house. Together. We can do anything together."

"Did you sneak something into your tea, and if so, can I get some?" Had I spiked her tea and couldn't remember?

She laughed.

I had planned on finishing grading the essays by the end of the night, but that wasn't going to happen now. "I'm going to order new Christmas light organizers so we can avoid this disaster next year."

I'd expected Sarah to say not to because she'd find the old organizers, but she only responded with a nod.

My stomach growled.

"Time to make dinner. I think it's your night, isn't it?" She quirked an eyebrow.

Groaning, I consulted my daily tasks, but before I could, my phone buzzed, and the make dinner reminder appeared on my home screen.

"Pizza it is. No. How about Chinese? Not all the kids like it, so they're not missing out."

Sarah rolled her eyes but didn't argue.

Had getting the lights done truly lifted the weight off her shoulders, or was she finally coming around to my ways? The easier way was the best way, I'd always said. Would she let me run out and get new lights instead of trying to unbundle what I was becoming more and more convinced couldn't be salvaged? Because honestly, at this point I was less concerned with the future of the planet than my own sanity.

Except that would involve leaving the house and dealing with people. One of my least favorite things these days. Besides, this was a puzzle of sorts, and I liked puzzles.

I would not be defeated.

CHAPTER FOUR

A WEEK LATER, I WAS PUSHING A CART AT WALMART, while Sarah tossed items into it with almost reckless abandon. The kids were at home with Eloise, our au pair. "What do you think of this sweater for my holiday party?" She held what had to be one of the ugliest sweaters I'd seen. It had two pink flamingos sipping through red and white striped straws from a Frosty the Snowman mug. That part was okay. In fact, the more I studied it, the more I liked the sweater. The flamingos wore striped tights and Santa boots.

"I wish it wasn't so busy," I said even though the design was growing on me. "Why can't it just be the flamingos and not the star patterns along the arms?"

"But you'll wear it?" Sarah held it up to me, pinning it to my shoulders to check the fit.

"Me? Why?"

"My holiday party."

"We're having a party?" The last holiday party Sarah threw, my brother got arrested. Not because of the party itself, mind you. But the cops still came into my home to arrest Peter, and ever since then, the thought of another Christmas party made my heart race like I'd snorted all the caffeine in the world.

"No. It's a work party." She raised an admonishing finger as my lips parted. "Before you say you can't make it, you're going. Leonard will be there. You get along with him."

"Because he considers hot dogs a proper meal. Who can hate a man like that?"

"It's odd how differently we think about food." Sarah tossed the sweater into the cart. "Now we need ones for the kids."

"Are they going to the party?" If they were, I'd fake the stomach flu. Even if I'd have to eat an entire bar of Ex-lax to give me diarrhea, it was a sacrifice I was willing to make. Taking the kids to grown-up parties was the definition of hell, if hell was filled with tarantulas, rattlesnakes, and piranhas.

"For their school parties," Sarah clarified to my immense relief. "Don't forget their holiday concert. Calvin and Demi's class is up first, then Fred and Ollie's."

"How many songs does each class do? One?" *Please, oh mighty Christmas Spirit, let that be the case.*

"One? Hardly. They do several, I'm sure."

"But, like, four songs tops, right?" I bobbed my head in agreement with my reasonable suggestion. "I can handle that. Four songs, boom, boom, boom, boom, and then we're out of there. I can manage a fifteen-minute appearance, I guess."

"Lizzie!" She bopped the back of my head. "We have to stay for the entire performance, you numbskull."

"Why? We only have kids in two grades. Why do we have to suffer through an entire night of kids singing off-pitch?" *Some of us have lives*, I added silently, knowing this part was probably pushing it in terms of Sarah deciding whether or not to punish me in some way for my attitude. But I stood by the sentiment. Since summer, I'd been meaning to put a puzzle together while listening to an audiobook, and I still hadn't managed it. Now was the time. Or not now, but whenever this holiday concert was taking place. That would be the perfect time.

"How would you feel if the parents of the older kids didn't show up until it was their kid's time?" Sarah prodded.

"Like we're kindred spirits and I'd like to buy them a drink."

She threw her hands in the air. "You're impossible. You know that?"

"You love me, so what does that say about you?" I stuck out my tongue.

She ignored my childish behavior, like she normally did. "You're going to sit your butt in the chair the entire time, and you're going to like it."

"You can't force me to like something. It's physically impossible."

Sarah pressed her fingertips to her forehead and took a deep breath. "Fine. Just don't look miserable, or you will break the children's hearts."

"You know I don't have a poker face. This is why I should duck out." I pressed my palms together, trying to put on the best *throw me a bone* expression.

"Not happening." Sarah held up a Darth Vader Christmas sweater that read: *I find your lack of holiday cheer disturbing*.

"I don't think it'll fit." I pouted.

"It's for the boys." Either I was imagining things or Sarah's tone was growing more exasperated by the minute. "What do you think?"

"They'll love it, but it sucks for me. I wish they made kid clothes for adults."

"You're literally wearing a Snoopy shirt." She held up a Nightmare Before Christmas sweater with Sally on it. "The girls?"

"Yes, but I'd like to lodge a complaint." I jabbed a finger in the air. "I have to wear silly flamingos while the kids get the fun ones."

"Kids should have fun." Sarah tossed the sweaters into the cart.

"It sucks being an adult."

"At least you're being a brave little toaster about life." Sarah's smile oozed sarcasm.

I wasn't going to let her get to me. "You know I tried finding a T-shirt with the brave toaster on it in adult size and failed."

Sarah started to speak, stopped, and flapped her lips a few times in vain. Finally, she managed to say, "Let's go to the toy section. After that, we can get the baking stuff before heading out."

"We've been here for over an hour." I shifted my weight from my left to right leg, not alleviating the pain in either foot. My mind flew once again to that flashing red 30 on Willow's stupid smart scale. Was that why my feet always seemed to hurt lately?

"Buck up. We're halfway done."

I glanced at the cart, which was more than half full. "Should I get another cart?"

"Probably. I'll be in the LEGO aisle."

It took me way longer than I thought it would to track down an empty cart in the parking lot. Everyone on the planet seemed to be shopping. I trekked back through the store to the toy section, stopping at the jigsaw puzzles. Spying one I wanted to add to my collection, I placed it in the cart.

"There you are. I was getting worried." Sarah held a Star Wars LEGO set. "Do you think Freddie can manage one that's intended for a nine-year-old?"

"Absolutely. Heck, he could probably do one that's a hundred times harder."

Sarah started to put it in my cart, but her eyes spotted the puzzle box I'd intended to hide with some more stuff before she could see it. She let out a sigh. "Another puzzle?"

"I like them." I clenched my teeth, determined to get the puzzle or die trying.

"You like buying them, but when's the last time you put one together?"

"This puzzle is going to change that." I held up the box. "It has an old red truck with a Christmas tree in the bed, parked in front of a stone cottage that's covered in lights and snow. You can't get more Christmassy than that. I thought Fred and I could work on it this season." Despite my clever invocation of parent-kid bonding, she didn't seem sold, so I kicked it into a higher gear. "Look. It has a red door with a wreath." I circled a finger in front of the box. "It's Christmas adorable. I need to surround myself with cuteness to survive the holidays this year."

"Why is this year different than others?"

"They seem to get harder and harder."

Her head bob confirmed she was on the same page. About things getting harder, that was. Not the puzzle. But then her firm expression faltered, and she let out a slow sigh. "You can get it as long as you don't utter one complaint at the holiday concert."

"Not a single one?" My shoulders sagged. "You're asking the impossible."

"No, I'm not."

"This doesn't seem fair. Complaining is ingrained in my personality. It's like you want to hack off a piece of my soul."

"Complain all you want when you're by yourself. Like during your quiet times hiding in our closet."

"I don't do that anymore."

"Maybe you should start again. Do we have a deal?" She stared pointedly at the puzzle.

"I don't think you understand. I need all the help I can get to survive. Complaining helps me do that." I pressed my hands over my heart. "I don't know who I am if I don't complain. It's my identity."

"I don't think *you* understand. I also need all the help I can get, and having to cover for your outbursts in public is the last thing I need this season." She started to put the puzzle on a random shelf, not where it belonged, which rubbed me a million wrong ways at once.

"What's to stop me from coming back on my own and buying it?"

"It would be wrong, and I'd return all of your Christmas gifts."

"The punishment seems to be increasing." I swallowed.

"It does. If I was you, I'd zip it. Now and at the concert."

I mimed zipping my lips, and when her back was turned, I added a Baby Yoda LEGO set to my cart to replace the puzzle, covering it with a gift for Ollie. If I wasn't going to be allowed to complain even once during the concert, I would need a much bigger reward than some silly old puzzle. I needed a prize that was worth the pain.

LATER THAT EVENING, SARAH CAME INTO THE library with an Amazon box in her hands. "Do you know what's in this?"

I glanced up from my laptop. "Is this a new guessing game for the holidays?"

"I don't think I ordered it, but it has my name on it. Did you buy a gift, but forget to change the shipping name?"

"A gift?" I scratched the top of my head. It was only early December. Buying a gift this early definitely didn't sound like me. "I don't even know what you want for Christmas this year."

"This isn't a gift for me, then? It's safe to open?"

"I don't think it's a gift." I searched my memory bank, coming up empty.

Sarah took the letter opener from my desk, sliced the tape on the box, and ripped open the flaps. Her face squished into the deepest frown I'd ever seen. "It's a scale."

"What?" I blinked, that word clawing a memory to life. *Oh, shit.* That scale was supposed to be a secret I took to my grave.

"Did you order a scale for me?" Sarah accused.

"No."

"Did you order it for yourself?"

This answer was trickier because I didn't want to confess about the BMI reading on Willow's scale. Not to the woman I wanted to find me attractive. If I said the word obese, I'd probably never have sex again. Besides, Willow's scale was also a secret; therefore, I was not at liberty to discuss any of it.

"There are healthy eating books in here as well." Sarah pulled out the plastic bubbles, clearly on the hunt for more healthy-lifestyle contraband.

"Silly me. Of course, that's right. I did order the scale. As a… gift. The books are for… research. For the podcast." That last bit was weak, but it was all I could come up with.

"You ordered the scale as a gift for whom? If you say me…" Her eyes landed on the letter opener, a piece of the packaging tape stuck to it. I was pretty sure the implication was that letter opener would soon find itself lodged in an uncomfortable and possibly fatal part of my anatomy.

"Dad."

"You bought your father a scale for Christmas? Why would you do such a thing?"

I pushed up the sleeves on my sweater. "What's the heat set on? I'm sweltering."

"Why would you get anyone a scale for Christmas?"

"I thought he might like it. What else do you get a man who has everything?" Sure, that was a pathetic reason, but my brain wasn't kicking in. Anyway, I deserved some credit. It was marginally better than trying to claim I bought healthy eating books for a history podcast.

"He likes fun slippers. I would go that route."

"Fun slippers. Got it. I'll return that." I motioned for her to set the scale down on my desk.

She held onto it. "You didn't even remember buying it. I think I should send it back to make sure it happens."

"I'll put a reminder in my phone." I picked up my device to do that, not that I actually intended to send the scale back. I hadn't gone through the trouble of ordering it to let it slip through my fingers without discovering the truth of my BMI measurement. Not this time.

Sarah hesitated before leaving the box with me. "I think from now on, you should run your gift ideas past me. A scale for your father? Really, Lizzie. It's like you don't even try." She left the room, shaking her head the entire time.

I stared at the scale like it might be an ancient talisman or a fortune teller. Would this one be smart enough to have better news for me?

Not that I could strip down right there in my office to weigh myself naked. What if someone barged in? Also, Sarah was on high alert right now. She had a way of sniffing out things, so if I tried to smuggle the scale upstairs, she'd know. She always knew. Okay, not always since I still got myself into jams, but she sussed things out on the regular, keeping me on my toes.

I needed a foolproof plan, but my mind went blank.

What was the best way to get everyone out of the house so I could find out the truth about my health?

I could suggest a movie. But how could I hang back, expecting Sarah to manage all the kids on her own? That seemed unwise.

I'd just have to wait until everyone fell asleep, which would be six long hours from now. I tried turning my focus back on work but failed.

Getting up, I found Fred in the front room. "Freddie, wanna help me put a puzzle together?"

He nodded vigorously.

"Me too!" Calvin popped off his beanbag like a rocket.

"The more the merrier. Girls?" I glanced at Demi and Olivia.

"Do we get hot chocolate?" Ollie asked.

"Puzzles aren't punishment necessitating a treat." Then again, hot chocolate sounded pretty darn good. I needed to pivot fast. "But hot chocolate is a Petrie family Christmas tradition. So, yes."

"Since when?" Sarah jutted out a hip.

Where had she come from? This was even more proof she knew when I was up to something I shouldn't be. "Hi, I didn't see you there. And, since when is hot chocolate not a Christmas tradition?"

"It's dinnertime."

"Great!" I patted my belly, regretting it immediately. It felt weirdly soft and squishy, like dough. When had that happened? "After dinner, I'll make hot chocolates for dessert, and then the kids and I can start on the puzzle. And you said I never put them together." I waggled a finger at her. "You should never doubt me."

"Is that right?" Her expression was undecipherable. "Kids—that includes you, Lizzie—wash your hands."

"What's for dinner?" Calvin cocked his head to the side, making it clear the answer could possibly be a deal-breaker.

"Lasagna."

"I love it when it's your night to cook." Calvin zipped off toward the downstairs bathroom.

"I thought kids liked pizza," I asked, bewildered.

Sarah didn't answer, heading back into the kitchen but

stopping short to announce, "I'll be up late tonight grading essays."

That was twice in under five minutes Sarah had thrown a wrench into my plans.

CHAPTER FIVE

"That's mine!" Calvin swatted Demi's hand from the mug in question.

"The empty one is yours," Demi corrected our youngest family member.

"No, it's not. This is." Calvin tried to wrestle the mug from Demi's hands, resulting with spilling it all over the puzzle pieces. "Look what you made me do!"

"Calvin, go get paper towels," I said in my calmest voice as Freddie scooped pieces out of harm's way.

"It's Demi's fault!" Calvin tucked his hands into his armpits, scooting down in the chair.

"Go. Now!" I jabbed my finger toward the kitchen.

Grumbling, Calvin stormed off.

"It was mine." Demi's bottom lip trembled.

"I know," I soothed. "Would you like the rest of mine?"

"Then you won't have any left."

What could I say? Demi was the sweetest kid. "It's fine. I'm not that big a fan of hot chocolate."

"Liar," Demi giggled, but she did take my mug.

I should have made Calvin make a new one for Demi, but I

wasn't in the mood for that battle. There had been a time when I would mentally critique the parenting skills of strangers in public. Then I had four kids and learned the hard way that most parents were simply trying to make it from one day to the next. Style points didn't matter. Survival did.

"There!" Calvin tossed the paper towel roll on the table.

"How's the puzzle going?" Sarah strolled in, stretching her arms over her head, exposing a small patch of her creamy skin on a belly that most certainly did not resemble dough in any way.

"Swimmingly. Literally." I ripped off a section of paper towel and handed it to Calvin. "Clean, and if you utter one more complaint, you'll never have hot chocolate again in your life." I seemed to have overcorrected on my parenting skills, but Sarah didn't admonish me.

Calvin opted not to risk his chances.

Demi and Freddie helped with the cleanup while Olivia got up for quiet time in her beanbag. I couldn't blame her.

When most of the damage had been repaired, Sarah announced, "Time to get ready for bed, kiddos."

I yawned.

"You, too." Sarah winked at me, making me go all gooey inside even after all these years.

After getting the kids tucked in, I climbed into bed. "I think we should get hot chocolate mugs that have the kids' names on them."

"Way ahead of you. They're ordered and will be one of their gifts."

"When did you have time to do that since the puzzle incident?" I yawned again.

"I did it days ago. Mom mentioned a scuffle over hot chocolate at her house last week."

"Was it Calvin?"

"Olivia."

"Those two are in a competition to see which one will make it to adulthood." I snuggled a little closer. "I thought you were staying up late to grade."

"I should, but I'm fading." Sarah rested her head on my chest. "We need to limit the amount of sugar the kids are consuming. We all need to get better." She draped an arm over my stomach, and I was immediately aware of how big it felt. Did it feel that way to her, too?

"Is this your way of telling me to go on a diet?" I asked, my stomach muscles contracting in an effort to firm things up.

Her head popped up. "Do you think I'm like that?"

"How do I know you didn't buy the scale for me?" I have no idea why I said this because I did know she didn't, but that didn't stop me from stupidly tossing out the accusation.

Sarah's face reddened with anger. "I thought you said you bought it for your father."

"I did… it's… I'm tired. You're confusing me." Why was it that whenever I made rash accusations, they never went well for me?

"Right. Go with that." Sarah rolled over onto her side, but I could tell from her breathing she wasn't close to falling asleep now.

Sadly, I was, so my date with my new smart scale would have to wait until another day.

DECEMBER

CHAPTER SIX

IN THE DIMLY LIT CLOSET, I GAPED AT THE NUMBER displayed in yellow on the scale beneath my feet. That couldn't be right. I stepped off, waited for the screen to clear, tapped it back to life, and then stepped on the stupid thing again. It was the same number.

29.8.

Only two-tenths of a point away from obese. I'd only recently learned about BMI, but I loathed the entire concept. Ignorance could truly be bliss.

As it turned out, Willow's scale hadn't been defective after all. Worse, my new fancy one not only provided me with my weight and BMI, but it went deeper. According to the scale, through some magical calculations, I had a metabolic age of forty-five years old.

I was only thirty-eight! Sure, during the summer I had thought I was turning forty, but as Sarah pointed out, I had two years of my thirties left. I was finally settling into that fact, and now this stupid scale was trying to blast me to my mid-forties.

This meant that the weight I'd been adding wasn't only

impacting the number on the scale, but my life expectancy and quality of life, too.

Well, fuck.

"Lizzie, we're going to be late. What are you doing in there?"

My heartrate took off like a rocket at the sound of my wife's voice. Even so, I continued to stare at the scale, unable to move. 28.6. This was bad.

How had this happened? For the majority of my life, I was super skinny because of my thyroid. In fact, it tried to kill me, and I had to take meds for years to stabilize it. All the while losing weight to the point I looked like a skeleton with skin.

Now this number was staring me in the face. My mind spun.

The walk-in closet door rattled but didn't open. Probably because I had it blocked with a chair.

"Lizzie! Open the door. It's stuck."

I shoved the scale under my suitcase below the rack of clothes and then opened the door. "That's weird. How'd it get stuck?"

"You're n-naked." Sarah spluttered.

"Correction. I'm getting dressed." Why had she spluttered? Was she disgusted by my almost obese body?

"We have to leave in three minutes for the kids' holiday performance, and you're standing in the middle of our closet buck naked. What the fuck is wrong with you?"

"I'm old."

According to the scale, who would henceforth be called Meanie Pants (MP for short), I was forty-five. Seven years closer to my death. Was that how it worked?

"If you want to get any older, you'll stop standing there like an idiot. Put your clothes on. Now!" Sarah placed a hand on each hip and stared me down. I'd seen her do this when prompting Calvin to get dressed for school. Now I understood why it was so darn effective.

"I think I need to make some changes in life." I yanked on my underwear.

"Are you taking requests? I have some suggestions where you can start." Sarah checked her watch. "I'm going to load everyone in the car. If you're not downstairs, ready to go, in two minutes, I'm going to skin you alive. I know you're not excited about tonight, but the kids are. This isn't about you, Lizzie. Jesus Fucking Christ." Sarah stormed out of the closet.

In retrospect, the evening of the school holiday music concert probably wasn't the best time for me to strip down and weigh myself. In my defense, I kept forgetting to do it, until Sarah told me my sweatpants and hoodie wouldn't cut it for the night. Truth be told—and I would never admit this aloud—I'd forgotten about the performance, too, just like the scale. Probably because I was actually a forty-five-year-old in a thirty-eight-year-old's body.

Or was it the other way around? Math was hard, and this scale was making things even harder for me to grasp.

Shoving my arms through my flamingo Christmas sweater, I flew down the stairs, holding my socks and shoes. Everyone was in the car, with Sarah in the driver's seat. I sprinted across the dusting of snow that coated our lawn, the sting on the bottom of my feet shocking me fully awake.

"Why do I have to wear shoes if Mom doesn't?" Calvin asked from the back row of the car.

"She does." Sarah adjusted the rearview mirror, presumably to give Calvin the death stare before turning it fully on me. The heat from it had me wishing I was standing naked in a snowbank.

"I'm putting my shoes on now, buddy," I told Calvin, though the assurance was mostly for Sarah. As much as I was not looking forward to the concert, I was looking even less forward to the lecture I would receive if I caused any more trouble. "Everyone looks nice. Let's get our jingle on!"

There was a cheer from the kids and an anguished sigh from Sarah. Whether in response to the noise in the back or my dumb statement, I wasn't sure. Frankly, I was on the verge of some serious sighing myself as I contemplated the upcoming season. I still hadn't figured out what to get my wife for Christmas, and at the moment, I was considering an Alaskan cruise all by herself. Maybe with her mom who used to cruise with her friends, until Rose fell in love with Troy, the son of one of the cruisers. It tore the group apart, sadly.

I was about to start fishing around to see if the cruise idea would be received in the right way when Sarah announced, "I need you to wear black on Friday."

"For punishment?" I eased a sock onto my foot, not liking the way my stomach and the tight space made the task more difficult.

"We're going to a funeral."

"Mine?"

Sarah actually laughed, which didn't really answer my question.

Before she could respond with more details, Demi asked a question about the evening, but I wasn't paying attention.

Had Sarah spied the scale and put two and two together? Did she know I had lied about who I'd purchased it for and about returning it? I couldn't remember the account I'd purchased it from. Mine or the joint account. I always screwed that up, and you'd think I'd learn the lesson after so many missteps. Was that another warning sign? Was my weight gain also impacting my memory? It seemed like I used to be better at intrigue. Questions kept infiltrating my mind, making things even more muddled.

CHAPTER SEVEN

"Remember, no complaining," Sarah whispered in my ear, nibbling on the lobe.

I was 93.25 percent certain she'd used her breathy voice and nip on my lobe as a distraction technique to decrease the odds of my whining. I'm ashamed to admit it worked.

Also, it was adorable to see my kids in their respective classes. Even Calvin did his best, although, he shoved the kid next to him with his shoulder. In Cal's defense, the kid seemed to be falling asleep on his feet, and our son may have saved the kid the embarrassment and possible bodily injury of falling off the riser and faceplanting in front of an audience of hundreds.

I admired the child's ability to tune out to the point of practically falling asleep. The one notion I came to the show with was the singing would be hard on my ears. And I wasn't wrong. Twenty kids singing off-key and not in time to the music, or even each other, was an assault on my auditory senses.

The school only had five grades, plus kindergarten. When we reached the fifth graders, I was able to see the proverbial light at the end of the tunnel. Two more songs, maybe three, and I was coasting to a new puzzle and Baby Yoda LEGO set.

How hard could it be?

To help pass the time, I started to count backward from one thousand, but whenever I got to the 800s, I got confused and had to start over. No worries. It was still working.

923, 922, 921…

The sound of clapping interrupted my task, but I didn't mind. In fact, I wanted to leap out of my seat and applaud like my life depended on it. Also, standing would make it easier to make a fast getaway. There were so many people in a tight space, and I wasn't exactly the popular parent. Sarah tried to get me to interact more with them, but that hadn't turned out all that well. Hopefully, Sarah learned an important lesson.

Before I could make a mad dash for the door, the principal stood at the mic, tapping it in that way that made it clear we were about to get a speech. Who knew there would be closing remarks at a kid's concert? But whatever. I was that much closer to freedom. As long as the principal didn't plan to sing, I didn't mind.

"Now we'd like to welcome Mrs. Wilson's fourth grade violinists," the principal said.

My insides went cold.

"Vio-what?" I asked Sarah as quietly as possible.

"You'll see." Her smile could only be described as wicked.

"You knew about this?" I pressed in a hushed voice.

"It's in the program."

"What program?" I fumbled around, seeking some sort of folded paper even though I couldn't remember being handed one.

"It was emailed," Sarah said, picking up on my confusion. "They're trying to go paper free."

"I miss Covid times," I said with a sigh.

"Careful, Lizzie. You're bordering on complaining." Sarah moved a finger back and forth, admonishing me.

"I'm only stating a fact," I argued. "I didn't think there was anything good about Covid. Now there's one thing I miss. If you ask me, I'm being optimistic. I feel like I didn't appreciate it enough."

Sarah glared at me until I turned my head to face the music. Literally.

Now on the stage sat fifteen violinists. The odds of more than one or two of the children being decent at this age were bad enough, but with fifteen, I was doomed.

The music teacher raised her hands like a conductor. The first strokes of bows on strings could only be described as the death of a thousand cats. That reminded me. Did I clean Hank's litter box? The violinists hit a particularly difficult part, at least I assumed, given how much worse they sounded. Did the music teacher have tenure? Was that why she was still able to call herself that?

Would sticking my fingers into my ears count as complaining? It was more about self-preservation. From the amount of shifting in seats, I wasn't the only one experiencing auditory pain. But a quick scan of the crowd told me that none of the other adults were covering their ears.

Mother ducker.

Closing my eyes, which hopefully looked like I was sinking into the experience, I restarted the countdown trick. 999, 998, 997...

Again, there was clapping, but I wasn't going to be fooled this time. Fool me once, shame on me. Fool me twice, I wished you a fiery and painful death.

"Are you sleeping?" Sarah shook my arm.

"I'm enjoying the festivities. I concentrate better with my eyes closed."

"It's over. I can't believe you. You're worse than that little boy. He's five. What's your excuse?"

From the fire in her eyes, I knew playing the autistic card wasn't going to cut it. "Seriously, I was focusing on making the experience more enjoyable, and I kept losing count."

"Losing count of what?"

"Uh, the names of the reindeer and Santa's helpers," I ad-libbed, knowing that if I admitted I had been counting backward from one thousand to endure this hellish evening, I would never hear the end of it.

The expression on Sarah's face suggested she didn't need to know all the details in order to be disappointed in my behavior. "It's refreshment time."

"What?" I pictured another rousing chorus before serving red punch or whatever they offered in an elementary school.

"There's a bake sale."

I jumped out of my seat. "There better be cupcakes. Otherwise, this night has been a complete wash."

A woman in her thirties whirled around, tutting at me.

"I like to raise money for the children," I explained.

Sarah bit down on her bottom lip, all the blood drained out of it.

I had a feeling that comment was going to cost me roughly a five-hundred-dollar donation to redeem myself. Not to the woman, but to Sarah.

CHAPTER EIGHT

"The violins get me every time. Like why?" I could only see Leonard's back, but he was voicing a sentiment that reminded me why we were kindred spirits. That he was saying this to Ingrid, his twin sister, was brave. That woman scared me.

The twins had gone to a birthday party at Ingrid's house, and all I can say is there's regular over-the-top, and then there's Ingrid. Her party was in a category all by itself. Women like that always made me feel smaller than a dead ant at the bottom of a swamp.

"People can hear you," Ingrid said in a singsong voice, her fake smile spread across her face, looking more like a demented housewife on Halloween. "Hello, Sarah."

"Always lovely to see you." Sarah tossed her arms around Ingrid as if they were the closest of friends.

My skin crawled. Was I expected to do the same routine?

"Lizzie," Ingrid said coolly, and I wanted to break out into a Snoopy happy dance.

No fake hug necessary!

Leonard whipped around, looking ecstatic to see me. "Here's someone who'll understand. Why the violins?"

I gulped, looking at Sarah as I attempted to calculate a safe response. Would an honest answer count as whining?

"They… uh… took me by surprise." I was pretty sure Leonard was more than capable of filling in the blanks.

"It's Christmas carols, not a violin recital." Leonard wasn't willing to let it go, even with his twin tossing some serious shade.

Would Olivia and Fred be like this in thirty years?

"I'm going to mingle with people who won't ruin my reputation." Ingrid fled without elaborating, but I got the feeling she had lumped me in with Leonard.

"She's no fun." Leonard dismissed the conversation with a wave of a hand. "This is quite the week. First the holiday concert and tomorrow a funeral. What whiplash, huh?"

"My heart breaks for Edna's family." Sarah's expression quickly changed to one that was full of remorse. "It's never easy to lose a loved one, but right before Christmas…" Her voice trailed off.

"Yeah, but the old girl had a good run. Not sure I want to live until one hundred and three."

I mouthed *wow*, before adding, "All the history she witnessed firsthand. The depression, the rise of the Nazis, two world wars—wow."

"And she had the good sense to check out before the next war with the Nazis." Leonard grabbed two red punches from one of the servers passing by, handing one to Sarah and me.

"You're terrible." Sarah laughed, raising her glass in thanks.

"How come he can say that, but I can't?" I demanded in a harsher tone than necessary.

"Because I'm not responsible for Leonard."

He laughed, but inwardly, I fumed. I couldn't really refute Sarah's statement. She was always telling me that my presence was like adding another child to her responsibilities. I would agree because I am fun and love life. However, this is apparently not what she means. It's more like because if you let me loose in a store, I get lost and then buy the one thing Sarah told me not to buy.

"How long did Edna work at the school?"

"She didn't." Leonard snagged a red punch for himself.

"I thought the funeral was for a coworker?" I didn't say what I really wanted to say, which was, "Why the fuck do I have to go?" I'm not saying I wished anyone dead—well, not without good cause—but I was pretty indifferent to whether or not most of the human population lived or died, and it seemed unfair to have to pretend otherwise in front of a bunch of people I didn't even know.

"Edna's daughter is one of the teachers." Leonard guzzled the juice before continuing, "Edna would come in every year to share about her life. I should have invited you, Lizzie. I didn't think of that until now, and it's too late. She was a real kick. I've always loved old ladies who swear. It makes me giggle like a little boy. The students loved it, too, and none of the parents would complain about Edna. Everyone in town loved her."

"I would have liked to talk to her, but I'm confused as to why I have—"

"It's the decent thing to do to show our respect." Sarah wore her watch-it expression. One wrong step and she'd squash me.

"Trust me, Lizzie." Leonard's eyes sparkled with enthusiasm that wasn't usually associated with someone dying, or at least not openly so. "If you only go to one funeral in your life, this is the one you want to go to. There'll be hot dogs."

"For the kids?" I guessed, my spirits deflating.

"No. All of us." Now I understood why Leonard had looked so excited, because I was feeling it, too. "Ms. Edna wanted all the food she loves to be there. Hot dogs. Hershey bars. Oranges—"

"Oranges?" One of these things was not like the others, at least in my estimation.

"When she was a kid, her family was poor, and they couldn't afford things like oranges," Sarah explained. "She actually had scurvy as a child."

"Get out!" It was impossible for me to contain my enthusiasm. "She really did experience everything. What a shame I never got to speak to her."

Given the way Sarah's eyes bulged, that wasn't the best way to put it. It amazed me how Sarah didn't understand the intricacies of my historical mind. I'd never known anyone who literally experienced scurvy. I thought only pirates did. Could I go around saying, "Argh, matey," at the funeral? Would the others get it?

Leonard guffawed and clapped a hand on my shoulder. "This is why I love you. We both run our mouths without thinking and get into trouble. We can be each other's wingmen —er—women."

"I'm not sure I want you two hanging out together at the funeral," Sara said. "Or anywhere."

"Don't be that way, Sarah. No reason to ruin the funeral of our lives. Did I mention the ice cream cake?" He let out a whistle. "I hope when I go out, someone other than Ingrid plans my funeral. I want people to enjoy themselves and help me say goodbye to the things I love." He shook his belly. "I wonder if there'll be craft beers. I would want those. And the best whiskey money could buy." His expression darkened. "If you'll excuse me, I'm being beckoned." He walked across the room like a man heading to face the firing squad.

"You better behave at the funeral," Sarah warned, her tone scolding even though I hadn't done anything to deserve it. At least not yet. Had she sensed my desire to talk like a pirate?

How cool would it be if the funeral was held on Talk Like a Pirate Day. "Don't eat too much and puke in the casket or something."

"There's going to be a dead woman around the food?" My stomach twisted in such a way I thought I'd never be able to eat anything ever again. Alas, another dream died. I'd never make a good pirate because I think they were around dead people a lot, and I couldn't stomach the thought.

"No, but I'm not convinced that could stop you. If anyone could manage to do something like that, it would be you."

"I won't go near a dead body." I shivered, all the while internally practicing my pirate impression. Halloween was over, but would the party store have an eyepatch and peg leg? I was willing to bet Ms. Edna would get a kick out of it. Sarah, on the other hand, might beat me senseless with the peg leg.

Sarah met the eye of one of the moms in her friend group, leaving me to my own thoughts.

A funeral with all the best foods? The idea spun in my head. Was that what I needed? Not to die. My entire goal was to get into better shape to avoid dying prematurely. But did I need a food funeral as a way to start my new life of nothing but healthy shit that made me gag?

CHAPTER NINE

"Did Santa's workshop explode in here?" Sarah stood at one end of the kitchen, her eyes bulging out of their sockets as she took in what was admittedly a much messier room than I had realized until just that second.

"Willow, Maddie, and the kids are helping me do all the baking." I rubbed my hands on my apron, stained with frosting.

"I see that." Sarah entered the frenzied chaos with trepidation.

"The kids are frosting the cookies. Willow's making seven-layer bars—I frigging love those. Maddie's been in charge of the fudge, toffee, and…" I spun around. "What are these?"

Maddie looked up from the mixing bowl. "Bourbon balls."

"Right. Not kid or Lizzie approved."

"Suit yourself." Maddie kicked the mixer back on.

"This is amazing." Sarah swiped a piece of fudge, moaning after a tiny bite. "Maddie's forever in charge of fudge."

"That's what all the girls say after tasting—"

"Little ears…" Willow cut off her girlfriend before she could finish.

"I wasn't going to be offensive." Maddie's face reddened. "Not overly, at least."

The twins, Fred especially, had started to understand a lot more than the previous year, making it harder to carry on lewd adult talk in their presence. Not that Sarah and I did that much, but Maddie was a loose cannon.

"I hope you don't mind that I spearheaded all the baking." Appreciating anew the complete mess we had made, and being honest about how much of it Sarah would likely get stuck with, I hung my head. "I should have asked you first."

"Are you kidding me?" To my surprise, Sarah seemed genuinely pleased. "This is one thing off my list."

"That's a relief." Considering her good mood, I decided to get a few other things out in the open when I was least likely to get reprimanded. "I've also done some shopping for all the food between Christmas Eve and New Year's Day. We've got pigs in a blanket, little smokies—"

"Aren't those the same thing?" Sarah frowned.

"One's naked."

Fred cranked his head toward me, reinforcing in my mind once again just how quickly the kids could pick up on the slightest thing that might be construed as naughty.

"Maddie's making her famous meatballs—" I made a zip-it sign to Maddie and jerked my head to Fred. "Hot dogs—"

"Since when did we start having hot dogs during the holidays?"

"This year," I replied with an airy laugh. "Allen's even volunteered to grill them outside. Gabe wants burgers."

"What about the grown-ups?" Sarah asked, not entirely joking.

"Your mom and Troy want Chinese on Christmas eve, which we'll order, obviously. I don't have enough time to learn that. Helen and Dad have requested turkey and all the trimmings on Christmas day. And, I was thinking prime rib on New Year's." I prayed she approved of the menu choices since all the food had been paid for, which was only dawning on me in real time. Once my mind set on having a food funeral, or as many as possible, before the calendar ticked to 2024, I went into action mode.

"What about bonbons?" There was a hint of sarcasm in her tone, but I chose to take the comment at face value.

"I've never understood what those are, but I can look at the store. Do you need them right now?" I started to untie my apron.

Sarah gave a slight roll of her eyes. "I was kidding. What have I done for all of you to spoil me this year?"

I was confused for a moment because I hadn't actually taken Sarah into account when planning a menu of all my favorite foods. I was about to respond along those lines when Fred came to the rescue.

"You take care of us every other day in the year," Fred shouted from the table, a sugar cookie in hand that he was spreading green frosting on.

I owed that kid a twenty for saving me from whatever I would have said.

"You do." I put my arms around Sarah's waist. "I want this to be the best holiday season. Ever." I knew I couldn't tell her my real plan. That this was my bon voyage party to tasty food for the rest of my life. She'd tell me that was unreasonable. Sarah, though, didn't truly understand my plight. Nor did she appreciate the way I tackled problems head-on.

For decades I'd been the skinny-mini, especially during the years when my Grave's Disease wasn't under control. I never had to watch what I ate and could eat anything and everything in sight and not gain a pound.

I still ate like I used to, but I hadn't simply put on an extra pound or two. Now I worried about complications of being overweight. Diabetes, heart problems, and a million other possibilities.

It was possible I was overdoing it. Something I'd been accused of many times before. The problem was, I didn't know how not to do that.

"What's for dinner tonight?" Sarah asked, knocking me out of my head.

"Uh… pizza." I motioned to the oven. "It's booked for the rest of the night, right kids?"

"We want all the cookies!" Calvin raised his cookie in the air, before chomping into it, smearing red frosting all over his face.

"Can Mom have one?" I put a hand out.

Calvin shook his head, wearing an evil smile.

Demi popped out of her seat, bringing me one of her creations.

"This is beautiful, Demi. Almost too pretty to eat. Almost." I bit into it enthusiastically, getting it all over my face.

"You're just as bad, if not worse, than the kids." Sarah shook her head, but fondness softened her expression.

"We have great kids, so I'm taking that as a compliment."

CHAPTER TEN

"What is it?" Sitting in front of the shining Christmas tree, I shook the box Sarah gave me, listening for clues.

"Open it to find out, duh!" Olivia rolled her eyes.

"Ollie." The warning in Sarah's tone got our oldest to paste on her *I'm innocent* expression.

I ripped the Disney wrapping paper off the box. "It's a FitBit. But I have one." I raised my left arm as proof.

"You mean the one that's not counting all your steps, and you keep complaining about it?" Sarah smiled fondly. "This one pairs with your new scale."

"What scale?" I laughed nervously, wondering how long she'd known, or if this was a bluff. It seemed especially cruel to call me out on Christmas morning with the entire family there. "Are you trying to send me a message?"

"Who's next?" Calvin scrounged under the tree, looking for more packages.

"Gramps," Sarah directed Calvin before turning her dark browns to me and lowering her voice to a whisper. "The one hiding under your luggage in the closet, that's what scale."

"You snooped!"

"I was hanging up clothes and busted my toe on it. If you're going to try to hide things, do better. I also know you've been buying more healthy eating books because they're sitting on top of the scale. You practically have a library now." The muscles in Sarah's face relaxed. "I support you. We can get into better shape together."

"Not now, though, right?" My pulse raced as I thought of all the food I'd bought and most certainly planned on eating before the clock struck midnight on January first. "I want to enjoy this week and not think about what the new year holds."

"No one should diet during the holidays." Sarah's laugh was light and breezy, and I joined her with relief.

"Now who?" Calvin popped his head out from under the tree. How did he fit there?

"Freddie," Sarah responded without missing a beat.

How did Sarah remember the order of all the gifts? Or maybe she was shooting from the hip because the rest of us were hopelessly lost. Either way, I was impressed.

Fred ripped the paper off. "Baby Yoda!"

I straightened on the couch to look over the table, my heart sinking ever so slightly at the familiar box. "That's a very cool LEGO set, Fred."

Sarah winked at me, raising my suspicions. Did that mean she knew I'd meant to buy that for myself and not Fred?

Given the amount of shredded wrapping paper on the floor, we were nearing the end of the gift portion of Christmas morning.

Sarah had a small pile of gifts next to her chair. A new robe from her mom. Slippers from Maddie and Willow. A portrait of the kids from my dad and Helen.

My gift was missing, and it was becoming clearer and clearer.

After Demi opened the last gift, Sarah met my eyes.

I pulled an envelope from my old bathrobe, not having put on my new one. "It's still... in process. I need to know some dates."

Sarah scrunched her nose. "For what?" She opened the envelope and read the coupon I had scrawled in my terrible handwriting. "It's an IOU for an Alaskan cruise." She held the paper closer to her face. "It's for one?"

"Yes." I bit my lip, wondering why her voice had gone up at the end, like a question. "Isn't it great? I really had to think to find you the perfect gift. Seven days all by yourself on a cruise." I had a feeling of déjà vu. Had I given Sarah a similar gift? Was that why she was so confused? I should keep track of the gifts to avoid repeats.

"By myself?" There was that questioning tone again. And she didn't seem as excited as I'd expected.

"You're always rushing around, taking care of all of us and your students," I explained. "I thought you'd like some Sarah time."

Sarah blinked slowly as if trying to understand something. "Why would I want to spend seven days on a boat without anyone to talk to?"

"There will be other passengers, I'm sure. Right, Rose?" I hoped Rose, the former cruise fanatic, would come to my rescue.

Rose simply nodded, her expression guarded. I was beginning to think I had stepped in it somehow.

Gabe and Allen left the room after announcing they wanted to check on the grill for the hot dogs and burgers later in the day.

This was bad. Even my brothers knew I was in the doghouse.

"Did you want to go with someone?" My voice squeaked. "I can get a pen and add another ticket." I gulped air like a fish about to say adios to the world. "What name should I add?"

"Yours, you idiot." Sarah fixed me with an expression that was filled with both humor and disbelief. "If I'm going on a cruise, I want to go with you."

"I drive you insane." Should I hold up a mirror so she could see the murder in her eyes?

"No need to tell me that. I'm aware."

"You want me to go on the cruise with you?" I wasn't understanding because it went against what I was pretty sure I would want if I was in her shoes.

The kids were too busy playing with their new toys, so they didn't pick up on my gift fail, but Maddie wore an odd expression. Like she wanted to pass out. Had my gift been that bad? Would I need to break into a jewelry store to save face?

"Uh…" Maddie got to her feet. "Uh…"

"I know, I know. I'm bad at gifts." I cupped my forehead.

"You are, but that's not—Willow." Maddie turned to her girlfriend, who was sitting on the floor next to Demi, playing with the new ballerina Barbie dolls.

"You want to go on the Alaskan cruise with Sarah and Lizzie?" Willow joked.

Or I hoped it was a joke, because apparently no one understood my meaning. Sarah needed Sarah time. I was trying to respect that. I'd love a week on my own with all the food I can eat. Diets weren't a thing on a cruise, right?

"You're so amazing," Maddie pressed on, her voice shaking.

Sarah reached for my hand, using her other hand to smother her mouth. Had she swallowed her hot cocoa wrong? I could see tears of pain glistening in her eyes.

"I can't imagine my life without you." Maddie's voice grew stronger.

Willow's jaw dropped. There were tears in her eyes, too, and it started to dawn on me that maybe Sarah hadn't choked on hot cocoa after all.

Demi bounced the two Barbies in the air, oblivious to Willow's tearful eyes.

"I had a whole thing prepared, but—"

"Yes." Willow jumped to her feet, launching herself at Maddie. I really hoped this was what she thought it was, because if she was as bad at reading Maddie as I was with Sarah, this could go very wrong.

"You haven't even seen the ring yet." Maddie held onto Willow tightly.

"It can be made from construction paper for all I care."

"Because it'd come from the heart," I whispered into Sarah's ear. "Like the cruise."

I thought I had made a pretty good point, but Sarah made a *shut it* motion with her hand.

"It's a little fancier than that," Maddie said with a laugh. "Although, not much, since you're opposed to gold and gems."

"I won't wear blood on my finger." Willow hid her hands behind her back.

"I'm aware, and while you'd probably prefer one made from scraps of construction paper, because you're against consumerism, I couldn't propose with a handmade ring."

Sarah shot me a look, and I sunk into my seat cushion. Could I go on the cruise by myself?

Maddie continued, "So I looked high and low for the right ring." Maddie pulled a box from her bathrobe.

Sarah nudged me in the side. "She looked high and low."

She probably meant something by that, but I was too busy watching as Maddie slowly opened the lid to give it a lot of thought.

"It's beautiful!" Willow clasped a hand over her mouth.

"It's made of wood, green hydrangea, mint, wildflowers, spikelet—whatever that is," Maddie chuckled. "Oh, and wheat."

"It sounds like a science experiment gone wrong," I whispered into Sarah's ear. This earned me a sharp look.

Maddie continued. "The green symbolizes nature and love."

"It's something a fairy would wear. I love it." Willow kissed Maddie passionately.

How had that gone over better than my handmade Alaskan cruise ticket? I'd never get people.

All the adults sprang to their feet to offer congratulations and hugs. The kids seemed amused by everything but were too engrossed in their new toys to ask questions.

"Is everyone ready for breakfast?" Sarah got to her feet.

"Yes, but after that, we need to get on wedding planning!" Willow squealed, hopping up and down, with the kids joining in.

I was willing to bet the kids still had no idea what was going on. They simply liked jumping.

Willow beamed, shouting, "This is the year of our wedding!"

I closed my eyes, wishing the morning had gone differently where my gift was concerned. Why couldn't I get it right?

"Would you like a ring like that?" I asked Sarah once we were alone in the kitchen.

"I love my wedding ring." Sarah kissed my cheek. "And, we'll have a lovely time on the cruise. I'm cashing in on that coupon."

I swallowed, feeling a little shaky inside. "You like it, then?"

"Yes and maybe someday, I'll send you on a vacation all on your own."

"Really?" Whoops. I had sounded way too excited about that prospect.

"You're impossible. You know that." Sarah kissed the tip of my nose. "Lucky for you, I like a challenge."

JANUARY

CHAPTER ELEVEN

"Three, two, one. Happy New Year!" I jumped up and down with the kids, each of us blowing into our noisemakers. As the festive music from the television echoed through the room, I couldn't help but smile at the joyous chaos unfolding all around me.

"Here's to 2024!" Willow raised a glass of bubbly, clinking it against Maddie's.

"It's going to be the best year!" I pulled Sarah close and kissed her cheek.

"Best year ever." Calvin did a little dance that resembled a locomotive on amphetamines, his arms flailing wildly.

"Ever!" Demi shouted in agreement as she did a ballerina turn, twirling toward the center of the room with a gracefulness that caught me off guard.

I cocked my head, wondering if I had imagined it. "Demi, do that again."

She paused for a moment, her eyes twinkling with mischief, before she twirled once more, her movements fluid and elegant. It was as if my little daughter had transformed into a professional dancer before my very eyes.

I caught Sarah's attention with an urgent look. "Did you teach her that?"

"Where would I have learned such a thing?" Sarah replied, her brows furrowing in confusion. "Maybe she's just naturally gifted."

"Actually, she's been watching YouTube videos with me," Willow explained before taking a sip of her drink. "I'm considering taking a class, and I think Demi has promise."

"I want to take a class, too," Demi announced, her voice filled with determination. "I want to dance like the ballerinas in the videos."

My buzz, which was not from alcohol, but from all the sugar I'd consumed over the holidays, crashed. I suppressed a groan. Just what we needed. Another thing to drive one of the kids to. I tried my best to hide my hesitation, putting on a supportive smile for Demi's sake. After all, it was important to encourage our children's passions and dreams, even if they seemed fleeting.

At least, I was pretty sure that was what Sarah would tell me if I dared to squash our little one's dreams.

"I'm sure we can talk about this later," I said, stalling for time. Maybe she would forget by morning.

But Demi pressed her hands together, batting her lashes. "Pretty please?"

I couldn't resist that innocent plea. My heart melted on the spot at the sight of her hopeful eyes, and I caved faster than a sandcastle at high tide.

"Alright, my little Demitasse," I sighed, wondering just how much this new passion of hers was going to set me back. "We'll look into dance classes for you."

Demi squealed with delight, jumping up and down as if she had just won the lottery.

With a grin, I blew into my noisemaker. Demi did the same. Sarah massaged her forehead with a pained expression, knocking her black and gold party hat to the side. "Is it bedtime yet?"

"Ha!" I exclaimed with genuine glee. "Finally! I'm not the party pooper this time." I blew my noisemaker in her face, and she swatted it away with a look that told me if I planned on doing it again, she would rain down retribution upon me that I couldn't even imagine.

I have to admit, I was tempted to find out just how bad the consequences would be. After all, it wasn't often that I got to be the fun parent. I was willing to push my luck a little and savor the moment.

Luckily, Fred rescued me from my own foolishness by grabbing my hand to join all the kids in a riveting round of Ring-Around-the-Rosie. It took everything I had to stop myself from giving a history lesson about the song that, apparently, they still taught to kids. Not about how the song was about the plague because historians didn't know if that was the case. The theory that it was about the plague didn't appear until after World War II, and the symptoms didn't fit.

But, no. Dissecting the origins of a somewhat macabre children's nursery rhyme on New Year's, when I was legitimately the fun mom of the moment, seemed a sure bet to knock me back to fuddy-duddy status. Also, I had a slight headache from the insane amount of sugar I'd consumed during the holiday season.

So, I just let go of any lingering thoughts of historical analysis and threw myself into the game with the same childlike abandon as the rest of them. We spun around in a circle, laughing and stumbling over our own feet, until we all collapsed in a heap on the floor. The room was filled with a chorus of giggles that almost made up for the increased pounding in my head. Being the fun parent was way more exhausting than I'd anticipated.

By the time we tucked the children in and Sarah and I

retreated to our room, I could feel the weight of exhaustion in my bones. The remnants of laughter still lingered, echoing in my mind as I settled onto the edge of the bed. Sarah joined me, her expression a mix of amusement and weariness.

"You're oddly chipper these days." Sarah pulled her Rudolf sweater over her head, dropping it on the floor.

"Why shouldn't I be?" I asked, tapping my fingertips together. "2023 is in the books, and 2024 is all sparkly and new. Promising nothing but happiness."

"Nothing but happiness?" Sarah pressed a hand to my forehead as if checking for fever. Her touch was cool against my skin, soothing in its own way. If it wasn't already well after midnight, it may have given me some ideas.

I smirked and leaned closer, enjoying the way her eyes widened in anticipation. "Maybe a little mischief thrown into the mix," I whispered, my voice low and playful, before pulling my head away so I could remove my Frosty sweater. "I think I'm finally getting the hang of this."

"Getting the hang of what?" She kicked off her slippers, groaning a little as she rose from the bed in order to undo her jeans.

"Life."

"Why do I have this feeling 2024 is going to be hell?" Sarah let out a soft chuckle as she unzipped her jeans. "You always find a way to make things interesting. By which I mean disastrous."

"Not this time. I promise. I have plans in place." I gave her my best trust me expression.

"Do you not remember the Summer of Lizzie?" Sarah groaned. "By the time it was over, you thought I was going to divorce you."

"Look," I dropped my pants, struggling to kick them off gracefully.

"Nope. Not going to work." Sarah crossed her arms, jutting

out one hip and wearing an expression that said she wasn't buying a word I was saying.

"What's not going to work?" I glanced down, belatedly realizing I'd never finished my sentence, and she might have gotten the wrong idea. "I wasn't trying to seduce you."

"Oh really? The year's looking up already." Sarcasm dripped from every word Sarah spoke, but it was accompanied by a playful glint in her eyes.

She stepped closer, wrapping her arms around my waist and resting her head against my chest. I could feel the warmth of her breath against my skin, sending shivers down my spine. Maybe I'd been a little hasty about that no seduction thing.

"I was just trying to say that I studied where I went wrong with the Summer of Lizzie, and I have safeguards in place for 2024. There is absolutely no reason for you to worry. I've got this!" I jerked my thumb into my chest, a little too hard, but I didn't want to let on I'd injured myself trying to reassure her.

Sarah's expression said she was anything but reassured.

I wanted to raise holy hell on my behalf, but even I knew it was pointless. Truth be told, I'd put zero thought into the Summer of Lizzie, and it had shown. But I had this amazing ability to block things out of my head completely. Especially things better left in the past.

You'd think driving Sarah bonkers to the point I honestly thought I might receive divorce papers would've prodded my memories, but no. Instead, I had shrugged it off as a turbulent phase in our relationship that we had overcome. But Sarah, with her impeccable memory and her keen ability to put my mistakes into context, wasn't about to let me off the hook that easily.

She pulled away from me, her eyes narrowing as she crossed her arms once more. "You really believe studying your past failures will prevent you from repeating them?"

Is that what I thought? If so, I believed it without a shred of evidence. I was the type who always drove Sarah to the brink, resulting in me thinking she would leave me more times than I cared to admit. Yet, somehow, she always found a way to forgive me. Maybe this time would be no different.

Or maybe it would be different, because I would finally get it right. I was going to live my best Lizzie life in 2024. Become the best me.

"Just you wait, Sarah. I'm going to be a whole new Lizzie by the time we ring in 2025. I have plans. Big plans. I want to be a better parent, wife, teacher, and Lizzie."

Sarah raised an eyebrow. "Lizzie is its own category?"

Her skepticism was warranted. I could admit that to myself, if not exactly to her. I knew I had a long history of making promises I couldn't keep. But this time, I was determined to prove her wrong.

"I need to work on myself, and that's what this year is all about. The Year of Lizzie!" I gestured with my hand, imagining each letter of the phrase glowing and exploding across the sky like the fireworks that had celebrated the beginning of the new year not too long ago. "I'm going to nail 2024. Just you watch."

Sarah's expression softened, and she let out a sigh.

"I want nothing more than for you to succeed," she said, her voice tinged with a hint of caution. "But let's be honest, trying to change overnight is a recipe for failure."

"I know that. I'm not planning on changing overnight," I reassured her, my determination seeping into every word. "This is going to be a journey, a journey that starts with acknowledging my flaws and taking small steps to improve."

"Huh. That actually sounds… sensible."

I grinned, triumphant that I'd managed to sway her even a little. Sarah was always the voice of reason, the one who could see through my grand declarations and hold me accountable for my actions. If she found even a hint of sensibility in my plan, then maybe, just maybe, I was on the right track.

"I'm glad you think so," I replied, stepping closer and wrapping my arms around her in a tight embrace. "Now, about that seduction thing. I—"

"I thought you said you weren't trying to seduce me," Sarah interrupted, pulling away slightly to meet my gaze with a teasing look in her eyes. I chuckled, my confidence building with each passing moment.

"Well," I began, my voice laced with playfulness, "I never said I wasn't open to the idea."

"Is that right?"

I nodded, a mischievous glint in my eyes. "Absolutely. The Year of Lizzie is all about exploring new possibilities and pushing boundaries. And who better to embark on this journey with than my beautiful, intelligent, and incredibly enticing wife?"

Sarah's cheeks flushed with a mix of surprise and delight as she leaned in closer, her lips hovering just inches away from mine. There was an electrifying tension in the air, anticipation building with each passing second. I could feel my heart beating faster, matching the rhythm of the fireworks exploding in the distance.

"Maybe I was too hasty in dismissing this Year of Lizzie idea," she whispered, her warm breath tickling my ear. "It seems 2024 is already off to a surprising yet unforgettable start."

"It certainly is," I replied, my voice barely a whisper as our lips finally met in a tender, passionate kiss.

That settled it. 2024 was going to be the best year ever. I'd basically already conquered it, and we were still only on January first. With such a strong start, the rest of the year would be a piece of cake.

CHAPTER TWELVE

"Care for some cantaloupe, my dear?" I forked a chunk of melon, offering it to Sarah, who'd finally made an appearance downstairs. Sure, it was only 7:06 a.m., but she wasn't going to win any awards for being an eager beaver if this was the best she had to offer on the first morning of the year. I, on the other hand, had been up since before the sun, ready to tackle the world.

"Caffeine," she grunted, brushing by me to the coffee maker.

Apparently, giving up her morning brew was not one of her resolutions for the new year. It was probably just as well. If I wanted 2024 to be the best year ever, I had to live to see the end of it. My chances of this happening were much higher if my wife didn't go through caffeine withdrawal.

I watched as she poured coffee into a travel mug that could fit most of the pot. With a sigh, she took a cautious sip, her expression morphing from drowsy to slightly more alive.

"Blueberries," I said as I looked at the notebook in front of me on the table, not offering an explanation as to the sudden twist in my train of thought. After so many years together,

Sarah should've been used to it by now. "Would you say they're more blue than purple?"

"Are you asking me if blueberries are blue?" Sarah took another sip before topping off the mug to the brim with what was left in the pot. "Is this a trick question, or have I just not had enough brain juice yet?"

"What about blackberries?" I pressed, my mind humming. "Are they purple?"

Sarah held her mug to her lips, giving me a quizzical stare.

Sensing she wasn't going to answer, I googled purple fruits. "Yes, blueberries and blackberries are both lumped into the purple fruit column." I jotted that down in my spiral notebook. "Uh-oh. That means I don't have anything under the blue category." I erased blueberries. "I'm going to add blueberries back to the blue row, and keep blackberries under purple."

"You know, there are very few, if any, naturally occurring blue foods." The fact Sarah was correcting me must've meant the coffee was kicking in. "Studies have shown being in a blue room suppresses your appetite. We know not to eat blue foods because they might be poisonous."

"How do you know this?" I massaged my chin, pondering this random fact. The woman was barely awake and already spewing out factoids like an encyclopedia. It was one of the reasons I loved her so much, not that I was planning to let on about it. It would just give her an ego.

"Naturally brilliant." Sarah batted her lashes and smirked, taking another gulp of her caffeinated elixir.

"Does that mean I should combine blue, indigo, and purple into one column?" I drew some arrows to solve my problem and then took a sip of my lemon water. "What do elderberries taste like?"

"I've only had them in gin."

"Would that count?" I mulled it over before laughing. "Of course not. I don't drink anymore."

"I think I could use a drink. Dare I ask what project you're working on?" The worry in her gaze spoke as loudly as a cannon blast on the front lines.

"Eating the rainbow."

"Can't you just buy Skittles like a normal American?" Sarah half-heartedly covered a yawn.

"That's the problem. I do eat like an American," I explained. "I'm getting closer to forty, and my waistline isn't where I'd like it to be, if I'm being a hundred percent honest."

"Is this about those diet books from the closet?" Sarah's eyes narrowed as she spotted the spine of one of said books peeking out from beneath my notebook.

"It's not a diet." I poked the book back into its hiding place with a guilty smile. "It's more like a lifestyle change. I want to live another forty years, at least. More, really. If I could last until one hundred, that'd be something, wouldn't it? That is, if the planet can last that long."

"Always the optimist." Sarah smiled and shook her head, the corners of her lips turning upward in a way that made my heart skip a beat. "But I worry that you're putting unnecessary pressure on yourself with all this rainbow-eating business. I thought you promised last night to take things slow. Small steps, remember?"

"Of course. How could I forget?" I consulted my scribbles with a frown, trying to decipher the next step in my rainbow-eating journey. The truth was Sarah had a point. I had a tendency to dive headfirst into new endeavors, often overwhelming myself in the process. But this time, it felt different. This time, it wasn't just about losing weight or adhering to a fad diet. This was about life and death. Didn't that deserve an all-in approach?

"I'm going to keep blue and indigo separate from purple," I announced, punctuating my decision with a tap of my pencil against the page. "Blueberries have blue right in the name. My brain kinda needs it to be that way. Although, I still don't get why there are two blues in the rainbow. That leaves purple, where I already have blackberries. Why do they have to keep giving foods the wrong color names?"

"Is this a resolution?" Sarah asked suspiciously as she swiped one of my cantaloupe chunks.

"Absolutely not! It's my new way of living. Resolutions don't last. This will. One hundred years! That's the goal. To live for a century." I tapped my pencil against the edge of the kitchen island. "Do I like beets?"

Sarah shrugged, studying me with an amused glint in her eyes. "I don't know. Do you like beets?"

I hesitated for a moment, my mind wandering to memories from my childhood of canned beets, which I had despised. The thought of their slimy texture and earthy taste made my stomach turn. But this felt like a challenge, a test of my commitment. I was determined to give beets a fair shake.

"Only one way to find out." I added them to my shopping list as Sarah's eyebrows shot up in surprise. "What about purple cabbage?"

"Lizzie," Sarah said, her tone full of warning.

I crossed my arms. "You don't seem all that interested in my reset."

"I thought you said it wasn't a resolution."

"It's not. It's a reset." I almost spelled out the word, but I suddenly couldn't remember if it had one S or two. "It's all here in the *Reset for Results* book."

"A diet book?" Sarah made a move to snatch it from beneath my stack of research materials, but I scooped it up out of her reach.

"Not a diet," I insisted. "This is a program by a real doctor, and not one of those ones that goes on talk shows. He's an expert. And he says I need to eat more fruits and veggies."

"I didn't go to medical school, and even I could've told you that."

"Specifically, I have to eat one pound of veg every day."

"Are you off your rocker? You call all vegetables the devil's weeds." Sarah offered up a smile dripping with sarcasm. "When does this reset start?"

"It already has." I pointed to the cantaloupe that had taken the place of my usual breakfast. "I need to go to the store for the rest of my items."

"You're doing this today?" Sarah's voice had taken on a high-pitched quality that filled me with alarm. I was almost certainly going to get in trouble, and I had no idea why. "It's New Years Day. All of our family is coming over for dinner."

"I can make my own meal, including beans," I assured her quickly.

"Beans?" Sarah's eyes grew squinty, and I would've sworn she'd never heard the word before.

"Legumes. That's my new main dish." I said it with an enthusiasm I didn't entirely feel, but that was okay. The doctor said I needed beans. I would grow to enjoy them. Eventually. Probably.

Sarah set down her travel mug. "Let me see if I'm getting this right. You want to start eating a pound of vegetables every day, starting today. Plus fruit. And only beans for your main course instead of meat."

"That is correct!" I tapped her nose with my mechanical pencil.

She swiped it to the side, clearly not finding the gesture cute. "Do you think—?"

"I try not to as much as possible. It only gets me into trouble." I flashed my cutest smile.

"I need you to alter that policy right now."

"I was joking. Have some more coffee." I gestured to her oversized mug with a grin.

Her deadly glare made me wonder if one of Sarah's resolutions was to ditch having any semblance of a sense of humor.

"You can't go from eating normally to—"

"The American diet isn't normal. This"—I held up my shopping list—"is normal. It's what humans consumed for centuries because it was what was readily available. Those"—I pointed to the cinnamon rolls on the cake platter in the center of the table—"are abominations. Filled with sugar."

"That's what makes them tasty." Sarah removed the glass lid, placing one of the pastries on a small plate. "They go perfectly with coffee."

And tea, a little voice in my head whispered, but I paid it no attention. Frankly, I was irked Sarah was being this way. I'd just said I wanted to eat better, and now she was eating a cinnamon roll, which smelled delightful, right in front of me. My cantaloupe didn't seem nearly as appealing anymore.

"Don't give me that hurt look. I know you're thinking I'm not being supportive, but I am. I think all of us could do a better job eating healthier. My concern is you're jumping into this plan—"

"I'm not jumping in. I read a book on it." I avoided pulling the reset book out from the hiding spot, not wanting Sarah to get her hands on it. Why, I had no idea.

"That might be the case, but you can't flip a switch and suddenly eat completely perfectly all the time. It's going to do a number on your stomach."

"I've been incorporating more fruit for weeks. I've even put lemon wedges into my water." I made a ta-da motion to draw her attention to my glass. "I'm surprised you haven't noticed."

"I did, but I had no idea garnish was part of your master plan."

"I'm sensing sarcasm."

"From me?" Sarah placed a not-so-innocent hand on her chest.

"You're going to be eating your words in two weeks."

"Which is more than what you'll be eating. You're talking about only eating fruits, veggies, and beans. Beans, Lizzie? I know your digestive system. You're going to be blowing holes in your underpants."

"I can also have seeds," I informed her, ignoring her dig at my delicate insides. "I can add sunflower seeds to my salads." I jotted down the addition to my grocery list. "I appreciate your concern. But I've been planning for this. I even read the book twice. I've got this." My eyes landed on the cinnamon roll, a sense of loss roiling through me. Not that I wanted to admit that out loud.

I didn't have to, because my internal thoughts didn't escape Sarah's notice. "Want a bite?"

I shut my eyes. "No. I need to go shopping for real food."

"You can't go shopping today."

"Why?"

"It's New Year's Day, Lizzie. Everyone in the family will be here in a few hours. Please. We just need to survive this day. It's been a long holiday season. I'm exhausted. Don't be the reason I crack on the last day, okay?"

"Fine." I yanked the lid off the serving platter and snatched a cinnamon roll. "One more day of crap. But I'm going to the store first thing tomorrow morning. I'm doing this reset, and I'm going to get results."

"What you'd better get is some Beano. You're going to need it." She left the room with her cinnamon roll and coffee before I had a chance to argue.

"Oh, ye of little faith," I muttered to myself as I sank my teeth into the last cinnamon roll I would ever eat.

CHAPTER THIRTEEN

"Who knew strawberries are so hard to slice?" I gritted my teeth as I pressed down hard with the knife, causing strawberry juice to splatter across the cutting board. The vibrant red liquid trickled down the sides, resembling a macabre scene from a horror film. Fitting, considering that after nearly a week of healthy eating, I was on the verge of committing murder almost constantly. "These are ripe, aren't they?"

Sarah set her morning coffee down slowly, as if not at all bothered by my culinary emergency. "Can I see the knife?"

"Do you think it needs to be sharpened? Do we have a knife sharpener?" I tapped my iPad screen and pulled up my favorite shopping app. "I can order one. Oh look. I'll also need to get a special glove." I squinted at the picture on the screen, intrigued by the model's metal accessory. "Looks like chain-mail. I'll be your knight in shining armor."

"Or you could just turn the knife the right way and use the blade side." With that, Sarah turned the tool over, slicing through one of the strawberries with ease.

"Lookee there. Problem solved." I took the knife back, doing my best to hide my annoyance. "How many strawberries do you think I need to cut for the breakfast spread? Which kids like them again?"

"Four."

"Does that include you?" I pointed the knife at her, realizing too late that the move seemed rather hostile. "I didn't mean it that way. Do all of us like strawberries? Six individuals? Plus Dad and Helen."

"Yep." Sarah rolled her neck side to side. "What day of your reset is this?"

"Five." I glanced up, practically glowering but quickly plastered over it with a wide grin. "And I feel fantastic. I know you were worried, but honestly, I've got this in the bag. No stomach issues, whatsoever, by the way."

Claiming to feel fantastic was a stretch, considering I was on the verge of a murder spree over slicing fruit. But surprisingly, the stomach part was true, as long as you didn't count the constant gurgling as my digestive tract attempted to break down more fiber than it had ever encountered before.

But I wasn't about to let Sarah in on that little detail. Not when she was already looking at me with those skeptical eyes, always ready to question my latest foolproof plan.

Before Sarah could voice her opinions, of which I was certain she had many, Calvin ran in, his sweater on inside out and the tag tickling his chin. "How much longer? I'm starving."

"Have a strawberry to tide you over." I motioned to the bowl.

Calvin pressed his lips together, making a disgusted face.

"More for me, then," I happily chirped.

Sarah took one of the strawberry slices, placing it in Calvin's hand. "You love strawberries."

Calvin popped it into his mouth. "More please."

"Less for me," I joked as I cut the last strawberry in the container. "If we all keep eating like this, I'll need to go to the store every other day." I blocked out my aversion to grocery shopping, and said in a forced cheery voice, "Which is just fantastic. What matters most is we're all eating healthier."

"You know what? I'm actually really proud of you, Lizzie." Sarah put a hand on my shoulder, and I tensed, waiting for the punchline. "I'm serious. You're sticking with this, and it's helping all of us."

I scrutinized her face to suss out the snark but saw only support in her eyes. "I think this is going to be a life-changing experience for all of us. And, I'm happy to report breakfast is ready. Cal, round up the troops!"

The boy saluted and shot out of the kitchen, screaming, "Great news, troops! We're not going to starve!"

"Maybe I should start getting up earlier. Prepping everything takes time." I opened the reminder app on my phone. "I have an opening at 5:30. I can start cutting fruit then, and hopefully be done by my next appointment at six."

"What do you have scheduled at six?"

"A walk with Gandhi. My doctor says it's the best way to help with that pain." I massaged the tender spot right above my left butt cheek. "The on/off motion is supposed to be good."

"You already take him for a walk after school with the kids," Sarah pointed out. "Are you sure the doctor meant for you to do that much more exercise all at once?"

"The dog's got to pee." I picked up the tray with all the fruit bowls and plates for the kids, kicking off a twinge in my back, but I pressed on. "Exercise is good for me. I'm not getting younger, you know."

Halfway to the table, the twinge in my lower back shifted with a pop, setting off a stabbing pain, stopping me in my tracks. Sarah almost rammed right into me.

"Keep going," Sarah prodded me.

"Can't." I closed my eyes, seeing white lights.

"You okay?"

"My back."

She worked around me to ease the tray from my hands, taking it to the dining room table, because my dad and Helen were expected any second.

I remained put, the pain radiating up and down my left leg.

Sarah returned, putting two pills into my palm and holding out a glass of water.

"I don't think I'm supposed to take these. Not with the reset. Medicine isn't natural." I closed my eyes, trying to remember what the section on pain relievers said, but nothing came to mind except a silent shriek of agony.

"Don't argue. Or do you plan on never moving from this spot?"

"It's starting to let up." I wished that were actually true.

"Lizzie," Sarah admonished, seeing right through my lie. She pressed the pills into one hand and a glass of water into the other.

"I hate when you use the mom voice." Without further argument, I swallowed the pills. "Please don't tell my dad. I don't want to worry him. I think I can get to the table now."

"Only if you promise to slow down some. You don't have to go full steam ahead with every plan you get in your head. Like this reset thing."

"The reset isn't causing my back pain," I argued. "If anything, dropping some pounds will help."

"I knew that was what this was really about," Sarah said in that way that told me she was, as usual, two steps ahead of me. "You're beautiful just the way you are."

"I'm pudgy." Or, according to the fancy scale in my closet, almost obese.

Sure, it had only landed on thirty BMI for a second before

settling just below, but talk about a wake-up call. Plus, it had happened on three separate occasions. I didn't know how to explain it to Sarah, how that made me feel. Like I was losing control of my own body. Like I couldn't trust it anymore.

With my Graves' disease, I had never had to worry about being overweight. Quite the opposite. But while being in remission for so long was a blessing in many ways, for the first time in my life, I was realizing my body was as vulnerable to the fluctuations of weight and appearance as anyone else's.

Sarah's eyes softened with empathy, understanding the turmoil that brewed within me. She reached out, gently squeezing my hand. "You are not pudgy. We just need to eat better, which you're doing, and get regular exercise. But you don't have to do it all at once. Have you been lifting weights?"

"Maybe," I muttered, not wanting to admit to something that would certainly get me into trouble, considering the state of my back.

"Lizzie," she started cautiously. "I know you want everything to be corrected at once, but that's not good for your body. Little changes have a better chance of lasting."

I tried taking a step forward, the pain subsiding. "I'm fine. Trust me. I've got this."

The front door creaked open, snagging Sarah's attention.

"Good morning, Petries." The voice didn't belong to either my dad or Helen, which made me frown.

"Who's that?" I asked.

"I forgot to mention something." Sarah's face paled.

"Are we having a party?" My eyes widened as panic set in. "After the holidays, I'm partied out. Not to mention we're out of fruit. I'll have to run to the store if there are more mouths to feed."

"It's not that—Leonard." Sarah stopped short to greet our guest as he entered the kitchen. "How are you this morning?"

He held a pet carrier, a broad grin on his stubbled face. My dad and Helen brought up the rear, with Helen cooing to whatever was inside.

"Is that a new pet?" I asked Leonard, stopping myself from asking why he brought it over to my house bright and early on a Saturday.

"Yes," he answered. "Yours!"

As I tried to make sense of his words, Sarah took the carrier.

"You're a doll for bringing her by," Sarah said.

"It's the least I could do for Ms. Edna's poor cat. Can you imagine making it to nineteen and losing the one person you lived with all your life?" Leonard asked.

My brow crinkled as I struggled to work through the numbers. "I thought she lived to one hundred and three."

"Edna did, yes." Sarah gave me a smile. "Her cat is the one who's nineteen."

"That's amazing." I nodded my head to express my admiration. "I wonder what the secret is. Does the cat only eat fresh foods?"

"Is Fancy Feast fresh?" Leonard laughed. "There's a lot of that in my car. I'll go get it."

"Why is he going—" I began but was interrupted mid-sentence as Calvin shouted from the dining room.

"We're going to starve!"

"We'll take care of the kids." Helen gave Sarah a supportive squeeze on the arm, as if picking up on something I wasn't piecing together.

Once alone, I whispered, "Is Leonard feeling okay? I know you said he's been under a lot of stress at school. Is this cat like an emotional support thing?"

"Not exactly," Sarah replied. "You see, Edna's daughter tried moving Snickers into her home, but it didn't work because, as it turns out, her daughter is deathly allergic. She was going to take Snickers to a shelter, but she's nineteen so..."

"So, Leonard saved her." I smiled. "That's nice of him."

"No. Actually, he can't." Sarah paused for a second. "No one could but U-S."

Sarah said these letters without explanation, and I tried to think who in our circles went by those initials. And then it dawned on me. She had spelled the word us. I had a sneaky suspicion she did it to give herself another second or two of reprieve in hopes Leonard would return to save me from flipping out. Which he did with a blue IKEA bag on his shoulder.

"You have enough food for months, and the instructions for all her medications are typed out in the binder along with pictures. I gotta run, or Ingrid's going to kill me. You two are amazing for taking Snickers in. See ya, Monday." He gave Sarah a quick hug and waved at me before darting out of the room.

"You did that on purpose," I accused. "You knew I would be too confused by spelling in my head, denying me the chance to say no." I'd meant to spell it out for her, N-O. Only I got confused, inadvertently proving my own point, if only to myself.

"Want to meet Snickers?" Sarah wore a hopeful expression.

"I'm trying to avoid Snickers this year, and you've gone and adopted a cat with that name?"

"I'm going to let her out in the library," Sarah said, ignoring me. "That's the quietest room in the house. She's going to have to adjust."

"In my library?" I tailed Sarah, not willing to roll over and give in just yet.

"In *our* library," she corrected, and not for the first time. "She's nineteen. We can give her a loving home for her final days."

"In the library?" I felt like a record with a skip in it, but I feared it was the only way Sarah would see the problem with her plan.

"Hopefully, that's not permanent. I'd like Snickers to become part of the family." Sarah waved for me to shut the library door before she unzipped the carrier.

A tiny ginger feline stuck a nose out, before retreating back inside.

"I'll get her some food to see if we can coax her out. Stay with her, Lizzie."

I eased onto the floor next to the carrier so I could casually peer inside. My heart melted a tiny bit despite myself.

"I know what it's like, not feeling like you have a place with loved ones. I felt like that for years until I met Sarah. She has a way of saving people. And animals." I let out a quiet chuckle.

Snickers stuck out her nose again.

"It's okay, little one. You're safe here." I didn't have the best introduction to the situation, but I loved animals. Always had. It was one of my weaknesses, according to my mom.

She climbed into my lap, shoving her head against my hand with more force than I was expecting.

Sarah returned, not making much noise. "I knew you'd love her. Isn't she sweet?"

"You've met her before?"

"I've only seen photos. Ms. Edna would give us wall calendars with Snicker photos for each month. I feel like I know her." Sarah set down a bowl with food. "Shall we join the family for brunch?"

"I'll be there in a bit." Tentatively, I scratched Snickers behind an ear. "I can't tell if she's purring or shaking."

"Both, probably. I'll bring you some food."

"Looks like we're alone again," I joked to the cat as Sarah closed the door.

How had I found myself in this predicament? Welcoming a

cat into my life was never a part of the plan, but here I was. Despite all my careful planning, Sarah had a knack for disrupting my perfectly calculated world. She had a way of finding the things that were broken and putting them back together. Including me, on occasion.

I couldn't decide how to feel about it—annoyed or grateful.

CHAPTER FOURTEEN

I SAT AT MY DESK, STARING DAGGERS AT THE GLASS bowl beside my laptop. It contained baby carrots, snow peas, cucumber, radish, and cauliflower. There was so much veg in the bowl I felt I'd been sentenced to a lifetime of rabbit food. The thought of consuming all those vegetables made me cringe. I despised vegetables. But here I was, trapped in a lifetime of torture that was entirely my own doing.

The worst part? The veg only weighed five ounces. Five! How would I ever consume sixteen ounces a day at this rate?

Nibbling on a carrot, I tried to focus on the task at hand, emptying my email inbox.

"Mommy, can I have some hot chocolate?" Demi stood on the other side of the desk, giving me the sincerest face I'd ever seen. Too sincere, maybe. Suddenly, I suspected foul play.

"Did you ask Mommy, and she said no?" I guessed.

Demi shook her head, and she wasn't the type to lie. I considered the prospect of hot chocolate for a moment, wishing I could count it toward my vegetable total.

"It is pretty cold," I conceded. Cocoa came from beans, right?

"Brrr." Demi wrapped her arms around her torso.

"You know what? Sure. Why not?" I got out of my chair to head to the kitchen.

Before I got there, all of the kids had appeared out of thin air and were following me like ducklings.

"Let me guess. All of you want hot chocolate?" Each child nodded solemnly as I pulled four Swiss Miss envelopes from the stash on the top shelf of the pantry. "Okay. Fred, get the mugs from the shelf."

He climbed onto the step stool, carefully getting down the personalized unicorn mugs Rose had gotten them for Christmas.

"Ollie, add one packet to each mug." I finished filling the electric kettle, putting it on the base and hitting the on button.

While Ollie got on a stool in front of the mugs on the counter, I asked Calvin to get a spoon.

He did so, without too much grousing. The kid must really want hot chocolate.

"All of you are very quiet. What gives?"

Freddie and Ollie shrugged like they had no idea why I was asking. Odd, but I decided to let it slide for now. After all, there was hot chocolate to be made, and I didn't want to spoil the moment with unnecessary probing.

The kettle clicked, and I poured water into each mug. "Demi, can you stir each one?"

Demi climbed onto a stool, stirring her heart out.

"What's going on?" Sarah stood in the kitchen, with a laundry basket in her arms and a scowl on her face.

I swallowed, certain I was about to get grounded. "We're making hot chocolate."

"I see that, but what I don't understand is why. Calvin asked for some, and I said no because it's almost dinnertime."

Demi stopped stirring the minute my eyes met hers.

"Is that right?" I asked.

Demi's face turned red in response.

"If it makes you feel better," I told Sarah, "I'm not having any, and the kids helped with every step."

"It's already made, Mommy," Calvin said in a snotty tone, and I held my breath. That kid was going to get in so much trouble, and he was going to drag me right along with him, the unrepentant rascal.

The other three knew not to press Sarah's buttons when trying to get away with a hot chocolate crime. But our youngest was turning out to be an even bigger handful than Olivia.

Sarah's eyes narrowed as she set the laundry basket down on the counter. "Calvin, what did I tell you about sneaking snacks before dinner?" she scolded, her voice stern but tinged with exhaustion.

Calvin shuffled his feet, avoiding eye contact with her. "But, I didn't sneak it. I had parental supervision the whole time."

"Such as it was." Sarah directed this comment toward me, and I couldn't really argue. It hadn't even occurred to me to check the clock to see if it was close to dinner.

"Those mugs have lids and are meant not to get cold. Each of you can have yours after dinner. Do you understand me?" She met everyone's eyes, even mine.

I stuck my hands in the air. "For the record, I already said I wasn't having any, so I don't think I should be in trouble."

"You helped them break the rules." Despite her stern tone, Sarah's lips twitched, and I suspected at least part of her was amused by this situation. "We need to stand united."

"Why does hot chocolate have to smell so good?" I stared longingly at the mugs for a few seconds before I realized Sarah was glaring at me, waiting for me to back her up in that whole unity thing. "Rodger, dodger. Kids, only Mommy in Charge can okay hot chocolate going forward. I get played too easily."

Sarah rolled her eyes but left with the laundry basket.

"Whose idea was it to send Demi into my office?" I crossed my arms, studying each one of their faces.

None of them said anything, but Calvin became suddenly interested in his dinosaur slippers like he'd never seen them before.

"I'm going to remember this because now I'm on Mommy's naughty list, and that's not where I want to be."

"Will you get coal next Christmas?" Freddie asked, seemingly upset on my behalf.

"I hope I can get back on Mommy's and Santa's good sides by then. It's only January tenth. Plenty of runway." I crossed my fingers, making Fred laugh. "All of you scoot."

After sealing each mug of hot chocolate with the lids and placing them out of reach on the off-chance Calvin tried to tempt fate, I returned to my office.

Sarah entered not too long after.

"I'm sorry about the hot chocolate." I told her. "I didn't realize the time, and I don't appreciate the kids using Demi like they did. She's the sweet one, and they take advantage of that."

Sarah furrowed her brow, so I explained how it had all gone down.

"I think we need to strengthen the rules because we're outnumbered, and it's only going to get worse going forward." Sarah laughed, her eyes landing on my Baby Yoda glass bowl that read, *Protect, Attack, Snack.* "Holy Baby Yoda veggie snacks."

I sighed in agony at the reminder.

"What's wrong? Struggling with the reset?" She tried not to snicker, and it seemed like a mighty battle going on inside.

"Guess how many ounces of veg are in here?" I stabbed my finger at the bowl.

"Ten."

"Half that," I said with a groan. "I need to finish all this and still have eleven more ounces for dinner. This isn't a way to live."

"Look at it this way. For centuries, this was how people did it. They survived mostly on fruit and veg. You're living through a history experiment. Does that help?"

"No because if this was all I ever had for the rest of my life, I wouldn't want to go on. This is misery. Pure misery." My stomach made a weird, churning sound, and I clenched my butt cheeks in a sudden rush of blind panic. What the hell was that?

"You can stop anytime, you know. No one is putting you up to this."

"And admit defeat? Never." Snickers jumped onto my desk for a head pet.

"She's settling in. Speaking of, we're having a family meeting." Sarah waved me over to the sitting area.

"How many times can I apologize for the hot chocolate?"

Right then, Maddie, Willow, and Eloise, our au pair, entered the library.

"Not about that. Next week Demi's starting ballet class. Freddie has his music lesson, and Ollie and Calvin are in karate. Both of those are at the same center. Not ballet. Eloise can't be at two places at once, so we need to come up with a battle plan."

I got up from my chair, a tiny fart escaping me. To cover up, I made a show of coughing into my shoulder.

"Are you getting a cold?" Concern etched into the corners of Sarah's eyes. "I can't afford to get sick."

"We have four kids in school. Having a cold is the state of being this time of year." There was movement again in my stomach, forcing me to perch on the side of the couch instead of the actual cushion as buttress. I sniffed, my nose wrinkling as an unpleasant odor reached it. Had that come from me? "How long is this meeting going to be?"

"Until we figure things out," Sarah snapped. "You're the one who signed Demi up for ballet."

"Willow got her interested in it by watching YouTube videos," I argued, shifting again as things shifted inside my body in a most alarming way.

"Speaking of," Willow said, "I also signed up for a class. I can take Demi there, but I can't bring her home because my class is two hours long, not one. I don't think Demi will want to wait an hour, if that's even allowed." Willow snapped her fingers in a sorry Charlie way.

"What night is this?" I asked, unable to focus on anything other than the growing pressure in my abdomen. Was it an alien trying to escape?

Sarah let out a tiny groan. "You're literally the person who signed Demi up. You don't remember the day?"

"It's in my phone." Desperate to avoid another scolding, I hopped off the couch to retrieve my phone. That turned out to be a fatal mistake because I ripped the loudest fart that had ever been heard on earth.

"Lizzie!" Sarah waved a hand in front of her face as the air around us turned green from the noxious fumes.

"What? That wasn't me," I insisted, instinct taking over. "It was this ancient cat. I think Snickers needs new food."

"You're trying to tell me that horrible sound and smell came from Snickers?" Sarah's eyes landed on the tiny cat sitting in the middle of the library, cleaning a front paw.

"Afraid so," I lied, demonstrating exactly where our children had learned their skills. "She's been letting them rip all day."

I only felt slightly guilty for throwing poor Snickers under the fart bus. It was self-preservation. Grabbing my phone, I settled on the chair off to the side to keep everyone out of firing range in case it happened again.

"Why does the cat's fart smell like rotting cabbage? This has nothing to do with all the veggies you're eating?" Apparently,

Sarah wasn't willing to let my—er, Snicker's—flatulence go without a full-scale investigation.

"Wednesday night. I can pick Demi up." I ignored Sarah's question and avoided looking in the direction of Willow, Maddie, and Eloise.

It was bad enough that I had farted in front of Sarah, Willow, and Maddie. But our au pair was the quiet type, and I hadn't really gotten to know her all that well. This wasn't exactly how I wanted to break the ice. Or melt it. To be honest, I was pretty sure if I farted again, I might start peeling the paint off the walls.

"Does that work?" I added. "Willow takes Demi, and then I pick her up?"

"Only if you drive with the windows down," Maddie quipped. "Or she might die."

"Luckily, Snickers hates the car, so we won't have to worry about that." In fairness, I hadn't driven with Snickers, but I was fairly sure that my assertion about hating cars was not a lie. I hadn't met a cat anywhere who liked them.

"I admire your dedication." Maddie got to her feet.

"To Demi?" I cocked my head to the side.

"To the lie." Maddie leaned down and scooped Snickers into her arms. "Blaming a sweet, old kitty for your fart."

"I didn't fart!" I stomped a foot, not thinking of the potential danger. Thank goodness, nothing came out of my back end.

"With that, meeting's over. Thanks, Lizzie." Sarah gave my cheek a peck.

"Are you making a fart joke?"

"What—no, never mind. I don't want to know how you got there from a kiss on the cheek. Thanks for offering to pick up Demi. She's excited."

"I'd do anything for my kids." That was entirely true. On

average, I was doing fairly well in the truth department, no matter what Snickers might have to say about the matter.

Luckily for me, cats can't talk, but the reproachful look she cast in my direction filled me with instant shame. I grabbed my phone and started typing. "How do you stop farts from smelling bad?"

The internet delivered.

CHAPTER FIFTEEN

A WEEK LATER, I STOOD IN THE LIBRARY, HOLDING UP a pair of thick black underpants, eyeing them suspiciously. "How do they work?"

Snickers was the only being in the room, and she didn't offer up an explanation, but I recalled the website had claimed the underwear contained activated carbon to combat the smell of flatulence.

"Do you think they're soundproof?" I eyed the fabric doubtfully. Once again, Snickers stayed mum.

Over the past few days, my stomach issues had only worsened. I had hoped things would level out, but each hour only brought more misery. How did people live on veggies for so long? No wonder once modernity hit, things had changed. In my opinion, for the better. Aside from the obesity epidemic in areas where processed foods reigned supreme. Oh, toss in the increased stroke, heart attack, and diabetes risks...

I was back to the need to eat veggies and wear fart-proof underpants. I wasn't always the smartest about things, but even I knew I could only blame Snickers one or two more times before the jig was up.

"Looks like I don't have a choice, Snicks. It's put on the weird underwear or confess. And that's not happening."

By way of response, Snickers climbed into her bed on my desk, wrapping her front paws around her head.

Sarah's voice came through the speaker on the bookshelf behind me. "We need to leave now for the store."

"Okay. I just need to pee first." I gave Snickers a pat on the head before shoving the underwear down my pants. Clearly, I was doing this to hide them before stopping in the bathroom to slide on my fart-blocking miracle thingy—at least I prayed they were. Even I knew they wouldn't work just by shoving the item down my pants. Especially, since they were in the front, nowhere near close enough to the danger zone.

With the thick, slightly scratchy undergarment securely in place, I joined Sarah in the garage. "Where are we going again?"

"The kids need new clothes, and I want you to try on some pants. The ones you have now are getting loose."

"It's the veggies." I tried pulling my waistband away from my stomach, but my belt was super cinched.

At the mall, after buying clothes for the kids, Sarah said, "Your turn."

"Should we buy new pants now? I'm hoping to lose more weight. It's only been a couple of weeks."

"True, but when was the last time you bought clothes?"

I scratched the back of my head, thinking. "I don't really like clothes shopping."

"I'm aware, dear. But I don't know your size anymore. Which is why you're here."

"Not for my charm?" I swear to all that was holy that was when my body released a fart. Tiny, but it still happened. I tensed as a cold sweat broke out across my brow. Any second now, the aroma of toxic waste would envelop us.

Except Sarah didn't react.

I risked a shallow sniff, detecting nothing. I inhaled deeply, overjoyed. It didn't smell!

Had it actually made a sound, or was I just aware of it because I felt it? Maybe the underwear were soundproof after all. Not that I wanted to put the fart pants to the test right there with Sarah handing me several pairs of jeans. But I couldn't wait to get back home and tell Snickers she'd been wrong and that flatulence pants really did work.

"I'm going to look for some slacks," Sarah announced.

"Why?" I fumbled one of the pairs of jeans, and they fell to the floor. Fearful to bend over, I asked, "My back is still bothering me. Can you help?"

Sarah retrieved them, giving me an odd look. "We have some parent events at the school, and jeans won't cut it."

"Let me see if I'm understanding. My university employer doesn't care if I wear jeans, but going to a back-to-school night for elementary students has a dress code?"

"Life sucks. Go try them on." Sarah waved me toward the dressing room.

There wasn't an attendant, so I leaned over to spy which ones were free.

Naturally, I farted instantly.

Luckily, no one was in any of the stalls. And once again, the experience was completely odor-free. These new underpants were nothing short of a miracle. I was so overjoyed I let another fart escape to relieve some of the pressure in my belly.

And that was when I heard someone clear their throat behind me.

There stood Sarah with a pair of black slacks.

"How did you find them so quickly?" I asked, my cheeks burning with the intensity of a million suns.

"I can shop in my sleep." She wore an exasperated expression, making it hard for me to determine whether she'd heard my fart or was just mortified for all the usual reasons.

In the dressing room, I quickly tried on everything, ditching most of the choices, aside from one pair of jeans that didn't cut off circulation to my bits. I'd never understood tight jeans. Never.

"Did any of them work?" Sarah called out.

"These." I placed the jeans over the door.

"Only those? Not the slacks?"

"Too tight in the hips."

"Stay put. I'll grab other types."

I stood in the dressing room in my socks, sweater, and fart pants. Despite them looking mostly like normal underwear, I still cut a ridiculous image, so I turned away from the mirror.

There was a tightening in my belly.

Would I be able to convince Sarah to stop at the drug store on the way home and stay in the car? I was in desperate need of something to make the gas go away. It was like I was a helium balloon, filling and filling well past my capacity.

Did this mean I was allergic to vegetables?

I couldn't decide if that would be a good or bad thing.

I missed my normal food, but I was enjoying looking better. My energy levels were improving. I could focus on work for longer periods. The only downside was the stomach pain. And the embarrassing moments, although my new miracle pants were a godsend where that was concerned.

"Here's a pair." Instead of setting them on the door, Sarah tossed the pants over.

Not expecting that move, they billowed to the floor as I looked on, displaying not even a hint of athletic ability. I shook a fist at the door, but I didn't really want her to see me in my fart pants, so I braced for bending over.

And released a seismic wave of flatulence that put the fart in the library to shame.

Could I live the rest of my life in this small room?

The car ride home from the store took place in total silence.

Which kinda made things worse. Like Sarah was too embarrassed on my behalf to even say a word. She didn't need to be because I was plenty mortified all on my own.

At home, I disappeared into the library without speaking to Sarah.

Snickers was still sleeping. Not surprising. She slept about twenty-three hours a day.

Sitting at my desk, I started googling home remedies for flatulence. Apple cider vinegar, baking soda, betel leaves—what the heck where those?

I sighed.

"We need to talk." Sarah entered the room, holding a book in the air. "I skimmed the intro to this reset diet—"

"It's not a diet," I said wearily. "It's a way of life."

"Yes, eventually. You do know, the steps outlined in the book are supposed to happen over twelve months, right? You've crammed an entire year's program into a few weeks."

My shoulders slumped. "I want it over with. This is miserable."

"That's not how it works. You can't simply change everything and not expect…" The word she eventually landed on was, "Consequences."

It was pretty charitable, considering.

"I just wish my fart pants had been soundproof," I said with a sigh. "That's what I need."

"Your what?" Sarah blinked excessively, as if trying to erase an image from her head. "Honey. I know you like to charge headfirst into a problem—"

"You think my weight's a problem." I slumped even more.

"No, I don't—"

"You just used the word problem."

"It was the wrong word. What I need you to focus on is—"

"I think I'm allergic to veggies. I never want to eat one

again." I rubbed my stomach, only causing more pain. "I might explode."

"Oh no you don't," Sarah scolded. "For once in your life, you need to follow the actual plan. Like I said, I skimmed the book, and this actually sounds good. Not all at once, though. Small steps, like you promised on New Year's."

"It's not fair."

"What isn't?"

"Why can't I like them?" I cradled my belly, the pain intensifying.

"What?"

"Veggies. Millions of people do. Like you. When we go out to eat at a steak place, you always get Brussels sprouts, asparagus, or broccoli as your side. And, it's the first thing you eat, instead of the steak."

"Clearly, the universe and I want to fuck with you." Sarah chuckled, but I almost believed that was true sometimes with the way my life tended to go.

"I want to be healthy. I don't want to worry about my heart. I just hate it. With all my being. I hate all of this. I love fruit. I could easily live on fruit, but vegetables—not only do I dislike the taste, but they make me feel like I can blast off into space."

"We need to tackle this together. Slowly. I'm sure I can find ways to get vegetables into your meals without you knowing."

"How?" I perked up at this possible solution.

"If I tell you, it won't be a secret." Sarah winked at me. But not a saucy one. More like a pity wink.

"I don't like to take things slow."

"I'm aware. Everyone under this roof is aware. Poor Snickers." Sarah scratched the cat's ear. "She might not be able to smell—"

"I knew the pants were too good to be true."

"What pants?"

"If I tell you, it won't be a secret." It was a weak attempt, but Sarah kindly let it go.

"We can do this together. I just need you to listen to reason." She quickly added, "To me. We can see a nutritionist and come up with a plan."

"I guess I don't have much of a choice, or I'll never leave this office. Snickers, doesn't though. So can it be that bad?"

"You're not a geriatric cat."

In defiance, I stared at Snickers, who was lazily stretching out on the cushion. She blinked back at me, as if to say, "Don't you dare compare yourself to me, human."

I couldn't help but chuckle at the absurdity of it all. But amidst the laughter, there was a flicker of determination. Maybe Sarah had a point. Maybe it was time to face the reality of my unhealthy eating habits head-on and take it slowly, step by step, the way I had promised to do.

After all, if Snickers could maintain her health and vitality into old age, then why couldn't I?

FEBRUARY

CHAPTER SIXTEEN

"Lizzie, honey." Sarah tiptoed into the library, looking like a cartoon character trying to get away with... something. I could almost hear Looney Tunes music in my head as I watched her.

"Nothing good happens when you say both my name and honey in one breath." I leaned back in my desk chair, pushing down the urge to bolt from the room with my fingers shoved into my ears. After being with Sarah for so many years, I was proud of myself for having learned to control the urge. To be honest, I didn't think I ever got enough credit for it.

"No need to panic. You're not being marched out in front of a firing squad. I promise." Sarah took a seat, leaning forward to scratch behind Snickers's head as the cat snoozed on the fluffy pet bed I'd placed on my desk. "I didn't want to wake the kitty."

"I'm adding fear of firing squads to my never-ending list of things that might be in my terrible future." I pretended to scribble on a mental list. Mental being the key word. The older I got, the more insane I believed I'd become. Not to mention stupider.

"Dramatic, much? I simply came in here to tell you I'll be working late one night next week." Sarah relaxed in the chair, letting me believe that was all she wanted to say. I knew better, however. This was some kind of trap. I was sure of it. It seemed everything under the sun was out to get me, and I was constantly trying to game out how. Was it exhausting? Sure, but necessary.

"Why?" I asked, not sure if this was the smart move. Did she want me to ask, or was I supposed to accept what she said without question?

"I'm going to be a chaperon at the school's Valentine's Day dance."

Snickers rolled onto her back, covering her face with a tiny paw in a way that drew a smile to Sarah's lips.

"She's so cute."

I nodded in agreement, but my mind was firmly focused on the school activity. "Is the dance during the day on Valentine's Day?"

"No. It's that night, hence why I'll be working late." She tried, but not very hard in my opinion, to curb a smile. It was the look I got when I was being a lovable idiot, which happened a lot.

"But it's Valentine's Day," I whined, despite not having it on my radar until this very moment.

"That's why it's called a Valentine's Day dance." Sarah's brow knitted as if she had no idea why this was upsetting me.

And, honestly? It was. If I had to explain right then and there why it was, I wouldn't have been able to. But I was irked beyond all reason at this news, like I was being denied something I hadn't known I wanted until it was taken from my grasp.

"What if we have plans that night?" I demanded with a pout, knowing we didn't. I mean, I certainly hadn't planned anything. And Sarah wouldn't double book herself. That was something I would do and not realize until I had to be in two places at once. But not Sarah. If her calendar said she was free, she definitely had not planned anything for us either.

"Don't worry. We don't." She didn't seem bothered by this statement.

Which annoyed me all over again.

It wasn't because I expected her to plan something. I knew that wasn't fair. But she was so convinced I hadn't planned anything either. Probably based on the fact I never had before, and history had a good chance of repeating itself because, truthfully, I hadn't.

But still!

"You give me no credit. You're assuming I haven't planned a thing." I tapped my fingers on my desk, villain-like. Don't ask why because I have no idea. "You didn't even ask."

"It seemed a safe bet. You gave me a coupon for Christmas and need me to give you a detailed list of items if you have to stop at the grocery store. Details aren't your department, dear." Her voice wasn't accusatory. More like she was reading the weather report.

This made my suspicion levels go to DEFCON 4. First she called me honey, and now dear? I wasn't sure if I was being majorly condescended to or was so far in the dog house I'd never find the door, but either way, I smelled trouble.

"That's not right. Assuming I haven't put a thought into Valentine's Day. What day is that, anyway?" I reached for my calendar and started flipping the pages.

"February fourteenth," my wife informed me with a knowing smirk. "You know, the same day it is every year."

"Of course, I know that! I was just testing you," I scoffed, pretending to be insulted. And I should have known that, but that's not how things work for me. To avoid total humiliation, my brain latched on to a final hail Mary. "It's because this is a leap year that I got thrown off."

"You're a historian, and you don't even know how calendars work." Sarah rolled her eyes and crossed her arms. "Not that it's relevant in any way, but leap day is the twenty-ninth of February, which happens after the fourteenth. Do you need Calvin to help you learn your numbers?"

Okay, that should have been obvious. Clearly my ruse was only backfiring, digging me in deeper. A common element of many of my deceptions, come to think of it. I switched gears. "I meant, what day of the week is it?"

"Wednesday."

"Aha!" I raised my arms in the air as if I'd just crossed the Boston Marathon finish line and everyone should applaud my greatness.

"Wednesdays get you hot? How did I not know this?" Sarah's smile was a mixture of amusement and annoyance. That it was not one hundred percent annoyance was a fairly big win in my mind.

"I switched my night class from Wednesday to Tuesday this semester," I said triumphantly.

"I'm aware—" The penny seemed to drop, and Sarah started laughing. "Are you trying to convince me that you rearranged your entire teaching schedule just to accommodate Valentine's Day? That's rich."

"As a matter of fact, I did," I lied. "And now you've gone and ruined it. Too bad. I had plans. Big plans. Spectacular love plans because I'm like that." I flicked my fingers to imitate fireworks. Was that tempting fate too much? When I planned things, they tended to cause fires that Sarah had to put out.

"Is that right?" Sarah stared deeply into my eyes, and it took everything I had not to whither under the intense glare and admit the truth.

That would have been the right thing to do. I mean, she'd have to be an idiot to believe a word I was saying. She did know me, after all. And part of me felt horrible about laying it on so thick. But I didn't like that she assumed it'd never entered my mind to make romantic Valentine's Day plans, like I was totally incapable of it.

And that's why I decided at that moment to leap across the Rubicon without fully engaging my brain. A nasty habit of mine.

"Because I'm the romantic one." I pressed my hand to my chest. "You recently informed me I wasn't trying hard enough to keep the magic in our relationship alive. This might shock you, but I listened. Look what that got me. I did all this planning, and you've gone and ruined it."

Yikes, Lizzie. Don't be a total jerk.

It may surprise you to hear that lecturing myself didn't lead me to correct the record and admit I was lying my ass off. Shocking, I know.

"Okey dokey," Sarah chirped. "I'll let Leonard know I can't chaperon the dance this time. No biggie, and I wouldn't want to ruin all of your hard work."

Panic set in. Had this been her plan all along? Trap me into saying something stupid, which let's face it is almost a given, and then leave me no choice but to follow through? I was playing checkers to my wife's three-dimensional chess game.

That didn't stop me from back pedaling.

"Didn't you already say you would? It doesn't sound right to back out now after giving your word." I felt a stabbing sensation in my heart. It was the feeling of my impending doom. I know this because it was not the first time I'd experienced it.

Sarah shrugged like none of this was any big deal. "I told him I would see if it worked with my schedule. As it turns out, it doesn't. I'll go to one of the dances later in the year to make up for it. I wouldn't want to miss these spectacular love plans."

She was calling my bluff. This was my last chance to confess and save my bacon.

Now or never, Lizzie.

Tell her the truth.

Save yourself…

"Yeah," I said as I wagged a finger at her. "I wouldn't either if I were in your shoes."

There was something seriously wrong with me. She knew I was full of shit. I knew it. Even Snickers was probably aware of the situation. Sarah had given me an off-ramp from my own madness. And I'd doubled down like a moron.

Sarah gave me a quizzical look as if still waiting for me to come clean. Again, this would have been the wisest course of action.

Instead, I doubled down again, making it a quadrupling down. I think. Math is not my strong point.

"I myself can't even believe what I pulled together." Why, oh why, couldn't I stop my mouth from digging the hole deeper and deeper?

Sarah offered a bemused smile, her eyebrow quirking slightly. "I'm proud of you, Lizzie."

"You are?" I swallowed hard, my mouth suddenly dry. Was she actually starting to believe me? That'd be foolish. "Why?"

"For hearing my words and putting a plan in place to let me know how special I am to you after all these years." Sarah paused, her eyes searching mine with total sincerity.

My palms grew clammy, and I struggled to maintain eye contact.

"That's me. The romantic listener."

That statement made no sense. Not even for me, a person for whom common and sense were never in the same zip code.

Apparently neither was a rudimentary grasp of the English language.

Sarah stood and worked her way around the desk to plant a kiss on the top of my head. "It's my night to make dinner. See you soon." At the door, she stopped, batting her lashes as she said, "I love you."

"Ditto." I gulped.

I couldn't decide at this point if Sarah still suspected I was blowing smoke out my ass. Given my recent flatulence issue, blowing anything out from there was dangerous.

I tapped my fingertips on my forehead, trying to figure out a solution. Could I convince Sarah that the dance was more important? That her students needed her? That I was willing to sacrifice all my hard work for their well-being and happiness?

She would see right through that. I was 89.786 percent sure she already knew I was stretching the truth, but a whopper like that would seal my doom. How did I repeatedly get myself into these situations?

The only solution, aside from building a time machine to go back and redo that whole conversation, was to do now what I said I'd already done.

How hard could it be to plan a spectacular Valentine's date ten days… no, nine days out? Hold on. It might be only eight days.

I started counting on my fingers but gave up as the gravity of the situation pressed down on me like all the oxygen was being sucked out of the room.

As a side note, if we ever lived on a spaceship, I was darn certain someone on the vessel would shoot me out of the air lock. To be completely honest, it'd probably be me who did it, totally by mistake, but it might end up saving humanity.

Why had I run my mouth knowing I hadn't put one thought into Valentine's Day?

Snickers let out a deep sigh. It was like the cat was

connected to my thoughts. Or she was so old that everything warranted that kind of sigh.

"Why do I have this feeling I'm going to be frog marched before a Sarah firing squad, Snicks?"

This time Snickers stared at me with dead eyes.

Not a good sign.

CHAPTER SEVENTEEN

"Mommy!" Demi ran to Sarah right as she stepped into the kitchen after returning home from work.

"Demi!" Sarah hunched down to hug our daughter. "Why can't everyone be this excited to see me?" Sarah's gaze met mine over Demi's head, and I had the distinct feeling that she was referring to me.

I gave her a quick kiss on the cheek, but this earned me an eye roll from my beloved wife.

"Too little, too late," she told me.

Make a mental note, Lizzie. Next time she comes home, run across the room and throw your arms around her legs—er, shoulders.

"I have homework," Demi crowed as she did a twirl. She wore a little pink skirt that spun out around her like a tutu, her face a picture of pure joy.

"Finally, one of our kids is excited about school." I grinned at Demi, trying not to give the three others a disappointing glare as they "helped" me make the dinner side salad. "What kind of homework, my little Demitasse?"

"Valentines!"

Valentine's homework? My eyes narrowed in suspicion. No

way was that a real thing. Had Sarah put Demi up to this? I suspected my wife knew I hadn't made any progress on our spectacular plans since our conversation two days ago, and this was her way of rubbing it in.

Planning things wasn't exactly my specialty. Especially when it came to dates.

Was it still romantic to go to dinner, see a movie, and then have dessert someplace? Because that was all I could think of, and it didn't seem all that amazing.

Especially not when you saw people on social media posting pictures of extravagant surprises and over-the-top gestures for every little thing. You couldn't even have an ordinary, heartfelt moment without someone setting off fireworks or hiring a flash mob to turn it into a production.

Valentine's Day was likely to bring out all the big guns, and I was feeling the pressure.

"Yes, that's right," Sarah said to Demi, playing along with this Valentine's homework farce. "All four of you do. Demi, let me take a look."

Now I really didn't believe Sarah. It was one thing for a single child to come home with Valentine's homework, but for all four of our kids to have it? That seemed highly unlikely.

Sarah put her hand out as Demi brought her the bright pink homework folder that came home in her backpack every day. The one I'd neglected to pull out of her bag to check, despite Sarah having told me to do so at least a dozen times in the past. I made another mental note not to forget again.

Too bad there wasn't an app on my phone that could connect directly to this mental list. It would probably require a microchip implant, but I didn't care. I needed all the help I could get, no matter how close it came to mirroring the plot of a dystopian novel.

I was falling down on every front right now. Parenting. Homework. Even the salads I was making looked a little wilted.

How was I going to pull off a spectacular love date? A trickle of sweat wended down my back.

"You should show this to Mom. She's in charge of Valentine's Day this year." Sarah waved to me, as if the kids needed to know I was the mom she was referring to, and not Eloise, our au pair, who had the night off and wasn't even in the room but would probably still be better at everything than I was.

Demi gave me a worried look. It was time for me to rally.

"That's right, Demi. I'm the 2024 Valentine's mom-in-chief!" I tapped my chest like I was a four-star general getting ready to conquer...what? I had no idea. Love, maybe? War was probably not the right image for me to project, considering I was about to destroy Valentine's Day forever.

"We need Valentine's cards." Demi presented me with the folder. "And treats."

I mustered a smile and took the pink homework folder from my daughter's hand, opening it to find a photocopy of hand-printed instructions. The teacher's handwriting was neat enough to be mistaken for a computer font, except for the little hearts that had been used to dot all the Is.

"What kind of treats?" I eyeballed the sheet of instructions, the words swimming in front of me. Why were there so many words on the page? What Valentine's hell was this?

"Not stickers!" Fred shouted loudly enough to be heard in the next room despite the fact he was standing next to me, parceling out spinach leaves into the bowls. "Those are stupid."

"No stickers, got it." I gave a salute, once more returning to my military theme. Maybe this was a sign from the universe. What extravagant Valentine's date could be inspired by war? There had to be something. What about a romantic candlelit dinner in a bomb shelter? It would be unconventional, but it could certainly make a statement. I wasn't entirely sure it was the right one, but Sarah did marry a historian. It would be kinda her fault.

"What do you want Mom to buy?" Sarah's smile had bite, as if she knew this would open the kid floodgates. I braced myself for the coming onslaught of ridiculous requests.

Sure enough, Calvin soon blurted, "Signed football cards!" He stopped counting cucumber slices, not that I had asked him to, but Eloise had just taught him how to count to ten in German, and he enjoyed showing off his new skill.

"Signed cards, huh? This is starting to get expensive," I joked. "Wouldn't unsigned ones work just as well?"

"Whatever you do, don't get the rulers like Susie's mom did last year. We'll be toast." Ollie squirted salad dressing into the bowl that Calvin had scooted over to her in their makeshift assembly line.

"What do you mean?" I asked, starting to get a little nervous about this task. I hadn't anticipated so many potential pitfalls in buying Valentine cards.

"The kids still say, 'Who rules? Not Susie,'" Fred explained, using a high-pitched voice to imitate Susie's tormentors.

"That's not nice. Rulers are a lovely idea." I was amazed I got those words out without swallowing my own tongue, because I also thought rulers were lame. But to make fun of a child over them? That was just mean. I didn't like mean. Not one bit. Probably because growing up, my classmates hadn't been particularly kind. Not that I could remember any instances. Just vague memories that fed my nightmares.

Even so, Sarah slanted her head as if certain I'd meant to say something else but temporarily had been taken over by an alien presence.

"I mean. Picking on a kid for a gift isn't nice, and rulers are helpful when you need to you know... measure stuff. You two don't taunt Susie, do you?" I watched the twins closely. Fred shook his head, but Ollie didn't confirm or deny.

Instead she said, "We all have rulers in our kits." She groaned as if I was as lame as Susie. Or Susie's mom. I wondered if Susie's mom got taunted by other parents. Maybe this was a multi-generational faux pas.

"No stickers or rulers," I said. "And, getting signed football cards this late in the game isn't going to happen, little man. Hit me with the next best thing."

"Candy!" Demi did another ballet twirl before returning to the crouton station at the counter.

"Everyone likes candy," Fred confirmed.

"I can do candy," I said solemnly as if this was the most important topic of the year.

"Kids, after dinner, don't forget to give Valentine's mom-in-chief your homework sheets so she can follow each of them to a T." Sarah's eyes were definitely twinkling with mischief as she said this, and I could tell she was enjoying my discomfort in trying to navigate the treacherous world of Valentine's Day gift-giving.

"What else do I need to know aside from buying the loot?" I slipped on oven mitts to pull out the lasagna from the oven.

"How many cards to buy and what the directions are," Sarah informed me. "It's an actual homework assignment. For grades."

"For Ollie and Fred, I only need to buy one box, right? They're in the same class," I pointed out, one of the advantages of twins.

"No, because they each have to fill out their own cards." Sarah swiped a crouton off one of the salads.

"They can't fill out the same card?" I challenged. "It's what we do when we send a Christmas card."

"Careful, Lizzie. You might be stepping into the ruler zone." Sarah walked two fingers in the air.

"Don't, Mom!" Fred exclaimed in all seriousness. "Or we'll have to eat lunch with Susie."

I frowned. "Doesn't anyone eat with Susie?"

"The new kid does." Ollie hopped on one foot for some reason. I might have asked why, but I was too preoccupied with Susie.

"I think you two should sit with Susie. It's not nice to feel left out." I scooped lasagna onto the plates, the steam momentarily blurring my vision.

"Mom's right. Kindness and honesty will get you far in life. Right, Lizzie?" Sarah gave me a look I didn't understand.

I nodded, trying to figure out why Sarah tossed in honesty.

"I'm so glad you're the one overseeing their Valentine's homework. Far be it from me to get in the way of the love expert." Sarah placed a hand on my shoulder, giving it a firm—almost too firm—squeeze.

Now I knew. The reference to honesty had to be a dig at my claims to be organizing the best Valentine's Day date ever.

She was definitely on to my Valentine's hoax.

CHAPTER EIGHTEEN

THE FOLLOWING MORNING, I DROVE TO THE WALMART in Framingham to take care of buying the Valentine's Day cards for the kiddos. And to see if I could find some inspiration for the Love Spectacular night—I shook my head. I still wasn't getting the wording right. Not that it mattered. I sincerely doubted Walmart had an aisle for idiotic spouses who let their mouths run and now had to deliver a once-in-a-lifetime romantic experience.

Walmart wasn't exactly known for being a romantic haven, but that didn't mean there wasn't a company somewhere out there that could deliver on what I had promised. It occurred to me that there were businesses specializing in just about anything you could need. Why not one that created extravagant and over-the-top romantic experiences on behalf of spouses who had fallen down on the job?

I pulled up Google on my phone and typed in *once-in-a-lifetime romantic experiences*.

A bucket list from someone's blog appeared at the top of the search results. Their number one item was cage-free shark diving. Like I needed to present an opportunity for Sarah to feed me to the fishes. Thanks, but no thanks.

Given it wasn't that much after eight in the morning, I was surprised to see a handful of moms scouring the seasonal aisle.

One frazzled brunette said, "It's really picked over."

I had to agree with her. The big day was a week away, but it looked like vultures had hacked the Valentine's carcass dry.

The woman reached for a plastic-wrapped packet, proclaiming with excitement that she'd found heart-covered rulers.

"Don't get that one unless you hate your kid," I said, trying to be helpful.

Apparently, the woman did not consider my advice all that useful. In fact, she glared at me, told me what I could do with my advice (I'm still trying to figure out if it's even anatomically possible), and then marched to the checkout area with the box of rulers I had tried to warn her against.

"Your kid's funeral," I muttered to myself as another mom backed away from me.

Okay, I wasn't making friends today, but I wasn't here for that. I needed to get cards so special my kids wouldn't be bullied. What a world we lived in when a child's entire social life rested on the correct choice of a printed piece of card stock.

Had my mom bought the lame ones, and that was why I never had friends? I was beginning to suspect this was the root of all my issues. Was this why I always blocked Valentine's out of my thoughts? And why I was going to disappoint Sarah?

Just as I was about to give up in defeat, I spied a section that wasn't depleted. When I saw the prices, I understood why. How did little slips of paper with cartoon drawings cost that much? Although, they did come with chocolate. With the others, I'd have to buy the treat separately. Maybe it was worth it.

I reached for one box, and looking closer, I realized it only contained eighteen cards. Considering we lived in a good school district and still none of the class sizes were below twenty kids, I questioned who these cards were intended for. Had I stumbled into a special selection of cards made for snooty private school kids? And if so, would buying them improve my kids' social prospects or hinder them? It was impossible to tell.

Right now, I had a bigger problem. Namely, math. If there were eighteen cards in each box, but twenty or more kids in each class, I needed two boxes per kid. Eight boxes? Could that be right?

Surely, I could just buy one box for each kid and an extra box to make up the difference. But that'd mean I'd have to buy the exact same type for all four kids to avoid disagreements. Which was fine, except we'd been avoiding buying identical items for the twins so they didn't feel like we were undermining their individuality.

And now I felt guilty for suggesting they sign the same card last night.

My mind returned to the task at hand. If I bought eight boxes, it was going to cost me over one hundred bucks. This was Valentine's Day extortion!

Letting out a Snickers-like sigh, I wondered how much therapy for four kids would cost me if I went the cheap route and ultimately destroyed their social lives at such a young age. At the average hourly rate of a psychologist, a hundred bucks seemed like the better option. Even if my sensibilities bristled by the consumerism we were teaching our children. This was what was wrong with society. The need to outdo others. Sure, I was trying to wow Sarah for Valentine's Day, but that was different... somehow.

Then I slipped on the solution. Literally. My foot landed on something slippery, and I went skidding across the slick floor.

When I caught my balance, underfoot was a package that had to have been sent from the heavens.

Adorable cards that weren't like the others. That appealed to me instantly. Maybe even more than the deeply discounted price on the clearance tag. And it turned out there was a whole basket of this style with different graphics hidden on a bottom shelf, so I could get enough for everyone.

These particular packs didn't come with anything fancy, like candy, but I could buy a pack of Tootsie Roll Pops and the kids could tape the stick to the envelope. It was a perfect plan!

The only thing concerning was the size of the card. They were longer than the others, but—

My phone trilled.

"Hey, Willow. What do you know about Val—"

"Snickers is making the most god-awful sound. I think you should come home."

"On my way!" I grabbed a handful of the discounted card packs and Tootsie Roll Pops and paid for them at the self-checkout, which mercifully went smoothly instead of the red light flashing above my head to alert a staff member I'd done something stupid. Receipt in hand, I ran out of the store.

I'm pretty sure I broke about ten traffic laws as I sped home.

Bursting into the library, I saw Willow standing next to Snickers, who was sleeping peacefully on my desk.

"What's wrong?" I whispered.

"Nothing, now," Willow whispered back. "She hacked up a mother of a hairball and then went back to bed. I'm so sorry I scared you. It's just—Hank doesn't make that sound when he's ready to expunge a hairball."

"No, you did the right thing. I want to know if there's something off with anyone under the roof." I moved into a squat to be eye level with Snicks.

She let out a contented sigh as I scratched behind her ear.

"She's so sweet, isn't she?" Willow said.

"That she is, and everyone keeps saying it. Hey—" I straightened, extending one leg and then the other to work out my protesting muscles from being in the squatting position. "Do you and Maddie have plans for Valentine's Day?"

"Yes, and I'm so excited. Maddie booked us a room in a Vermont inn."

"Wow, that sounds nice." It sounded perfect, actually. I needed to find out how to get in on this Vermont inn action.

"This place goes the whole nine yards for the holiday. Wine and cheese. Five course meal. Champagne. Every couple gets their own heart-shaped cake. And, they get to use a private hot tub."

"Wow, did you have to book it like a year in advance?" I forced a laugh, even though this was an accurate reflection of the state of the Valentine's market from what I could tell.

"No. It was a last-minute thing. We're looking at it as a possible wedding venue, so we'll get to see what we think."

"That's amazing. What's it called?" I whipped out my phone and pulled up my browser, my heart thumping with relief. "I think I'll book a package there, too."

"Oh… uh… I doubt they have room."

My spirits fell as quickly as they'd soared. "But I thought you said you just booked it."

"Yes, but they're usually booked a year out. It's just that Maddie did some design work for them a while back, so when they had a cancellation last week, they offered her the spot. They also know we're wedding venue shopping…" Willow let her voice trail off apologetically, clearly picking up on my disappointment.

"Dang," I said with a pout. "But I'm happy for you. It sounds like a great venue. Unfortunately, I'm in charge of Valentine's Day, and it's—do you know you can't book a decent restaurant anywhere in the greater Boston area for dinner that night?"

"It is the biggest night of the year for some places." Willow softened her expression, but I detected a hint of disappointment in her eyes. Disappointment but not surprise.

My shoulders slumped as I let out a sigh. "I had no idea. I can't even get a fancy flower arrangement. I missed the deadlines at every florist I've called. One place said the only thing they could do was a funeral wreath, and I seriously considered it."

"Does Sarah even want flowers? They drive your allergies insane. I doubt she wants you to suffer."

"Good point." Even though I wasn't quite as confident about my wife's lack of desire for me to suffer under the present circumstances, I drew a line in the air as if crossing flowers off the to-do list. It was the only item on that mental list that could be marked done despite me having focused on nothing else the entire time.

"If you had to plan a last-minute night of love, what would you do?" I asked Willow.

She thought for a moment. "I like simple. That speaks volumes."

Says the woman going to Vermont for specially made heart cakes. Miraculously, I managed not to say this out loud.

"The kids really like Friendly's." I flicked a helpless hand in the air, knowing this suggestion was not one of my best.

"Ice cream is not a bad way to go, but Friendly's is more of a family restaurant. Have you considered staying in with Sarah? Make a picnic at home?"

"With Sarah and the kids?"

"Right. The kids." She frowned, her eyebrows scrunching, as she pondered this additional wrinkle in the plan. Suddenly, Willow's face lit up. "What about your dad or Rose? Would they watch them?"

"I could ask, but—"

The light in her face extinguished like the flick of a switch. "But it's Valentine's Day for them as well. And they're the romantic type."

Yes. What I needed was a non-romantic type. Did I know anyone like that? Other than myself, that was.

"Allen?" I tossed out, basically because I was out of options.

Did my brother have plans? He was back in Boston for school, but he was also in his early twenties with a girlfriend. Surely, he hadn't been as stupid as his older sister and forgotten to plan something. Unless romantic failure was a genetic trait.

There was always Eloise, but we tried to respect our au pair's hours. Just because she lived with us and her job was to take care of the kids, that didn't mean she was on duty twenty-four seven.

"I better get to campus." And start sending out SOS texts.

CHAPTER NINETEEN

"That's wonderful, Calvin. I love the football after your name." I patted his head as I worked my way around the table. "And, Ollie, that heart over the I in your name is very creative. Kiddos, you are smashing this homework assignment! Your penmanship is wonderful, and you're showing your personalities. Tick, tick, tick!" I was about to say hot chocolate all around, when Eloise, who was dressed to go out, stopped and held up one of the discarded attempts from when Fred had misspelled a classmate's name.

"What's this slit for?" she asked, pulling at it with a finger.

"What slit?" I picked up a different card from the whoopsie pile and gave it a closer look. "I didn't notice that before. Do you put candy in it?"

"It's for the gift card," Sarah said, setting down her bag. She'd been so quiet coming into the house, and we were so engrossed in the Valentine's cards, no one had realized she was there until she spoke.

"You're home! Kids, Mommy's home!" I said with way too much enthusiasm. Not that I wasn't glad to see her, of course. In fact, I may have been a little too relieved after realizing exactly how hard it is to oversee four children doing a somewhat tedious task at the same time.

"Done!" Calvin tossed the pen down, rubbing his hand like he'd just signed thousands of cards for seventy hours without a break. In a way, I couldn't blame him. It had sure felt that way to me.

"Me too!" Fred tossed the pen in the air, caught it before it fell to the ground, and grinned.

"I like how you show up right when the hard work is done." I winked at Sarah, or attempted to. I'd learned in my nearly four decades on this planet that there were people who could wink and then there were people like me, who looked like someone stabbed them in the eye with a mechanical pencil.

"These are the cards you got for all the classes?" Sarah took the one from Eloise, who still wore a befuddled expression.

"Yes. They're different from the others I saw. We're Petries. You can't put us into a box. Right, kids?"

"No way!" Ollie tossed her pen down. "Done!"

"But, Lizzie, they're for gift cards. You have to put a gift card here. If you don't, it's really obvious." Sarah held it open for me to see what she was talking about.

"That can't be right." I studied the card again, this time with Sarah's explanation in mind. The concept was slowly seeping in, filling me with a low buzz of anxiety. "They're fine. It'll be obvious to grown-ups, but the kids won't know."

"Some might, and their parents will." Sarah bored her eyes into me as if daring me to dismiss the very real danger of being judged by a horde of Wellesley parents. "Did you get gift cards?"

"I got Tootsie Roll Pops." I forced a smile, but a chill ran down my spine. I could almost hear a few of the snarkier moms pointing out my faux pas. "Can the kids slide one into the slot instead of taping them to the envelope like I'd planned?"

"Have the kids addressed the envelopes yet?" Sarah asked

in a way that made me think she was enjoying my misery, because it was pretty obvious from the stacks of pristine white envelopes on the table that not one had been filled out. That step in the homework assignment had totally slipped my mind.

Oh!" I boinged my head in an exaggerated way that I hoped would cover up this latest in a string of mistakes. "Team, you still have to write the names on the envelopes."

"No more writing!" Calvin shook a fist in the air.

"Sorry, kiddo. It's written out in your homework assignment. You don't want to fail valentines, do you?" Not like your mom, I almost said. Because I sure was going to when the big day came and I had nothing to show for the big fuss I'd made.

"I hate valentines!" he shouted, crossing his arms and giving me some serious shade.

Yeah. Me too, buddy.

I didn't say that, of course. Instead, I returned my attention to Sarah. "About the gift card thing. What if the kids write out coupons for each card?"

"Sure. You mean like a promise for a cruise?" Sarah's eyes fluttered innocently as her dagger hit home. More proof I was the least romantic person on the planet. Why hadn't I kept my mouth shut instead of pretending I could become competent at this love stuff overnight?

"No, like—I don't know. Fred what type of coupon could you write for a classmate?"

"Jason hates to eat his carrots. I can eat them for him one day," he replied. Unlike his brother, Fred was already starting to address the envelopes.

"Perfect. That's no stinking thinking, Freddie." I gave him a high five.

"I can do Sam's math homework," Fred went on.

"No. No. No." Sarah glared at me. "We can't have the kids

be indebted to their classmates because you bought the wrong cards."

Wow. Way to go placing blame. Like I was supposed to know the cards were different from the rest just because they looked different. And were in a clearance basket. And no one else had bought them even though there had been half a dozen desperate moms in the aisle around the same time as me.

Okay. I was starting to see the situation the way it must look to Sarah.

"Fine." I shoved some colorful words deep down. "I'll go back to the store and get different cards."

"No!" Ollie registered her complaint.

"You can't make them redo all of their hard work," Sarah admonished. Once again, she had a point.

My mind raced to come up with an alternative plan. "Can we put a dollar bill into the slots?"

"You have eighty ones on you?" Sarah boosted her eyebrows in a gotcha kinda way. If I didn't know better, I'd almost think she was enjoying watching me squirm through this self-inflicted predicament.

Oh, who was I kidding? Of course, she was enjoying it. I guess that was fair. She might as well have a good time now because this was as much fun as she was going to get out of Valentine's Day.

"No," I admitted after checking my wallet and finding nothing but a single twenty. "But I can run to the bank."

"Valentine's is tomorrow. Or have you forgotten?" Sarah's sing-song voice kinda scared me, even more so than the realization I was off by a full calendar day.

I could've sworn it was only the twelfth. And Sarah was enjoying this way more than I'd realized. I almost didn't feel bad about having no plans for us yet.

"Of course, I haven't," I lied, because actually I'd honestly thought I still had some time. "It's why we're doing this now.

The reminder on my phone went off." Because I had set it incorrectly, apparently. Now I was really in trouble.

"You can't buy much with a buck," Calvin, who was only in kindergarten, supplied.

The kid wasn't wrong but still.

"You're going to have to get gift cards, Lizzie." Sarah seemed extremely giddy to deliver this news. The joke was on her, because she'd be lucky to get a box of chocolates tomorrow from me at the rate I was going. "I haven't met a kid who doesn't like a donut."

"Donut gift cards." I said this like I was speaking a foreign language, the words unfamiliar in my mouth. "Where do I get those?"

"Seriously? It's like you don't live in Massachusetts. There's a Dunkin on every corner."

I consulted my phone. "The lowest price is five bucks! What's five times eighty?"

"Not eighty. Don't forget the teachers and aides."

"How many are there?"

"The two homeroom teachers, plus art and music. I'm not sure how many of the aides will be there tomorrow. I know some of the parents will be there to help with the parties, but we don't have to give them anything." Sarah squinted as she did mental math. "Get ten extra just to be safe. We can keep the extras for emergency gifts."

I punched in ninety times five into my phone calculator because I didn't attempt mental math when there were other options available to me. "That's four hundred and fifty dollars!"

"Everyone's going to love us!" Ollie darted her hands in the air. "So much better than Tootsie Roll Pops."

"You should still give them the suckers, Ollie. We don't need those around the house." Sarah took one as she said it. "Because I don't have willpower."

I gaped at Sarah, who smirked as she unwrapped the sucker. I was about to insist that no way was I spending that much on gift cards, but then my eyes scanned the kids. All of them were staring at me with pleading eyes as if they didn't want a Susie debacle on their hands.

"I don't like how our kids' social lives depend on the quality of a Valentine's Day card," I declared, knowing I was defeated and about to be out a ridiculous sum of money.

"I don't either," Sarah replied, giving me a ray of hope that was quickly dashed when she added, "I also don't want our kids to suffer because of it."

With perfect timing, Demi's bottom lip quivered. I had no choice, and I knew it.

"Okay, okay. I'll go to Dunkin and get ninety gift cards. That will solve the world's problems." I dug my car keys out of my jeans pocket as I grumbled.

"It's a start." Sarah gave me a kiss on the cheek. "Get a box of munchkins for dessert."

"Best day ever!" It was Fred's turn to dart his arms in the air.

"They might have heart shaped donuts for tomorrow," Sarah not so subtly hinted.

I was so bad at Valentine's Day even this simple detail had never occurred to me.

CHAPTER TWENTY

I sat at my desk in the library, holding my head with both hands, rocking back and forth. Sarah would be home any minute, and all I had managed to scrounge together was shuffling the kids off to my dad's, a picnic-style meal I thought we could eat in bed, and an ice cream cake.

"Are you sick?"

I glanced up at Sarah, my heart clenching in anticipation of her utter disappointment in me. "No. Just thinking."

"I'm so sorry, Lizzie." Sarah looked bereft, and I hadn't even told her our plans yet. This was going worse than I thought.

"About what?" I asked, my stomach tightening.

About divorcing me because I had failed Valentine's after boasting I'd plan the best one ever? That sounded about right. At least she was being kind with the news. I probably wouldn't have been able to show that kind of restraint if our roles were reversed.

"Two of the chaperons are sick. I have to get changed and head back to school for the dance. There's no one else to cover for them."

"Really?" I almost sprang out of my chair to do a victory

dance but thought better of it. No reason to injure myself. Or give the game away, at least no more than I already had by the expression of complete glee on my face. Too late, I tried to smooth my face into something neutral.

"You're excited about me ruining your extravaganza." This was not a question. Her knowing smile made it crystal clear she'd been aware I was full of shit the entire time.

"Of course not. I'm so sad," I bluffed. "But it's a worthy sacrifice. The kids should have their dance."

"Uh-huh. Why don't you come with me?"

"To the school dance? I don't know if you noticed, but I'm a grown-up."

"I see glimpses from time to time that you might be," she teased. "Come on. It's Valentine's Day. We should be together tonight, at least."

"We will be when you get home," I pointed out, praying this would be the end of it.

"You're coming with me." Sarah placed one hand on her hip, making it clear my prayer would go unanswered. "Or I'll make you tell me what you had planned for the night. And before you say a word, I know it's not a night at an inn in Vermont."

"Willow ratted me out!"

"She didn't mean to. She felt bad mentioning it to you after learning you were trying to plan an epic night and had zero idea what to do."

"I d-did—I got an ice cream cake." If only Sarah was one of our kids, all would have been forgiven on the spot.

"What kind? Only ice cream or does it have cake and ice cream?" Sarah's eyes narrowed as if everything depended on my answer.

"The second," I said, dreading being wrong. I was starting to doubt myself about the most basic facts of life. I was one step away from not knowing her name. Or mine. I wasn't equipped for such a spectacular failure. "Cake with ice cream."

"That's my favorite kind."

My body remained tense.

"I know." I swallowed, still unsure if I'd live to see another day. I'd remembered the right cake, but was that enough?

She smiled ear to ear. "We'll eat it when we get home. You have ten minutes to get upstairs and change into your dancing duds."

"Is that a thing? Or did you make it up?" My mind reeled as I tried to figure out what dancing duds looked like and where I might find mine.

"Doesn't matter. You're wasting time. We have to help with the setup, not the takedown. I can almost taste the ice cream cake."

"This isn't fair! I'm being punished for—"

"Spending time with your wife and the mother of your four kids is punishment?" She cocked her head, watching me intently.

"I didn't say that." This time, my throat was too dry for swallowing, and I nearly choked.

"Sounds like you did."

I started to argue my case, but Sarah offered up her *take no prisoners* glare. I shut my mouth and headed for the stairs to change. "Will jeans and a sweater work?"

"Perfect. Don't forget comfortable shoes for the dance floor."

This was the worst night ever. Would it be too soon to book the Vermont inn for next year? Because I never wanted to end up in a situation like this again.

My nose hairs curled as we entered the school gym. I'd never liked gyms when I was a student, and I still didn't as an adult.

"Mrs. P!" A teenage boy high-fived Sarah, who slapped his hand emphatically.

"Mrs. P, huh?" I raised my eyebrows.

"Petrie is a tough name with this crowd. Too many jokes."

"Tell me about it. I've been a Petrie all my life. Middle and high school had been particularly cruel."

"It was character building, and you're quite the character." Sarah bumped her hip into mine. "Help me with the balloons?"

"Where are they?"

"We have to fill them."

"With what?"

Sarah cocked her head. "Helium. What do you normally fill balloons with?"

"I don't know," I muttered. "I didn't want to blow them up myself with just air."

"Don't sell yourself short. You have enough hot air most of the time to fill a thousand balloons." She grinned cheekily and handed me a bag full of unfilled balloons that she retrieved from a box of decorations near the bleachers.

"I see bullying is tolerated at this school," I said pointedly as I grabbed the bag from her.

"Good natured teasing, dear." We stopped at a table nearby where a man was sitting. "Malcolm, this is my wife. She'll be helping you with the balloons."

Malcolm had an impressive goatee.

"Are you one of the teachers?" I asked him once Sarah charged across the gym to take care of something.

"Senior."

"That's an interesting subject matter."

"That's funny." He clapped me on the back. "Give me the pinks."

I handed him a pack of pink balloons as I put the conversation together in my head. He was a senior in high school? His facial hair was impressive considering he wasn't old enough to vote.

"Ever inhaled helium?" Malcolm asked as he filled the first balloon, staring at me through his black-framed glasses.

"Nope. You?"

"Every dance. It's why I volunteer." He spoke with a serious air, and I had to give him credit for his dedication.

"You give up a night of your free time just to sound like a chipmunk?" I wasn't judging. I was intrigued.

"It's a kick. Here." He handed me the balloon. "Try it."

"I don't think I should. It's probably not in the rules." I glanced around nervously as if the helium balloon police would swoop in at any second.

"Would it go in your permanent file?"

"Would it?" I wasn't a student, but— "Oh, wait. You're joking. That's funny."

"How's it going?" Sarah reappeared, putting her hands on my shoulders.

"Peer pressure," I said, half joking.

"You or Malcolm?"

"I would never." Malcolm filled another balloon.

"Be easy on her. High school wasn't her thing."

"Only for you, Mrs. P," Malcolm called out through cupped hands as Sarah made her way across the gym floor.

"She's right," I told him. "I didn't fit in much then. Or now."

"I get it. Life is hard." His shoulders sagged like his own life was on the cusp of something bad. It made me wonder how any of us ever made it safely through these years.

I held out my hand. "Give me a balloon."

His face lit up. "Are you sure?"

I shrugged. "Only one way to find out."

"I like you, P2."

P2. Was that my new nickname? Had I ever had one before? A fuzzy, warm feeling stole over me, the first time I'd ever had a positive experience associated with a gym.

I inhaled and said, "Four score and seven years ago," because it was the only thing I could think of saying. I sounded like a record on too high a speed.

Malcolm busted up. Sarah glanced over her shoulder, laughing. I shrugged, continuing what I could of the Gettysburg Address. You can't just start reciting Abraham Lincoln and stop midway, after all.

By the time the dance started, I was pretty wiped out. Not from the preparation, but the older I got, the harder I found social situations. Maybe they always had been taxing, but in my younger years, I'd simply avoided them. Sarah ensured I didn't do that all the time, and it wore me out.

"Wanna dance?" Sarah held her hand out to me.

I looked at her askance. "Don't you remember our wedding? That's the last time we danced together. For a reason. I'm terrible at it." At least I think the wedding was the last time we danced, but who knew if I was right. That was becoming a rarity these days.

"No, you're not. You just have your own style." She fluttered her lashes, making my tummy go all tingly. I could safely say that had never happened in a gym, either. "Besides, it's Valentine's Day. You can't say no."

"Why can't I?" I demanded, refusing to give in to her spell without a fight. "Isn't it a holiday for me?"

"It is, and we have the house to ourselves tonight, thanks to you. Do you want to spend it sleeping on the couch in the office?"

"There's a guest bedroom," I couldn't help pointing out.

Not that I wanted to sleep there, but I wanted to be accurate about my options.

Sarah chuckled quietly. "You're impossible. Dance with me or no ice cream cake."

"That's just mean." But effective because I followed her out to the floor.

"It's a slow song. Put your hands on my shoulders and move side to side."

I did, feeling like Frankenstein's monster, only one that had been constructed using two left feet.

"You're dancing!" Sarah rested her head on my shoulder. "It's only February. I feel like I've already lived three years in a month and a half."

"Having kids and working full-time does that to a person." I surprised myself by letting out a happy sigh. "I wouldn't change a thing, though. Would you?"

Sarah raised her head. "Not one. This isn't a bad way to spend the evening, is it?"

I glanced around the dance floor, spying Malcolm with a boy roughly his age. Whether friends or young love, I wasn't sure, but either way it made me feel good to see. "It's kinda life affirming, being around kids who have their whole lives ahead of them."

"It is, but don't start thinking we're old. We're not even close. You better get used to the idea we have a lot of years together." Without warning, Sarah dipped me. I clawed at her arm like I imagined Snickers would if I tried to put him in the bathtub.

"Are you trying to kill me?" I laughed.

"Way to go, P Squared." Malcolm screamed between cupped hands.

"I think I'm finally cool to high school students. Only twenty years too late." I gave Sarah a kiss on the cheek. Oddly, this might have been the best Valentine's Day I'd ever had.

MARCH

CHAPTER TWENTY-ONE

I ENTERED THE KITCHEN, SPOTTING SARAH AT THE table with a cup of hot coffee in her hands.

"Are you ready for date night?" I asked. "Or should I say date day?" I attempted to waggle my eyebrows, causing my eyes to strain and necessitating an eyebrow massage.

"What are you doing?" Sarah studied me like I was having a medical emergency or something. It wasn't an emergency per se. But I was pretty sure I felt the beginnings of a headache, which was exactly what I didn't need. Not when I had a whole day mapped out for us that Sarah knew nothing about.

"I don't understand how people can manipulate their eyebrows without causing serious injury. And don't get me started about how some can arch one eyebrow perfectly. I'm jealous as hell." I counted not being a smooth eyebrow communicator as another failing that I couldn't seem to get over. Odd considering it wasn't a life or death skill. Even so, it was one I would have given anything to possess. But alas, my eyebrows remained stubbornly uncooperative.

Sarah ignored all of that, focusing on the topic I had raised before my eyebrows distracted me. "What was this about a date?"

"Oh, that!" I palm-slapped my forehead, a major mistake. The eyebrow fail hadn't been enough to whip up a headache, apparently. I needed to inflict more bodily harm. "I planned a date."

"For whom? When?" Sarah's confusion was understandable as I had sprung this surprise on her out of the blue. I took a seat across from her at the table.

"Right now." I playfully tapped my wrist, relieved this action didn't cause me any additional pain. If I kept injuring myself at this rate, I wouldn't make it through the day.

"And you didn't think to give me any warning?" Sarah slanted her head to the side as if me planning a way for us to spend time together was so foreign a concept it had never crossed her mind.

I mean, after the Valentine's debacle, she had a point. Although, if she truly knew me, she must have known I would go into overdrive to rise above that train wreck. I could've pointed this out to her, but I opted to be the bigger person and not mention how she didn't know me as well as she thought she did.

"If I had told you ahead of time, it wouldn't be a surprise, silly. What's the matter? You got another hot date?" I bounced on the edge of my seat, as if expecting to get a treat for good behavior.

"Maybe I do." Sarah's words knocked the wind out of my sails, but I put on a brave face.

"Oh. Okay... I can reschedule—hold on." I raised a finger in the air, my brain whirring. "What is this other date, exactly?"

"If you really want to know, I'm dying for a luxurious soak in the tub."

Relief flooded me as I splayed my fingers across my chest.

"In that case, I'm pretty sure you don't want to skip the date I planned."

"Is it upstairs in our bathroom?" Sarah craned her head, an expression of concern settling over her features as her eyes narrowed. "Wait. Where are the kids? I haven't heard any screaming or bickering in at least five minutes."

"Maddie and Willow took them to the park," I announced proudly. "After that, they'll have lunch at Friendly's. Then they're seeing a movie. Fingers crossed Ollie and Calvin behave." I crossed my fingers with both hands and looked heavenward. Despite not being religious, it couldn't hurt to cover all my bases. "It's a big ask."

"How come I don't get ice cream?" Sarah crossed her arms. Playfully, or so I hoped.

I tried not to let her pout get to me. "Because you're getting a day at the spa."

"Is this a Sarah-only date?" Her eyes widened like she was really excited by the prospect, and once again my spirits deflated as I tried to cover it up with a brighter than necessary smile.

My Christmas gift, which didn't initially include me, had been a failure because of that fact. But now she seemed excited for just Sarah time. I'll never get women. "It can be. I mean, I was going to go with you, but if you'd prefer a Sarah day—that's fine. Totally okay. I get it."

The truth was, while she'd been begging me to go to a spa with her, it wasn't really my thing. I usually sent her with her mom or Maddie, but I thought this time I would suck it up and go. Apparently, I had missed the subtext. It was a regular enough occurrence it shouldn't have surprised me.

But before I could figure out where I'd guessed wrong, Sarah rose and came around the table, wrapping her arms around my neck. "Of course, I want you to go with me. Does this have anything to do with Valentine's Day?"

My heart began to race as blind panic overcame me at the mention of that holiday and the fact that I sucked at reading her body language. I could have sworn she was happy about the thought. How was I going to stay one step ahead?

"Is it Valentine's again already? No. That can't be right." I swallowed, trying to remember today's date. Did Valentine's Day happen more than once a year? Just the name of this most dreaded of holidays was sending me into a tizzy—like I'd effed up majorly again. It also proved Sarah did indeed know me, so it had been wise not to have called her out earlier. "We're in March right now, right?"

Sarah nodded.

"That's a relief. While I've learned I'm bad at the love holiday, hopefully I'm not so hopeless that I could fail to notice an entire year passing instead of a month. Yes, time flies, but that would be impressive even for me."

"You aren't bad at love." Sarah gave me a kiss on the cheek as if to reassure me. "I should get ready for this date you've planned."

"I've already packed your bag. We have a couple's massage scheduled at two."

"Oh." Sarah glanced at the clock with a frown. "It's only nine. Should I find something to do for the next several hours?"

"Only if you want to skip everything else the spa has to offer," I said, pleased I could offer her more surprises. "From what I understand, there's a salt room, two different saunas, a hot tub, and a cafe. I really don't know what a salt room is, but Willow said you'd love it."

Sarah's eyes widened as she put together the clues I'd offered. "Are we going to Rapture?"

"Yes. Er, I think so." I consulted the confirmation on my phone to double check the name. "Yeppers, it's that place. I'm about 89.67% sure it's the place you've mentioned several times since Valentine's Day. Wait. Does that mean I am bad at the love holiday? You need an entire spa day to recover from my epic fail?"

"Or—and listen carefully. I'm a mother of four with a full-time job, and I simply need a spa day to rejuvenate." Her expression softened. "You're amazing, Lizzie. Simply amazing. This is exactly what I want to do today."

"I aim to please!"

Three hours later, I was wearing a swimsuit and sitting in a beach chair in a room with walls made of pink salt. I was utterly confused. Was the salt from the Himalayas? How did it get here? Was that where the name came from, not the salt? Was it simply the whole concept of the room? And what about the chairs?

On further reflection, I was pretty sure those were not Himalayan in origin. They looked more like standard issue pool chairs. The tricky ones that reclined in such a way you had to extend your feet just right to avoid tipping over.

"Isn't this wonderful?" Sarah had her hands behind her head, showing off her tricky beach chair skills. I, for one, was impressed. Or would have been if my eyes weren't stinging.

"There's salt everywhere." I used my arm to wipe my mouth, resulting in me getting more salt all over my face and on my tongue.

"Salt in a salt room? Imagine that. I wonder if that's how they came up with the name." Laughing at her own joke, Sarah reclined further in her chair and let out a satisfied sigh. "This is sublime. Absolutely sublime."

I nodded, not quite agreeing. Personally, I found it difficult to breathe. And the air tasted salty. But it was a rare occasion for Sarah to use wonderful once and sublime twice in a matter of a minute to describe something I had done. I wanted to bask in the soft glow of victory.

I'd planned this day for her, and she was in heaven. The

best, or worst, way for me to wreck that would be to say how much I hated the salt room. It'd only been a couple of minutes, but this was some type of salt torture. One with a time limit, though. Surely, I could keep my thoughts to myself for twenty-something minutes, couldn't I?

As it turned out, twenty minutes was a very long time to breathe salt into my lungs. Was there such a thing as salt lung? I imagined it was like black lung, only pinker given the walls in this place.

No matter what the website had claimed, this experience wasn't like sitting on a beach at all. Even I could enjoy listening to the waves while surrounded by a lightly salty air. This was more like being on the receiving end of an overzealous McDonald's employee who was salting a fresh batch of fries. There was so much salt it coated everything in the room.

It wasn't solely the salt that wore on me. The music they were playing could probably be classified as relaxing, but it was not to me. It was the new age type, and I strained my ears trying to figure out what people liked about it.

This got me to wonder what was wrong with me because from our time at the spa, every other person seemed to be utterly relaxed and enjoying themselves. I would have preferred being at home, working. That was my happy place.

As I was thinking about this and wondering how I could get myself out of the rest of the spa day, Sarah sneezed.

"Bless you. Should we get you into fresh air?" All she had to do was say yes, and I'd leap out of my chair and make a break for it. Heck, I'd do my best to carry her if need be. I needed to get away from the salt, the music, and the forced la-di-da feelings.

"You're going to have to drag me out of this room." Sarah let out such a contented sigh that I didn't know how to say I was miserable.

Still, I didn't want to give up hope for freedom. "Because you can't breathe?"

"Because I'm totally relaxed for the first time in I don't know how long."

"Right. Me too," I lied, but I felt justified with this one. I wasn't good at sitting in a chair and doing nothing. I didn't have a book, phone, notebook, or anything to hold my attention. Was this a thing other people enjoyed? Doing nothing while drowning in salt? I probably could have lived a very long time without learning this oddity about humanity.

Personally, doing nothing had always stressed me out. I couldn't stop my brain from reminding me of everything I needed to do. For work. Household chores. Things with the kids. How did Sarah look like she was in pure bliss all the while panic was setting in for me? I studied her from the side, trying to detect a hint that her mind was racing. A twitch of an eyebrow. The tightening of the lips. But there was nothing but happiness.

It boggled my mind.

According to the brochure, the salt room was supposed to lower my stress, ease headaches and inflammation, boost my respiratory tract, increase my energy, and enrich my sleep patterns.

All I thought it was accomplishing was driving me mad. Could salt drive a person insane? I was willing to bet it could because I was about to lose it in epic Lizzie fashion.

Closing my eyes only made things worse when it came to settling my thoughts, but it kept the salt from burning my retinas.

"You ready for the hot tub?" Sarah asked.

"Absolutely." Maybe I could drown and end this relaxation torture. This experience was teaching me one thing. I'd been right all along sending Sarah with other people. I was not the spa type. I only had to last another four hours and fifty-eight minutes.

Not that I was counting.

CHAPTER TWENTY-TWO

The following morning, I was still spitting out salt as I prepared my first cup of tea for the day. Given the exhaustion pressing down on me, it'd be the first cup of many. Should I write the salt people and tell them I was immune to their so-called benefits? Maybe that would help them adjust their expectations. Not everyone liked their salt room, and I was certain I was literally worse for the wear.

I spit more salt into the kitchen sink and blasted the faucet to get rid of the evidence.

Sarah limped in.

I gaped at the redness around her eyes and nose. Her bedraggled hair. Hunched shoulders.

"Dear God, what happened to you?" I exclaimed. "Did a truck hit you on your way downstairs?"

"Such a charmer." Sarah sneezed into her robe.

I took a step back, instinct kicking in as I put my hands in the air to block my face. "Are you sick? You can't be sick. I don't have time to be sick, so you can't give me any germs."

Sarah crossed her arms and gave me a look that could've

melted a hole through a steel beam. "At least I know where I stand."

Belatedly, I came to my senses. "You shouldn't be standing. You should be in bed."

Behind a hermetically sealed door so the rest of the Petrie clan doesn't come down with the terribles, I wanted to add. I was smart enough not to. But I'd barely survived the last round. One thing I hadn't known before sending kids to school was the constant threat of illness. Kids were germ machines, and putting so many into a small space was the worst type of experiment. Was it too late to start homeschooling? Sure, Sarah wanted the kids to have friends, but at what cost? Always being sick?

Sarah, quite possibly in tune with my thoughts, continued to glare at me.

"You look miserable. What do you need?" I lowered my germ-blocking hands, knowing once germs were in the house, they were nearly impossible to avoid. Not that I was resigned to getting sick. I made a mental note to eat a pound of citrus and not to touch my eyes or nose under any circumstances.

"That's more like it. Herbal tea." There was another sneeze, which made me wince.

"Anything to eat?" My eyes scanned the pantry in hopes of finding a mask from Covid times. Not that the pandemic was actually over, but we'd become regrettably lax these days. Clearly, considering something that would probably turn out to be a completely new and deadly variation had made it into the heart of our home.

"Some toast, maybe," Sarah offered in a near whisper. She was fading by the second.

"Tea and toast. I can manage that. Please, go back to bed." I pointed toward the ceiling, sorta in the direction of our room.

She started to protest, but a coughing fit overtook her.

"This is my fault." I ran a hand over my head. "And so soon

after the twins brought home the flu. We zombie our way from one illness to the next in this household."

"Zombie our way." Sarah's chuckle turned into a sniffle. "How in the world did you get to this being your fault?"

"You started sneezing in the salt room. If I hadn't taken you there, you wouldn't be sick." I should add this to my complaint letter. Dear Salt People. You suck. Let me list the reasons why.

Sarah's faint smile worried me. Should I have kept my mouth shut and not ratted out the cause of her ailment? Would she actually blame me? I mean, if I were in her shoes, I would. But she wasn't like that. Not normally. Did her illness dent her usual martyrdom?

Although, to be fair, the source still could be the children. None of them were sick—or it could be the teenagers at Sarah's school.

"Not everything is your fault," Sarah said as if reading my thoughts. "Nor can you control everything under the sun. FYI: This Sunday is Easter."

"But, today's Sunday. It's Easter today, and you're only telling me now?" Considering this was the second holiday in as many months that I was totally destroying, I could barely keep my cool. I scouted the kitchen, trying to find signs of the kids' loot as my blood pressure skyrocketed. "I need to get the Easter baskets out."

"Not today." Sarah had to cough to clear her throat to speak. "This Sunday."

"I told you, today is Sunday." I scratched my head, completely lost. "How are you defining the word *this*? I need you to be crystal clear like I'm an alien from a different planet."

"It's not such a stretch," Sarah informed me. "And I mean *this* as in this upcoming Sunday."

"So, seven days from now. Is that right?" I started to count on my fingers. "Monday, Tuesday…" my voice trailed off as I was unable to keep count while simultaneously listing the days of the week.

"Don't hurt yourself," my wife teased.

She was right, so I stopped counting. "Let's not worry about Easter right now," I told her. "The worst thing that can happen is I'll be in charge."

Sarah's eyebrows shot up to her hairline, and I realized that the worst-case scenario of me being in charge of another holiday was the cause of her dismay.

"I know Christmas and Valentine's weren't my best showings, but I can handle Easter," I told her in a tone that hopefully didn't let on about how little confidence I had inside. "First things first. We need to get you better. It looks like the cold from hell. I'll bring you some medicine. Now go. It's hurting me to see you." I rushed to add, "Like this. I don't like seeing you like this." I'd also meant it the other way because I had a feeling this is what I'd look like in T minus two and a half days.

"You're adorable when you think you're in trouble. And I don't want you to worry. It's not that bad. I probably just need a day of rest, and I'll bounce back. I better because Easter is in seven days." She moved closer like she was going to give me a wet and sloppy kiss.

It took everything I had not to back away and crane my neck to avoid her lips, but Sarah simply patted my arm before retreating upstairs.

I made her breakfast and checked out our cold medicine supplies, discovering in the process we were dangerously low. That would have to be rectified once I got the kids fed and Eloise took them to a neighbor kid's birthday party.

I said a silent prayer for Eloise not to be ill, because if I had to take all of the kids to the store for cold medicine, it'd be a nightmare. One thing I'd learned about shopping with kids, even if you told them we were only going in for one item, they'd find a hundred things they wanted to buy and then throw an epic tantrum if I said no. That always warranted disapproving stares from strangers. Some would seem upset I couldn't control the kids. Others probably thought I was being mean not buying the kids yet another toy or sweet they didn't need.

It was hard to determine if Ollie or Calvin was the worst offender when it came to this. Maybe I should take just those two along with me and see who misbehaved the most. Take notes. Although, wouldn't I have to repeat it several times to get a better data set? Then again, was this really an experiment I wanted to take part in? Not just once but many times? The answer was a resounding no. I loved learning things, but this was something I could live without knowing.

Maddie appeared in the kitchen, not looking her best.

"You too?" I made a cross in the air with my fingers. "Stay back. No germs."

"I'm not sick. Just hungover. After watching the kids, I needed to unwind last night. It's possible I overdid it. Do you have Gatorade?" She cradled her head with both hands as if willing her brain to stay inside her skull.

"Yes, the powdered kind. Help yourself." I pointed to the container on top of the fridge. "I need to get this to Sarah." Before I left, I said, "You might want to put on a mask. We have the plague in the house. You've been warned."

"What else is new?"

I didn't like this attitude. As if everyone expected to be ill all the time. I hated being sick. Loathed it. We needed to try harder to avoid these situations. I was more than willing to never ever go to the spa again if it would help in this mission. And I was completely convinced it would.

CHAPTER TWENTY-THREE

Later that night, I tiptoed into the bedroom with a bowl of homemade chicken noodle soup. Willow had made it from scratch. No packets or mixes or anything.

Like, who knew that was possible?

I could barely manage heating up soup from a can without causing utter destruction and the possibility of food poisoning. Not to mention inflicting physical harm on myself. On more than one occasion, Sarah had said she didn't trust me with a can opener, and I couldn't really blame her.

Snickers slept on the bed next to Sarah, who was watching something on her tablet.

"I thought Snickers would love a day in bed." I set the bed tray down over Sarah's lap, before sitting at the foot of the bed, petting Snickers in the guise of wanting some distance from Sarah. Did she buy the ruse?

"She hasn't left my side. Gandhi and Hank were here for an hour tops." Sarah yawned.

"How are you feeling?" And then, just to be certain we were on the same page, I quickly added, "You're not allowed to die."

"I'm not dying," Sarah protested. "I just have a little cold." She punctuated her statement with a loud sniff.

My eyes widened. "Little? You look awful."

"Thanks, darling." She took a sip of tea, reaching for her throat as if in excruciating pain after swallowing.

"I'm serious." I looked away, unable to bear watching her try to swallow again. "You're disgustingly pale."

Sarah laughed—sorta. "You aren't helping yourself right now."

"You can't die. I'd rather you just divorce me if you want out. Not this." I circled a finger in the air. "This is going too far."

"You have to stop thinking everything will lead me to divorce you. It's not healthy."

"Says the woman on death's doorstep."

"I'm not dying from this cold," Sarah argued, "but from boredom."

"What?"

Snickers rolled onto her back, allowing me to rub her belly.

"I'm bored."

"How is that possible? You didn't do a thing all day yesterday, and not once were you bored."

"We were at the spa. It's different."

"At least here at home you can listen to a book, watch documentaries—the possibilities are endless." Now I kinda wished I was in bed with a cold. Not a bad one, but enough of one to justify having a bed day. In my book. That was a hundred times better than a spa day.

"I was being pampered at the spa," Sarah pointed out. "No way could I get bored while being pampered."

I tugged on my earlobe like I couldn't believe what I was hearing. "I don't see how. You're watching—What are you watching?"

For the first time I focused on the screen and tried to puzzle out what it was that had failed to entertain my wife sufficiently.

"YouTube videos on religious cults."

My face scrunched into an expression similar to the one I made when people offered me vegetables. "Why in the world are you watching those?"

Sarah shrugged. "They appeal to me."

"Apparently not much if you're bored. And I didn't think I'd ever have to say this, but if you join a cult, I'm divorcing you and taking the kids." I said the words slowly and with force behind them.

"Is that supposed to be a threat?" Sarah gave me a look that said she was anything but convinced. "You're always begging me not to divorce you, and I'm supposed to think you would carry through on that?"

"Consequences are not threats. Every action has a reaction. A cult action results with divorce." I joggled one hand in the air and then the other, like a scale. "I'm pretty sure every judge in the country would be on my side."

"Don't be so sure. I think some judges are downright cultish. Look at the matching robes they wear, let alone some of their rulings."

She had a point, but I couldn't focus on that. Was she trying to distract me with the robe thing so I couldn't put a stop to her joining a cult?

"I can't fathom why an intelligent woman would waste her time with these types of videos. Why don't you watch something educational? Try learning Mandarin. Make the most of your sick time."

Sarah shook her head in that way she sometimes did when she thought I was being a particularly adorable idiot. "Only you would say that."

"I don't know about that." I stroked my chin as I tried to come up with someone else who might've been on my team. "I have a hard time envisioning someone like Leonardo da Vinci wasting a good opportunity."

"That's what we need in today's world. A renaissance woman." Sarah looked down, eyeing the soup with trepidation. "Where did this come from?"

"Don't worry. I didn't make it. Willow's been helping me feed the kids and now you. Did you know there's soup that doesn't come from a can?"

"Yes. It's called homemade. And Willow is a saint." Sarah stirred the soup with a spoon, the delicious scent filling the room.

"That she is, especially after watching the kids yesterday. Oh, Maddie has the hangover from hell. Apparently, being with our kids for a day drove her to drink." I let out a tiny laugh. "Do you think she and Willow will have kids?"

"If Willow has it her way, they'll have their own brood." Sarah sampled the soup, a grin spreading across her face. "This is yummy."

"That's good to hear, because when I saw her taking the meat off the bones—" I made a disgusted face as my brain filled with images of the unnatural things Willow had done to that bird. "That may be one of the reasons why I hate cooking. You have to get your hands dirty and do unspeakable things. What exactly is a gizzard? No. Don't tell me. Ever."

Sarah put her hand to her head, massaging her temple with the tips of her fingers. "Do you ever wonder if you would have survived a hundred years ago?"

"I know for certain I wouldn't have." My tone was matter-of-fact. "I have Graves'. Without meds when my thyroid numbers were bad, I would have been dead years ago."

Sarah's expression grew wistful. "I always forget that fact about you. That you could have died before we met."

"You might have had some peace and quiet in your life." I ran a hand over my head. "Although, we wouldn't have our kids. We wouldn't have adopted Hank, Gandhi, and Snickers." I scratched the cat's head, eliciting a purr. "Did you text Leonard to let him know you can't go to work tomorrow?"

"I'm starting to feel better."

"No. Don't be that person." I shook my head adamantly as I scolded her. "Stay home."

"You, Lizzie Petrie, are telling me to be lazy?"

"Yes, but by all means, read something edifying." I looked her in the eyes, trying extra hard to convey that I was serious about what I was saying. "I just don't think you should spread germs. After covid—it's not right to go to work sick. We—I mean Americans—were so clueless about things. It used to be a sign of dedication going to work with an illness. When in reality, we were putting others at risk. I'm embarrassed by how many times I suffered through a cold out in the open. I insist, for the sake of your students and colleagues, stay home a day or two."

"I know you said you can handle Easter, but I think we should cancel—"

"No." I held up a hand to stop her from completing her thought. "That seems extreme. I can't take that away from our kids. You must have a fever to suggest such a thing. Should I get the thermometer? Or call an ambulance?

Sarah chuckled. "I don't want to cancel the holiday. We're supposed to host it this year, but we might have to ask someone to take over."

"Why can't we host?" It wasn't like I enjoyed hosting family events, but I felt more comfortable at home, which was a big incentive for doing what it took to keep the celebration here.

"I don't think I'm going to be up to doing it."

"But it's Easter. The kids like being here." Translation, I liked being here. I was about two seconds away from stomping my foot.

"I'm aware. But who's going to do all the shopping, cooking, and decorating?"

I glared at Sarah, waiting for her to realize her mistake. When she didn't, I said, "Me. That's who."

"Lizzie—"

"I might not be able to make chicken noodle soup from scratch, but I can manage Easter. It's one of the easier holidays. Buy candy and a stuffed animal for each basket. Dye eggs. Get a ham dinner."

"It's not as easy—"

"Is this because of Valentine's? I can admit it now with some distance—I whiffed that one this year. That only makes me more determined to land the Easter plane." The more I talked about it, the more I became excited by the prospect. "How hard can Easter be?"

"Don't get brown eggs."

Was this more proof of a dangerous fever? Spouting nonsensical things about eggs?

"For what?" I asked with trepidation. If she said because the aliens don't like them, I was dialing 911. "I don't like eggs."

"You can't dye eggs with brown shells."

What a relief. She was giving me Easter tips, not babbling.

"You think I'd make that mistake?" Silently, I added "again."

"I'm sure Helen would love to take over. Planning is in her blood." Her voice was getting weak, and her eyelids grew heavy.

"I'll have you know my plans make plans. Don't you worry about a thing. I got Easter. It's the least I can do. Get some rest." I removed the tray, letting her drift off to sleep.

It was time to map out Easter. This was going to be the best one yet.

CHAPTER TWENTY-FOUR

"Are you sure you want to do that, buddy?" Turning from the kitchen sink, I stared down Calvin, who held a boiled egg in his right hand, aiming it at Olivia.

"He doesn't dare." Ollie, also armed with an egg, stuck out her tongue. She was standing four feet away from her youngest brother and watching him with a gleam of challenge in her eyes.

I quickly moved my body into the middle, blocking their shots. "No one is going to throw an egg. You got me?" I held a hand out to each. "Give me the eggs or else."

They both shook their heads. My jaw tensed.

"She started it," Calvin said in a tone that could only be described as a whine. "She called my egg stupid."

"I called you stupid." Olivia stretched her neck to lock eyes on Calvin.

"I'm not stupid. You're stupid," Calvin shot back. "It's a football."

"It's an Easter egg," Olivia taunted. "Not everything has to be a football, dummy."

"Olivia! Apologize this instant for calling your brother a dummy." I stomped a foot to show her I meant business.

She glared at me, still holding her egg like she planned to lob it at Calvin.

"Now, young lady!" I snapped my fingers.

"Not until he puts his stupid egg down," she demanded.

I clapped my hands together as loudly as I could, hoping the noise would startle them into behaving. "If you two don't knock off this behavior right now, both of you will miss Easter!"

"I see we've entered the threat stage of the art activity." Shuffling into the kitchen in her robe and slippers, Sarah came over and leaned against me.

"You keep suggesting consequences are a threat. They're a fact of life." I kept looking from Calvin to Olivia, not wanting to let either one of them out of my sight. "We can always donate your candy to kids who don't get Easter baskets."

"I'll take them," Fred piped up.

"Me too," added Demi.

"And me." Sarah tilted her head in her mom-like way. "What's the cause of all this? I could hear you upstairs."

"I truly don't remember," I admitted with a shrug. "Why are you out of bed?"

"I wanted to see how things are going. Clearly well. I can go back to bed." She chuckled quietly, and I could tell I hadn't come anywhere close to convincing her I had this mess in hand.

I snorted, not even bothering to try to lie my way out of it. "Alright, you two. What's your decision? Give me the eggs and apologize to each other, or—" I made a slicing motion over my throat. "No Easter."

"She's always picking on me," Calvin's voice quivered, and his eyes started to brim with tears.

"Ollie," I said in a stern voice. "What do you have to say to that?"

"I'm sorry." She dropped her eyes, and it was hard to determine if she was truly embarrassed and remorseful or simply doing what she had to do so as not to miss out on the Easter festivities.

"And?" I narrowed my eyes, despite her not looking at me. "You'll stop picking on him?"

"He's my brother." She gave a half shrug, still avoiding my eyes. Had she noticed Calvin was crying? Not that I wanted to call him out in front of everyone. It was okay that he was crying, or at least I wanted him to know he could cry if he wanted to. But I didn't want him to feel like he was being pitied or ridiculed.

"Correct. Which is even more reason to be nice to him. When you grow up, he'll be there for you." I turned to Calvin. "And she'll be there for you. We're family. We help each other. We do not throw eggs at each other."

It wasn't the best speech, but I was exhausted. Planning Easter hadn't exactly been a cakewalk, but all in all, the egg standoff notwithstanding, I was smashing the holiday. In a good way. Not like what would happen if eggs started flying through the kitchen.

They both slowly dropped their arms, giving me their weapons. Inside, I was flabbergasted I'd managed to defuse the situation, but I did what I could to maintain a calm exterior.

"Wise choice," I told them. "Because Easter is going to be epic!"

"Mommy. It's purple." Demi held up the one egg she'd kept in the purple dye for so long I was sure it'd be that color through and through.

"It's so vibrant!" Sarah oohed and aahed as she made her way around the Operation Egg Dye table. She still hadn't decided to head back upstairs, despite the fact I clearly had everything under control now.

"Where's yours, Lizzie?" Sarah asked.

I pointed to my contribution, dipping my head. I hadn't quite smashed this part of the Easter preparation ritual out of the park. My egg was a disaster. "I tried making it pink and purple, but after getting the pink part perfect, I dropped it into the purple."

"I like it." Fred picked up the egg.

"That's why you're my favorite," I told him, quickly correcting myself to say, "One of them," as soon as Sarah shot me a withering look. She could claim not to have any favorites, but I didn't believe her.

"Am I one?" Demi looked up from her chair.

"You absolutely are. Along with Ollie and Calvin." Even if they were going to drive me to an early grave.

"What about Mommy?" Calvin asked, wiping his nose with his shirt sleeve.

"She's everyone's favorite," Fred said like that was the most obvious fact of life. He wasn't wrong.

"I agree one hundred percent." I kissed the side of Sarah's face.

Sarah rested her head on my shoulder. "I can't believe everything's going smoothly. Aside from egg threats."

"That's pretty normal for this family." I chuckled. "I keep telling you not to worry."

I had to admit, if I was Sarah, I would worry. It wasn't like I had the best track record when it came to holidays or planning, but this time, I was determined to come through. Sarah went above and beyond for us all the time. I could do the same for her. And by that, I meant, not eff up Easter. Even if that meant I had to do something I didn't normally do.

CHAPTER TWENTY-FIVE

A LITTLE BEFORE SUNRISE ON EASTER MORNING, I stood in the family room like a general ready for battle. I had spent the past week preparing, determined to pull off this holiday celebration in a way that would make Sarah proud.

Pencil in hand, I consulted the list of tasks on my clipboard. "Baskets. Cinnamon rolls in the oven. Plastic eggs scattered around the house." I crossed off the tasks one by one.

"What time is it?" Sarah rushed into the room, her robe billowing behind her. "I meant to get up much earlier to get everything—" Her eyes scanned the room, belatedly taking in the scene around her. "Hold on. Are those the baskets? They're adorable. Is that Demi's?"

I nodded, a swell of pride warming my chest. "I couldn't believe my luck when I found a stuffed Easter Bunny wearing a tutu. Check out Fred's. He's playing the drums. Calvin's is a football player, and Ollie's has a tennis racquet."

"These are perfect!" She squinted into Demi's basket, her eyes widening as she took stock of the contents. "It doesn't have black jelly beans."

"She hates them. With a passion."

"You remembered!" Sarah straightened, a look of pure delight on her face.

"Peter hates them as well." My own smile was laced with a hint of melancholy.

Sarah nodded thoughtfully the way she always did whenever I referenced my older brother. Peter and I hadn't been particularly close, but certain memories came back to me at odd times. Like his hatred of black jelly beans.

"What's that smell?" Sarah sniffed the air like a bloodhound.

"Is it me?" I not so casually inhaled my left armpit.

Sarah gave my shoulder a playful slug. "Not you. Is it cinnamon?"

"Right. That." I laughed over my error. "The rolls are in the oven. They have—" I checked the timer on my phone. "Six more minutes."

"Color me impressed."

"Everyone is coming over for brunch at eleven, but I thought we could use a snack to tide us over—hence the rolls. It's Easter after all. The ham needs to go in the oven at nine." I consulted my clipboard just to be sure I had it right. "Here are all the times for heating up the food I got from Cracker Barrel."

"You ordered dinner from them?"

"I know it's cheating, but I didn't think cooking on my own would be in the interest of everyone's health."

"It's not cheating." She narrowed her eyes. "You're holding a clipboard."

"It has my Easter battle plans."

Sarah nodded slowly. "It looks like you don't even need me."

"I don't know about that. I found a few mommy blogs that outlined minute-by-minute plans for the perfect Easter. But, uh, more laid back." That had been the part I didn't want to admit, that simpler was actually better. It took some major rewiring of my brain to get that thought to penetrate my hard skull. Ever since I could remember, I had a maniacal passion for being better than everyone else. One of my therapists told me this was because I'd always wanted my mother's love, which I never really got. Logically, I understood that. Putting that thought into action—er, by not attempting to best everyone—turned out to be impossible for me. Until now.

Sarah took the clipboard from my hands. "This is amazing."

"It's your clipboard. Usually, you're the one wielding it."

"I know. I—I owe you a huge apology, Lizzie. I didn't think—" Her eyes landed back on the baskets.

"That I could pull it off? Yeah, I'm with you there," I admitted. "If I hadn't found those blogs and YouTube videos, I would have been lost. It's amazing what you can find on YouTube. Come look at the table." I took Sarah's hand to lead her into the dining room.

Her jaw dropped as she took in the way the table was set. "There's a centerpiece."

"Cool, huh?" I kept my tone level, but inside I was crowing like a rooster at what I'd pulled off. "I took the best eggs the kids dyed for it. Here's Calvin's football. Oh, I signed him up for spring flag football. It starts on April twenty-eighth. I thought we could tell him together this morning."

"You remembered the deadline to register him." I couldn't tell if Sarah meant it to be a statement or question, but it was clear the information was rapidly overloading her brain circuits.

"Luckily, I had a reminder on my phone. I knew he'd be heartbroken if I dropped the ball."

"I spaced it completely, but you didn't." Again, it was hard to tell if she meant to ask a question or not.

"You were sick," I said simply. "Speaking of, how are you

feeling? Should you be up and about? Thank goodness no one else came down with your cold."

"Mommy!" Scrambling down the stairs, Fred ran toward Sarah, followed by the other three kids.

They were even more rambunctious than usual, and I wondered if the kids had assumed, just like Sarah had, that an Easter morning I was in charge of would suck big time. Maybe I should have felt insulted by this, but they had every reason to think it. I was just grateful to be able to prove them wrong for once.

"Did the Easter bunny come?" Demi pressed her little hands together, looking almost angelic.

"We should go check." Sarah took Demi and Calvin's hands, bringing them into the family room.

"I should get the rolls out of the oven." I headed for the kitchen.

"We'll wait for you," Sarah announced in her *there won't be any arguing* voice.

Not that it was needed, because Fred concurred along with Demi.

I mouthed *I love you* to Sarah, who responded by blowing me a kiss.

When I returned with two cups of tea, I handed Sarah one of the mugs and asked, "What should we do first? The baskets or find all the eggs?"

"Eggs!" Fred jumped up from the floor.

"I see one!" Demi ran off to get the plastic egg I'd placed behind the curtain in the living room.

"Good job!"

Sarah and I observed the egg hunt while enjoying our tea.

Maddie and Willow made their appearance, Willow grinning with excitement every time one of the kids shouted *aha*! Meanwhile, Maddie rubbed the sleep out of her eyes. If the two of them did end up having kids someday, I had an inkling which of them would be the Sarah in their relationship and which one would be me.

Sarah whispered something to Willow, who disappeared from the room.

"Look at my basket!" Freddie tilted it so I could see all the eggs he'd found.

"Excellent work, little man!" I put my hand up for a high five.

"Anyone want a cinnamon roll?" Willow came in with a platter.

The kids and I shot our hands in the air.

"We should sit at the table." I got off the couch, putting a hand out to Sarah. "Part two of Easter will commence soon."

"This has been the best Easter already. You really outdid yourself this time, honey." She leaned in to give me a quick kiss on the cheek. "Thank you."

"Check this out!" Calvin tossed his Easter bunny like it was an actual football, instead of a football player.

"It gets better," Sarah said to Calvin. "Mom signed you up for flag football."

"You did?" He stared up at me with massive eyes that melted my heart.

"The season starts in less than four weeks. We need to get you ready." I looked out the window, the rain splattering the glass. "They have an indoor facility for bad weather."

"I need to get into shape." Calvin dropped to the ground to do a push-up.

"I can help you." Ollie did the same.

My heart stopped, part of me wondering if she was going to pull a nasty trick, like pushing him over. She didn't, though. She started to count off as they did push-ups together.

"This really is the best Easter ever," I whispered in awe. The best part was I could see the genuine happiness and unity in my family's eyes. And, for once, I had gotten out of my own way long enough to make it happen.

APRIL

CHAPTER TWENTY-SIX

"Holy shit, this isn't good." I squinted at my phone while lying in bed.

Despite knowing doom scrolling before bedtime wasn't good for mental health, I still couldn't kick the habit. Acknowledging something wasn't good for me and actually doing what was good for me—well, let's just say I wasn't a role model for anyone in that department.

And, yes, I understand that as a mother of four, I should try harder to set a good example. I must note, though, none of the kids own smartphones yet. Technically, this means they have several years to forget my bad behavior before it applies to them. A pathetic excuse? Probably. But it was all I had at the moment.

"What's not good?" Sarah set her tablet down to switch all of her focus onto me. This was unlikely to be a good thing.

"Nothing. Just an article I'm reading." I should have said an email for work and then made up something if she pressed. I found whenever I alluded to a department brouhaha, Sarah stopped listening. Saying it was an article wouldn't throw her off the scent. Sarah wasn't exactly a news junkie, but she liked to stay informed, which meant she was less likely to tune me out.

"About one of the wars?" There was a hint of fear in her tone because none of the wars were going particularly well, and each piece of news added more heartache and frustration over the death and devastation.

"No." Again, I should have said yes. More than likely, Sarah would let it go, not really wanting any details beyond the latest headlines.

"What's it about, then?" Now she was curious. And an inquisitive Sarah? That never turned out well for me. Not at all.

"Me. Not me, *me*... but also it is, kind of." I skimmed the article again, getting chills, as things were hitting me over the head. Sadly, not heavy things in real life, like frying pans—because if I was unconscious, I wouldn't have to explain anything else about why I was so unsettled.

Sarah blinked. Like a lot. "Why can't you ever tell me what's going on the first time I ask?"

"Because... here. I think this will explain." I handed her my phone so she could see for herself why I was the way I was. I think the official diagnosis was: fucked-up.

"Signs you had a troubled childhood," Sarah's voice trembled as she read aloud the heading of the article. "What's this all about?"

"I have every single trait except one that's listed in the article." My hand stretched toward the water glass on the bedside table as my mouth became unexpectedly parched.

"Which one?"

"See if you can figure it out." I guzzled the water. In about four hours, I'd regret that decision as I stumbled half-blind to the bathroom, but that didn't stop me.

Sarah let out a little frustrated groan but started to click through each screen, nodding after reading each one of the traits. She paused when she got to one closer to the end. "You don't have alcohol or drug problems."

"Ding, ding, ding!" I licked my dry lips before remembering that doing so only dried them out even more, but I didn't have a lip balm near me. So I licked them again, naturally. "I'm almost forty. You'd think I'd be over my childhood trauma by now. Isn't there an expiration date on being pathetic?"

"You're not pathetic, and if only it were that easy, a lot more people wouldn't be so fu—struggling."

"You were going to say fucked-up, weren't you? It's okay. I already figured out what the article was telling me without being so blunt."

She shook her head, thinning her lips, her eyes going wide as she struggled to find the words to put my mind at ease. The joke was on her. Nothing would put me at ease.

"I know I'm fucked-up. You don't have to tell me that." I added. "I knew before I read this. It simply outlined all the ways, like always expecting someone to knife you in the back."

"I wouldn't ever say that about you. That you're fucked-up."

I noticed she didn't correct my statement about me always expecting the worst from people. Because it was true. My mind always whirred into action, trying to game out someone's next move and how much it was going to hurt, either physically, emotionally, or cosmically. I didn't understand how the last worked, really, but it sounded good, so I was sticking with it.

"You probably would be too polite to say it, but come on. On a scale of one to ten, how fucked-up am I?"

There was a lot more blinking before Sarah set my phone onto the comforter. "I don't think that's the right question to ask."

"Because you don't want to answer it. Because I'm *that* fucked-up." I stressed the word that. For some reason, I was a little pleased by this prospect. If I was fucked-up, I might as well excel in that department. Don't ask me to explain how my brain works.

"No, honey. I admit you possess these traits, but you're getting better at recognizing them." She offered a slight smile, accentuating the feebleness of her argument.

"Not in the moment. It usually takes—"

"Three days. Everything with you takes three days." Sarah chuckled. "Even when I ask you what you want for dinner."

"That's not true!" I got defensive but quickly calmed down. "Okay, that was funny."

"You see! You didn't take three days with that one." She was practically glowing with victory.

"You did that on purpose, didn't you?" I frowned. "I don't like it when you trick me, even if you're trying to make me feel better."

Sarah pulled me into her arms. "You don't have any proof I was tricking you."

"I have good suspicious instincts. It's one of the traits." I tapped the phone, the screen black now.

"You know what you need? Correction. Do you know what *we* need?" Her voice was doing that thing when she was getting excited about something I wouldn't be too keen on, so she was overdoing it some.

I gave her a dubious look. "What?"

"A weekend away. For a nice catch-up."

"A catch-up?" I spoke the words, not quite comprehending at first until they sunk in. "God, yes. I—we do need that." I was so far behind on absolutely everything when it came to work it seemed like I would never catch up. Considering Sarah had been grading papers in bed, she was probably in the same boat. "I would love a catch-up weekend. If only we could." In an instant, the dream faded away, leaving a bitter void in my heart. "When can we ever get away without a lot of complications?"

"Willow mentioned these tiny cabins you can rent in the

middle of nowhere. I'm going to book one." Naturally, Sarah ignored the heart of my statement. She had a bad habit of doing that.

"What about the kids?" I pressed as if I wanted them to be a complication. I didn't, but my voice made it seem like that, even to me.

"Should I get them their own cabin?" She wore a teasing smile.

But it wasn't the worst thought, was it? "Is that legal?"

Sarah jabbed an elbow into my side. "No. I'm sure my mom or your dad will watch them for a weekend. Think, Lizzie. It'll just be you and me in the middle of the woods. Doesn't that sound lovely?"

"It sounds like the setup for a horror movie. Is that where you plan to murder me? I imagine it'd be easy to dispose of my body without many witnesses." I could picture exactly how that would play out.

Sarah shook her head. "If I was planning it, I wouldn't tell you. To answer your question, though, no. I never plan on killing you."

"Why not?"

"Many reasons."

"Such as?"

"Do you think about killing me? Should I be worried?" With a single arched eyebrow, she sent shivers down my spine.

Not that I ever planned out her death, obviously. I loved her. But I had fantasized about it in depth for others. One thing usually stopped me in my tracks, which I stupidly admitted out loud, "I'm not organized enough to carry it out, let alone avoid getting caught."

Sarah burst into laughter.

"Does that mean you agree I couldn't pull off a murder?"

"Sometimes I'm simply baffled how you get from point A to me murdering you. It's not the first time you've brought it up."

Sarah was back on her tablet. "Here. What do you think of this view?"

There was a lake, which I had to admit seemed nice.

"I could see us there." Sitting at a desk, overlooking the lake, getting caught up with work. Ah, heaven.

"Me too. This is going to be the best catch-up weekend ever."

"Will this place be big enough?" I didn't have to bring all my books to prepare the lectures I'd been meaning to write but hadn't gotten to yet. There was also the article I needed to fine tune. But I'd need some space, and the cabin was tiny if the pictures were to be believed. Hence the tiny cabin label.

"It's perfect. You're perfect. We're perfect." Sarah let out the most contented sigh. "I simply can't wait."

"You seem really happy considering you just read confirmation of how fucked-up I am as a result of my miserable childhood."

"It made you who you are, and I happen to love you." She gave me a peck on the cheek.

"As is? You know, like they say for used cars. You can't return me now."

"All of us can make improvements. Even me." Sarah wiggled under the covers. "This weekend away will help with that."

CHAPTER TWENTY-SEVEN

I PARKED THE CAR OUTSIDE THE TINY CABIN, LETTING out a contented breath, although still clutching the steering wheel because I hadn't yet recovered from the massive holes and tree branches that made the last half mile of the dirt road tricky to navigate. "This is going to be a fantastic weekend."

Sarah rested her head against the car seat, peeling my right hand from the steering wheel to thread our fingers. "It really is. We've needed this for so long."

"I second that." I lifted her hand to my lips for a soft kiss. "Thank you for bringing me here. For knowing me better than I know myself."

"Wow. We're already off to a great start." She batted her lashes at me, grinning like a lovesick fool. It was fantastic to see, and it'd been such a long time.

"Why don't you go inside, and check it out? I'll start unloading the car." I glanced over my shoulder at her smallest travel bag. "Is that really all you brought?"

"Yep. Won't need much while we're here. I don't care if we ever leave the cabin."

"This is sounding better and better." I could practically see the weight being lifted off my shoulders. For weeks, my worry about getting everything done had been pressing on me to the point I was surprised I was still able to stand upright without my knees buckling. Or not burst into tears whenever someone inquired how I was doing.

Stressed. Hopelessly stressed. Thanks for asking.

I brought Sarah's bag to the entrance before opening the back of the SUV to grab my first box of books. Hefting one of the small cardboard boxes onto my shoulder, I waltzed inside the cabin, feeling like I could take on the world. "This place is really cute."

Sarah didn't respond, too busy gaping at my box, before finding the words. "Sometimes you amaze me."

"In a good or bad way?" I scrutinized her face, determining the answer could go either way. Was I losing my ability to guess what my wife was thinking? That didn't bode well for the next forty or fifty years.

"We have so many bags for travel, yet you packed your stuff in an old delivery box." She shook her head as if I had zero clue.

"This doesn't have my clothes or anything in it. Those are in a proper bag; I promise. I haven't brought it in yet. I have one more of these, though." I tapped the box on my shoulder. "I tried packing light so I don't throw out my back."

"Is it the food?" Sarah's expression started to shift from amusement to outright confusion.

"Right. I have two more boxes to bring in. The one with the food and the other—"

"What's in the box, Lizzie?" Now, she seemed annoyed.

"It's not a head, if that's what you're thinking." Maddie had made us watch *Seven* the other night, so I laughed at my own silly joke.

"It might have one in it soon." She narrowed her eyes, and

her warning tone set off alarm bells for reasons I couldn't fathom.

"Just books, journal articles, and stuff." Her cheeks started to turn red, and I didn't think it was from embarrassment. I quickly added for clarification, "For our catch-up weekend."

"You're planning on reading all weekend?" She crossed her arms, readying for battle.

This wasn't going well, but I couldn't quite figure out where I'd gone wrong. This entire weekend had been her idea, after all. Was I supposed to only bring one box of books? If that was the case, she should have said so right off the bat.

"I won't be reading all of them in their entirety, silly." Sometimes being easy breezy got me out of jams, so it was worth a try now. "But I need all of them to prepare my lectures."

"Prepare your—" Sarah squeezed her eyes shut and then balled up her fists. "What kind of catch-up weekend are you envisioning?"

"The best kind. I'm so behind with work, and I'm hoping by the time we leave, I'll be ahead. I know we've been parents for many years now, but I'm still not used to the idea of finishing everything at the last minute. Truth be told, it's slowly driving me insane." I set the box down on the desk, which had a lake view. "I can't thank you enough for getting this place for us. Did you want the desk? I can work on the couch. All I need is peace and quiet."

She didn't answer, I assumed because she was taking my need for peace and quiet to heart.

"We don't have to make a decision right away." I was starting to worry she wasn't getting enough air into her lungs, because her chest was heaving up and down, but her complexion was turning a purplish color. Or was it blue?

"Let me see if I'm understanding. Your plan is to spend this weekend with me, in a romantic cabin with a lake view, and all you want to do is work?"

"Of course not! I thought we could go for a morning and evening walk. It'd be a shame not to, don't you think?" I glanced out the window, letting out an appreciative whistle.

"I do think. More than you, apparently." Her eyeballs were turning red. Was that even possible, or was my mind playing tricks on me?

"Why are you upset? This weekend was your idea." I tapped my fingers against my leg, wondering if I should bolt before my head did end up in the box and then got tossed into the lake for good measure.

"I wanted us to come here to spend time together, alone. No work. No kids. No chores. Just you and me. So we can catch up with each other." She motioned to me and then placed her hand over her chest.

"Each other," I repeated as her words slowly sank into my brain. "So, I wasn't meant to bring work." I stared at the box with longing.

Sarah cleared her throat.

I returned my attention to her. "Catch-up doesn't mean work? Or at least not the way you used it?"

She moved her head to the right and then to the left so slowly it was hard to tell if she was indicating no. I really needed her to be clearer right now, but I was fearful if I asked her for absolute clarification, my death would be the only item on the agenda. Well, and getting away with it. I had faith in Sarah, though. She could totally plan the perfect murder. Which only made my predicament all the more precarious.

CHAPTER TWENTY-EIGHT

"Should I put the books back in the car?" I gazed at the box, feeling the weight of dashed expectations. Yet, I hesitated to express my disappointment. The hurt in Sarah's eyes was unbearable.

"If that's what you want to do this weekend, knock yourself out." To her credit, Sarah's voice held zero trace of sarcasm or anger. If I were in her shoes, as angry as she seemed to be, I wouldn't have been able to pull it off. Should that terrify me? Her being too calm?

I sucked my top lip into my mouth to avoid speaking too quickly. Sure, Sarah was giving me permission to do what I had intended to do this weekend. But—and it was a huge but—was that what she actually wanted from me? This seemed to be one of those times in life when I had to make a decision to make my wife happy. Again, the pain in her eyes, even when she tried not showing it, sliced right through me.

Besides, even in my head, my internal dialog sounded really bad. I should always want to make Sarah happy. Did I accomplish that on a regular basis? No, I didn't think I did. Far from it.

That needed to change and pronto.

I scooped the box back into my arms and carried it to the car.

By the time I returned to the cabin, Sarah had poured a large glass of red wine. It wasn't five o'clock here, but it must be somewhere as the song went. I'm sure I wasn't the first spouse to drive their partner to drink, but it wasn't something I wanted to be responsible for.

"Wanna sit with me?" Sarah waved to the couch facing the lake.

"I'd love to. Let me get some water." I poured it into a wine glass, eliciting a smile from Sarah when I took my seat. "It tastes better from a fancy goblet."

Sarah rested her head on my shoulder, releasing a tortured sigh. "Did you really think I wanted to work all weekend?"

"I admit I may not have understood your definition of catch-up." I took a hesitant drink of water.

"It's possible I wasn't exactly clear." She spoke slowly, as if I struggled to understand the English language. I did understand words, it was the subtext I often tripped over.

She was giving me an out, but it was too soon to let out a relieved breath. I'd been fooled before.

"I feel like we're going a hundred miles per hour in opposite directions all the time." Sarah's neck straightened, allowing her a chance to sip her wine. "It's not just the kids and work. I have to ask. Do you not find me attractive anymore?"

My head reeled back like she'd tossed a flaming turd at my face. Not only was it ridiculous, but I had a feeling it wasn't the first time we'd had this conversation. More proof I was an absolute shitty partner. "You're kidding, right?"

She stared at me. "I'm not."

"You have to know you're the hot one in this partnership." Which I had told her many times. But when was the last time? I was beginning to see the inkling of the issue.

"Hot one?" Her expression wavered from proud to annoyance.

I probably could have put it more delicately—no, that wasn't the word I wanted. Something with more heart… but my brain was sputtering. It always did in situations like this.

So I said, "Out of the two of us, you're the one everyone appreciates. And then they look at me and wonder how I landed you."

"People don't do that." There was a crinkle of merriment around her eyes. I may not have landed on the heartfelt way of saying this, but my clumsier method was still having an impact.

"Yes, they do. I see it in their faces all the time."

"Lizzie, that's not true."

I didn't want to focus on that because I never really liked the way it made me feel. Actually, it always gave me mixed feelings. Amazed to be with a woman like Sarah but frustrated that people assumed she was attracted to me for money or something. Sure, I had my trust fund, but Sarah had money, too. So it couldn't be that. Did they make a T-shirt that read: *She's not with me because I have money*?

There was the niggling thought in the back of my mind about how most days I didn't understand why Sarah was with me. The best way to ignore that thought was to change the subject.

"How could you think I don't find you attractive?" I reached for her hand, giving it a squeeze.

"One reason might be that I booked a romantic escape and you'd rather work all weekend."

"It's not so much that I rather do that. I—I'm drowning, Sarah. More and more each day. Some days, I don't know how I'll last until I can collapse in bed. Even that isn't much of a relief because I know I have to do it all over again the next day." I hated sounding pathetic, but it was also true.

"That's not good, honey." Now her eyes blazed with worry.

"You can't say you don't feel the same."

"Our lives can be exhausting." She quickly added, "In a good way. I just wish we could find a better balance." She joggled two palms in the air.

"I'm not good at that." I mimicked her, but instead of seeking middle ground, I suddenly dropped one to my lap to show the imbalance called Lizzie's life.

"I've noticed. Do you ever think you're doing too much?" Sarah's tone wasn't accusatory. Instead it was soft, like she was nervous to broach the topic.

"No. I'm worried I'm not doing enough. I'm not getting any younger, and there's still so much I want to accomplish in life." I could practically hear a ticking clock in my brain.

"Like what?"

"Everything. I want to do it all." I'd make a list, but I would need a never-ending scroll. And seeing it all in writing would probably drive me over the edge.

"Why?"

"What do you mean? Aren't there things you want to cross off your bucket list."

"I'd love to see giraffes in Africa."

I gaped at her.

"I take it your bucket list isn't like mine." She half smiled and half grimaced.

"I wouldn't say that. I was thinking more along the lines of a professional bucket list."

"I'm aware, but you've already accomplished so much. What more do you need to cross off that list, and *why*?" She emphasized the last word.

"To prove her wrong," I foolishly blurted.

"Prove who wrong?" Sarah asked, but before I could answer, she nodded with understanding. "Lizzie, honey, your mom has been dead for years now. Do you think it might be time to let some of… that go?"

"Like snap my fingers and poof, it's gone? Why haven't I thought of that before now?" I didn't exactly say that in a polite way. Defensive laced with anger would be the best description.

"I know it's not that easy, but maybe your time would be better spent working on the things that truly matter, not proving a dead woman was wrong about you. She came to her own ridiculous conclusions when you were just a child."

"A strange child." Thank goodness my mom wasn't around after my autism diagnosis. She'd never let me live it down. Hell, she might ask for a refund for a defective child.

"You weren't."

"You didn't know me then." I hugged my torso.

"I know you now."

"And I brought boxes of books for our weekend away. I'm always getting the wires crossed. How was I supposed to know catch-up was code for sex? Is there a manual for this?" I wasn't kidding. "It is code for sex, right?"

Sarah's shoulders were shaking with laughter.

"What's so funny?" I crossed my arms.

"You. You are always making me laugh."

"You're always laughing at me."

"That is not true. I find you adorable, and I like being around you." Sarah tugged on one of my arms, but I pulled away. "Even when you're pouting."

"I'm not." I tried to keep my lip from jutting out, but it was a losing battle.

"Wanna know what I packed for this weekend?"

"I hope some Hershey kisses. I could eat a hundred of them."

"Seriously?" Sarah shook her head in disbelief, but there was a sweet smile on her lips. Like she couldn't help loving me, no matter how big an idiot I could sometimes be.

CHAPTER TWENTY-NINE

She dropped her backpack onto my lap. "There aren't any Hershey kisses, but check it out."

"I feel like I'm about to fail yet another test." I didn't move to unzip the bag, my stomach twisting at the thought of letting Sarah down again somehow.

"It's not a test. I just want you to know what I have in mind for this weekend. To remove any doubt." She continued when I stayed frozen. "I'm not mad, Lizzie. I can see how you got the wrong idea."

Slowly, I undid the bag, reaching a hand in like it was filled with half-starved piranhas who had a special kink for my blood type. Nothing bit me, thankfully. I wouldn't have blamed Sarah for setting a trap. She wasn't like that, though. Fortunately for me.

"Whatever it is, it's soft. Silky, even." I pulled out a clump of fabric, my eyes bulging as it unfurled to reveal a very sexy piece of lingerie I hadn't seen before. "You haven't worn something like this in a very long time." I held the thin straps with my thumbs, my pulse skyrocketing in a delightful way.

"Correct." Sarah's eyes twinkled. "I miss those days."

"Me too." I swallowed. "What's it called? Besides Va-va-voom."

She laughed, her shoulders immediately losing all the tension she'd been showing from the moment when she clasped eyes on my box of books.

"It's just a nightgown. Or I guess you could call it a negligee."

"Negligee. That might be my new favorite word." I repeated it again slowly, as if able to taste how delightful it sounded. I was practically salivating, and I hadn't even seen the thing on Sarah yet.

"There's more." Sarah motioned for me to continue emptying the bag.

"Massage oils and…" I plunged my hand back into the bag. "Candles."

She waggled her eyebrows.

"Wow. I really read this weekend all wrong." I laughed. I mean I truly laughed. "I can't even imagine what you thought when I traipsed in here with all of those books. And there are more in the car!" I slapped my knee, laughing hysterically now, tears forming in the corners of my eyes.

Sarah rested her head on my shoulder. "You do amaze me sometimes."

"Is catch-up a thing everyone else knows? Like do other couples say it at the dinner table, 'We need a catch-up weekend,' while the kids are eating chicken nuggets?"

"Now there's an image. To answer your question, I'm not sure. It's just what came to me in the moment. Like you said, I haven't purchased a sexy outfit in I don't know how long. I don't want to lose sight of this part of our relationship." She squeezed my hand. "Yes, we love being parents, but that's not our sole identity. We're still Lizzie and Sarah, two people who are madly in love."

"Even more in love after all of these years. I know why I stay." I pointed to the silky thingy, waggling my brows trying to look naughty. "Wait. That came out wrong. It's not the only reason I stay. I love you, Sarah. You simply dazzle the hell out of me. Kind, loving, intelligent, brave, snarky, and so much more. Why in the heck are you with me?"

"I can't explain my love for you. I'm just happy we're with each other." Sarah took the silky thing—I'd already forgotten the word despite saying it at least half a dozen times—from my hands. "I'm going to change. Would you like to light the candles to set the catch-up mood?" There was a saucy wink.

That didn't stop me from saying, "It's not dark." After a slight hesitation on her part, I immediately corrected to, "I'd love to."

"Good girl." She winked at me again. And, I can't lie. It did things to me. She could do nothing but wink at me the whole weekend, and I'd be in heaven.

While Sarah changed in the bathroom, I found a lighter in Sarah's bag, because of course, she'd packed one. Before I could google the expression catch-up, Sarah stood in the middle of the cabin, wearing only a bit of blue silk with creamy lace that covered everything but in a way that it seemed to cover nothing at all.

"Wow." My eyes wandered over her body, the silk clinging to all the right spots. "I may come simply from looking at you."

"Is that right? I feel like that would take some of the fun out of it." She stepped closer. "I also feel you are way overdressed." Sarah flicked the collar of my shirt.

"I'm not—can people see in?" I glanced over my shoulder.

"A bear might be able to, but we're out in the middle of nowhere."

"There are bears here?" Now I really studied the surroundings outside the window. "Oh, look. There's a chipmunk. I love them. They're like squirrels with racing stripes. I want to come back as a chipmunk in my next life. Imagine how many smiles they spur every day. We need more smiles in this world. Too bad they don't come in rainbow colors. That'd be perfect."

"Lizzie!" Sarah clapped her hands to get my full attention. "Get naked!"

I swallowed the rest of my words, my eyes wide.

"Anyone ever tell you you're bossy?" I started to unbutton my shirt. "I'm wearing flannel."

"I'm aware." She eyed me with skepticism, like she sensed bad thoughts were going through my head.

"Do you ever wish I'd wear…" I pointed to her lacy nightie.

"It's not really your style."

"You haven't ever said truer words."

"You need to get it through your head that I like you the way you are." Sarah inched closer to me. "Let me help."

While Sarah unbuttoned my shirt, I worked on my jeans.

"You're doing well," Sarah said, confusing me.

"They're just jeans. I've been taking them off for years now." Was this how she wanted to build my confidence? Compliment me on something so simple? Honestly, I couldn't decide how that made me feel. I liked hearing something good, but undoing jeans? What idiot couldn't do that?

"What? No. I mean, you're looking very good. Slimmer, more toned than you've been in a while."

"I mean, I haven't really done anything," I said, recalling how badly my start to the year had gone. "Nothing drastic, anyway."

"That's probably why it's working. You look good, Lizzie. So very good." She leaned close for a kiss while her hands eased my shirt off my shoulders.

"You're amazing. Truly amazing." I cupped her cheek. "I adore you."

"Ditto. Now take the rest off, and join me in bed. Pronto. It's officially time for our catch-up weekend to begin in earnest."

"Catch-up. I'm really starting to like this idea."

CHAPTER THIRTY

"Now you're decent." Sarah patted the bed, not taking her eyes off my undressed form.

"I'm literally naked. I think that's the opposite of decent." To be honest, I wanted to disappear. I'd never been one who was comfortable with being naked. Sure, Sarah and I had been married for some time now, but it was hard to overcome growing up with forced shame for natural things.

"Depends on who you're asking and the situation. It'd be really hard to give you a massage if you were fully clothed." She squirted massage oil onto her hand.

"I'm getting a massage?" My voice squeaked, probably rounding out the scared mouse image.

"As soon as you lay down." She jerked her head to the spot on the bed.

"What did I do to deserve this?" I didn't move a muscle, like this was a trick of some kind. My heart—or was it my brain?—knew it wasn't but… what if it was?

"You might be the only person I know who would try to talk their wife out of giving them a massage." There was a sad shake of a head and a sympathetic smile.

"It's just I messed up this weekend. Big time. Shouldn't I be giving you a massage?" I covered my heart, causing me to remember I was buck naked and just standing there for all the bears, squirrels, chipmunks, and weirdos who stalked the woods to see.

"You should, and you will. Right now, I want to help you relax." It was more of a command.

"Good luck with that." I got onto the bed, resting my chin onto my hands. "I think I was born stressed."

Sarah's hands began working on my shoulders. "Ooof, I may need some help with these."

The next thing I knew, Sarah was straddling me.

"You're not wearing underwear," I said, looking over my shoulder.

"Didn't see the point. Besides, I should get something out of this, too."

"Major points for that. You'll get a bigger tip."

"A tip, huh? I have a tip for you." She dug deep into my shoulders. "Don't even think of putting clothes on this entire time. We're having a naked weekend."

"If you'd said that before, I would have known exactly what this trip was for, you know." I let out a sigh, partly of frustration but also because Sarah pressed the air from my lungs with her palms. "It took me ages to select all the books I needed."

"Not sure that's my fault," she argued. "Not entirely."

"I wasn't blaming, I swear. Oh, that feels good." My hands dug into the comforter as Sarah really worked on a knot.

Sarah leaned down and nibbled on my earlobe, my weak spot, in the most delightful way. She didn't linger, returning to massaging my shoulders, her touch just enough to make me squirm but not enough to hurt. At least, not in a bad way.

I lost all sense of time as I gave myself over to the sensations.

"I like the way you move." Sarah placed soft kisses along my back.

"You do things to me."

Sarah scooted down, sitting on my thighs. "If I remember correctly, there's a spot on your lower back that really gets you hot and bothered."

"That rings a bell." I knew the exact location, but I wasn't about to give it up so quickly. Not when she was kissing and touching me with such abandon. It might have been the one time when I kept a thought to myself. Should I be proud about withholding this information? Sarah didn't seem to mind, exploring the area with her fingers and mouth.

It didn't take her too long to land on the spot, and I let out a moan.

Sarah trailed a hand up and down my sides. "I think you might finally be relaxing a smidge. That's some progress. Not a lot, but…"

"Rome wasn't built in a day."

"Let's hope you don't collapse like the empire."

"It hung around for a thousand years. That's a pretty good run." I would've shrugged, but I couldn't move. My muscles had melted into a thin goo.

"I'd like to keep you around forever." Sarah's mouth was next to my ear. "Stop killing yourself with work and things you can't change."

"You're teaching me a bad lesson, though. Look how you're treating me right now. I just may book this cabin every month."

"Now there's a fantastic thought!" Sarah rolled me onto my back, repositioning herself over my midsection.

I ran my hands up the silky fabric, my hands landing on her breasts. "I love your body. I always have."

"You're not so bad yourself." She winked, leaning down, capturing my lips with a soft and sensual kiss.

I could kiss her for all eternity.

Her hip rocked into my center, the silk rubbing against me just right.

We didn't stop kissing for what seemed like an hour, and I couldn't remember the last time we'd done that. We were always rushing to get from one place to the next. Not this weekend.

Finally, when we broke for air, I said, "I love catching-up."

"And it's only just started."

"Can we never leave? You see, that's one of the problems when I do stop long enough to enjoy not being busy. I don't want it to end."

"Worse things could happen."

"Like losing our house, not being able to feed our children, and what if one of us gets sick? How would we afford health care in this miserable country?" My heart buzzed with dread.

"It's amazing how quickly your mind leaps to all the worst possible outcomes." Sarah slipped her negligee—oh, right, that's what it was called—over her head. "Does this calm you?"

"Your tits always do." I squeezed one of her nipples, only enough to get it to harden.

Sarah closed her eyes as I rocked my hip into her center. This was met with a *fuck me* moan. One I'd heard many times, but it still had a powerful effect on me.

Before Sarah knew what was happening, I had her on her back on the bed, her arms above her head.

"Is your massage over?" she joked.

"On hold. There's something I need to do." I clamped my lips around her areola, her nipple pebbling in my mouth.

There was another moan.

I loved this woman, more than I understood. And I wanted her to be putty in my hands. To get her to scream my name. Not yet, though. We had all weekend, and there was so much skin to explore with my tongue and fingertips, wanting to connect with her in the only way I truly could.

Sarah writhed underneath me, murmuring her approval and urging me along with the jolt of a hip, leg, and arm in rapid succession.

I still couldn't believe Sarah chose me. I wanted to show her how much I cherished her love.

By the time she came, I was spent in the most delightful way.

"I think I've been doing this wrong," I said through ragged breaths, lying on top of Sarah.

"Not sure about that. It was pretty hot." Sarah struggled to get the words out.

"Not sex. Hopefully, I'm halfway decent on that front. No. I mean this year. I've been determined to be the best Lizzie I can be, but I've been focusing on all the wrong things. Like starting off with the food reset. That didn't work out to my favor."

Sarah chuckled but tried not to look like she was.

"I want to be a better person. I want to be a better wife, mother, family member. I want to put all of you first."

"You don't think getting out of bed at ungodly hours is your way of putting others first? You work so hard. I don't always understand your drive, but I do appreciate it." She rested her hand over my heart.

"Yes and no. Like this weekend. My brain immediately went to what I could do to help myself, not noticing what you needed. Even though it should have been obvious when I look back on it. I want to do better. I'll need your guidance, though."

Sarah stared deeply into my eyes. "You don't have to be so hard on yourself all the time. You're already a good wife, mother, daughter, sister—"

"Not all the time. I have my selfish moments."

"We all do. There's nothing wrong with that."

"I want to find a better balance."

"That's something I can get on board with, but promise me you won't tip over into overdoing it."

"When have I ever done that?"

We both burst into laughter, knowing there was little chance I would manage to get it just right. But I would try.

MAY

CHAPTER THIRTY-ONE

I glanced up from the sandwich I was preparing as all four kids trooped into the kitchen with an exhausted looking Eloise bringing up the rear.

"There are my beautiful children!" I exclaimed.

"Why are you being weird?" Ollie shot me a puzzled look, reminiscent of Sarah's typical expression in such situations. The resemblance was enough to send a chill down my spine. If both Sarah and Ollie were scrutinizing me so intensely all the time, I knew I was facing trouble for years to come.

"It's just how I am." I pressed the top slice of bread onto my ham and cheese, which was devoid of mustard, mayo, or veggies. I definitely preferred my sandwiches simple, no frills attached. "We have a big weekend, so you four better get going on your homework."

"I don't have any." Calvin casually dropped his bag in the middle of the kitchen floor instead of hanging it on the hook next to the fridge. It seemed like a daily routine for one of us to remind him to utilize the hook. How he could miss it every time was a mystery, especially considering it had his name clearly labeled above it.

"Hang up your bag, please, and I'll take a look in your homework folder to make sure you don't have any this weekend." I took a big bite of my sandwich, relishing the plain, unadulterated flavors of meat, cheese, and bread.

"I don't have homework," Calvin vehemently insisted, his cheeks flushing crimson with the weight of his assertion.

"I still need to check your folder for messages from the teacher. I do that every day." I took another bite, trying to stave off the feeling of my stomach devouring itself. It was so much easier to parent when I wasn't starving.

"Don't go into my bag!" His expression was deadly serious, and he crossed his spaghetti-noodle arms for added emphasis.

Now I was suspicious. I eyed my youngest son, contemplating if this showdown could wait until after I finished my sandwich. I decided it couldn't. Perhaps it was my hunger that had me rearing for a confrontation. "Like I said, I check your homework folder every day, young man. Today is no different."

At this point, Fred lurched with his arms spread wide in front of all the bags hanging on their hooks, minus Cal's which still sat in the middle of the kitchen. "No, you can't!"

Now my curiosity was beyond piqued. Even Fred was refusing? This was unheard of. Freddie wasn't the defiant type. "Dude, are you guys drug mules now or something?" I laughed at my own joke while the kids looked thoroughly confused by the question.

"What's a drug mule?" Demi asked as she twirled around, arms raised like a ballerina.

Eloise tried not to snicker.

"Why are we talking about drug mules?" Sarah stepped through the garage door, hanging her bag on her proper hook without any prompting. Her eyes zeroed in on the sandwich in my hand like two heat-seeking missiles. "Lizzie! It's almost dinnertime." She motioned to my half-eaten sandwich, giving me a look that said she was very disappointed in my life choices.

I took another ginormous bite on the off chance this would be the day she'd rip it from my hands. "I didn't have lunch," I mumbled around the bite. Answering her previous question, I said, "The kids."

"The kids what?"

"They're the drug mules." It came out garbled since I was still stuffing my face.

"What's a drug mule?" Demi repeated, tossing her arms in the air and mouthing the word "Hello!"

"Nothing, honey. Mommy was making a bad joke."

"That means naughty." Ollie's eyes sparkled with a knowing gleam as she gave me a thorough once-over, silently implying she had doubted my abilities on that front.

"The kids are being weird about me looking in their backpacks for their homework assignments. We have a busy weekend. I want them to get everything done before dinner." I took another bite of my sandwich.

"At the rate you're going, we won't be eating until midnight."

"I didn't have lunch!" I growled.

"Why are you in a bad mood?" Sarah rounded the kitchen island and kissed my cheek, probably in hopes that would calm me down.

It didn't.

"Hunger and disobedient children do that to me."

"You must be hungry every second," Olivia quipped, wearing an expression that practically dared me to retaliate.

I couldn't fathom how my simple inquiry about Calvin's homework had escalated a typical interaction with the kids and Sarah into what felt like a showdown at the O.K. Corral.

"Demi, do you have homework?" Sarah pulled the cabinet

behind my head open, and I ducked. "Steady, Lizzie. I just want some water."

"No," Demi answered Sarah before heading out of the kitchen, probably to avoid getting whacked in the head by cupboard doors or glassware.

"Fred?" Sarah placed her glass under the ice dispenser in the fridge.

He shook his head, maintaining his protective stance. I had to admire his commitment, even though I couldn't quite grasp the rationale behind it.

"Why don't you take the backpacks upstairs to your room, Freddie?" Sarah gave him a wink.

The boy grinned with relief, loading up with the backpacks and scurrying out of sight. Eloise tailed him, picking up Calvin's bag from the floor.

Everyone took that as their cue to scram, except Sarah.

I shoved in the last bite of my sandwich fearful Sarah would take this moment to snatch it.

"Rough day?" Sarah tilted her head, giving me full access to her stunning eyes.

"It wasn't the best, but it's over. The work part, at least." I stared at the empty hooks. "All I wanted to do was be a good parent. Why couldn't I look in the bags?"

"What weekend is this?" Sarah mysteriously replied.

"Uh, like the date?" I reached into my pocket to retrieve my phone.

"No, the holiday."

"Oh, that. It's Mother's Day. We have brunch with the family." I gave her a puzzled expression, silently questioning what was going on.

"Do you remember when you were the kids' age?" She was staring at me like the answer was right before me, but all I saw were crumbs on my sandwich plate.

I shook my head. "I've pretty much blocked out most of my

childhood, so please enlighten me." I silently added, "Oh wise one." But I knew better than to say it out loud.

"More than likely, you made gifts for your mom and were sent home with them the Friday before."

"What'd I make? Sculptures out of dog turds?" The image pleased me. Odd considering I hated dirt of any type. But it would have been a suitable gift for the woman who raised me.

Sarah snorted. "I'm betting the kids have their creations in their bags, and they don't want you to spoil the surprise."

"Why didn't they just say that?" I thought for a second, and the answer jumped right out at me like a snake in the grass. "Because it's a surprise. Got it."

"You're adorable when confused." Sarah gave me a soft kiss on the lips.

"Glad you think so because these days, my synapses are misfiring all the time, leading to more and more of these situations." I snapped my fingers with both hands, but my left didn't exactly work out. Proving my point, which hadn't been my intention.

"I wondered how you got to drug mules."

"That wasn't my best joke," I admitted, followed by, "What's for dinner?"

"You're not full?"

"When stressed, I get snacky."

"What can I do to help you destress?" Sarah nibbled on my earlobe.

Right then, Olivia screamed from the front room, "Stop doing that, Calvin!"

"Rain check." Sarah stormed out of the kitchen to deal with whatever had Ollie worked up.

CHAPTER THIRTY-TWO

I crossed through the family room, and all four kids fell silent, their eyes following me as I headed to the kitchen. There, I found Sarah pouring herself another cup of coffee, her expression clearly indicating that if she didn't get more caffeine pronto, she might not make it through the next hour, let alone the day.

"I think the children are plotting something." I filled the teakettle, also in dire need of some *wake me up* juice.

"Aren't they always?" Sarah blew into her mug, the steam swirling around her face.

"I miss the catch-up cabin." I waggled my brows at her. "Three weeks back home and it's almost like it didn't happen."

"But it did." She wore a dreamy expression.

"Should I be worried about—?" I hooked my thumb over my shoulder. I couldn't see them still huddled together, but my motherly senses said they were.

Sarah shook her head with unwavering confidence, prompting me to wonder if she was somehow involved in the plotting. If that was indeed the case, I realized I would need a significant boost of caffeine to keep up.

"We need to leave in ten minutes." Sarah rinsed her mug and placed it on the top dishwasher rack, closing the door.

"So I need a to-go mug?" I added. "Where are we going again?" Despite all the reminders on my phone, I'd never fully mastered keeping track of all the kids' appointments.

"We're dropping off three of the children at my mom's, and then we're taking Demi to the dance studio for an open house."

"Do I need to wear a tutu?" I couldn't help but chuckle at the thought, finding it difficult to imagine such a scenario.

"Oh good. I thought you were going to fight me over that detail on today's agenda." Sarah leaned against the fridge.

I scrutinized Sarah's poker face, desperately hoping beyond hope that she was simply bluffing. The intensity of my gaze seemed to only reinforce her blank expression, which I couldn't help but find both impressive and oddly attractive. It made me question what that said about my own character.

Finally, I broke. "Please tell me you're kidding."

"I'm kidding. Maybe. Why don't you go upstairs to see what outfit I set out for you today? Hurry, though. We really need to leave soon."

"You love torturing me." I was about 97.65 percent sure she was pulling my leg.

"It helps pass the time." With a playful twinkle in her eye, she continued, "I would love to see you in a tutu, though. How do we make that happen?"

"We don't. And seriously, wouldn't you lose all respect for me?" No way was I going upstairs now to see if she had set out clothes for me.

"Not a chance. Tutus are hot!" The expression on her face made me question her sanity.

"You need help. Serious help." If she thought I was going to wear a tutu, she was most definitely out of her mind.

"Kids!" Sarah hollered. "We're leaving in seven minutes. Shoes on."

A flurry of movement erupted as Calvin pushed Freddie, who in turn countered with a stiff arm. While I knew I shouldn't revel in it, witnessing Fred stand up for himself brought a sense of satisfaction. He possessed a gentle spirit, yet also demonstrated resilience when the situation called for it.

Sarah and I observed their interaction closely, relieved that it didn't escalate any further. This was undoubtedly one of the most challenging aspects of parenting—allowing the children to resolve their own conflicts without butting in. Sometimes they managed it on their own, but there were occasions when, by the time we intervened, the situation had deteriorated into such chaos that it required considerable effort to persuade the bickering parties to let go of their grievances.

With four strong personalities, it kept us both on our toes. Toss in Sarah, and I was a goner.

"Shoes, Lizzie." Sarah snapped her fingers.

"My flip-flops are by the door."

"It's not that warm out," she cautioned.

"It's May, and I'm not at work." I stuck out my tongue at her.

Sarah's gaze swept the children, seeming relieved that none of them screamed they wanted to wear flip-flops, too. Then Sarah returned her stare with a quirked eyebrow that conveyed even the children knew it wasn't flip-flop weather. In my defense, I'd never claimed to be smarter than the children.

On the drive over to Rose's place, the sky opened up, and it started pouring rain.

"Regret the flip-flop choice now?" Sarah checked her makeup in the visor mirror.

"I never regret flip-flops. It could snow, and I'd still revel in not wearing shoes. I keep telling you they're prisons for the feet. My toes want to be free. Free, I say." I rapped my thumbs against the steering wheel.

"And if you get frost bite?"

"It's going to be in the fifties today. No chance of my toes falling off."

"I wanna see it if they do!" Calvin sounded too pleased by the possibility.

I quirked an eyebrow at Sarah to convey, "See what you've done."

She smiled, not seeming to care our son hoped my toes turned black and fell off.

Not wanting to focus on that, I looked in the mirror, making eye contact with Demi. "Anything I should know before going into the dance studio?"

She nodded solemnly. "Whatever you do, don't talk to Miss Deidre."

"Why not?"

"Uh, it won't go well." Demi squirmed in her seat.

That didn't give me much to go on.

Demi seemed to catch on that I wasn't following. "She's mean and makes people cry. Don't talk to her."

"She makes people cry?" I repeated this intel to Sarah. "Why are we sending Demi to a dance school with a teacher like that?" Furthermore, the classes came with a hefty price tag. Not that I minded footing the bill; after all, Demi absolutely adored her dance class. But I fervently objected to paying for people to be mean to my kid.

"It's a part of life," Sarah answered, not seeming particularly concerned.

"Crying?"

"Dealing with difficult personalities."

Drawing from my own tumultuous experiences with my mother, who was quite a character, I could empathize with that sentiment to some extent. However, those same experiences fueled my determination to shield my children from the cruelty of individuals who took pleasure in demeaning others. These conflicting notions waged a battle within my mind.

Maybe I'd put Miss Deidre in her place. After all, I was the customer and didn't that mean I was always right?

CHAPTER THIRTY-THREE

THE DANCE STUDIO WAS AT THE END OF A BLOCK OF four businesses. Naturally, one of them was a Dunkin. I had it on good authority it was illegal in Massachusetts to have a Dunkin further than a five-minute walk from every residence.

I killed the engine and unclicked my seatbelt. "Okay, gang. Let's tutu!"

Sarah chuckled, but when I glanced at Demi in the back seat, her expression was one of shock and dismay. I was pretty sure she was coming up with ways to explain that she'd never seen me before in her life.

"Don't worry. I'll behave in there." Despite my efforts to reassure Demi, her expression remained strained and unconvinced. This indicated either that my attempts at reassurance had fallen short, or she'd experienced being in public with me enough times to know the term best behavior was relative.

Sarah gave my shoulder a squeeze.

I wasn't a complete disaster, but situations like these tended to highlight my awkwardness. Evidently, the kids had picked up on it.

Inside, there was a stern looking woman across the room, and Demi whispered, "That's Miss Deirdre."

"The scary one?" I whispered back.

Demi moved her head up and down.

I casually shifted my gaze back to Miss Deirdre, who leaned on a cane, a chill creeping over my body. It was no surprise why all the kids were terrified of her. I had seen rattlesnakes with less intensity.

Sarah started chatting with one of the other moms, and Demi drifted over to some of her friends, leaving me on my own. I shifted on my feet, my left one hurting. Glancing down, I noticed that my toenails were in dire need of attention. Did I have a pair of clippers in the car?

When I looked up, Miss Deirdre stood right in front of me.

Now what, Lizzie?

I made several attempts to capture Sarah's attention, hoping she might step in and rescue me from what seemed like an impending disaster. Whether she didn't notice or chose to stay out of the brewing situation, I couldn't be certain. However, one thing was clear: if everything unfolded as I feared, it wouldn't end well.

Swallowing, I stood frozen to my spot like I was about to get caned by the woman.

With a rigid posture and piercing gaze, the elderly ballet instructor exuded an aura of icy authority, sending shivers up and down my spine. I pictured her barking out sharp criticisms during classes, leaving no room for error or mercy.

"Are you Demi's mom?" she demanded.

"No—er, yes. One of them." Again, I tried to get Sarah's attention so she could rescue me. I'd only just opened my mouth, and things were already going downhill.

"I want to talk to you about her."

I simply nodded, dreading whatever would come next.

"She's got talent."

This unexpected turn of events caught me off guard. Was she trying to soften me up before delivering a blow? Deciding to feign ignorance seemed like the best course of action, and truth be told, it wasn't much of a stretch for me. I knew Demi enjoyed dance, but it had never occurred to me to wonder if she was any good at it.

"She's always dancing at home," I said, not knowing what was expected of me in this situation.

"What are your plans for her?"

"For Demi?" I was baffled. What kind of question was that? I planned for her to grow up healthy and happy.

"Yes." Her steely eyes dug into mine, but she didn't give me any clues to help narrow down what kind of plans she was looking for.

Finally, I asked, "What do you think we should do?"

"More classes."

I blinked, not wanting to blurt out that of course she'd say that. Her livelihood depended on filling her dance classes. I wasn't born yesterday, Scary Dance Lady. I could smell a scam when I caught a whiff of one.

"We haven't had a student as promising as Demi since Tonya."

"What happened to Tonya?" I asked, though I would have rather asked what happened to her parents. Bankruptcy after paying for years of extra classes?

"She's with ABT now as a principal dancer." When I simply stared, Miss Deidre followed up with, "The American Ballet Theater."

"You think Demi could be a professional ballerina?" Was it the flip-flops or because my toenails were in such a dire state that made her think I was a sucker?

Just then, a mother approached Miss Deidre to inquire about additional classes. To my astonishment, Miss Deidre, typically intimidating, cautioned the mother against enrolling her child in too many classes. As she spoke, she seemed to lock eyes with me, almost as if she were aware of my skepticism regarding her advice where Demi was concerned, and this was her way of showing she was being genuine.

Was this a setup? Was this "mother" an actor, and they were pulling some kind of dance-class con?

Sarah motioned me to her side, and I hightailed it to safety. "Lizzie, this is Susan. She's one of the moms."

"Hi." I nodded in greeting, furtively keeping watch for another Miss Deidre attack to my flank. Did she really need the cane? To walk? Not for punishment?

"Demi's the star of her class." Susan spoke with awe in her voice. "I hear about her at home every week."

My gaze sought out our daughter, who was giggling with her friends. When she first joined our family, following her mother's death and my brother's arrest, I fretted that Demi might struggle to find her voice or fit in. Yet here she was, standing tall and conversing with confidence. Witnessing her in this moment was truly remarkable.

"Miss Deidre was just telling me Demi should be in more classes." I laughed like that was ridiculous. She wasn't even in the first grade yet. But Sarah and this other mom stared at me like I was missing something important. "Isn't she too young for all that kind of thing?"

"My daughter is in jazz, ballet, and modern."

"Isn't that… a lot?" I pressed.

"If Janie had it her way, she'd take classes every waking moment." The woman excused herself to speak with Miss Deidre.

"Are these people insane?" My eyes swept the room. "Shouldn't we let Demi be a kid, not a dance robot?"

"Dance robot?" Sarah repeated before saying, "She loves it. Look at her."

I did, and I was simply amazed by how she fit in here. This

was her domain, but did that make it okay to force her to take so much on at such a young age?

"She looks happy, doesn't she?" Sarah asked.

"She does, but I don't want to put too much pressure on her to be perfect. I don't want to be like…" I let my voice trail off.

"I know, honey. I don't think she feels that way. Demi's mentioned a summer camp. She can't do the intensive until she's thirteen—"

"What do you mean intensive?" I imagined Demi confined to some institution for weeks, Miss Deidre wielding her cane, resembling a lion tamer instead of a ballet instructor.

"It's for kids who want to be ballerinas."

"Is that sexist? Shouldn't we say ballet dancers? Like how we don't say actresses now." I ran a hand over my head, knowing that this wasn't really what had me concerned.

"I'm not sure. What I do know is Demi wants to take more classes. We've talked about it."

"Jazz?" I'd seen Demi tap her little feet earlier this morning. "And modern."

"How many nights a week would she be here?"

"Three." Sarah added, "There's also an acting class, but that's on Thursday after ballet."

"Hold on a second." My head was spinning. "You're telling me we should sign Demi up for a total of three dance classes and acting?"

"It'd boost her confidence." Sarah picked up some of the brochures from a table. "I hope it's not too late to get her into a summer program." With that, Sarah sought out Miss Deidre. Like, on purpose. My wife might be the bravest person I knew.

CHAPTER THIRTY-FOUR

I shifted onto my back, the bedroom shrouded in darkness. After a silent countdown from fifty, I flung the covers aside, determined to rise before anyone else in the house and tackle some work.

"Where are you going?" Sarah asked groggily, her hand reaching for the lamp on her bedside table.

"Downstairs to the library." I stretched my arms overhead. "Go back to sleep. It's Sunday."

"Not today." She patted my side of the bed.

"I'm pretty sure it is." Unless I slept through a day. I hadn't ever done it, but that didn't mean there wouldn't be a first time.

"Get back in bed. Now." Sarah's instruction carried a bossy tone that didn't sit well with me.

"If you're trying to seduce me, that's not the way to go about it." I crossed my arms, readying for battle.

Sarah sat up, and despite my eyes not adjusting to the soft glow of light coming from her side of the room, I sensed she was pissed. "I wasn't asking for that. You have to stay in bed this morning."

"Because?" I couldn't afford to entertain whatever this was. I had a pile of papers waiting to be graded.

"It's Mother's Day."

"Yeah, so shouldn't I be able to do what I want?"

"Not if you want to avoid disappointing your children."

I massaged my eyes with the heels of my hands. "What do they have to do with when I get out of bed? We're past the age of them waking us up all night long. Unless they're sick or had a bad dream."

"Because they want to surprise us this morning with breakfast in bed."

"How do you know this?" I stayed rooted in the middle of the bedroom, reluctant to return to bed knowing that the work I had planned to tackle the previous night remained untouched.

"I found their menu."

"What menu?" Why was Sarah speaking in riddles this time of day?

"One they'd written up to go with the breakfast." Sarah laughed quietly. "Every single word was misspelled, by the way. Even menu."

I let out a puff of air. "There's no way I'm getting any work done today, is there?"

"Not a chance. Stop being a baby, and come back to bed. What happened to the woman in the cabin who declared she wanted to be a better mom?"

"She has twenty papers to grade before Wednesday and has about fifty other tasks that need to be done." My eyes welled up, as if on the verge of spilling tears.

It was Sarah's turn to huff out a breath of air. "I understand. I'll make sure you have all the time you need on Monday and Tuesday. No cooking or dishes. Just you and your red pen."

"What about you?" I climbed back under the covers. "Aren't you drowning in work?"

"Next week, I will be."

"I'll do the cooking and shit next week if you help me this week."

"Deal." She snuggled next to me. "No complaining."

"We just made the deal. Now you think I'll start whining?"

"I meant about whatever the kids are making. You have to eat what you can of it, and no complaining." Her words were delivered like a hammer to the head.

"Wait. You never said they were doing this on their own. Isn't an adult helping them?" Now I was worried about this situation, and not just on behalf of my stomach. "What if they burn down the house?"

"Then they'd be taking after you."

"It was only an oven!"

Sarah chuckled. "Shush. I hear little feet. Pretend you're asleep." She killed the light.

I ducked my head under the covers. "It's still dark. They only get up this early on Christmas."

Sarah covered my mouth. With her hand, instead of her lips.

The door opened, and there was a shout of "Happy Mother's Day!"

Sarah and I sat up. The sudden flick of the overhead light left me momentarily blinded.

"What a surprise!" Perhaps Sarah ought to lead the acting workshops at Demi's school because that was some stellar bullshitting without any coffee to spur her brain into action. "You made us toast."

I glanced at the slices of bread resting on the tray that Freddie placed on the bed. They appeared untoasted, and there was a noticeable absence of butter or jam.

"It's raw toast," Fred said, a smile spreading across his face.

"Is that a new trend?" I inquired, observing the absence of any beverages to wash down the untoasted bread. While I usually preferred my sandwiches simple, consuming dry bread at this hour seemed like a recipe for disaster.

"It is now!" Ollie squealed.

"We couldn't get the toaster working," Fred confessed, his shoulders slumping.

"It's perfect just the way it is." I flashed him a reassuring smile.

"There's fresh fruit." Sarah plucked the unpeeled orange from the plate, starting to remove the rind.

"There's also an apple." Demi gestured toward one that appeared to have been inadequately cleaned.

"Don't forget the raisins." Calvin rattled the small boxes as if they were maracas.

I would have preferred grapes, which we had in the fridge. But I'd been told not to complain, so I kept the thought to myself.

"And cookies," Demi climbed up onto the bed, snuggling between Sarah and me.

"My favorite breakfast food." I swiped one of the cookies before Sarah had a chance to voice her opinion.

Sarah shot me a glance as she took a bite of the untoasted bread, emitting a contented sigh. Honestly, with that talent, she might have racked up twenty Oscars by now if she'd pursued acting as a career.

"We forgot the orange juice!" Freddie zipped out of the bedroom.

I continued to nibble on the cookie, coughing when a bite went down the wrong pipe.

Sarah passed me an orange slice, and I appreciated the tiny burst of juice it provided.

"This is the best orange I've ever tasted." It may not have been Sarah-caliber acting, but I thought I was pretty believable. Probably because, in the moment, it was true. Although, I would have done anything for a sip of tea.

Fred came back with the carton of orange juice but forgot

the glasses. It was almost as if they were intentionally overlooking the details, which struck me as amusing.

"Don't forget the gifts," Calvin pointed to a plain paper bag.

"It's lovely." I chewed on another orange slice for some liquid.

Sarah shot me a glance and then peeked inside the bag. "Look at these, Lizzie."

The projects spelled MOM with a handprint as the O. "These are so cool!"

All four kids were on the bed now, giving us cuddles.

"I'm not lying when I say this is the best Mother's Day ever." I kissed each of the kids and then Sarah.

CHAPTER THIRTY-FIVE

As I entered the kitchen, I announced with pride, "I have my flip-flops on."

"It's like you're all grown-up," Sarah said without looking up from the salad she was prepping to take as her lunch for school tomorrow.

That wasn't the response I was hoping for. "What time is our Mother's Day brunch? I'm ready to go right now." I rubbed my belly. "I'm absolutely famished since we ate super early." Not to mention, most of what the kids had prepared for breakfast, and I was using the term prepared lightly, had been unappetizing.

"Two o'clock."

"In the afternoon?" My stomach sent up a Mayday flag. "Are you sure it wasn't morning?"

"If it was two this morning, you would have missed it." Sarah hit the lid on the dish to ensure it was sealed shut.

"If it's that late in the day, can it still be called brunch? Isn't that solidly lunch? Or even an early dinner?"

"It's not my fault you didn't eat much this morning."

I took a few steps closer, whispering in an urgent voice,

"The kids served us raw toast. You know what we usually call that? Bread. Just bread."

"They did their best." Sarah's smile contained a warning. "My mom wanted to eat later in the day, so that's what we're doing."

"Should I eat something now?"

"I thought you didn't want to ruin the buffet experience so you can gorge yourself to the point of nearly passing out." Sarah's expression fell. "If it makes you feel better, I'm not happy about it either. The kids are grumpy. So are you. It's bloody fantastic. I told my mom this would happen, but she doesn't listen to reason sometimes."

"I'm sorry. I know it's not you."

Her mother had been getting stranger and stranger ever since Covid. Honestly, I was surprised Rose had agreed to go to brunch. She'd been avoiding public places like the… well, for lack of a better word, plague.

"It's driving Troy crazy how Mom doesn't want to do anything outside of her comfort zone, which is limited to her house or ours."

"How do you know that?"

"Troy talked to me about it, hoping I can talk sense into my mom." Sarah's expression screamed that it was like asking a crocodile to grow wings and fly.

"Good luck with that." I froze, unsure how that would land. Over the years, I'd learned digs at her mother weren't appreciated sometimes. Other times, she'd guffaw.

Sarah laughed, a bitter one, but it wasn't directed at me. "The place we're going today has a pond. Let's load up the kids so they can feed the ducks. The restaurant offers day-old bread for patrons. Mom and your dad always arrive early. We might luck out and get seated before our reservation."

"This is why I married you. Not only are you stunningly beautiful, but you're also wicked smart." I attempted my best

Masshole accent, but it paled in comparison to Ollie's imitation. Although, the kids weren't so much mimicking the accent as learning to speak that way.

After a short drive, I was delighted to discover the restaurant was in a charming old mill building. A placid pond gave way to a roaring waterfall that ran past the wheel that used to power the mill. Flowering baskets hung from the building's porch, and there were ducks in abundance in the water.

"Ducks!" Freddie shouted from the back seat.

"That's right, Fred. We're going to feed the ducks." Sarah got out of the car. "I'll go inside to get the bread and let them know some of the party is here."

I pointed to my head to indicate she was brilliant and then made a heart with my fingers.

The smile Sarah gave me in return made my knees go weak. Or it would have if I hadn't been seated.

"You know what, kids? We're all lucky to have Mommy in our lives." My eyes got teary for some reason.

"Yeah, don't screw it up," Ollie flashed me a wicked grin.

I laughed, not only amused by her statement but her colorful vocabulary was growing. "I'll do my best, Ollie Dollie. Now, let's get over to the pond."

I didn't have to repeat the order. One thing about our kids, they all loved ducks.

Sarah returned with a plastic bag. "Line up and put out your hands."

I braced for the arguments and jockeying to be first, but the kids simply filed into line with their little hands out.

"What is that?" I watched Sarah rip the chunks up to disperse them.

"Stale cinnamon rolls."

"Lucky ducks," I gazed at the creatures, jealous they were

getting a better offering from my children than I had. "Is that good for them?"

"Is it good for anyone?"

I was about to say something but thought better of it. The last thing Sarah needed—after all the kids were behaving for once—was for me to pop off and ruin the magic of Mother's Day.

"You want some?" Sarah shook the bag.

"How stale is it?" I eyed the bag with longing. The scent of cinnamon filled the air and was making my mouth water.

"Not to eat, Lizzie." She laughed. "To feed the ducks."

"Right." I bobbed my head. "Nah, I'll let the kids enjoy it." I stared up into the dark blue sky. "What a beautiful day."

Sarah rested her head on my shoulder. "It is. I'm sorry you're stressed about work."

"It's fine. All part of being a professor. I'm sure my students won't mind if I have to skim the papers and not do a deep dive, missing some of their mistakes."

"Do you think they've figured that out? How we're also rushing to meet deadlines just like they are?"

"Or that we don't really care as long as they try their hardest? I don't think that's a secret that should be let out of the bag." I squinted at a car pulling into the parking lot. "My parents are here."

"Go say hello, and you might want to mention the grandparents' tea while my mom isn't here." Sarah pushed me toward our SUV. "Don't forget your card."

"Happy Mother's Day, Lizzie." My dad pulled me into a hug as soon as I approached.

"Thanks." I stepped back. "Happy Mother's Day." I handed Helen a card.

Without reading the inside of the card, Helen tossed her arms around me. I had to stop myself from flinching because in my experience, moms weren't warm and fuzzy but scary creatures.

"Can I ask for a favor?" I shuffled in my flip-flops.

I had their full attention.

"There's a grandparents' tea at the kids' school at the end of the month. Can you go?"

"With bells on." My father laughed.

"You'll have a fab time," Helen patted his cheek.

"Uh, I was hoping both of you would go. The kids might be disappointed Rose—well, you know the issue there, but having their other set of grandparents might ease the blow, ya know." It was becoming more difficult to explain to the children why Rose wasn't as involved as she once was.

"You want me to go?" Helen placed a hand on her chest.

"Yes. You're their grandmother." I thought that had been clear, but then I realized what she was really asking because Helen was my stepmom. This was a big deal to her, and I'd blundered the invite. What did it mean I hadn't considered she'd think she wasn't included? I added, "I always think of you as their grandmother and my mom—if that's okay."

"Okay? That's fantastic. This is the best day ever." Helen gave me another hug.

It was quite possibly the first time I received a mom hug the way they should be. My eyes watering again, I croaked, "Ducks. We should feed the ducks."

My father wiped his own eyes, saying, "Ducks are great."

I laughed because my father and I could be so incredibly awkward with this stuff, but it didn't stop us from trying to be better people.

JUNE

CHAPTER THIRTY-SIX

"Look! It's a wolf's paw!" Freddie's excitement echoed from the rear of the SUV as I navigated the vehicle around the bend.

Much to my relief, it was not any part of a real wolf he'd spotted but a display of flowers planted in the shape of a paw near the entrance to the wolf-themed water park where we would be spending a short family vacation.

There was another wave of elation when the kids caught sight of the massive water slides that sprang from the sides of the lodge's building like exposed plumbing.

At least, I thought it was the lodge. I couldn't be sure. All I could see were tubes jutting out everywhere. There were green ones and a red and yellow combo that had something drum-like at the end. It looked to me like an alien spaceship, a thought that prompted a foreboding sensation deep within my belly.

"That looks pretty intense," I remarked, swallowing hard, wondering how many people had met their end in that drum. Or was it more like a toilet bowl? I assumed that going down that slide was like flushing one's life away.

"I can't wait!" Sarah declared as if she were plotting to make me a widow before I turned forty.

"How many days are we staying?" I parked the car, the kids flinging open the doors without waiting for any prompting. I couldn't help noticing that was the opposite of how they acted at school drop off. Now that classes were out for the summer, they had a lot more pep in their steps.

"Watch out for other cars." Sarah unbuckled and was already out of the vehicle, directing the children and ignoring my question.

Whatever the answer, it felt like one day too many. Even if it turned out we had only booked a twenty-four-hour visit, I stood by my assessment.

"Grab your bags, kids," Sarah instructed, opening the back of the SUV and orchestrating Operation Great Wolf Lodge.

"That's mine, Calvin." Ollie shoved him.

"What?" Cal's attention was fixated on the red and yellow death trap, not on the teal backpack with Ollie's name embroidered on it.

Sarah caught my eye. Was she as worried about Calvin's intense stare as I was? He wasn't quite forty-eight inches tall, a requirement for some of the riskier activities at the water park. Were we in for an epic meltdown once he realized he couldn't join the twins, who had both just squeaked past four feet, for the more intense slides?

I shook my head, refusing to worry about it. That was a problem for future Lizzie. Right now, I needed to get everyone inside, checked in, and changed into their swimsuits so the "fun" could begin. Whoever designed this family fun center clearly had it in for the likes of me.

"Hello, Petrie team!" My dad approached from the next parking row over, waving. "Ready for some fun?"

I detected no irony in his tone, and when I caught sight of his attire, I couldn't believe my eyes. My dad, whom I had only ever seen wearing three-piece suits during every single one of his working years, stood before me in pink flamingo swim shorts, a mismatched Hawaiian shirt, and a pair of flip-flops. As a fellow flip-flop wearer, I approved of pretty much everything, but one detail stood out.

"Your toenails are painted in rainbow colors." I pointed to his feet, trying to remember all the rainbow colors in order. Roy G Biv. That was seven colors for ten toes, which perhaps explained the two shades of pink and an extra purple. I already knew he had a penchant for silly slippers, but this was a new layer of the enigma of my father, and I can't lie. It was doing my head in.

"Olivia and Demi did them for me," he said proudly, wiggling his toes.

"We can paint yours," Demi offered. "I'm not allowed to have painted toenails, but you can."

"Why not?" I asked her, certain neither Sarah nor I had made such a rule.

"Miss Diedre." Her little face was grim.

"Your ballet teacher doesn't allow painted toenails?"

She shook her head. "No."

I didn't approve of a teacher telling my kid what to do with her toes, but Sarah gave me a *not now* glare. So my mind went back to my father.

I struggled to reconcile everything I thought I knew about my father with the image of him with painted toenails. Sure, everyone should do what they wanted. But it wasn't merely the flamboyant ensemble or the unconventional nail polish that caught my attention; it was the underlying shift in perception, a glimpse into a side of my father I had never fully realized existed. Here was a man who, in my memory, had always been the epitome of professionalism and stoicism. Now he was embracing a carefree spirit and a willingness to step outside the boundaries of societal norms. What was next? Would he go shooting down the red and yellow slide while shouting "Geronimo"?

"Let's get checked in because I want to go on that," Dad said, gesturing to the red and yellow death trap and reinforcing my fears. "It's called the Howling Tornado."

That name was even worse than I could have imagined. As I surveyed the scene unfolding before me—the frenetic energy of the kids, Sarah's unbridled enthusiasm, and even my father's newfound adventurous spirit—I couldn't shake the nagging thought that perhaps, just perhaps, I was the sole bearer of common sense on this escapade.

I couldn't help but wonder if anyone else shared my concerns about safety, practicality, or the looming specter of potential disaster. I studied Helen for a sign she was on Team Lizzie, but she was excitedly talking to Ollie about the slides.

That officially made me the adult in this situation, and I didn't like it one bit. At the age of thirty-eight, I understood there was no arguing the technicality of my adult status, but since when did I have to be the voice of reason in a group? It wouldn't end well. Let's just say I was getting images of the Donner Party in my head. This was proof that historians have too many real-life dark examples of the shit hitting the fan at the ready.

"Do you want us to paint your toenails?" Demi asked, recalling her earlier offer.

"If I say yes, can I skip going on that?" I gestured toward the tornado thingy.

"You never have to do something you don't like," Demi said solemnly.

"Except eat veggies," Sarah added, wearing a wicked grin.

"Yes to rainbow toes, and I wouldn't be opposed to doing my fingernails, either. No to the tornado. And"—I turned to face Sarah—"it depends on the veggies. I'm almost forty, and you can't make me eat the gross ones. Which is most of them."

For emphasis, I stuck out my tongue. More proof as to why I shouldn't be the adult in a group.

"Such maturity." Her words didn't just drip with sarcasm; they swam in it.

"Let's get inside." I winked at her.

CHAPTER THIRTY-SEVEN

If I found the outside of the building intimidating, the inside of this hotel and amusement park combo was a true nightmare. Kids ran to and fro, squealing, crying, or full-on melting down. It was a scene straight out of a horror movie.

We'd checked in using the kiosks. Rather, Sarah entered the details into the computer while I tried to keep the kids from climbing a ten-foot bear statue, the presence of which confused me. Bears weren't related to wolves, so what was the connection? Living in the wild? The chandelier was made of antlers. Again, not wolf related. Just when I thought I had the theme all figured out, they went and made it difficult.

Sarah handed out our light-blue wristbands, which were printed with the slogan *Strengthen the Pack*. So, now we were back to wolves, unless some other type of animals also had packs.

After changing into our swimsuits in our cabin-themed hotel room, complete with bunk beds in a simulated wolf den for the kids, it was officially time for the Lizzie torture to commence.

Navigating through the lobby again and shepherding the children past the gift shop to avoid spending hundreds of dollars right out of the gate, we reached the water park area. It was chlorine-scented pandemonium.

"There are two sections," Sarah said to the children, her voice raised to carry over the din. "Over there is the wave pool and some of the slides. That's where your grandparents headed, and on this side is the lazy river and another slide."

"Lazy river," I said, very much liking the sound of that option.

To my surprise, Calvin nodded in agreement. Sarah and I exchanged a quizzical glance. Was it possible our fearless younger child was actually more fearful than we'd expected? Did he know he wasn't tall enough? Or was he in the mood to be lazy? I could relate on two fronts.

"Any other takers for Team Lazy?" I asked.

Demi raised her hand, which wasn't surprising. She always opted to be with Calvin.

"Alrighty, then. We're going to the lazy river," I said to Sarah. "Do we need a time to meet up someplace?"

"We'll find you." Sarah and the non-lazies trooped off to the left.

Demi peered up at me, waiting for me to do something.

Since we stood next to the towels, I requested three. After providing my wristband to be scanned, I proudly declared, "Commence laziness."

Both children groaned, with Calvin palming his face with both hands.

"Tough crowd."

Inside, the indoor space was even more utter chaos than I'd anticipated. Was going back to the room and taking a nap an option?

"Look at that!" Calvin pointed to a shallow pool that had

some platforms little ones could cross on their own, and there was also a massive bucket overhead with water filling into it.

"Why are they filling the buck—?" I didn't need to finish the statement since the bucket tipped over, drenching the kids underneath it, much to their squealing delight.

"The Bucket of Death!" Calvin proclaimed, making me ponder if he had witnessed the look Sarah and I exchanged earlier and wanted to make it clear that nothing scared him.

"It does have a deathly quality," I observed, wondering how my lazy option had become more ominous sounding.

"Can we stand under it?" His eyes didn't exude much confidence, making me rethink my gut reaction of *Hell no!*

"Yes. Go on."

I stood back to let them enjoy it on their own. Okay, fine. I chickened out at the end and had no desire to go anywhere near the thing.

"No, Mom. You have to join us." Calvin tugged on one of my hands, Demi pulling on my other.

Let me be clear. Was I the type who enjoyed having gallons of water dumped over my head? Nope. Honestly, is that even a type? I'd call that more of a personality deficiency. Personally, I was even careful in the shower to avoid getting my face too wet.

But, did I adore my children? Yes. That meant I didn't have a way out of this. Or did I?

"The lazy river sure looks inviting." I stared longingly at the people sitting on big inflatable tubes, floating by without any worry in their expressions.

"Later. I want the Bucket of Death." Calvin pressed his palms together, begging.

"Bucket of Death it is." I didn't want to know if that was the actual name or if Calvin had come up with it. Either way promised trouble. The way I saw it, I was truly about to drown to death, or my son was obsessed with the concept. Neither option was great.

Holding hands, the three of us stood in the danger zone, Calvin peeking up. "It's getting close."

"How do you know?" I looked up but quickly thought better. It was like looking upward with your mouth hanging open while a flock of geese flew overhead. Trouble was sure to follow.

"I just know." He continued to keep an eye on the situation, finally screaming, "It's happening!"

Right then, both children fled, leaving me to get the full brunt of the water. Much to their amusement.

Spluttering, I asked, "Why did you two run away?"

"That's the game." Calvin shrugged as if I should have known that all on my own, but the way he avoided my eyes gave his true reason away. Water scared him. He could stand in the ankle-deep water but didn't want to get wetter.

"This is a game?" My mind spun with a way to deal with this situation.

"Everything's a game," Demi said with such a serious air I had to laugh. At least, I didn't have to worry about her being afraid of water.

"New rule. No one can move when it dumps the water."

Demi and Calvin exchanged a look before retaking their spots.

It took an extraordinary amount of time for the Bucket of Death to refill, my heart rate inching upward with each passing second. I hadn't exactly enjoyed the first time, but it wasn't the worst thing that had happened to me. At the moment, I couldn't think of what that would have been, but this probably wasn't in the top ten of terrible Lizzie events.

When Calvin squealed, a good enough indication it was about to spill, I held onto each of their hands. Demi didn't try to escape. Calvin squeezed my hand hard but held steady. I was proud he didn't try to break free.

The water rained down on us, and Calvin and Demi howled in delight.

After, Calvin wiped his eyes, exclaiming, "I want to do it again."

"Sure thing, buddy. We can do it as many times as you want." I wanted to announce over the PA system that I had the bravest son on the planet, but I refrained. Instead, I smiled at both my kids, who wore ear-to-ear grins.

Maybe our wristbands were on the right track. There was strength in the Petrie Pack.

CHAPTER THIRTY-EIGHT

"How's it going?" Sarah stood next to me as I sat in a lounge chair watching the people float by in the lazy river.

"This is exhausting," I told her, as if she couldn't tell from my slumped posture in the chair. I was too tired to prop my foot up on the railing in front of me to keep from sliding onto my ass.

"Watching the lazy river is exhausting?" She laughed, taking the seat next to me. "Try hiking up seven flights of stairs over and over with the twins to go down the water slides. My glutes are getting a workout."

I craned my neck over the back of my chair to check out her butt.

"The results aren't instantaneous!" She swatted my hand, but I detected a sense of pride that I was checking her out.

And let me tell you, the action almost did me in. I might not have climbed a million stairs, but my body felt like it had been through the ringer nonetheless.

"Being here is tiring. There's so much going on at all times." I waved to the people, the water features, the bar behind me, and the snack shop to my left. It was like the entire place had been designed to overstimulate.

Sarah jumped to her feet to wave at the twins as they floated by in inner tubes. "I know you!"

"Hi, Mom!" Freddie waved back enthusiastically while Ollie looked away as if having a parent was the uncoolest thing ever to happen to her.

Was it time to chat with Ollie about how she had ended up on the planet? Because without me or Sarah, she wouldn't be here.

"She's going to be really fun in her teen years." Sarah chuckled, retaking her seat.

"Thoughts of teenage Ollie literally keep me up at night."

"You aren't the only one."

My dad floated by, sprawled out on an inner tube, his rainbow toes on full display. Helen was right behind him, her eyes closed. How did she do that? I hadn't been able to zone out once.

"You know, when I was growing up, not once did I imagine I'd have four kids to take to a water park while my father, sporting painted toenails, would look so relaxed." I added, "Kinda gives me hope for retirement. My dad and I are a lot alike."

"I have an idea." Sarah slo-mo turned her head to me, probably for emphasis. "Don't wait for retirement. Start relaxing now."

"Do you know how many times I stood under the Bucket of Death?" I held up both hands, all my fingers on display. "Ten."

"The Bucket of Death? Do I even want to know?" She narrowed one eye.

I pointed to it. "I'm pretty sure Calvin came up with the name. After he got used to water raining down on him, he couldn't get enough."

"He actually joined me in the wave pool."

"The fact that he was scared gives me hope. With his love of football and his bravado, I imagine him begging us to take him to the Running of the Bulls for his tenth birthday because he'd be in double digits and not a child anymore."

Sarah grinned while also shuddering at the thought. "He's a character."

"They're all characters." And I wouldn't change a single one of them, unlike my mother who desperately had tried to cram a round peg into a square hole my entire life. "What's the food situation?"

"For lunch?"

I nodded.

"I'm guessing chicken strips and burgers." She let out a contented sigh, resting her head on the back of the chair. "For dinner, there's a restaurant. But right now, I can't be bothered to change out of my wet swimsuit to be presentable. I doubt it's expected, but you know me."

I glanced in her direction, my mind zipping back to the first time I met her in Dr. Marcel's office so many years ago.

"Are you okay?" Her eyes flashed with worry.

"Yes, why?"

"You look like you're about to cry." She leaned close. "Is all the noise too much for you?"

"No. It's a lot, but I'm managing. That wasn't it, though. I was remembering the moment I met you."

Sarah blinked, as if not believing me, but after examining my face, she said, "You were wearing a sweater vest."

"I can't remember what you had on, but I remember your eyes. So dark and inviting. Like a pool of chocolate."

She placed a hand to my cheek. "Just for that, I'll let you get a giant pretzel with cheese dip with your lunch."

"Only because you want some of it!" I kissed her cheek.

"Guilty as charged. But I understand what you were

referring to. I never thought that when we met, we'd end up here."

"I didn't even know places like this existed back then." I wiggled a finger in my ear, trying to dislodge some water that didn't want to leave my body.

"It's pretty intense, isn't it?" From the way she said it, it wasn't a complaint.

The twins charged us. "We're hungry!"

I stood, motioning for the rest of the troop to get out of the river.

"I don't want to," Calvin shouted, settling into his inner tube like he never planned on getting out.

"That's fine. You don't have to eat a burger and fries with the rest of us."

He rolled out of the tube, splashing into the water, dragging his tube behind him to report for lunch.

My father wore the biggest smile I'd ever seen on him, and when his eyes met mine, somehow, his smile widened.

CHAPTER THIRTY-NINE

"Okay, each of you gets to fill your own container with candy. I've written your names on the cups, so don't try claiming one that isn't yours. If you do, you forfeit your own." Sarah parceled out the plastic containers. She swatted my hand away. "You don't get one."

"It's rough being an adult," I joked. Fine, I was only joking a little. A part of me wished I could fill a whole bucket of candy and not suffer any consequences from consuming it all. I missed the days when my metabolism was supercharged. "What's the next activity after candy?"

We'd showered by this time and all sported shorts and T-shirts, so going back into the waterpark wasn't an option for now.

"The kids' passes include some kind of quest game, the arcade, a climbing wall, ropes course, mini-golf, and an adventure club." She tucked the paper away after reading off the list.

"I'm exhausted just hearing about all that." I watched the kids fill their cups with candy, noticing Fred didn't cram his completely full, unlike Ollie and Calvin who struggled to seal the plastic lid on top. Demi's was fuller than Fred's but not overflowing.

"How much can I have right now?" Fred held his up to his eye level, waiting for an answer.

"Three pieces," Sarah replied, adding, "then hand the cups to Mom to hold."

She jerked her thumb at me because I wore a backpack, which meant I was the one who got to carry everything.

After cramming the cups into the bag, I swung it over my shoulder. The combined weight of the candy added several pounds. "I'm going to be stronger than the Hulk after toting this around all weekend."

"No one's stronger than the Hulk," Fred argued, wearing a serious expression.

"You're going to be just as green as the Hulk if you eat all your candy tonight." I tickled his side. Before kids, I wouldn't have been able to tell you something as basic as how Spider Man got his powers, but now I was becoming well versed in all of the Marvel and DC comics. Sadly, I didn't think it was something I could add to my resume.

That gave me a thought, but before I could chase it, my father said, "What's first?"

"Magiquest," Fred waved around a plastic wand that we'd procured moments ago from the shop.

"Look what I found," Helen rounded the corner, coming from the gift shop area, holding headbands with fuzzy wolf ears. She was already sporting a pair, and she placed one on each kid and then one on my father's head as well. She held out two more. "Lizzie? Sarah?"

"When among the wolves." I slid the headband in place, as did Sarah. "There's one for Magiquest."

"Two!" Ollie stuck her wand high in the air.

"Arcade!" Demi screamed, and this was one of the places where that was totally acceptable behavior even if it made me jump.

"Rock wall," Calvin proclaimed, crossing his arms as if waiting for one of us to argue with him.

I waited to see if Demi would change her selection given her preference to hanging with Cal, but she didn't. Had they spent too much time together today? Or was she showing some independence?

"Good thing there are enough adults. I call arcade with Demi." I reached for her hand.

"We'll take the twins for Magiquest." Dad motioned for the twins to join him before he took Helen's hand, following behind Ollie and Freddie, who presumably knew what the heck Magiquest was.

"That leaves you and me for the rock wall." Sarah patted the top of Cal's head and then kissed my cheek as the others left.

"Can I have another piece of candy?" Demi looked up with imploring eyes. "I'll give you a piece."

The kid had my number. I made a show of checking over both shoulders, whispering, "Don't tell Mommy."

Demi giggled as she gave me a Hershey Kiss, my favorite.

The arcade was smaller than I was used to, which made all the flashing lights and sounds more intense.

Naturally, Demi chose a dance game. I was starting to wonder if the kid dreamed in dances, not words. I checked my phone to see if there were ballet performances coming up, but the only kid-appropriate one I could find was *The Nutcracker*, and it was half a year away.

I added a note in my phone to consult Sarah about what date we should buy tickets for, before I started down a different rabbit hole.

"Whatcha doing?" Sarah bumped my shoulder.

"Research." I glanced up, seeing Calvin hopping onto a motorcycle video game. "Yeah, that tracks. Demi's dancing, and Cal is riding a hog."

"I'm shocked you know what a hog is." Her smile was affectionate. "What kind of research?"

"Marvel comics."

"Liar!" Sarah wagged a finger in my face.

"Shall we take a bet?"

"You know the answer. How is that fair?"

"Says the woman who just called me a liar. If you're right, I'll do the tea and coffee run in the morning before breakfast. If you're wrong, you have to. Do you agree to the terms?"

"Fine," she laughed, her eyes losing confidence in her accusation.

I showed her my phone. "Captain America made his first appearance in 1940."

"Do I even want to know?"

"I thought it could be an interesting side project. Learning about comics. Something the kids and I could do together. And, there might be a historical angle I can take for work."

"You'll literally research anything and turn it into a history project." She playfully rolled her eyes.

I shrugged.

"Promise me this won't consume you. No more podcasts."

"Hey now, Willow and I enjoy doing the podcast. What if the kids want to podcast? Would you say no to them?" I rocked back onto my heels as if delivering a kill shot.

"You're impossible, you know that?" Her expression morphed from playful to wary. "Remember our chat at the lazy river? You don't have to wait until retirement to slow down."

"It's a project I can do with the kids. Fred loves comics. It wouldn't hurt me to show an interest in something he likes. That reminds me. When we get home, we need to buy tickets for *The Nutcracker* in December."

Sarah shook her head, but she was chuckling. "For a woman who was afraid of commitment in the beginning, you've sure committed to being the best mom."

"Don't know about being the best. I think that's an impossible goal, but I'm giving it my all."

CHAPTER FORTY

It was our last dinner at the lodge before heading home. The eight of us were sitting at a table in the main restaurant, each looking bedraggled and exhausted. We'd stayed three nights, and let me tell you, that was a lot of family fun time in this type of environment. Even Calvin was finding it difficult to muster the energy to complain about anything.

"Is it time for fancy desserts?" Demi sat up straighter in her chair on the off chance good posture would be the deciding factor in her favor.

"It's always time for fancy desserts." Sarah set her napkin on the table so she could lead the kids to the buffet.

When it was just my dad, Helen, and me, Helen said, "I love that they think pudding in a plastic cup with a cherry on top is fancy. I hope they never lose that feeling."

Dad rubbed the scruff on his chin. "This has been fantastic. Did you have fun, Lizzie?"

I nodded. "Not sure I want to stand under the Bucket of Death again anytime soon, but there's something about watching your family let loose and have fun that makes it all worthwhile."

He reached for Helen's hand. "It's a gift."

She returned his squeeze of the hand. "Next time, we should bring Gabe and Allen."

Dad bobbed his head, looking away, and I had to wonder if his mind wandered to Peter, because mine certainly had. The one missing member of the Petrie family puzzle. Soon, his parole would be over, and he'd be free and clear to leave Colorado. Would he choose to come here?

The sadness in Dad's eyes confirmed we were on the same page.

"Do you think Peter will ever visit?" I tried to keep my voice from betraying my fear. Before Peter was sentenced, he'd renounced his parental rights so Sarah and I could adopt Demi.

Dad's gaze sought out Demi, standing on tippy-toe to get a better look at the desserts. "He hasn't mentioned it."

"Would it be too much for him to be around Demi? We haven't mentioned her adoption to her."

"He doesn't want that." Dad met my eyes.

"I know, but he's also the uncle of my children. They're growing up fast. I don't want him to have regrets, or not more than I imagine he already has." Peter worked for my dad's finance company when he got busted by the feds. It forced my dad into early retirement because the board wanted to bury the Peter fiasco, and having the name Petrie associated with anything became a liability. In that line of business, fiduciary responsibility trumped everything.

"You'd be okay with him visiting?" Dad shifted in his chair, giving me his full attention.

"He's made mistakes, but he's served his time." Not all of it in jail, as he'd been released on house arrest during the worst of Covid, but that wasn't the point. I imagined what he'd gone through had changed him. "He wasn't always the best brother. That doesn't mean he can't be."

Dad rubbed his throat, and I wondered if he was fighting off his emotions. "You keep impressing me, Lizzie."

"Don't be too impressed. It worries me. When he sees how amazing his daughter is—what will he do?"

Helen sniffled, nodding.

I pressed on. "I've put a lot of thought into this. I think it's a risk we should take. Demi is amazing. Peter played a role in that. The older I get, the more I learn you need all your people to love and support you." I flicked my eyes to the kiddos and Sarah. Judging by the fullness of their dessert plates, we had about forty-five seconds left before they returned, and we'd have to change the topic. "I'm sure her answer will be yes, but I'll ask Sarah if it'd be okay to invite him for the Fourth of July bash."

"You don't have anything to worry about." Dad patted my hand. "I understand your concerns, but Peter has been honest with me. He knows Demi is better off with her siblings and you and Sarah. I'm sure he misses her, but he doesn't want to fuck up her life."

My father wasn't the type to swear much, so I assumed that was Peter's phrasing. It actually made me feel a bit better to hear it.

"Do you think he wants to see her?"

"The thought terrifies him."

As if sensing the unease at the table, Sarah glanced across the room, checking in with me with a nod. I smiled at her. A weak one, which only made her eyes crinkle with worry.

"What about it terrifies him?" I swallowed.

"Facing his biggest regret."

"Having Demi?" I asked, aghast. Maybe I had been too quick to give my brother a free pass.

"No, not at all. Letting her down." He sighed with a touch of sadness. "Being a parent is the hardest job, even when you're not actively parenting."

I had to wonder if he was speaking for Peter or himself.

"Look at these." Demi waved at the deserts on her tray. "Have you ever seen anything more beautiful?"

"I have." I pressed a finger into her belly. "You and your siblings. Each and every one of you is perfect."

Calvin let out a well-timed belch.

I shook my head and laughed. "Still perfect, little dude."

Dad and Helen chuckled.

Sarah retook her seat, whispering in my ear, "Everything okay?"

I simply said, "Peter."

Sarah squeezed my leg under the table, letting me know she understood. Whenever Peter's name came up, she knew it caused my brain to kick into overdrive with worry.

No matter what, he was still Demi's father, and he had the right to see her. That didn't mean it didn't scare the shit out of me.

Being a good person was nearly an impossible task. No wonder so many didn't even try.

JULY

CHAPTER FORTY-ONE

"I shouldn't be in here, Snickers." I scratched the cat's head as I sat on the floor of the walk-in closet I shared with Sarah. "I keep doing this. Hiding. When things get tough, my instinct is to disappear. Like that'll solve a problem. I know it's stupid, but…" I could only muster the energy to shrug one of my shoulders.

Snickers briefly lifted her head, only to let it fall as if she was exhausted by my antics. It was adorable and nearly brought a smile to my face.

It didn't stop me from saying, "Try being me. You'd be even more tired."

"Are you telling our geriatric cat that your energy levels are worse than hers?" Sarah leaned against the door jamb with her arms crossed, but the softness in her eyes betrayed her stern posture.

"She gets to sleep all day." It was a weak defense. If I had three days, I would have been able to craft the perfect response. Sadly, life didn't work that way.

"Because she's old," Sarah pointed out with a chuckle.

"I'm almost forty." I jutted out my bottom lip. It worked for the kids. Well, sometimes it did. Usually only with me.

"You're not even thirty-nine. Don't jump to being forty before you have to. Not again."

That finally brought a smile to my lips, because this time last year, I'd been freaking out about the big 4-0 only to discover on my birthday I was, in fact, turning thirty-eight. I still had plenty of time to have a meltdown before forty, but that wasn't the reason why I was here.

"Why are you hiding?" Sarah asked. "It's just us here. Usually you do this when people are arriving for a party or something."

"What do you mean it's only the two of us? Where are the kids?" I got to my feet, worried. Frankly, I was shocked Sarah wasn't. "Do I need to organize a search team?"

"Relax. They're downstairs with Maddie and Willow. I meant it's only the usual suspects here at home. No house guests."

"I got a text from Peter." I plopped back down onto the carpeted floor. Now that I knew the kids were safe, I wasn't quite prepared for life outside of the closet. Not the metaphorical closet, of course. I was fine with living my best gay life. But the physical comfort of a small space was surprisingly appealing right now.

"Is he coming for the Fourth?" Sarah actually looked excited by the prospect.

"I don't know." I stared at my slippered feet, wondering if it was time for a new pair given their shaggy state.

She tilted her head to the side in that familiar way that said, talking to you rarely makes things clearer. Perhaps seeking a new perspective, she joined me on the floor.

"I haven't read the text message," I explained, wishing they or any type of communication, didn't exist. Life would be so much easier if people couldn't get a hold of me, expecting things.

"Honey." Sarah took each of my hands in hers. "He's not going to take Demi back."

"Has he told you that?" I countered. "Definitively? Not to Dad or anyone else, but specifically to you."

"No, but we legally adopted her. He can't just snap his fingers and make that go away. Even if he wanted to, which we have no reason to believe is true."

"My brain tells me that, but…" Since she had my hands firmly in hers, I could only glance down at my heart. "I don't know what I'd do if he even hinted that we should give Demi back. That it's the biggest regret in his life."

"I have no doubt it's his biggest regret, but I also don't think he would change it. Read the message. I'm sure it's not bad."

"I can't." I broke free from her clasp and fished my phone out of my pocket. "You read it."

She shook her head, as way of admonishing me but not refusing my request. She insisted on getting across that I was impossible sometimes. Like I didn't already know that. Then she held the phone up to my face to unlock the screen.

After a second she said, "I have good news for you."

"He's not coming?" I was about to jump to my feet for a Lizzie-style happy dance, which resembled a baby giraffe attempting its first steps. At least, that was what the kids told me the last time I did it.

"No, he is coming, and he's bringing a surprise."

"Like a lawyer?" My shoulders slumped.

"I don't think he's flying out here with a lawyer."

"True. He could have hired one here." I raked a hand over my head.

"I suppose, but I'm having a hard time believing he'd do that."

"Old Peter would do that." Tucking my face between my knees, I added, "He wasn't the nicest of brothers."

"I'm aware, but I don't think he's cruel like that anymore." She either believed that, or she had perfected her acting skills.

"He outed me to our uncle to get my inheritance."

She pulled me into her arms. "I know it's hard to trust anyone in your family. Why did you invite Peter to this party anyway?"

"Because it was the right thing to do." My tone was sullen. "I always do the right thing, and it's annoying. Why can't I be the asshole for once?"

"Please don't make that a life ambition." I couldn't see her eyes, but I imagined they were filled with worry.

That didn't stop me from saying, "Why not? It's probably easier for assholes."

"Considering your former asshole of a brother literally spent time in jail, I can assure you being a jerk won't improve your life. You did the right thing in inviting him to visit so he can get to know Demi," she continued, probably to get my mind off the wrong subject. "He's made so many mistakes, Lizzie. Too many to keep track of, but we can't ignore the Peter problem forever. He's a Petrie and a part of our family. Nothing has changed that."

"I get that. I do." I sniffled into her shoulder. "The kids and you are my whole world."

"I know."

"I can't lose any of you." I held onto her tightly.

"You're not going to."

I pulled back to stare into her eyes. "You promise never to die?"

"I'll do my best. Please respond to Peter because he's probably going through hell on his end. Don't be the cause of more pain."

"I hadn't thought of that." I dashed off a text, simply saying, "Great news!"

She gave me a smile.

"On a scale of one to ten, how much would you hate me if I became an asshole?"

"One hundred."

That didn't sound good for my prospects of turning into a raging asshole. "On the bad end?"

"Yes, Lizzie. On the bad end."

CHAPTER FORTY-TWO

"Are you sure about this?" I stood in the driveway with the key in my hand, jabbing the not pointy enough end into my palm to keep from screaming. "All of us are going to the airport?"

Sarah, wearing a sun dress and looking like nothing in the world could rattle her, nodded. "None of us has seen Peter since we left Colorado. Him coming here is a big deal."

"But Dad and Helen are giving Peter and Gabe a ride home. Isn't this overkill? We can't even meet them at the gate. There are six of us in our car."

"Look at you doing math without your fingers." She gave me a saucy wink, completely ignoring the substance of my argument.

I blew a raspberry at her because I really couldn't claim I was a math whiz. Not without fear of upsetting the entire universe and being struck with a thunderbolt by Thales of Miletus. He was known as one of the first mathematicians from Ancient Greece. Although he wouldn't be the thunderbolt-throwing type, since he didn't look to mythology for explanations, but natural philosophy.

Luckily, I didn't say any of that out loud because Sarah was already staring at me like she expected me to meltdown at any second.

Sarah gave me a buck-up grin and then shouted inside the front door, "Get moving, or miss out on ice cream later!"

That got my butt in the driver's seat. Probably not Sarah's true purpose, or perhaps it was part of it. In the past, she has said she feels like she has five kids. Which is fair to a point. I could be difficult to manage, but I would like to mention, none of the other children earned a full-time income and cleaned up after the pets. I stayed mute on this subject since it usually didn't go the way I intended it to.

Way too soon, after parking the car, we were steering the kiddos through Logan airport. Freddie was in charge of the rolled-up welcome sign, because we were that family, apparently. The type you see in a Hallmark movie. Peter wasn't coming back from a war or anything. Should we have made some sort of reference to him being a freed jailbird, just so no one got the wrong idea and thanked him for his service or something?

Dad and Helen greeted us, my dad hugging me tighter than normal. Had Sarah ratted me out about the closet incident, or did he just know me and my perpetual worries about absolutely everything?

There was a burst of activity, and my eyes were glued to the passengers streaming toward us, my body tensing for the first sighting of Peter. I'd convinced myself I would know his true purpose as soon as I saw him.

But when I did spy him, I had no idea what thoughts ran through his head. It was always weird seeing him, since we looked a lot alike. Even more so now, with my short hair. Although, I didn't have a neatly clipped graying beard. He was seven years older, and let's just say, after being in prison, he'd probably seen some shit. If I was looking at my future, I was going to need to get better about using daily moisturizer.

Sarah motioned for the kids to unfurl the sign that said, "Welcome Home Uncle Peter and Uncle Gabe!"

Gabe tapped Peter on the shoulder, pointing us out, laughing.

Peter laughed along, but his step slowed for a millisecond. So did my heart.

I followed his gaze to Demi, but it bounced off her quickly.

"Welcome home, sons." Dad wrapped both of them into his arms. "Did you have a good flight?"

"Not too bad." Gabe wrapped his arms around Helen and lifted her off the ground, making her squeal, hopefully out of delight. I prayed we wouldn't have to rush her to the hospital for a slipped disc or something.

Peter briefly met my eye, and I wondered if he had the same thought. Neither of us would have ever thought of doing such a thing with our mother. He gave me a shy smile. I returned it with even more awkwardness, which probably meant we didn't only look alike, but thought alike, too.

Sarah hugged Peter. "Do you remember everyone's names?"

She rattled off all the kids' names, not tripping over Demi's like I probably would have.

Peter hunched down. "Let me see. You're Fred." He tickled Olivia's tummy.

"I'm Ollie." She giggled.

"Are you Fred?" He asked Calvin.

"Calvin," said our youngest, sticking his scrawny chest out as if that trait marked him as Calvin.

He turned to Demi and visibly swallowed. "You must be Fred, then."

"I'm Demi, Uncle Peter."

I thought I saw him flinch just a little at the term uncle, but the next second it was gone as Demi squealed and launched herself into his arms like she knew that was where she belonged.

The other kids joined the hug, while all of the adults looked like they were on the verge of a cry fest, including Gabe and Peter.

I shuffled on my feet, not knowing if I trusted myself to speak. So when Peter was free, I simply gave him a hug. I couldn't remember a time when we'd ever done that. I'm sure we had, but it seemed monumental in the moment.

He whispered in my ear, "Thank you, Lizzie," using my nickname, not Elizabeth like he and my mom used to.

I held on tighter to him, wondering if this triggered another threat of a cry fest from the onlookers.

When we broke apart, I said, "Sarah promised all of us ice cream."

CHAPTER FORTY-THREE

We sat at a picnic table outside of our favorite ice cream place, the one where the cows lay in the field behind a fence. I probably should've felt guilty enjoying the fruits of their labor, but the cows seemed well taken care of, and that appeased me somewhat. Besides, the ice cream was truly delicious.

Gabe and my father were with the kids, feeding a handful of broken ice cream cones to an eager group of goats.

"It's beautiful here." Peter's eyes swept the green grass, a small stream, and the trees along the far end of the farm. "Sure beats the ice cream places in Colorado."

I spooned in a bite of frozen chocolate and peanut butter goodness, nodding in agreement. After swallowing, I said, "I miss the mountains sometimes."

Peter's gaze traveled back to the kids as he said, "Have they tried skiing yet?"

"Nope, but Calvin wants to try it."

"Gabe and I went to Breck a few times last season." Peter shortened the name of Breckenridge not because he was a snob but because that was how most Coloradoans referred to the ski town. And, I was surprised they'd gone there, not the fancier places like Vale or Aspen. Old Peter would have. Not to mention, it still surprised me that he was no longer under house arrest. Time really had flown by.

"Does that mean Gabe's been taking time off?" Helen asked. "Not just this week?"

"Occasionally." Peter shifted on the bench, as if not enjoying being put into the role of informant. Snitches get stitches, after all. He'd probably learned that in prison. "He wants to open a shop out here."

"Does he?" There was no denying Helen's happiness about this prospect. Allen, her youngest son, was in Boston, but Gabe had stayed in Colorado when everyone else moved. If I was a betting woman, I'd say it was because of Peter. Gabe was solid like that, despite Peter and I not knowing of his existence until fairly recently.

Another factor to Gabe staying behind was he took over the three flower shops Helen had started decades ago. Had she wanted to sell them and have Gabe here the entire time? Lizzie before kids would have thought that was asinine. But now, after having kids, it seemed perfectly reasonable. I would probably feel the same.

Peter had been working in one of the shops, and I won't lie. It was hard to envision my brother, the finance dude, trimming roses—or whatever it was florists did.

"What does that mean for you?" Sarah asked Peter pointedly, and I wanted to kick her under the table. Undeterred, she continued, "Would you come out this way as well?"

Again, Peter shifted on his seat. "I haven't put much thought into it, but it might be nice to get away from Colorado. I hear Vermont's nice."

"We should go for a drive," Sarah encouraged. "Lizzie's mad for a cheese shop in one of the villages."

"I'm pretty sure I'm not the only one who loves their cheese." I bumped my shoulder into Sarah. "There's a Christmas tree farm just down the road from the place. A charming general store, too, and the church has a white steeple. It's the quintessential picture of Vermont. I'd thought those Christmas movies were selling us a bunch of BS, but when it comes to the scenery, they're spot-on."

"Sounds perfect." Peter looked upward, where there was not a cloud in the sky. "No one will know me there."

I remembered the days after he'd been arrested. His face was splashed all over the news, along with my dad's and mine. Many people had lost a lot of money because of Peter's shenanigans and were rightfully angry. One person even spat at me as if I'd been a party to everything. Peter had probably received much worse treatment, and a stain like that wouldn't rinse out easily.

He hadn't mentioned his surprise yet, but I had to wonder if this was it. Was he leaving Colorado? For a Christmas tree farm in Vermont, perhaps. The kids would love it. To visit. I couldn't picture any of them doing farm chores.

Well, Demi, but…

It was a struggle, but I shoved down another wave of anxiety with a massive bite of ice cream, regretting it instantly when I got brain freeze.

Dropping my spoon, I cradled my forehead with both palms, moaning. Sarah rubbed my back, trying not to laugh at my stupidity. Did she suspect the cause?

"Lizzie, have you ever thought of doing another podcast?" Peter asked, seeming to ignore my distress, or perhaps trying to focus my mind on something else.

"I've been banned from that." Maybe he knew me better than I thought, because his question stilled the brain freeze, much to my relief. "Sarah doesn't want me to take on any new projects, in an effort to try to control my stress levels. Apparently, I'm wound too tightly."

That made Sarah, Helen, and Peter all laugh—with me, as it happened, because I was also chuckling.

Then something occurred that I hadn't expected, but now that it had, I was kicking myself for not predicting it on my own. Both Sarah and Helen got up to join the kiddos.

Only Peter and I remained at the table. It had all been an elaborate setup, one I'd been too slow to catch.

Was he ready to spring his surprise on me? Was there a lawyer lurking behind the red barn, ready to serve me papers?

"She's gotten big." His words came out slowly, like it took great effort not to break down.

I nodded, not pointing out Demi was still the smallest of the children. That wasn't what he meant. She had only been a baby when he went to prison.

"She's doing well?" He chewed on his bottom lip.

"Very. She lives and breathes ballet." Inexplicably, I blurted out, "We're taking her to *The Nutcracker* this December. You should come along. If you can swing it."

"That would be okay?" He perked up, and I would be lying if I said it didn't make my heart feel just a tiny bit of happiness to see it.

"Sure, especially if you buy a Christmas tree farm in Vermont. You'll be the kids' favorite person on the planet."

He belly-laughed so hard his shoulders shook. After a few seconds, he said, "I'm thinking more of a small cabin."

"By a river?" The thought sounded like a dream come true for the likes of me. Vermont didn't have many people.

"Or a lake. I might even take up fishing." He mimed casting a line.

"There's something I never thought you'd say." I chuckled over the image of Peter living off the land in the woods. He'd always been so focused on material things when we were kids, but how much of that had been my mother's influence? Had he always wanted to be a mountain man, living a simple life? Maybe there was more to my brother than I ever suspected.

"I need your help with something." Peter took a deep breath.

I gave him goldfish eyes, as if surprised to see the castle again as I swam by. I braced for the worst.

"I'm writing a book, and I'd like you to read it."

"A book?" Out of all the things that could have come out of his mouth, I didn't ever ponder this option.

"My story. I started it in prison out of boredom, and I've been tinkering with it off and on. I want to make sure I get it right. I want you to be honest about how much of a dick I used to be."

Well, he'd certainly come to the right expert if that was what he wanted.

"Is this going to be shelved in the horror section?" I joked but then blanched, feeling awful I'd actually said that aloud. He'd been through so much these past few years. Now I was the one being a jerk.

Luckily, that only made him laugh. "It's a shame we didn't get along at the start. I think things would have turned out differently."

"True, but then again, we might not be sitting here, enjoying the best ice cream on the planet, if that were the case."

"I wouldn't change it, then." He pointed to our entire family. "You know what gets me through the difficult moments? Knowing she's growing and thriving."

My vision blurred as my heart squeezed tightly inside my chest. "I think you should really consider coming here. What's keeping you in Colorado?"

CHAPTER FORTY-FOUR

"You actually said that?" Sarah held a pillow under her chin as she positioned the case at the bottom.

"It slipped out," I defended. "He's sad, and I hate seeing him that way. Despite how much he tortured me until not so recently."

"That." She pointed a finger at me, a smile spreading from ear to ear. "That is one of the many reasons why I love you."

"Because I'm weak? Mom wouldn't have forgiven him for stopping his torment of me."

"She's not the measuring stick for how to live, unless you want to grow up to be a bitter woman no one likes. You're not weak, Lizzie. You're caring." Sarah tossed the pillow onto her side of the bed. "I know your childhood taught you differently, but your mother was wrong. You're one of the strongest people I know. Stubborn as hell, but you also have a heart of gold even when it scares you." She walked toward me, wrapping her arms around my neck.

"My mom would be rolling over in her grave."

"Good. She can rot in—" Sarah pinched her eyes closed as she fought to keep in the remainder of her thought. "I'm glad you told Peter that. He needs your permission. You know that, right?" She let her arms fall to finish making the bed.

I worked on shoving my pillow into a case, not as successfully. "Why would he need my permission? He couldn't leave Colorado because of his parole. That had nothing to do with me. I don't control who can and can't live in the New England area." I quickly added, "Or anywhere. Even though I study dictators, I'm not a wanna-be one."

She gave me her knock off the stupid act expression. It irked me that she knew I was obfuscating.

So, I admitted, "Won't it complicate things? Having *Uncle* Peter around all the time?" I tried making air quotes but didn't want to let go of the pillow because I'd started to make progress. It only ended up making the situation worse, naturally. That was my specialty.

"Yes and no. We're going to have to tell Demi at some point."

"You're not suggesting we do it now, are you?" I sucked my lips into my mouth as if that would prevent those words from ever escaping me.

She took the pillow from my hands and easily shook it into a clean case. "I don't think now's a good time. When she's older. She has a right to know. And if Peter's in her life, it might be easier news to absorb." Her voice wasn't convincing. Neither was the confusion and fear in her eyes.

I sat on the edge of the bed. "He doesn't seem to want to intrude."

"He's not an intrusion."

"I know… I just mean… he doesn't seem to want to be more than Uncle Peter. He hardly ever takes his eyes off her, though."

"Would you if you were in his situation?"

"I wouldn't be in his situation," I shot back, certain of at least that much, thank goodness.

"Not what I meant." She waggled a *behave* finger in my face. I had a habit of changing the subject when the conversation hit areas that made me close to pooping my pants.

"I can't even begin to imagine what it's been like for him. When I try, my brain shuts down. The idea of not being able to parent our kids—it's unthinkable." I leaned back, resting on bent elbows, staring up at the ceiling.

Sarah settled on the bed next to me. "We should do everything we can to make things easier for the two of them. All the kids like him. He pays attention to them. Not all adults do."

"He wants to go to some of Cal's football games. It wouldn't hurt to have someone in the family with a lake house in Vermont."

"It sounds nice," Sarah admitted with the hint of a sigh. "I never used to think I could trade city life for a remote place, but the older we get, the more appealing that sounds. People are so people-y these days."

"Ain't that the truth, including our own family." It was a relief to know Sarah and I were on the same page. "Is your mom coming tomorrow?"

Rose hadn't been the most social lately.

"She says she is." Sarah's shoulders sagged with what had to be concern.

"Are you worried about her?"

"As much as I can be."

"What do you mean?"

"We have four children, full-time jobs, and she has a husband." She let out a frustrated sigh. "I love my mom, but I can't be a mom to her. I've suggested therapy. Troy's suggested therapy. I get that Covid scared the hell out of her, but hiding away—is that the solution?"

I pulled her down on the bed next to me, holding her. "I really hope you don't turn out like her."

"Thanks for that." She laughed while playfully bonking her forehead against mine. "And I hope you don't turn out like your mom, too."

"No way." My face scrunched at the very thought. "I hate the taste of scotch."

That really made her laugh.

"Pinky swear that we won't turn out like our mothers." She held hers out, and I locked mine with it.

CHAPTER FORTY-FIVE

"When are the fireworks?" Calvin pressed his cheek on top of one of the folding tables in our backyard, the humidity sapping his energy. At least for the moment.

Dad, Gabe, and Troy were in charge of grilling the hot dogs and burgers. Sarah was with her mom under a shady tree, while Maddie and Willow played some type of game with the twins. It involved a lot of squealing, but I'd failed to discern the rules or even the reason behind whatever it was they were doing.

"It's noon, buddy. Not until it's dark." I patted Cal's head.

"There should be fireworks all day on the Fourth," he pouted, pulling his head away, probably because he didn't want to be treated like a baby with Uncle Peter present.

"Wanna toss the football with me?" Peter got to his feet, a Nerf football in his hands.

I gave him a grateful smile. It wasn't that Peter was all that athletic, but he was trying to bond with all the kids, and I'd reached my limit of whining from Calvin. It truly was miserably humid, and there wasn't a cloud in sight to keep the sun's rays off us.

"I want to!" Demi jumped up and down.

"No way. Football isn't for girls." Calvin shoved Demi's shoulder as if to banish her from the situation.

"Hey now. Football is for everyone." I gave my son a shape up stare. "We do not discriminate in this family."

"I don't take ballet classes." Calvin folded his arms across his chest, readying for battle.

"Maybe you should. Professional football players do," I countered, folding my arms over my chest.

"They do not!" Calvin laughed at the preposterousness of that idea.

"They do. It helps improve their balance, strength, and agility." After dropping this bombshell, Peter fiddled with his phone, pulling up an article with a large headline, proving his point.

Calvin looked at the screen, which had football players participating in a ballet class, and then gaped at me. "Can I take ballet?"

I briefly closed my eyes, wondering how I'd gotten myself into this situation. Another activity for one of the kids? I was never going to escape having to ferry them all over town. He wouldn't be in the same class as Demi because she was with much older dancers now. Ms. Deirdre wasn't letting up on the promise she saw in Demi. Of course, knowing my luck, this meant there was no hope of any of the schedules lining up.

"We can talk about it with Mommy." Sarah was going to kill me for punting it to her, but I had a point. I shouldn't make the decision on my own. It was a family decision. Preferably one that didn't have to be made on a blistering hot day.

I left Peter, Calvin, and Demi to toss the ball around and joined Sarah, her mom, and Helen.

"Where's Gabe's girlfriend?" I asked Helen.

"She's flying in tomorrow. They're going to spend a few days in Maine."

"Sounds nice." I had to wonder why Gabe's girlfriend opted to skip family time, but I could sort of see it. We were a lot.

While the rest of them chatted about the possibility of Gabe popping the question on the trip, I watched Peter with the kids. Somehow the game had morphed into trying to tackle Peter to the ground, the twins joining in, tugging and pulling on Peter's arms and legs while he laughed, giving it his all to stay on his feet.

"I've never seen him so relaxed," I observed.

My father was also watching with a smile.

When it was time for lunch, Peter took a seat next to me at one of the far tables. "Cal really wants to take ballet now. Is he always like that? Once he gets an idea in his head, he doesn't let up?"

"Yes, and I have a feeling I'm going to regret blurting that out."

"Do you often regret blurting things?" Peter bit into a burger, getting mustard on his chin.

"All the time." I stressed each word.

"Does that include inviting me to *The Nutcracker*?" It sunk in why he'd started this conversation thread. Or perhaps he just saw an opportunity and struck.

"While I concede my mouth ran with the idea before I had time to think, no, I don't regret that. Sarah and I talked the other night. We want you in Demi's life. I don't have a blueprint for how this will go, but banishing you to Colorado doesn't seem like the right idea."

"You didn't banish me. My actions did." He looked down at his plate, his shame radiating from him. There was a time I would have reveled in it but not anymore. No one was more shocked to discover this than me.

"It's my understanding," I began with hesitation, "you're now free to leave Colorado. Sarah said you need my permission to move out here. I don't agree with her. You're free to live your life, but if you do need to hear this explicitly from me, you have my blessing. Not only for Demi. For all of us. We're family. Imperfectly so."

"The thought of her figuring things out scares me." He spoke barely above a whisper.

"Me, too." I let out a sigh.

"Maybe I should stay in Colorado."

I sucked in my bottom lip, carefully weighing my words before saying, "If you do and she still figures it out, don't you think that will be worse than you already being in her life? Or only occasionally visiting?"

"Should I know the answers?" He studied me like he wanted guidance.

"If you did, you should become a therapist or something. People would pay big money for answers to life, especially when it comes to atoning for our mistakes."

"Wouldn't that be nice. I need to think about it. I just don't know what's best."

I gazed into his eyes, the deep blue matching my own. "Whatever you decide, we'll support you. But don't make a decision because you think you need to be punished. Life's too short to beat yourself up every day."

He blinked away some tears. "I'll try to remember that."

"I've found setting up reminders on my phone helps me."

"What should it be?" He laughed, some of the stiffness in his shoulders relaxing.

"Forgive yourself or something like that. I have a daily reminder that reads, *Just Breathe*. It does help me calm down."

"I might try that." He took another bite of his burger, chewing carefully. After he swallowed, he said, "I do need your permission. Thank you. I wasn't a great brother, but I would like to make up for that now. If it's not too late."

"It's never too late. I'm on a mission to be a better person.

We can do it together. I'm sure Dad will join us. He's been making a big effort."

"I think having Helen in his life helps." Peter's eyes didn't wander to Maddie, who sat at a table on the other side of the yard, but I wouldn't be surprised if that was where his mind was, given they'd once been engaged and she'd ditched him at the altar.

"Love can strike when you need it most as long as you keep your heart open."

"All types of love." He sat up straighter. "Are you ready for my surprise?"

"As ready as I'll ever be. When I first heard about it, I thought you were going to spring a lawsuit or something."

He actually laughed. "You've always been suspicious and rightfully so, considering. No, lawyer. You know the book you're reading."

"The one you wrote?"

"Yeah, that one. When it's done, I want to dedicate it to you."

I blinked.

"Is that okay?" His eyes flared with concern.

"It'd be an honor, Peter. A true honor."

AUGUST

CHAPTER FORTY-SIX

"Do you know we're only a five-hour drive to Philadelphia?" Squinting with one eye, I looked up from the navigation app on my phone. The blistering sun overhead made it hard to see the screen, which seemed like a major flaw in the design. Had the designers never tested it outside of the lab?

"Is that right?" Sarah flipped a page of her paperback, glancing up, not at me, but on account of the squeal coming from Calvin as he cannonballed into my dad's pool.

"How did I not know this?" I adjusted my phone to see it better under the umbrella. "It's so bright out. Why is it so hot?"

"It's the first of August. These days, summers are pretty famous for being hot and miserable, especially when August hits." Sarah returned her attention to the book now that she knew the children weren't in danger.

"Aren't you even curious why I'm seeing how far away Philly is?"

Demi bobbed in the middle of the pool on her unicorn float, giggling as Freddie's cannonball drenched her.

"When it comes to you, curiosity really does kill the cat."

She softened the statement with a wink before whipping her head to ensure the shriek coming from Ollie was out of fun and nothing nefarious.

All was well. Our four kids were appreciating the pool while Dad and Helen jetted off on a quiet weekend away. Given our children, we rarely had quiet time. Although, I was getting relatively decent at blocking out the most obnoxious sounds, while staying tuned-in enough for a cry of distress. It was exhausting to be so on all of the time.

I ignored Sarah's dig. "A writer I admire is giving a talk in Philly, and I'm thinking of driving there to hear it."

I waited for a response, even if it was the *hell no* type. Instead, all I got was another turn of the page. I could be annoyed she wasn't paying attention to me, or I could use it to my advantage to snag some quiet time of my own. "Gettysburg isn't that far away. A little over two hours." I casually mentioned. "I might drive there, as well."

Another flip of the page.

"Wowzers. Valley Forge is in the area!" It was impossible to disguise my glee, and I hoped that wouldn't ruin my chances of going solo on this trip. Yet, I couldn't stop myself from spilling, "I know I'm mixing two wars, but I can't help that. There's so much to do and see." I swallowed. The next part wasn't going to be easy. "Did you want to go with me?"

"When is this?"

"Right before school starts."

"You want me to travel to hear a historian speak and then visit two battlefields in the middle of Pennsylvania during the swampiest of days?"

"Technically Valley Forge was an encampment. I don't think a battle occurred there. Granted, it's been years since I studied the Revolutionary War." I brought up Amazon on my phone. "I think this calls for reading some books."

Sarah restated her earlier comment. "Do you really want me to go to Philly with you?"

Actually, I wanted to go alone to allow myself to nerd out in epic Lizzie fashion, but saying that out loud seemed like a really bad idea. As if my wife might take offense to me not wanting her around or something. It was hard to tell with her some days. "It'd be lovely to have some time alone."

"What about the children?"

"They might like seeing a battlefield." What I pictured in my head was a battle, but not the Civil War type. More the *history is stupid; why are we here?* type from at least three of them. Freddie was easier going on this front, but he wasn't exactly gung-ho about history. Which killed a piece of my soul every time I thought about how much my own children hated my life's purpose—aside from being the best parent I could be, that is.

"I doubt that. Probably best to leave them home. How many days are we talking?"

I did some quick math in my head but thought better of it. Counting on my fingers, I blurted out the number seven. And regretted it instantly. No way would she let me escape on my own for an entire week. This wasn't even for work.

"Seven days of history?" Her eyes widened in obvious horror.

"There's other stuff to do in Pennsylvania," I offered. "I think there's an amusement park."

Sarah's expression remained deeply skeptical, and that was when I realized my mistake had benefited me. Personally, I didn't think seven days would be long enough. Not if I also wanted to do Philly justice. But it was way too long for Sarah to want to join me, and I could squeeze in a lot of history in that time frame.

Honestly, I hadn't been this excited about anything in I didn't know how long. Would it be wrong to make a list of things, like the births of my children, holidays, and this to see how all of them ranked? Yeah, probably. That wouldn't stop me from doing it, though.

"I'll think about it." Sarah picked her book back up, which I took to mean we'd never talk about it again unless I pressed her. Which I had no intention of doing. Since the trip was obviously her idea of hell on earth, she'd let me go alone and be more than happy to stay back with the kids. It was perfect.

Should I start making hotel reservations? Or maybe it was in my best interest to casually broach the topic later when she was about to fall asleep. That way I could say I really tried to convince her. It wasn't exactly kind to plot like that, but seven days to totally nerd out about history without any family responsibilities whatsoever? How could I resist this golden opportunity?

Olivia cannonballed into the pool, soaking Sarah and me.

I closed my eyes, imagining seven days of child-free, history heaven.

I opened my countdown app on my phone and started a new one for my possible trip. Seventeen days to go. Was there an advent calendar for this type of thing? Like each day revealed a historical fact about one of the regions on my itinerary? Why hadn't I thought of this earlier? I could have been getting daily trivia all year.

CHAPTER FORTY-SEVEN

"It's hot back here," Calvin whined from the depths of the SUV before sliding his headphones back over his ears.

Funny story. It turns out Sarah is not as sound a sleeper as I imagined. And also much more prone to saying yes to weeklong family road trips than she appears at first glance. Who knew? Certainly not me, or I never would have mentioned Philly again unless she was snoring like one of those old cartoon characters sawing a log.

Aside from my wife, everyone in the vehicle, including our au pair, had on headphones and their eyes were glued to their personal devices.

Sarah made some adjustments to the AC, basically depriving herself and me of even a wisp of cold air so the kids could have relief. As a parent, I shouldn't be annoyed. Shouldn't being the keyword. Sometimes, being the parent sucked. Massively.

"Isn't this family bonding experience great?" I asked in a not-so-nice tone. "Instead of me going on a vacation by myself to enjoy things I wanted to do, we're all crammed into this hot car, everyone with their headphones on, doing their own thing as we hurtle along a highway in Pennsylvania."

"Spending time with us isn't at the top of your list?" I couldn't see Sarah, but I sensed the fluttering of her lashes. Too bad they didn't have enough oomph to move the still air and provide me a momentary relief from the oppressive humidity overtaking the front of the car. I thought it was swampy in Massachusetts. Pennsylvania was ten times worse.

"Don't even try that tactic with me. All the kids are watching movies on their iPads. This isn't exactly starting off as a kumbaya family vacation." I glanced over my shoulder to check to see if I could merge into the left lane to get around a pick-up truck older than I was going at least twenty miles under the speed limit. There was always at least one.

"Things will improve when we get to the amusement park. Who knew there were so many family-friendly places to visit in this state?" She was laying it on thick, even using her most saccharine tone. But deep in my heart, I wasn't swayed.

"You completely hijacked my trip. You took all the history stuff off the itinerary. Valley Forge, gone. Same with Gettysburg."

"I never said we couldn't go to Gettysburg. I said I didn't think an eight-hour immersive tour with our own private guide at three hundred dollars per person was the best way to make lasting family memories. At least, not the kind of memories the children wouldn't have to go to therapy for. You're the one who decided it wasn't worth the extra drive for the ninety-minute highlight tour."

"What about the talk I wanted to hear in Philly?" I demanded, unable to defend myself against Sarah's point, since it was technically true. I stood by my assertion, however. Who in their right mind would turn down the full day, immersive tour option? "I don't even get to do that now."

"The author came down with covid and canceled. You can't blame that one on me."

"I can and do." I briefly turned my head to stick out my tongue at her. At the moment, I was blaming all the ills in the world on Sarah. If she'd stayed home with the kids the way I had fantasized about, I would have had the vacation of my dreams.

"On the bright side, the cancellation in Philly gave us an extra day to spend at Hershey. It has a zoo, roller coasters, a water park, and—"

"I don't do roller coasters." I let out an angry sigh. How could she be excited for rides and water parks but have no interest in spending eight hours with a Civil War expert? What was wrong with her priorities?

"Won't you go on at least one roller coaster with me?" Now she was whining.

"I have to watch the kids."

"That's why we brought Eloise," Sarah countered, and of course she was right, not that I wanted to admit it.

"It's her last week with us before she goes back home," I argued and quickly pivoted to the true travesty, which was certainly not my hatred of roller coasters but a different injustice of international proportions. "I thought the point of her coming to the USA was to see culture and history. You took all of that off the itinerary. Or have you forgotten? I feel like you keep skipping over the fact that everything I wanted to do ended up in the trash bin."

"How could I forget when you keep bringing it up and blaming me for it every five minutes? We talked about every single one of these changes together. It's not my fault you tuned out what I was saying and nodded along with it all."

I harrumphed, again recognizing that her version of events was factually accurate. I had to go to my happy place to avoid blowing my stack, devolving into an epic argument which would only result with the itinerary Sarah had, but a lot of hard feelings on both sides. Focusing on the road, I eased the car back into the lane on the right now that I'd left the truck in the dust.

"We're going on a tour through Amish country," Sarah said with a placating tone when the silence between us dragged on. "That's historical."

"How does that qualify?" I didn't bother pointing out I knew nothing about the Amish, and they were skimming one percent on my bucket list items.

"They live like it's the 1800s."

"Because they want to. That's their way of life, making it the present time. Would it have killed you to leave in Valley Forge? Give me one thing I wanted to do? We went to a water park earlier this summer. Why are we going to another?"

"We determined it was too far out of the way if you wanted to have time for Philly."

"But we're not going to Philly now that the talk is canceled," I reminded her.

"Have some more ice water. This heat is making you cranky." Sarah filled my cup from the jug on the floor between her feet.

"Did you see that sign?" I jerked my thumb behind me as the SUV continued cruising along the highway at sixty-five miles an hour. "Something about a cave."

"I missed it." Sarah didn't seem to understand the urgency coursing through me.

"It said it was the next exit." I looked for another sign, but there was nothing.

There was only one thing I could do. Take the exit.

"What are you doing?" Sarah asked. "Do we need gas?"

"Nope. I'm taking the family to see some caves."

"It's not on my itinerary." She tapped the binder squeezed between her seat and the console.

"What? You don't like it when someone overrides your plans?" I probably said that with too much annoyance in my tone, and frankly, I didn't care in the moment. Sure, it might bite me in the ass later. Things usually did, but that was why it was called instant gratification.

"I mapped everything out to the minute."

"Our goal today is to get to the hotel in Hershey. We don't have to be there by a certain time since you already checked us in on your phone."

Which had happened as I was trying to figure out what turn I needed and she hadn't been helping because she was trying to get that task done. I took the wrong exit, and somehow, that was all my fault instead of the GPS giving confusing directions.

"The kids will need dinner, dear. As of now, we won't be getting there until five."

"Make that six. We're stopping at the cave."

"You don't even know what type of cave it is." She flicked her hands in the air.

"Don't care. I love caves." I tightened the grip on the steering wheel.

"Since when?" She truly sounded floored by this fact.

"Since forever." How did she not know this about me? "It should be obvious I love caves."

"They're dark, dank, and filled with creepy crawlies. You hate all of those things."

"True, but I still love caves. Look it up on your phone. What does it say about it?"

With great reluctance and an anguished sigh, she consulted her phone. "It's called the Lost River Caverns. They don't know the source of the river. Oh, this is interesting…" She sounded excited but didn't complete the thought.

"What? Are there dinosaur bones or something?" I couldn't contain my glee over the prospect.

"No. The temperature is constantly fifty-two degrees. Sounds like heaven."

"Kids!" I perked up in my seat, motioning for them to take off their headphones. "We're making a detour to explore some caves!"

This time I didn't mind all the squealing, and I refrained from rubbing it in Sarah's face how excited they were about something I had suggested. Well, mostly I refrained. I did give her an evil grin. She blew me a kiss, and honestly, it made my heart melt. It could be annoying how easily I forgave her and vice versa. Sometimes, it seemed like holding a grudge could be really satisfying. Although, forgiveness was a hell of a lot cheaper than divorce. We'd both need houses large enough for all the kids, and real estate was insane right now.

CHAPTER FORTY-EIGHT

I HAVE TO BE FRANK. THE CAVES WERE AWESOME.

So far, Hershey Park wasn't. So many people, and all of them were being extremely people-y. Give me a cavern underground any day of the week.

We stood in our swimsuits right outside of the changing rooms in the water park section of the amusement park. I eyed the scene before us.

Calvin reached for my hand, squeezing it hard. "Look! They have the biggest Bucket of Death I've ever seen. And smaller ones, too. This is my new favorite place!"

Contrary to all the happy expressions on my children's faces, I didn't like what I saw. Not one bit.

Unlike Great Wolf Lodge, this was outdoors. It was miserably hot. No way would there be any walking barefoot from one water attraction to another. Not without ending up with third-degree burns on the soles of your feet.

That was the first strike against it.

In one section, there were rows and rows of beach chairs to sit on, but they weren't appealing. The chairs were sitting side by side, facing forward, like in a movie theater. How was that conducive to quality family time?

Strike number two.

The chairs under the shade were already taken, naturally. Getting our squad to do anything in a timely manner was impossible at best. No matter how many times I tried to cajole and outright threaten.

Not enough shade was the biggest strike against the park. It wasn't just strike three and you're out. It was game over for me. Sadly, I was only one vote, and I feared I was in the minority.

"Have you noticed the significant lack of shade?" I said to Sarah, who was struggling to get sunscreen onto Demi because she was dying to break free and make a dash for the splash area where Calvin had spied the massive Bucket of Death.

"I recommend staying immersed in water." Sarah shoved another bottle of sunscreen into my stomach. "Calvin."

Eloise was working on the twins, who weren't as squirmy.

I did as commanded, trying to remember that the soldiers at Gettysburg had to brave through much more horrendous conditions than anything Hershey Park could dish out. Things could be worse. Like dying on a battlefield with a cannonball hole in your gut. Was it this hot and sticky back then? Again, I wasn't wearing a uniform and inhaling gun powder, which I imagined burned one's throat and eyes. If only I had the time to create a comparison chart to determine who had it worse, the soldiers or me.

"Eloise and I are taking the twins to the slides. You have Calvin and Demi for that." Sarah pointed toward the Bucket of Death.

I would have argued, aside from some important facts. I hated slides. More than I hated water. Put the two together and I really, really hated them.

I simply glowered at her.

She returned it, not with her usual snark. I think the heat was getting to all of us.

Upon further inspection, most of the parents in the area looked bloody miserable.

I was willing to bet, when the majority purchased their tickets, they didn't know there would be a dangerous heat wave. Which seemed to be the norm every damn summer now. I was seriously considering taking up residence in a cave.

"What time do we meet back up here?" I glanced at my newly-purchased waterproof watch, because the idea of not knowing the time sent me into a tailspin.

"Noon for lunch." She jerked her head to the Nathan's shack to our right. "They have hot dogs."

"The day is looking up." I kissed Sarah's cheek before taking Demi and Calvin's hands to lead them away.

"Look at the baby Bucket of Death." Demi pointed and squealed.

Expecting a complaint from Calvin over such a tiny one, I was pleasantly surprised to be met with an eager face. Both of them grinned as if this was the best thing that had ever happened to them.

There was literally nothing I could do but to join in the fun. Not to mention, Sarah had been right. The best thing to do on a day like this was to stay in the water.

After placing our flip-flops in the shoe zone, we splashed our way through the area to hit all the Buckets of Death. Each of us squealing as we got soaked. It wasn't Gettysburg, but it would have to do.

CHAPTER FORTY-NINE

A WOMAN USHERED US FORWARD TO STEP INTO ONE of the cabins of the Ferris Wheel. Sarah and I ensured to have Calvin, along with Demi, in between us. Ever since exorcising his fear at Great Wolf Lodge, the boy now believed himself to be invincible. He probably was under the illusion he could fly if he willed himself to.

On the other side, Eloise, Fred, and Ollie were immersed in a conversation about what I think was the Reese's peanut butter cup ride they'd been on that involved shooting things with laser guns. At least, I prayed it had something to do with one of the rides and not a new fascination of obliterating candy with a machine gun. What a waste of perfectly good sugar that would be.

"That's one of the rides we went on." Sarah pointed to the water ride below us.

"It looks like the one at Great Wolf. The one I thought you were insane to do." I craned my neck to see a group of people in an inner tube shoot into what still looked like a toilet bowl to me. "Huh, it doesn't seem as scary now that I can see what happens. I'd imagined flipping over and nearly drowning."

"It's not terrifying at all," Sarah reiterated. "I wish you'd try one ride with me."

I swiveled my neck to her and pressed a hand to my chest. "A water ride? It's like you don't even know me or care about my feelings anymore."

"What about a different ride?" She pointed to the one we had a good view of. "That looks tame."

I readjusted my position to look over Calvin and Demi's heads as they chatted about the bear we'd seen in the zoo. I needed to judge the validity of Sarah's opinion of what constituted a tame ride. Unlike one of the rides Sarah had taken the twins on, this one didn't seem to have any flips or a massive climb up into the air.

In fact, the track had a simple, clean design. Just some simple back-and-forth curves. How bad could it be?

While I wasn't much of a ride person, I was getting tired of Sarah pestering me about going on one. I kept pointing out that coming here hadn't been my idea and I didn't see why I should punish myself with something I hated doing.

"If I go on it, will you stop badgering me to go on other rides? Peer pressure isn't nice, and it's really starting to make me mad."

"I'm sorry." Sarah bowed her head, but her contrition was momentary. "I think you'll enjoy them if you just give them a chance."

I was about to find out for myself.

As soon as we got off the Ferris wheel, Sarah dragged me into line for the ride. It was called Wild Mouse, but I kept referring to it as Mouse Trap because it reminded me of the game of the same name from my childhood. Also, because it drove Sarah crazy every time I said the wrong thing.

Each vehicle of the ride could seat four, and the twins took the front seat while Sarah and I sat right behind them. The security bar clicked into place, and then we were off.

It started slowly, but I quickly realized my miscalculation when I opted to go on this one. I had only seen a limited portion of the roller coaster's framework for the track and had erroneously assumed it meant it was tame. While I may not have been traveling at a lightning-fast speed, not having a support structure around it, like the old wooden roller coasters, made it all the scarier. Because each time we jerked around a corner at the last second, I was certain we were about to go over the edge and plummet to our deaths.

"I hate this!" I screamed, turning to Sarah with murderous intent. "Why do you have your eyes closed?"

"It's scary!" she yelled back but not sounding terrified. Thrilled was more like it.

How the fuck was she enjoying this agony?

So were the twins, both of whom held their hands up, squealing at every herky-jerky, hair-raising turn. Sarah slid into me, resulting in me whacking my arm against the side of the car. That was going to leave a mark. Perhaps permanently.

What was it about this that everyone else enjoyed while I wanted someone to rescue me via helicopter? Okay, perhaps not that route, because I was about to puke my guts out, and I didn't think being whisked away by a whirlybird would ease that sensation.

I tried closing my eyes like Sarah, but that only made the experience all the worse.

Honestly, all I had wanted to do on this vacation was mill around a Civil War battlefield where thousands had perished. I didn't actually want to die myself.

Finally, we jerked to a stop.

The kids turned around, saying at the same time, "Can we go on it again?"

"Sure!" Sarah edged out of the seat, going to the cubbies to retrieve our sun hats and bags. "Didn't you love it, Lizzie?"

I stared daggers at her but didn't speak, not wanting to ruin the twins' fun. Had she not understood me when I screamed, I hated it? Or maybe she hadn't believed me and thought I was exaggerating. Granted, I did exaggerate every once in a while, but not about things like seeing my life flash before my eyes. Sarah and I would be talking more about this later, and more than likely off and on for the next fifty to a hundred years, until one of us shuffled off to the Great Beyond. Considering Sarah's love for death-defying thrill rides, my money was on her biting the dust first.

Luckily, the kids were too amped to notice my death rays, but Sarah saw. Did she ever.

"I think Mommy has to help Eloise with Calvin and Demi, but I'll go on the ride with you again." Sarah put a hand on each of the kids' shoulders, leading them back into the line.

I made a beeline for the nearest bathroom, which mercifully wasn't too crowded, and puked up my guts.

All I could think was, "I could have been at Gettysburg."

CHAPTER FIFTY

MUCH LATER THAT DAY, THERE WAS ONE FINAL Hershey Park punishment to endure. Ironically, it was the part I had been looking forward to the most, but I'd miscalculated how much the kids would love it as well.

What was this torture chamber? Hershey's Chocolate World. It was a gift shop on steroids, a large building outside of the park where visitors didn't have to pay admission to enter like they did for the amusement park. Meaning, it was crowded as fuck.

Fred held a sweatshirt in his hands, his eyes imploring. Sarah had suggested the kids look for trinkets to take home.

The problem with this idea was the sheer size of the store. It had everything from chocolate, clothing, glass bowls, toys, and so much more. Every single kid was finding more than trinkets, and I couldn't help but see dollar signs each time one of them found something else they just had to have. Not to mention, how would we fit all their loot into the car? We still had Amish country on the itinerary, and I envisioned Sarah buying something like a bird house.

Not sure how to handle Fred, I asked, "Whatcha got?"

Immediately, I felt like an idiot. It was a sweatshirt. Only an alien who hadn't been on Earth that long wouldn't know what it was. Since covid, most Americans lived in sweats.

Fred, though, surprised me with his reply. "It's a hug from Hershey Park. I want to remember this trip for the rest of my life."

I hunched down to his eye level. "Why's that?"

Sarah was behind Fred, looking down with tears in her eyes.

"We were all together. I like experiencing things with my family."

I was so overcome with emotions I couldn't say no.

"You got it, buddy." I added his sweatshirt to the pile of spoils, no longer thinking about money at all.

He ran off, happy to have accomplished his mission. If it'd been one of the others, I would have felt played, but Freddie wasn't like that. There was sincerity, and then there was Fred, the sincerest of the bunch.

"He's such a sweetheart." Sarah threaded her arm around my waist, resting her head on my shoulder.

"The sweetest." I added, "You know what this means, right?"

"What?"

"More family vacations to amusement parks." I shivered, seeing my future stretching out in front of me, an endless hot summer of thrill rides and sweltering car trips.

"It doesn't always have to be roller coasters and water parks. I think next summer will be the history vacation. Gettysburg, Valley Forge, DC—"

"DC?" I broke free from her arm, needing to look at her full on to make sure I had heard correctly. "You're adding DC?"

"Yes."

"How far is Monticello from DC? I've always wanted to go." Not waiting for a response, I whipped out my phone, checking it on GPS. "Two hours." I did a little hop, almost dropping everything in my arms. "Wait!"

"Yeah." Sarah let out a solemn sigh. "I know. We'll have to handle the slave topic with the kids. I want them to know the full story, not just the glorified version of Thomas Jefferson."

"Yes, yes. Excellent point," I murmured, even though that wasn't remotely what I had been planning to say. "I'll look for a book on that."

What I had planned to point out was that the Battle of Bull Run had happened right outside of DC. Another battlefield to add to my growing list. This was already shaping up to be the best vacation ever. So many battlefields.

If I could have, I would have done a fist pump, but my hands were full, so I had to settle for imagining myself doing one.

"When are you thinking?" I demanded. "June? July? August? Maybe we need a few weeks next time."

"I'm going to regret this, aren't I?" Sarah chuckled softly, but there was some trepidation in her eyes.

"Making me the happiest wife on the planet? I hope you won't regret that." I did my best to bat my eyelashes, but I wasn't a pro like Sarah.

"You're not now?"

"Considering I'm trying not to puke again because you tortured me for the day, I'd say I'm going to have to deduct a few stars from my review."

"Will this cheer you up?" She held up a glass container in the shape of a Hershey's Kiss.

"It would if it were full of kisses."

Sarah held up her other hand, brandishing a large bag of the chocolates I loved. "Is this enough?"

"Two more bags like that and I might forgive you. Might."

Olivia and Demi rushed toward us. "There's another ride!"

My knees went a little weak. Surprisingly, getting sick from a ride lasted a lot longer than the two minutes of hell.

"It's historical," Ollie added.

Before I could scoff, Demi said, "It tells the story of Hershey."

"Really?" I asked.

"It's why I suggested we come in here." Sarah offered a smile. "One of the reasons. There's also the candy. I know how much you love Hershey's Kisses."

"History and kisses," I said in a wowed voice. "And a history vacation next summer. I might be the luckiest person on the planet, after all."

I would be even happier if I could find some caves between Massachusetts and DC before next summer, but Sarah probably didn't need to know about that right now.

SEPTEMBER

CHAPTER FIFTY-ONE

"Kiddos! You have less than sixty seconds to get your buttocks out the door!" I shouted up the stairs through cupped hands. "Would it be over the top to get a megaphone? Or maybe a whistle so I can train them to respond to a certain number of... whistles?" Was there a word for the sound a whistle makes? Beats wasn't right. Maybe blows?

"We still have ten minutes until the bus arrives." Sarah sipped coffee from her travel mug as we waited downstairs.

"You ignored my question." I narrowed my eyes in what I hoped was an intimidating way. "I want a megaphone."

"Let's just say I don't want you running around with a megaphone or a whistle. Little people with absolute power." She rifled through her work bag, trying to find goodness knows what. "And why are you lying to the children about how much time is left?"

"It doesn't hurt to put some fear into them. Besides, it's going to take all nine minutes and—" I checked my watch "ten seconds, no matter what time frame I give them, to get them down here. I miss Eloise."

"Sadly, she had to go back home. And with all the kids in school for a full day this year, it seemed silly to get an au pair." Sarah took another drink as if fortifying her belief that we'd made the right decision to go au pair free this year. After two years of having that extra help, it was going to be a big adjustment.

I'd been on board with the idea when we discussed it over the summer. But today, the first day of school, I was no longer so sure. Although, I was angling to move some of my stuff into the apartment above the garage, turning it into a real office and not allowing anyone in there ever. Perhaps Sarah, if she was on my good side. Her not letting me buy a megaphone didn't put a point in the *okay to visit* column, though.

"Don't even think it!" Sarah adjusted her blouse, making me wonder if she was talking to one of the buttons or to me.

When her fiery glare turned on me, I squeaked, "Think what?"

"The garage apartment. It's for guests, not you."

"I wasn't contemplating anything like that," I lied, only feeling slightly guilty. It wasn't right for her to know me that well. Like she was cheating somehow but I haven't been able to figure out how. Although, I did have a tendency to blurt out things that were best kept under wraps, so I was probably my own worst enemy.

"I know exactly what you were thinking. I saw that longing stare."

Foiled again. I blew a raspberry, thinking, not for the first time, I needed to develop some type of technology that kept Sarah from being able to see into my head. It was extremely frustrating when she blocked me from getting what I wanted before I even had a chance to make a move.

Ollie flew down the stairs, running toward the kitchen, screaming, "Lunch box!"

"First kiddo is almost ready! Who's going to be next?" I

shouted through my imaginary megaphone. I was definitely going to look online for a real one, no matter what Sarah said about it. And I would store it out in the garage apartment when it became my office. Just try to stop me.

"Did you get an email from a travel agent?" Sarah fished through her bag again. Was she looking for her phone or a toothpick to cram into my eyeball since my mind had wandered to the garage apartment again? "Something about a cruise? It seems suspicious, but it was addressed to both of us. Are scammers getting that sophisticated?"

"It's not a phishing email!" I proclaimed with pride.

She gaped at me as if her coffee hadn't kicked in for the past decade. "It was about an Alaskan cruise. How is that not a joke?"

"It's your Christmas gift, remember? The Alaskan cruise coupon I gave you."

"The one you wrote out by hand and attempted to draw a polar bear? I didn't think that was for real."

"The very one, and of course, it was for real. The year's almost up. I don't want to be one of those people who doesn't fulfill a gift coupon." I'd wanted to defend my polar bear drawing, but if she couldn't see the potential of greatness, that was on her.

"Don't stress about it. I assumed it was like the coupon books the kids give us for Mother's Day. It's the thought that counts. I never cash them in."

"What do you mean? I used one last night to get Calvin to sweep the kitchen floor." I sneezed into my shirt. "Excuse me. Just thinking about dust makes me sneeze." Which I did again. "Am I not supposed to cash them in?"

"I never have." Perhaps sensing danger, Sarah redirected the conversation. "When would we find the time for a cruise, anyway?"

"I'm getting open-ended dates. But this way the vouchers

are bought and paid for, which will force us to make use of them."

Fred ran by, heading for the kitchen, his backpack bumping up and down.

"Two more to go." I put a fist out. "Rock, paper, scissors for who has to wrestle with Calvin."

Sarah threw paper, while I selected rock.

"Paper smothers rock. Tough luck," she said without an ounce of actual sympathy in her tone.

Demi came down the stairs, grinning. "It's the first day of school!"

"It is!" Sarah kissed the top of Demi's head, before she ran into the kitchen presumably to get her lunch from the fridge. "That's the fifth time she's said that."

I looked up the staircase, girding my loins for the Calvin battle. "If I don't make it back, remember I love you."

"That's my Brave Little Toaster." Sarah patted my arm. "Remember, you're the parent. He has to do what you say."

"Can I get that in writing?"

Sarah laughed but wandered into the kitchen, leaving me with the task of getting our most difficult offspring to fall in line. There was a time when I thought Ollie would be the death of me, but as she grew older, the more reasonable she became. Would the same happen with Cal? Ollie still had her moments. If they ever joined forces—I couldn't bear to complete that thought.

It wasn't pretty, but Calvin and I made it to the bus stop right when the driver was closing the door. She stopped, letting Cal onto the bus.

"Have fun, our little sweetums! That's right. Calvin Petrie is such a sweetie pateetie." Sarah blew him kisses in the most exaggerated fashion I'd ever seen, causing Calvin's face to go up in flames as he had to walk to the back of the bus to find a seat next to Demi.

As soon as the bus door closed, I burst into laughter. "You did that on purpose."

"Maybe he won't be late tomorrow morning if he wants to avoid more mom humiliation."

"You're evil." I grinned.

"Speaking of evil…" Her voice trailed off.

"That never bodes well for me." I braced for whatever hell she was about to unleash.

"I can't make the gala planning meeting tonight."

"You're going to skip?" I blew out a whistle. "Ingrid's going to be pissed."

"Not if you go in my stead."

After a second, her words sank in, and my jaw nearly fell off its hinge.

"Don't panic. All you need to do is take notes. Don't make eye contact or raise your hand. These people can smell a sucker a hundred miles away. You're good at taking notes. You do it when we're watching television."

"Only when we're watching documentaries," I defended. "I'm not completely deranged."

She was about to make a rebuttal but seemed to rethink it.

"Why do I have to go?" I whined.

"Because I have to take Demi and Calvin to ballet tonight. Ms. Deidre is assessing Calvin. Do you want to handle that?"

I shook my head. "That woman is terrifying."

"Ingrid can be as well, but I think it's the safest option. Remember, no eye contact." Sarah pointed to both of her eyes with her pointer and middle finger. "Head down at all times, and don't you dare nod. You like to bob your head when confused. Don't do it. They'll take it as agreeing to do something you don't want to do."

"Pul-lease! You've obviously never been to one of my departmental meetings. I can handle the likes of Ingrid. I got this. Don't you worry about a thing."

If only I believed myself, and it was safe to say, Sarah didn't believe me either.

CHAPTER FIFTY-TWO

There were a few—okay, many—things I hated in life. At the top of the list, tied with veggies and fascists, was being late. It made me feel all sorts of discombobulated and cranky. And I was behind schedule when I edged into the school cafeteria for the gala meeting Sarah had saddled me with. It was a massive understatement to say I wasn't the gala committee meeting type, and this made it worse.

Another thing I hated, and I was only reminded of it upon entering this space, was feeling awkward as hell. It was how I usually felt because I was the perpetual square peg in a round hole, but when put into a situation that heightened it, my hackles immediately activated.

What was the situation, aside from being late to the meeting, that put me on my back foot? The tables. I get that they're made for humans half my size, but given that fact, why did we have to meet in a room that looked like it had been left in a hot dryer for too long?

Even worse, the cafeteria didn't have separate tables and chairs. It was all in one, like a picnic table at a park, except that instead of long benches, there were several individual stools lined up on each side. As casually as possible, I slid into one of the immovable chairs. This wasn't an easy feat and required more tummy tucking and breath holding than I'd ever done before. Had I really been this size once?

For a moment, I ignored Sarah's advice to keep my head down as I watched a woman in heels and a pencil skirt struggle even more than I had to take a seat across the room. I couldn't often win points against such a well put-together professional woman, but I was chalking this up as a major victory for wearing flip-flops and cargo shorts. No, I hadn't worn that to work, but I'd changed into them at my office before dashing to the meeting. Sure, the crowd at this school wasn't the type to dress down, but I didn't give a flying fuck about anything but comfort.

A man wearing practically the same uniform I had on joined me at the table. I nodded in his direction, which he briefly returned before staring at the table top. Had his significant other given him the same instructions? Keep his head down to avoid getting looped into something he'd regret? Or maybe he was a single parent and simply knew the rules without needing to be told.

Without raising my head completely, I noticed he was the only dad in the cafeteria. So much for smashing the patriarchy.

"Good evening, everyone." Ingrid's voice grated on my nerves, but I resisted the urge to glance up to shoot her the stink eye to end all stink eyes.

Instead, I summoned all my energy to strike her flat with whatever magical qualities I had coursing through my soul. It was worth a try.

"We're here tonight to plot the biggest and most important event of the school year." She really did use the word plot instead of plan, like we were accessories to a heist or something.

I am sad to report that I possessed zero magical abilities,

because Ingrid continued to drone on despite all of my energy focused on making her stop. All the times I'd been accused of being a witch of some type because I was different, only to have it turn out to be untrue when I needed it most, was a true injustice.

"As the PTA president, I want to remind all of you that every family is expected to attend the gala. Not just the people in this room. Oh…" She stopped speaking, and I made what could only be defined as the biggest mistake of my life. I looked up. "Lizzie, you're here instead of Sarah."

I nodded, breaking yet another rule, but what was I supposed to do? No eye contact or nodding was great in theory but impossible when someone called you by name. This evening was going from bad to worse. First, I was late. Second, my back was killing me from sitting in this idiotic chair. Now this. I had no idea how it was going to go sideways, but my gut told me I was about to step in it big time. Knowing this and being able to swerve the social meteor were two separate things that never seemed to conjoin for the purpose of good.

"I'm assuming Sarah sent you here in her stead this one time." There was a warning in her tone, as if to imply bad things would happen if Sarah, the competent one, did not show up for all future meetings.

Remember when I said I'd just made the biggest mistake of my life? Well, I decided to step in it even more despite every warning bell in my mental universe ringing.

"No," I told her defiantly. "I'm the gala mom of the Petrie family this year. Sarah did her time last year."

The man in cargo shorts let out a tiny snicker but then made a sound like he was a cat hacking up a hairball that would have made Snickers envious.

"That's wonderful." Ingrid's voice and glare said it was the exact opposite, so that made me feel slightly better even if I'd just volunteered myself to be in her presence more than was considered healthy for someone who cared about their stress levels and wanted to stay out of prison. We'd already had one family member go to jail. It wouldn't help the Petrie name to have a second be imprisoned.

I offered a cocky smile that I feared came across as more terrified than victorious. If I was going to last in this new gig, I'd have to practice in the mirror to become semi-proficient at flashing a *fuck off* grin.

Ingrid continued her spiel, talking about the playground equipment we were fundraising for. There was a lot of yapping about handcrafted organic Canadian pine and all Eco-friendly materials that were purified in special waters on Zoltar or some bullshit like that. At one point, someone mentioned a treetop fairy castle, and I wanted to raise my hand and ask if we were still talking about playground equipment, but I thought better of it. I'd already gotten myself into a pickle.

Sarah had been clear. Keep my head down, take notes, and do not be noticed. Shoot. I hadn't been taking notes. Pulling out my phone, I typed playground equipment into my notes app. Maybe that would keep whatever bad thing I was certain was about to happen at bay.

But Ingrid was like a lion stalking an injured zebra.

"So the grand total for everything will be two-hundred and fifty-thousand dollars," Ingrid proudly announced as if that was a completely normal price tag for some swings, slides, and a climby thing.

I burst into laughter, because who in their right mind would spend a quarter of a million dollars on things kids would dedicate their lives to destroying with their amazing child demolition skills?

Every head whipped around to glare at me.

I masked my laughter by coughing. "Sorry. Water went down wrong," I said, pointing to my empty water bottle.

Fortunately, it wasn't see-through, so there was a slight, and by that I mean next to zero, chance people may have believed me.

"We need to make this the best auction in the school's history in order to achieve this goal." Ingrid ground her teeth, her beady eyes staring daggers at me. I imagined she was thinking if we failed, it'd be all my fault.

Why hadn't I kept my head down and my idiotic mouth shut?

"To get the ball rolling, I'll be donating a week at my Maine lake house, including daily massages and a private chef, as one of the prizes to be auctioned off."

There was a lot of impressed murmuring. Of course, there was. That was what this whole thing was really about, after all.

Back in my day, we had zipped down metal slides that either burned our butts in the warm weather or were frozen solid in the winter. We were so grateful to be out of the classroom we never thought twice about it. This fancy playground wasn't about the kids as much as it was for the parents to win bragging rights.

It was madness, but I wasn't surprised given the birthday party the kids had attended at Ingrid's. She'd given every kid a prince or princess costume to take home instead of simple party gifts like stickers, bubbles, and temporary tattoos. Who the fuck did that? Aside from Ingrid. If she was that flush with cash, why didn't she simply pony up for the equipment and not torture all of us? I guess there wouldn't be much fun in that for the likes of Ingrid.

"Lizzie, will you be taking over Sarah's role as the chair of the donation committee?"

I swallowed.

"It's not too late—"

"Sarah has filled me in completely on what's expected. I've got this." I didn't even know Sarah had been the head donation person, but that didn't stop me from bluffing.

What was worse? Not knowing or trying to convince Sarah that I really wanted this role for this year's gala?

All I had to do was take notes, but now I was slowly spelling out my email address to the room so everyone could send me their donations for the silent auction. It'd also be included in the next school-wide communication, meaning my inbox would never be empty again.

Shoot. Me. Dead.

CHAPTER FIFTY-THREE

"If I have to tell you one more time, Olivia Rose Petrie..." Sarah let her threat trail off.

I'd just returned from the gala meeting, and I wanted to turn around and leave the house. But that wouldn't be right. The impulse to run still hummed throughout my entire body. It'd already been one hell of a night, I didn't need kid drama on top of that.

One look at Sarah and I realized that would be the absolute worst decision and only make whatever was happening much, much worse.

Luckily, Ollie backed down, and left the kitchen, her shoulders hunched around her ears as if whatever she was letting go was taking a physical toll on her.

It was good to know that the use of her full name still did the trick. I loved our oldest child, but Olivia put the fire into the word spitfire.

"What was that about?" I asked, giving Sarah's cheek a kiss.

"I don't even know where to begin." She rested her head on my shoulder. "When did life get so hard?"

"It's not a good sign when you start talking like me. Did you not have a good first day at school?" I kissed the top of her head and pulled her into a tight embrace.

"By good do you mean I have at least three kids who I already know are going to be the death of me? Or that our volleyball coach quit and, for some reason, I stepped up? Should I mention I have to chaperon three dances this year?" She sucked in a fortifying breath. "How am I going to manage everything? Do you think Eloise would come back if we put an SOS into the sky like they do for Batman?"

"There's a thought." I didn't have the heart to tell her there was no way that was going to happen. I couldn't even picture what image we'd beam into the night. A bat for Batman was easy. Would it be Eloise in a cape? That'd be hard to do, since it would simply be her silhouette. How would she know it was meant for her? Although, any au pair might do in a pinch.

But I was putting too much thought into a throwaway comment made by Sarah and not dealing with the situation at hand.

Willow crested the basement staircase, quickly assessing something was off. "Should I come back?"

"No, no. Don't mind me. Simply having a nervous breakdown, but it's passing. Gotta mom, ya know." Sarah tried smiling, but it turned more into a whimper.

"I can mom the rest of the night," I assured her. "Go take a bubble bath and hide upstairs."

"I'll help Lizzie mom. That's why I came up. Does anyone want to go for ice cream? It's been a day." Willow quickly added, "Not trying to guilt trip anyone into ice cream or compare bad days."

"Yes!" Sarah gave Willow a kiss on the forehead. "You're a saint! Ice cream is exactly what I need."

I tried not to interject that I had offered to mom for the evening and let Sarah take a bath and hide upstairs for the rest of the night. She seemed more fragile than usual and probably wouldn't like the reminder. Also, I didn't want to lose ice cream privileges because, in Willow's words, it had been a day.

An hour later, we sat outside our favorite ice cream place while the kids ran amok, hopefully burning off all the sugar they'd just ingested.

Sarah finished off her lavender ice cream, which I personally thought would make a better perfume than a flavor, dropping the spoon into the empty paper cup. "That was perfect. What a great way to finish a stressful first day back. But I'm still taking you up on that offer of a bath when we get home," Sarah added with a pointed look in my direction.

"Where's Maddie?" I asked Willow, still working on my chocolate and peanut butter scoop.

"She's working late on that house in the Berkshires. She'll be staying at a hotel for a few days." Willow laughed at the kids rolling down the slight hill. "Do you remember when that was fun?"

"Yes," Sarah said dreamily.

I answered, "No."

Sarah chuckled but didn't make a snarky comment.

It seemed like this was the perfect time to tell her about the meeting. Not everything that had happened but the part about me taking over her role.

"Ingrid has gotten it into her head that I'll be in charge of all the auction donations for this year's gala." I clearly neglected to tell her I was the reason for that confusion because I let Ingrid get under my skin. Sarah wasn't having the best day. Why burden her with the whole truth? Especially when it could get me into trouble.

Sarah's post-ice-cream glow started to fade. "I'll email her to straighten everything out."

"Don't worry about it. You have a lot going on this school year. Besides, isn't it my turn to handle the gala? The kids do have two parents."

Sarah stared at me as if I'd started speaking Swahili. "This really isn't your type of thing, though."

"Pretty sure I can learn it." I shrugged like it was no biggie, even if I wanted to puke up the ice cream that seemed to be curdling in my belly.

"You really want to do this?" There was a hint of hope in Sarah's eyes.

No was the brutally honest answer. However, there were a lot of things I didn't want to do, but I did them anyway. Being an adult and a mom had some major drawbacks. This gala thing ranked right up there with taxes and death. Hopefully, participating in the gala prep didn't lead to my death or Ingrid's murder. Unless one of the other parents did that. Who was I to judge?

To avoid betraying my true feelings, I responded with a nod.

"Thank you, Lizzie. Thank you, thank you, thank you!"

"Anytime." By which I meant, only this one time and then never again. Ever. Sarah had warned me about the consequences of nodding, but I thought she only meant around Ingrid. Apparently, I couldn't nod anywhere.

"What do you know about Roman aqueducts?" Sarah mysteriously asked, taking the conversation in a direction I never would have anticipated in a million years.

"Uh, I feel like this is a trick question that's going to have some dire consequences for me." I tried laughing, but my mind wouldn't stop trying to figure out how this was going to blow up in my face.

"It's an honest question. The twins have a project about them that's got Fred super excited. They need to build one."

"Seriously?" My eyes grew wide. "This is going to be so much fun!"

"Does that mean you can steer their project? I'll work with Calvin and Demi on their semester thingamajig."

"Is that the technical term?"

"I don't know what it is yet, but they'll have some big project to accomplish. They have a new teacher this year."

"Captain Roman Aqueduct Building Supervisor reporting for duty." I saluted Sarah, wondering if I could have a special hat made for my new role.

She gave me a hug before slipping away to stare at the cows lazing about in the field.

Although I suspected she was really trying to leave before I came to my senses.

"It's really kind of you to take over the gala. I can guess it's the last thing you want to do." Willow patted my hand. "You two are inspiration for me and how I want my marriage with Maddie to be. Full of honesty and love."

Let me tell you, it took everything I had not to break out into mad laughter at that one.

CHAPTER FIFTY-FOUR

"Nice hit, Olivia!" I cheered for my daughter during her tennis lesson while I scrolled through all the donation emails, groaning at each one. Box seats for a Red Sox game. A meet and greet with some quarterback whom I assumed was a big deal because even I vaguely recognized his name. Golf lessons with a pro.

Olivia let out a grunt before whacking the ball again, which whizzed past my head. Had that been intentional? If it was, message received. I put my phone away, giving my daughter my full attention. I hadn't known how important it was to pay attention during practice until my head was almost taken off. Literally.

When it was over, I said, "That was some impressive hitting."

"I imagine the ball is someone I'm mad at."

I wasn't sure if this was healthy or not, so I simply nodded. But I couldn't stop from asking, "How many of those balls were my head?"

"None." She added, "Today."

Laughing, I put my hand on her shoulder. "Let's go pick up

Fred from his music lesson, and then maybe we can talk your mother into getting pizza tonight. I'm not in the mood to do dishes."

"Pizza!" She waved her tennis racquet above her head, and I was 98.07 percent sure it wasn't meant to be a threat.

I still ducked.

By the time the three of us pulled into the driveway, Sarah was returning from coaching her first volleyball practice looking as if the entire squad used her as a target. Not that she had any physical marks, but she wasn't looking like her usual chipper self.

"Rough day?" I asked.

"Why did you make me go back to teaching?"

First, I didn't. Second, I was getting smarter. This was a trap. "Because I'm cruel, which is why I'm going to reneg on my cooking night. Tag—" I tapped her shoulder with a fingertip. "You're it."

Sarah looked me up and down before turning to the twins. "This is your mom's way of convincing me to order pizza, isn't it?"

They did their best to look innocent. At least Fred did. Olivia wore an evil grin. She pretty much came out of the womb with that expression. And yet again, Sarah had figured out my motive before I had a chance to reveal my plan. It was seriously getting spooky.

"Is it working?" I asked.

"I'll do you one better. I already ordered and—" She pointed past my shoulder at her mom and Troy pulling into the driveway. "Pizza's here."

Demi and Calvin tumbled out of the back seat, both carrying small plastic containers while Troy carried two family-size pizza boxes.

"You also requested baklava?"

"I did."

"You really are the best!" I gave Sarah a kiss on the cheek before giving Rose and Troy one-armed hug hellos.

Inside, we tore into the pizza.

I'd invited Willow to join us since Maddie still wasn't home.

"This place has the best pizza." Troy ripped off his third slice.

Willow bobbed her head in eager agreement.

"Lizzie, I hear you're in charge of the gala donations." Rose wiped a strand of cheese from her chin and then dabbed it with a paper napkin.

"Yeah. I have a million emails to read before bed." I glanced in Ollie's direction, but she wasn't paying me any attention. Maybe she hadn't noticed me on my phone during her practice after all.

"We want to add a weekend at The Elysian Spa in town. Do I need to email you?" Rose asked.

"Nope. I'll add you to the spreadsheet."

"That's very generous of you, Mom." Sarah licked the corner of her mouth to remove some pizza sauce.

"Yes. I should have said that. Sorry, I went into work mode." I added a reminder on my phone to add Rose's item. "Everyone is really going all out for this. What are we adding to the auction?"

"A dinner at L'Atelier des Saveurs."

"The French place?" I asked.

"Yes."

"Uh—"

"I'll help you spell it." Sarah winked at me.

"That would be helpful, but is it enough? Ingrid's giving away a week at her lake house in Maine."

"Sadly, we don't own a lake house." Sarah did seem down about this fact, but I didn't think it was because we couldn't give away a week's stay.

"Should we—"

"Buy a lake house simply for a donation?" Sarah laughed at the thought.

"I wasn't going to suggest it, but now that you have—"

"Stop right there, Lizzie. Only a few people will go over the top. A dinner at a place that'll easily cost several hundred bucks is plenty."

I wholeheartedly disagreed, especially since I'd been seeing the donations. But it didn't seem like the right time to raise an objection. Not when Sarah was about to dish out the baklava.

Besides, if I came up with a different idea, it wasn't like she'd know. At least not until the bill came, but that would buy plenty of time for future me to figure it out. I was the keeper of the donation spreadsheet, which meant I could see every donation that came in and assess my competition so I could win. My mind started to race with possibilities. Was Taylor Swift still touring? No way was I going to let Ingrid and a few other parents get all the glory. Go big or go home, as they say.

CHAPTER FIFTY-FIVE

The next gala meeting arrived much too soon. Sarah, to my disappointment, got a gift certificate to the French restaurant that everyone who was anyone raved about. Personally, I couldn't give a fuck. They literally had frog legs and snails on the menu. In my book, both are cute as fuck and absolutely not to be eaten as food. When I'm out walking, I move snails off the sidewalk so they don't get crushed. Sadly, I never saw frogs, but I did hear toads on occasion in one of the ponds off a rail trail where I'd take the kids for walks.

In my humble opinion, the French place with the unpronounceable name was barbaric, and I simply couldn't condone it.

There was another sticky point. Many others were donating extravagant gifts, but nothing compared to Ingrid's week at her Maine lake house. That rankled me more than it should.

This was about the children, after all. And their ridiculously expensive playground equipment that made me shake my head in shame for being part of such a blatant show of consumerism. But none of that mattered right now because of one fact.

I hated losing, pure and simple.

What should I do? Log the frog and snail murder place as our donation or conjure up something bigger and better?

If I chose the latter, what should it be, and how could I keep Sarah from finding out?

Ingrid was the last to swan into the cafeteria, standing in the front, clapping her hands to get our attention. "Welcome, everyone. You ready to get to work this evening?"

Did she mean shoot mental laser beams in an attempt to kill her dead? Yeah, I was all over that. Somehow that didn't seem as wrong as serving frogs and snails. It should be noted, frogs and snails had never ever made me feel insignificant. This seemed to be Ingrid's goal every single time I was in her vicinity.

It was a good thing I wasn't around when social rules were implemented eons ago because I would have knocked out stone tablet after stone tablet Fred Flintstones style about how to *take care* of annoying people. It was safe to say humanity wouldn't have survived if I had been in charge of things right from the beginning.

"Lizzie!" Ingrid snapped her fingers to get my attention.

I pictured myself etching into stone: *Those who snap fingers should have their fingers snapped.*

"Yes?" I did my best to appear completely engaged, despite sizing her up to see how wide her grave should be and considering if I had ride or die peeps to call in order to get her lifeless body into it in the dead of night. Peter had done time. Did he know someone nicknamed The Caretaker who, ya know…?

"I didn't see your donation on the spreadsheet. Your dad is donating a helicopter ride at sunset over Boston."

Did she think I wasn't aware of that information? I was the one who entered it into the spreadsheet.

"I didn't know I had to enter my own donation since it's

locked and loaded." I tapped the side of my head to imply *how goofy of me*.

"We need to make up the details for it so people know what they're bidding on. You have until tomorrow to figure out what you're going to donate."

Now she was accusing me of lying in front of everyone on the committee. I had a donation. I simply didn't want to use it. And what was the frigging rush? The gala wasn't until December. We'd barely tiptoed into September. *Slow your roll, bitch.*

"I don't need until tomorrow. I'll enter it right now." I opened my laptop, and typed it into the spreadsheet.

"Care to share with the class?" Ingrid tittered, glancing around for others to join in mocking me.

New social rule. *Those who tittered should be pecked to death by a flock of pigeons.* No. Have their legs broken by an ostrich and then have lions descend upon them. I wished I had a stone tablet to carve that into right now.

"It's okay. Every gift, no matter how small, is welcome." Ingrid seemed to offer a kind smile, but it looked more crocodile-like.

"It's an Alaskan cruise."

There was a gasp from everyone in the room, aside from Ingrid. Her crocodile smile faded into a grimace.

"A what?"

"An Alaskan cruise." Having picked up the vouchers from the travel agent earlier that day, I yanked them from my bag and slapped them on the table as proof, like a gambler producing the deed to an oil well to up the ante. Then I added, "Airfare included," because I was that much of a moron.

Not only had I given away Sarah's Christmas gift, but I'd tossed in yet another expense on an already pricey donation for a playground set I wholeheartedly objected to.

I was certain of two things.

Sarah was going to kill me.

The second didn't really matter because I'd be dead, but Sarah was never going to trust me with a committee of this type ever again.

While on the surface that didn't seem like such a bad thing, it also made me feel absolutely terrible. Sarah had so much going on right now. She needed me to mom-up.

The only thing I could do was come up with an elaborate ruse to explain this mess. Or run away from home and join the circus.

I wondered if it was too late to take up the trapeze.

OCTOBER

CHAPTER FIFTY-SIX

Capping and uncapping the red dry erase marker in my hand, I stared at the schedule on the white board in the library. "What about Thursday night?"

Sarah shook her head in such a way I knew she was convinced this news would break me.

She wasn't far off the mark. We'd been trying to figure out this problem for way too long, and the schedule on the wall looked more like a murder board with red string than our everyday lives.

"I thought Thursdays were free," I said with a pout. I'd been so certain I'd finally found the solution that it was hard to let it go.

"Usually they are, but there's a special thing going on at the dance studio that Demi doesn't want to miss." Sarah uncapped her green dry erase marker and jotted it into the Thursday slot, eliminating another day from the possibilities.

Which now stood at basically nil.

"How are we going to get all four kids and us in for our wedding outfit fittings?" I scanned the board again, trying to find two consecutive free hours during their awake time. It seemed cruel to schedule fittings at midnight, even if that was when I was getting a lot of my work done these days. "We're jam-packed every single second of our lives." I squinted at the board, hoping it would help me find the answer. "What about October 18? The day's wide open. How did we miss that?"

"That's the day before Maddie and Willow's wedding. We can't leave it that close."

In the moment, I was of a different opinion, but I knew I would lose the argument. I unwrapped a Hershey's Kiss from the container Sarah had gotten me at Hershey Park. It should be noted that the original candy was probably long gone, but by refilling the container every few days from a giant bag I kept hidden in my desk drawer, I was able to maintain the illusion that my chocolate consumption was reasonable.

"There's this day." Sarah tapped the board with the marker.

"Isn't that the Sunday of the thing?" As if not trusting my time-keeping skills, I double-checked the website on my phone. "I thought people didn't work on Sundays. You're always telling me I'm not allowed to. Is that not a rule?"

"All rules have exceptions. I know the woman who owns the shop. Her daughter's in my class. It doesn't hurt to ask, right?" Sarah added, "We can't skip the fittings. Fred and Demi are the flower kids, and Ollie and Calvin are the ring bearers. This is too important."

"But we have plans that Sunday." I circled the event on the board. "It's not blank."

"I know, but can you think of a different plan?"

"We can try taking each kid separately." My eyes went back to the board.

"How? One of us has to drive them and…" She finished her statement by waving to the board. "We're already stretched thin."

"That Sunday is when there's a Revolutionary War

reenactment in Newbury." I glared at her. "I got your approval to add it to the calendar weeks ago."

"I remember." She gazed at me with kind but trepidatious eyes.

Which didn't help me feel better. It wasn't like Sarah and the kids were purposefully destroying all my happiness in this world. At least I didn't think it was intentional. "Why does everything I want to do always get shoved off the schedule? Every. Single. Fucking. Time."

"It seems that way, doesn't it?" Her voice raised at the end, implying a question, but I think she was being more cautious about me blowing my stack.

I unwrapped another Hershey's Kiss. "Not seems. It happens all the time, and I'm really getting frustrated."

"I understand." Sarah wrapped me into her arms. "You might luck out. It's possible I can't arrange it."

"Don't tease me like that. We both know you'll convince the woman to do us a solid. You always have a way of working miracles." I barely stopped myself from saying *unless it involves me*. I still had some self-preservation instincts intact, no matter how disappointed I was.

But sometimes Sarah could read my mind.

"Not when it comes to you, though," she said, filling in the blank I had left. Her voice was soft, like I was about to have the biggest fit she'd ever personally witnessed.

"Did I say that last part out loud?" I closed my eyes, trying to conjure up what had been said and hopefully unsaid.

"No, but I can see the hurt in your eyes." She placed a hand on my shoulder. "I'll make it up to you."

"How? Throw another reenactment?"

"What if we got you little army guys, and you can—"

"That's not the same thing, and you know it!" I stabbed the air with a finger. "First Gettysburg. Then the apartment above the garage. Now this. I never get my way." If I wasn't so devastated, I might have used this opportunity to bring up the Alaskan cruise problem, as in I had donated her trip for the school charity, but I couldn't muster up the courage to admit what I'd done, and even I knew they weren't of the same caliber. Missing a reenactment that I stumbled upon in one of my New England history newsletters couldn't compare to me telling Sarah I was sending her on a cruise and then giving said cruise away to show up Ingrid. I hadn't figured out how to get myself out of that dilemma yet.

"What can I say? Life sucks, and then you die."

I rolled my eyes and said, only partially in a teasing tone, "Every single one of you is trying to kill my passion for history and life. Mark my words; it's not going to happen."

"I highly doubt you'd ever give up being a history nerd." She tried threading her arms around my waist, but I wasn't in the mood, so I took a step back.

"I thought June was wedding month. Why are Maddie and Willow getting married in October."

"October is overtaking June. Especially in New England when you have beautiful fall colors for photos."

"What's this day?" I tapped the calendar.

"Halloween."

"I knew that much. Why does it have so many reminders? It's after the wedding. When things should be settling down. That's what you keep saying."

Sarah let out a whoosh of air. "Because each of our kids wants to go trick or treating with one of their school friends, but we can't be in four different places. So all of their friends will be coming here for a party. But in four stages so none of our kids feel like we're not putting them first."

"Are you saying we're throwing four Halloween parties?"

"Yes, and each has its own theme."

"Uh, it's Halloween. What other themes are there?"

"Demi and her friends are dressing as characters from the

Adams family. Freddie and his buds are Japanese anime characters. Calvin's theme is football, naturally. And Olivia is going for Disney characters."

"Let me guess. Each party will have different decorations." I closed my eyes, doing my best to teleport from this dimension.

"It only seems fair."

"Fair." I said the word slowly. "Not sure I know the meaning of that word."

"I'll make up for the reenactment."

"Sure. There's always next year, right? Unless I die first."

"Please don't." Her eyes drifted to the board.

"Yeah, I know. How would you find the time to plan my funeral? Not with all this going on." I sucked in a deep breath, slowly releasing the air.

"Pretty sure that wouldn't be my first thought. Maybe the third or fourth."

I tried glaring at her, but a smile won out. "It seemed like a good idea in the beginning. Having four kids. Until you have to draw up battle plans for every week to make sure we don't miss a school or extracurricular activity."

"Look at it this way. Each one of them is on the hook for taking care of us when we're old, and they'll have to plan like this then. That's how we get even." Sarah emphatically recapped her pen after crossing out the reenactment. I wished I knew how to get even for that, but nothing came to mind.

CHAPTER FIFTY-SEVEN

"Ollie, stop squirming." Sarah gave our daughter a *you can do it* smile as we stood off to the side while the dressmaker worked on pinning Ollie's dress.

Ollie stuck out her tongue in return. At Sarah, not the woman with the mouthful of pins.

Sarah was about to say something, but it took her half a second to realize Ollie had indeed stopped squirming, allowing the woman to stick the final pins into the wedding outfit.

When Ollie hopped off the stool, I tapped Fred's shoulder. "Tag. You're it."

He gave me a toothy grin, jumping up on the stool and holding still without any prompting on what he needed to do. There were times I wanted to give the kid a ribbon for good behavior. Not only would he love it, but he deserved it. The issue would be Calvin and Olivia. Their complaints about how unfair that would be were too much to imagine, let alone live through.

"I hope you behave as well as Fred," Sarah whispered in my ear. Her tone suggested teasing, but I wasn't fooled. There'd also been a hint of a threat, because my wife knew me all too well.

I chewed on my bottom lip, not excited about my role as Willow's best person. Sure, we'd grown close since she'd moved in during the pandemic, but this would require me to give a speech. While I had no issue giving a history lecture, speaking from the heart for all to hear wasn't necessarily my strong suit.

There was another thorny issue. The irony of the situation was simply too rich. Maddie had been engaged to two of my brothers. Not that either were coming to the wedding, but their ghosts would be hovering over the entire day. For me, it most definitely would, and I had to believe for at least one of the brides, if not both of them.

Luckily, Willow had opted out of a bachelorette party, meaning I was off the hook for planning it. In fact, both Maddie and Willow decided not to partake in that tradition. Instead, they went away for a quiet weekend since Maddie had been spending a lot of time away from home for work.

"Why do they need best people anyway? What's the purpose?" I tugged on my sleeve, pulling it to my wrist, only to shove it back past my elbow again.

"It can be a short speech," Sarah said, invading my thoughts as was her specialty.

"I didn't say anything about the speech. You really need to stop reading my mind. It's getting creepy." I palmed the top of my head as if to ward off her invasion.

"Not sure I can stop. It's like being tuned into a radio station broadcasting at full volume even when you're silent."

"What am I thinking right now?" I closed my eyes, trying to clear my head of any thoughts, but kept focusing on Hershey's Kisses. When nervous, I craved them.

"How much you love me, naturally." Sarah batted her lashes.

I burst into laughter. "If I say that wasn't what I was thinking, then I look like a jerk."

"And, we both know you aren't a jerk." She threaded her arms around my waist.

"Stop that right now!"

Sarah stepped away. "Hmm. I might be changing my mind if you keep that attitude."

"Not you. Calvin." I gave him my determined mom face. "Stop climbing on the furniture."

Sarah slowly turned around, stifling a groan as she spied Calvin standing with one foot on each arm of a wingback chair.

"Young man, if you don't listen to your mother, you will not be playing in your football game next weekend. Do you understand me?" Sarah stepped closer, causing Cal's face to go white.

"I'm bored," he said but without much oomph given the football threat hanging over his head.

"Join the club, buddy." It probably wasn't the best response I could have offered, but it was hard to say the right thing when I wanted to throttle my youngest child. "Mrs. Carter is doing us a favor by seeing all of us on Sunday. The least we can do is not destroy the furniture in her own home." Seriously, why did I have to explain this to any of the children?

He carefully climbed off the chair while both Demi and Olivia gave him a shake of the head, looking so much like Sarah it nearly made me double over in laughter. It always amazed me how much the children could mimic others, and I doubted they knew they were doing it.

"Now apologize to Mrs. Carter," Sarah demanded, adding to my lecture.

Chin tucked to his chest, Calvin mumbled an apology.

Sarah and I added our own sorrys.

Mrs. Carter pulled two pins out of her mouth to say, "I only have one child, and I'm barely surviving. I don't know how you two do it."

"Neither do we," Sarah joked.

"They do have a habit of keeping us on our toes. That's for sure." I placed a hand on Cal's shoulder to keep him in place as his gaze became overly fixated on a mannequin in the corner. The last thing the day needed was for him to practice a football tackle on what almost appeared to be a piece of artwork and was certainly something vital for her business.

"You're so skibidi," was his response to my proactive step.

"What did you just call me?" My patience was wearing thin.

"Nothing," he muttered under his breath.

I turned to Sarah. "What did he call me?"

"Nothing."

"Are you taking his side?" First, I had to contend with the fact that I could almost read Calvin's mind, much like Sarah did mine, but now she was siding with the troublemaker. It was one step too far on a day that hadn't gone the way I'd wanted it to. I should have been at the reenactment right now. Why was it that every time I wanted to relive a historical war, I ended up battling with my family instead?

"No. It's a word that literally has no meaning, but Gen Alpha loves to say it. Mostly to get under our skin," Sarah explained.

"It's not like they need to invent new words to drive me batty," I whispered. "They can do that just fine with anything in the dictionary."

Calvin slinked to the corner, picking up his iPad before settling next to Demi on the floor.

"I don't understand why kids these days say words that literally have no meaning. What's the point?" For some reason, I couldn't let it go.

"Every older generation has thought the younger ones

sounded stupid. There was a time when *the cat's pajamas* was the hottest new phrase."

"Can we go back to that time? I could use some moonshine to survive today and every day after."

"Are you in your rebel era?"

"Like the Civil War?" I guessed, shuddering a little. Sure, I liked studying it, but no way did I want to travel back in history to witness a bloody time period without plumbing or antibiotics.

"Nothing so literal." She laughed. "It's more Gen Alpha or Gen Z slang. Personally, I'm thinking of entering my villain era."

"You want to ruin my life even more?"

Sarah slowly blinked her eyes, her cheeks turning pink, before shifting to a frustrated grin. "I'm going to ignore that. Besides, it's time for your fitting."

CHAPTER FIFTY-EIGHT

"Wow, that's such a drippy outfit!" I kissed my fingertips with a flourish like they did in movies to indicate smoking hot.

Inexplicably, Willow burst into tears.

"Drippy is a compliment," I rushed to explain. "It's what the kids are saying today. I watched a video on current slang terms."

This was what happened when I tried to be young, cool, and hip. I made women cry, and not in a good way.

"I know it is," Willow said through ragged breaths. "I know."

Well, if she already knew what the word meant, I was really confused.

"What's wrong?" I motioned for her to take a seat on the bench outside of the church before sitting down next to her.

"I don't know. I didn't expect this feeling." Willow twisted her top into her fist. "We've been living together for months now. But married? That's… like… a really big step. Isn't it? What does it mean if I'm questioning whether I'm doing the right thing?"

I searched the area for Sarah, but she was probably with Maddie. Who'd left Peter at the altar. I couldn't help wondering if Sarah was dealing with the same situation. Was Maddie getting cold feet? Would it be weird to text so I would know all the key data points before deciding how to handle this situation? If Maddie was of the same mind, should I advise Willow to run for her life to protect her heart?

"How did you know it wasn't a mistake?" Willow asked, looking at me through her tears. "You know, when you and Sarah got married."

"Sarah would have killed me if I didn't go through with it." I laughed, trying to picture what my fate would've been if I'd done a runner.

Willow's face scrunched with horror.

Clearly, humor wasn't what was in order at the moment. That meant I had to be heartfelt, which really wasn't my jam. Why was it so hard to communicate with the ones who wore their hearts on their sleeve? Probably because I was always so terrified of crushing them.

"I mean—" What did I mean? "I lost Sarah once by being a fucking moron—"

"When you kissed Maddie?" She interjected like it was a totally normal question that didn't pertain to the woman she was about to marry.

Only she got a key detail wrong. And while it still made me look like a fucking asshole, I couldn't let her version stand.

"Tried to kiss!" I stabbed the air with an indignant finger. Seriously, the Petrie and Maddie situation was soap opera level cray cray. Did Gen Alpha have a different phrase for that? "What I meant to say was when I thought Sarah would never speak to me again, my entire world crashed. She's my everything. Life without her would be meaningless. Is Maddie your everything?"

"I... I'm not sure. How do you know? Like, for certain, I mean."

"Try to imagine never seeing or speaking to Maddie again."

Willow shook her head vehemently. "I c-can't," she said in a shaky voice.

"Can't or won't?" Not sure why I sought clarification because I didn't really know what either scenario would mean in the grand scheme of things, or how to differentiate one from the other. Maybe I was buying time, hoping Sarah would wander by and save me. Why wasn't there an app on my phone for handling these emotional emergencies?

"I can't. It hurts too much to even think about it." Willow closed her eyes. "She's always there, even when we're not together."

"I think that's your answer, then." I patted Willow's thigh. "I won't lie. It's scary. To stand in front of everyone and to pledge your love to be with her for the rest of your life. Just know Maddie will be right there with you." That was, if she wasn't doing another runner right now. I was placing the odds at fifty-fifty, especially if even Willow was getting cold feet. Maybe sixty-forty. Not that I was going to tell Willow that at a time like this.

"What if I can't speak?" Willow grabbed onto her own throat.

"You'll find your voice. It may be shaky, but you'll find it." I chuckled quietly, nervous about all this bullshit spewing from me. Where was it even coming from? It was like I'd swallowed a radio that was tuned into some sort of pop-psychology call-in program, and every time I opened my mouth, you could hear it speaking instead of me. "Keep your eyes on Maddie, and forget the rest of us are there. If she's your everything, that means she's also your beacon."

Had I really just used the word beacon? I was becoming unrecognizable to myself.

My phone vibrated, causing my heart to sink. I was certain this was a message from Sarah saying Maddie had high-tailed it out of town. If she had, would that be a world record or something? Sadly, she hadn't left Gabe at the altar. Ouch. Even in the confines of my own head, that sounded terrible. I only meant, that might help with hitting the record for the number of ditched fiancées at the altar. If there was such a thing. There seemed to be a record for everything, like heaviest train pulled by a beard. Was there prize money for that kind of thing?

I checked my message with trepidation, but it was only my dentist's office reminding me about my upcoming appointment.

Music started to play in the church.

"It's time." I got to my feet, holding out a hand for Willow to take. "You ready?"

"As ready as I'll ever be." She let out a tiny laugh. "It doesn't instill much confidence, does it?"

"Trust me. We all felt this right before. If you love Maddie like I think you do, everything is going to be okay."

Just as long as Maddie wasn't trying to set a weird world record. No amount of prize money would be worth it.

CHAPTER FIFTY-NINE

I stood to Willow's side, staring at Sarah, who was standing next to Maddie. Our eyes locked, and so much was said without uttering a single word. One thing I was absolutely freaking certain about. Willow hadn't been the only one with cold feet. Yet, here they both were.

Before I knew what was happening, Willow and Maddie were kissing and then laughing.

They made it! For better or worse, and fingers crossed, for forever.

Of course, many say the first year of marriage is the most brutal, so it was way too early to know if this one would last. Luckily, none of that was in my speech, or at least it wasn't now that Sarah had heavily edited it the previous night. I would like to note that even I knew not to say certain observations aloud. No sense cursing the couple before they had a chance to fuck up everything all on their own.

The newlyweds made their way out of the church, with Sarah and I behind them, our arms linked.

Sarah leaned against me more than usual. I had to wonder if

it was because she was exhausted or feeling extra lovey due to the theme of the day.

Once we got outside and off to the side, I whispered, "Stressed?"

"That wasn't easy," she whispered back.

"Cold feet?"

Sarah nodded.

"Same with Willow."

She turned her head, her dark eyes searing into mine. "What did you say?"

"I lied to get her to the finish line." I shrugged no biggie.

"About?"

"I told Willow all of us feel that way on our wedding day."

"You actually said that?"

I couldn't tell from Sarah's tone if she was angry or— "Did you have cold feet?"

Sarah broke into a wide grin. "Not at all. I'm just glad we said the same thing. It'll be easier to keep our stories straight if it's ever brought up. Looks like I'm not the only one with mind-reading powers."

"You're not lying, are you? About not having cold feet?" She wasn't the liar in the family, but the expression she had moments ago—it had me worried.

"No. I couldn't wait to rush right in and make the worst mistake of my life." She arched one eyebrow just so and it worked on me in so many delicious ways.

I tipped my head back and laughed, releasing all the tension in my shoulders.

"Were you lying about having cold feet?" she asked once I settled down some.

"It wasn't my feet I was concerned about. My biggest worry was you'd come to your senses and not show up," I confessed.

"And miss out on all of this with you? Not a chance, Lizzie Petrie. You're the one."

"Why do you always have to say these things when I can't do anything about it?" I tried peeking down her dress, though I wasn't nearly as successful as I would've liked.

"Do anything, huh? Such as?" Mischievousness danced in her eyes, adding at least half a dozen things to my list of ideas.

"Guess you'll have to wait until tonight to find out."

I looked at the crowd, everyone speaking in hushed tones. It was the type of New England fall day that made tourists want to visit our part of the country this time of year. The sky was dark blue. The leaves on the trees were bursting with autumnal colors. The temperature was in the mid-sixties and utterly delightful. I truly couldn't imagine anything nicer.

"Whatever happens next, this has been a beautiful day." I threaded my fingers through Sarah's.

"Let's hope only good things happen for them going forward."

"Come on. That's not possible. Life loves to throw people shitty curveballs. Usually when you're already at your breaking point because the universe has a sick sense of humor." I eyed our children with my dad and Helen. "How long until they try for a baby? Not my parents. The newlyweds."

"Who says they aren't now?" Sarah winked at me, but people approached, so I wasn't able to push her on the question.

Surely, Willow would have mentioned something if that was the case. I was her best person after all. Didn't that mean she'd confide in me?

"You ready for your speech, Lizzie? It's almost time." My dad gave me a half smile.

"I'd rather give a history lecture."

Sarah, who was in the midst of talking to a couple I didn't know, turned to me and said, "Don't you dare," before easily transitioning back to her conversation.

"I wish I had her skills," I whispered to my dad. "I can't multitask like that."

He laughed. "You'll be fine. Just speak from the heart."

I did my best not to roll my eyes considering I now knew both brides had doubts moments before they tied the knot. Was that common or only something you saw in movies to up the angst?

Sarah reached for my hand, giving it a squeeze.

This time I didn't mind her reading my thoughts.

"Have you heard Peter will be here for Thanksgiving?" Dad asked in his quietest tone.

"Will he?" Sarah, returning to our conversation, gave my hand a squeeze again. "That's wonderful."

Just what the day was missing. Peter chatter. Not that it bothered me all that much these days. Years ago, I couldn't stand the man. Now I loved him and only wanted the best for him. From a distance, though.

It wasn't his doing. He was still a touchy subject though, considering the Demi situation.

"How long will he be here?" I asked, doing my best to sound breezy but secretly plotting how to avoid the holiday. Was it possible to get my appendix to burst on cue? Surely, I could get out of Thanksgiving if I was having emergency surgery.

"That depends if he finds a place or not," Dad said as if this wasn't earth-shattering news.

"What do you mean?" My mouth went dry.

"He wants to be closer to all of us, so he's looking for a place to live."

"He won't move in with you two?" Sarah asked.

Dad shook his head. "We've offered, but he wants more privacy. He specifically mentioned having his own kitchen and bathroom. Those seem to be his sticking points."

Was that a byproduct of serving time in prison? Or simply a

Petrie trait? I didn't really like sharing my bathroom either and only begrudgingly shared with Sarah. After a cake incident that nearly burned our house down, I wasn't really allowed to be in the kitchen unsupervised.

The photographer waved us down for snaps with the brides before the dinner.

"Gotta wedding!" Sarah threaded her arm through mine, whispering. "We'll deal with the Peter thing later. Today is about Maddie and Willow."

CHAPTER SIXTY

"Here's to love, laughter, and a lifetime of happiness for Willow and Maddie. Let's raise a glass to their wonderful adventure ahead. Always together." I raised my champagne flute, pretending to take a sip, fearful I might still choke on the final words: always together. Try as I might, I was unable to get the earlier doubts out of my mind.

Sarah gave me a relieved smile, probably because I had said the words she had approved and had not gone off script. I had a nasty habit of saying the one thing I shouldn't say out loud when I got nervous.

Honestly, though, I didn't remember much of anything that had come out of my mouth.

All I wanted was to go home with Sarah and the kids and put this day in the books.

Sadly, we still had a couple more hours of celebration to endure before we started rounding up the children to head for home.

As soon as we finally stepped foot into our kitchen, I said, "I can't wait to get out of my torture suit."

"It's a pant suit. Try wearing this dress and heels." Sarah

leaned down to remove one shoe and then the other, wincing. "I'm getting too old for heels."

"Trust me. You're not." I licked my lips, suddenly recalling all those ideas I had entertained so many hours ago.

Sarah winked at me. "I'll remember that later."

"I'm starving," Calvin whined, kicking off his shoes and practically flinging them across the room instead of placing them where they belonged.

"We had dinner at the reception," I reminded him, too tired to battle about the shoes.

"That food was terrible," was his retort. "It was covered in gravy. I want real food, like dino nuggies."

"Me too!" Fred's face looked hopeful.

Sarah met my eye, before caving first. "Who else wants dino nuggies?"

All of the kids raised their hands.

"Get changed into your pajamas, and then we'll eat." Sarah pulled the bag out of the freezer.

"Does that include me?" I removed my blazer, placing it on the back of one of the chairs at the island.

"Yes, since you behaved."

"Can I add a corn dog to my order?" It was my turn to look hopeful. "I had to give a speech. My legs are still shaking."

"Don't press your luck. Go get changed. Hurry, though. I'm dying to get out of this dress."

My eyes traveled up and down her body. "Me too."

Before dumping out a bag of nuggets onto a tray for the oven, she gave me another saucy wink that boded well for the dessert portion of the night.

By the time we all sat at the dinner table, the kids talked excitedly about the day.

"Why didn't Uncle Peter and Gabe come?" Freddie bit into one of the nuggets.

"Uh…" I took a sip of my water, desperate for a way to avoid answering that landmine of a question.

"They live in Colorado, and it was too far for a weekend trip," Sarah calmly explained.

"Will we ever see them again?" Calvin asked.

"Peter's coming out for Thanksgiving, and Gabe will be here for Christmas." Sarah sipped her water.

"Good. Maybe he can tell me who my father is." Demi reached for another nugget, plunging it knuckle deep into barbecue sauce while my heart nearly gave out.

"What do you mean?" Sarah asked, her face showing zero distress, but there was a slight wobble in her voice I hoped no one else noticed but me.

"For my family project at school. I need to know all my parents." Demi dipped another nugget into the sauce.

"We're sitting right here," I lamely said, waving to Sarah and then back to myself. "In case you missed the memo, we're your parents."

"Rachel said everyone has a father. Do we all have the same father?" Demi studied her siblings as if she'd never seen them before.

We were entering tricky territory, because three of the kids had the same sperm donor. Demi, obviously didn't, considering Peter was her biological father and Tiffany was her mother. Tiffany had died when Demi was a baby, which was yet another piece of news I didn't want to deliver to the child at such a tender age.

"We came from a parrot." Calvin stuck his tongue out at Demi. "Everyone knows that."

I covered the bottom half of my face to hide my confusion.

"You're referring to a stork," Sarah corrected him. She turned to Demi. "Why do you think Peter would be able to help you with… this project?"

I stared daggers at Sarah, not liking how she tap-danced along the no-go zone for this conversation.

"Because he's a boy and a grown-up." Demi's reasoning made my heart melt with the simplicity. "I don't want to fail my project," she continued.

I was about to counter that her grandfathers were also boys, but that didn't really solve the problem. More than likely, it'd compound the issue because there would be two more people who wouldn't know the right thing to say because... how could I put this delicately? It was complicated as fuck.

"You won't, honey. The school knows you have two mommies." Sarah gave her a comforting smile. Or was it intended for me?

"Rachel said—"

"Do you know what we're missing?" I got to my feet, really disliking this Rachel girl, whoever she was. "Corn dogs. Who has room for corn dogs?"

Everyone, including Sarah, raised their hands.

"What about pizza?" Ollie asked because of course, she did.

I was about to say absolutely, but Sarah cut me off. "We'll have that for lunch tomorrow." Sarah stood. "I'm going to help Mommy with the corn dogs—"

"Or she may burn the place down." Ollie giggled maliciously.

While prepping the food to go into the oven, Sarah placed a hand on my back. "Everything's going to be fine. We're fine."

"How is that possible? She's asking about her father. What do we do? Lie?" Personally, I was of the mind that lying was the frigging best solution for most things in life.

Sarah had different survival skills that truly baffled me.

"Lying isn't the right answer," she said, just as I'd suspected she would.

"It seemed to be earlier when we both told Maddie and Willow that everyone got cold feet."

"That's different, and you know it." The fact that Sarah didn't elaborate told me she hadn't quite worked out all of the particulars on how her argument was true, but that I would be wise not to call her out on it again. "It's going to be okay."

"You keep saying that, and it only tells me the opposite. This is a nightmare. We should have home schooled the children to avoid this. We wouldn't have assigned this project."

"Too late for that choice." Sarah seemed a little disappointed by this fact.

Which sent my freak out into overdrive.

NOVEMBER (AGAIN)

CHAPTER SIXTY-ONE

"Oh, no," Sarah said upon entering our walk-in closet. "Not again."

I glanced up from the scale. "Are you seeing what I'm seeing?"

"A naked woman on the scale I keep hiding?" Sarah crossed her arms, but it was hard to tell if she was angry or fearful.

"I knew you were hiding it! I wish you'd stop. According to the experts, I need to weigh myself at least twice a month. Preferably first thing on Wednesday mornings."

"Why Wednesdays?" Her arms fell to her sides, and she leaned against the doorframe like she no longer had the energy to keep herself upright.

"To give you time to undo some of the weekend damage, I think. Speaking of—" I waved her closer.

"It's Monday, isn't it? Please tell me it is. I'm not ready for Wednesday." Her voice wavered.

"Yes, it's Monday."

"Then why are you on the scale?"

"I stubbed my toe on it, and I was already naked because I just got out of the shower." I shook my wet hair as proof and then gave her a *duh* look. How had she not put all that together on her own? It was so obvious, yet sometimes I swore she believed there wasn't a rhyme or reason for my actions.

She continued staring at me like I was drunk or something. I didn't drink anymore, but there were days I wished I still did because I missed that slightly buzzed feeling. What I didn't miss were the nightmares and waking up feeling like shit.

"Do you see what I'm seeing?" I waved an excited hand in the air as I asked her this question again.

"I literally have no idea what's going on, and it's too early for this type of Lizzie quiz."

I blew a raspberry, which turned out to be extra wet and gross. Since I was naked, I couldn't wipe it on my shirt. Nonetheless, I pressed forward. "The number on the scale."

She took a step forward. "Y-yes," she stuttered. "Please tell me you aren't going to go hog wild with your diet again, eating nothing but veggies as your only food source. You know, the things you hate and that upset your stomach to the point we needed to buy air purifiers for every room?"

"It wasn't that bad." I did an exaggerated eye roll before a thought crashed through my skull. "Back up a second. Are you trying to tell me you think I'm fat and I should only eat veggies? That's mean. I hate them."

Her head snapped up from the number on the scale. "I have never said that. I never would. Never ever." She sighed. "I just know you. There's overboard, and then there's the Lizzie way, which is simply bonkers with terrible ramifications."

"I can't believe I'm saying this, but maybe the Lizzie way isn't always the best option, because the plan you helped me implement after the gas issue—it's working. Look!" I excitedly pointed back to the number on the scale.

"What plan?" Sarah wasn't following, or perhaps her brain was whirring at warp speed to figure out my next Lizzie move so she could stop me before I could implement it. Truth be told, if she had that power, it'd save both of us a lot of headaches.

"I'm losing weight. Not the buttloads I had pinned my hopes on at the beginning of the year, but I've dropped twenty-five pounds. For the past few weeks, I didn't think I'd hit this mark. The number kept going up and down, but never dipping to this point. It's finally here, and it's not even Wednesday. I wonder what it'll be in two days. Should I eat veggies until then?"

"No!" Sarah waved both hands in the air in a somewhat threatening manner. "Be happy about this. You're on a lifelong journey, like the rest of us."

She had a point. Besides, veggies were the work of Satan.

"Who knew moderation could work? When I devised the Lizzie weight-loss plan, I thought I'd never enjoy food again, but you saved me. I even get to eat the occasional Hershey's Kiss." I wrapped my arms around Sarah, forcing both of us to jump up and down.

"I'm very proud of you, but we need to get going. Getting four kids to the bus on time doesn't happen by wishful thinking."

I laughed. "Wouldn't it be nice if it did? Although, I bet in thirty years, when all of them are out of the house, we'll miss these crazy mornings."

Sarah took a step back, giving me a hard look. "You really are in a good mood."

"I am."

She gave me a kiss before saying, "We need to talk about Alaska."

I blinked, forcing a calm expression. Had she heard about me giving her trip away? Suddenly, I realized I was stark naked, and I had never felt more exposed in my life.

Mercifully, her phone started to ring. "Get dressed. I need your help."

She answered the phone as she closed the closet door, presumably to give me privacy to put some clothes on.

I leaned against the door, regretting it when the cold wood made contact with my backside.

Did she know what I'd done?

"I should have told her right away. No, I shouldn't have done it in the first place," I muttered to myself, ruing my Lizzie ways.

How was I going to explain that I'd let Ingrid get to me and donated the cruise to the school fundraiser. This was nothing like the time I only ate veggies and farted up a storm, blaming poor Snickers, our elderly cat. That caused a literal stink but paled in comparison to the stink that the cruise situation was likely to brew.

As if sensing I was thinking about her, Snickers crawled out from under the bottom row of clothes.

I knelt down to scratch behind her ear. "I thought of you, and you showed up. Earlier, a phone call saved me from the Alaska talk with Sarah. Does that mean I should try buying a lottery ticket? Then I could buy all the Alaskan cruises in the world."

Knowing my luck, all of these signs were simply ploys to lull me into complacency before something bad happened. Really bad.

I had a feeling I already knew what that bad thing was going to be, because Peter was coming over later today to discuss Demi. As in coming up with a plan to tell her he was her true father.

"Are you still naked?" Sarah crashed into the closet. "What's wrong with you today? We have to get the kids ready for school."

She clapped her hands like a teacher getting rowdy kids to line up after recess.

It worked.

I got dressed and went downstairs. As soon as I reached the bottom step, Demi flew down, her backpack bouncing up and down, as she laughed with such innocent joy. "It's a new school week!"

"It is, my little demitasse." I had to force down a sob. Would she still like me when we told her the bombshell news? Was it fair to tell her?

Demi took no notice of the turmoil flooding my nervous system, instead rushing toward the kitchen for breakfast. As she should, because she was only a child. I was the parent who should know how to handle things. The more I parented, though, the more I realized all of us were simply bullshitting our way through life. It was simultaneously a terrifying and comforting thought. Scary that none of us really had figured out this thing called life, but I liked the fact that I wasn't alone in my cluelessness.

Sarah watched me from the top of the stairs, her eyes trying to convey everything was going to be fine. How could she even think that? I felt like that dog in the meme saying everything is fine while everything burned around him.

CHAPTER SIXTY-TWO

I sat on the couch in the library, my right leg bobbing up and down like a turbocharged piston, wishing the cushion would swallow me whole. Why couldn't there be some fantastical portal that would whisk me away to a magical land with rainbow unicorns, where nothing ever went wrong and I could eat all the Hershey's Kisses in the world without worrying about a number on a scale?

Probably out of fear I'd launch us into space, Sarah put a hand on my thigh, forcing it to still. "It's going to be okay."

"Sure, sure," I responded, not really paying her any attention. I closed my eyes, trying to picture the magical place in my mind: The trees would have Hershey's Kisses instead of apples. It'd always be strawberry season. There would be an endless supply of peanut-butter ice cream at just the right almost-melted state I preferred.

The doorbell rang, forcing my eyes open, and my heart kicked into heart attack level.

"I'll get it." Sarah didn't bother giving me a chance to offer. Not that I would have. Maybe she feared I'd banish Peter from our home and lives forever.

Peter entered, looking like he'd rather be having a colonoscopy.

Right there with you, dude.

"Hey." He barely looked at me.

"Hey." I did a head nod back, dropping my eyes to my hands in my lap before forcing them to glance up to watch his every facial muscle as if that held the key to the mysteries of life.

He returned the same head jerk.

Sarah wore a bemused smile. "Sometimes it's odd seeing you two together. Your similar mannerisms. You also both look like you're about to be scolded and sent to bed without supper."

"Am I?" Peter asked in a whisper, and given the lack of color in his face, he wasn't joking.

"No." She waved for Peter to have a seat on the opposite couch while she retook a seat next to me. "We need to talk about Demi."

I scratched the back of my head, wishing Sarah had eased into idle chitchat first, instead of diving head first into the Demi conundrum.

"Is she okay?" Peter's face twisted with fear.

"She's thriving," Sarah assured him. "It's just that she has a school project that's got her asking questions, and we—" Sarah took my hand, squeezing it hard. Was she trying to tell me not to say I wasn't on board with this whole honesty tact. Because I wasn't. "We don't want to lie to her."

"About?" Peter's eyes screamed he knew exactly what Sarah was referring to, but his voice seemed to hold out hope it was something less scary. Like maybe she wanted to know the exact minute she'd come into this world.

"Her father." While Sarah didn't believe in lying to get out of a jam, she apparently didn't beat around the bush when it came to confronting a touchy subject either.

If I'd been in charge, first and foremost, we wouldn't be

having this chat. Second, and this wouldn't be a necessary step given the previous statement, but to round out the picture, I would have danced around the topic for two hours and would have to schedule a follow-up meeting to actually get to the point. Or three more meetings, until Peter stopped accepting my invitations to avoid my inane babbling. That would be better than this.

"Can't you tell her you don't know the sperm donor's name?" Peter tugged on the collar of his button-up.

I wanted to hug Peter. It was two against one, and while democracy was dying in this country, it still reigned supreme in this household.

Didn't it?

Sarah tossed cold water on my enthusiasm, saying, "She has a right to know, Peter. It won't be easy, but if she's already asking questions like she suspects something, she'll figure it out eventually. We have a short window to get this right."

I did see Sarah's point, and I think I'd said something similar last time Peter was in town. That didn't mean coming clean didn't scare the bejesus out of me. The thought of hurting Demi in any way tore my soul into a gazillion pieces.

"I'm finally getting to know her again. I don't want her to hate me." All the color drained from his face, which was a feat considering he already was pale.

"She won't." Sarah spoke as if she believed her words with her entire being.

I was of the opinion Demi would hate all of us and would sneak off in the middle of the night to live among the wolves. Were there wolves in Massachusetts? There were plenty of wild turkeys, but they were intimidating little beasts, and I didn't get a parental vibe from that at all.

Not that wolves gave me warm fuzzy feelings. Historically, however, there was some precedent for wolves raising human children. Take Romulus and Remus, for example. While more myth than real history, it was worth exploring. Was this an appropriate time to inject this topic into the conversation? Sarah wanted me to be truthful, and these were the honest-to-God thoughts running through my head.

Something told me she wouldn't appreciate my Lizzie-ness in the moment. That was my curse to bear. Never knowing the right moment to be fully me.

"Also, she needs her father. You have so much to offer Demi. I know it's scary. For all of us." Sarah met my eyes briefly before turning her gaze back to Peter. "We'll get through this rough patch together, as a family."

"What does that mean?" Peter licked his lips.

"The three of us will always be there for Demi."

"But she'll still live here with you two and the kids, right?" Peter leaned back into the couch with such force I worried he'd tip it over.

I'll be honest; the image in my head almost made me burst into a fit of laughter. But I pulled myself together to interject with "Yes" before Sarah asked for his opinion or something stupid like that.

Relief washed over Peter's face. "Don't get me wrong. I want to be part of her life, but I'm not equipped to raise her. Besides, she fits in here. I've messed up her life enough. I don't want to rip her away from her siblings."

I noticed he didn't say cousins, much to my relief.

"How's house hunting going?" Sarah asked, changing the subject.

That should have pleased me, but I couldn't figure out what game she was playing. Sarah would probably say she wasn't playing any games, but I wasn't born yesterday. Everyone had a motive for everything. Even my darling wife. She wouldn't agree with that statement, but...

"Not great. Real estate around here is outrageous." Peter drummed his fingertips on his knee.

"Tell me about it. I remember when Sarah and I had started looking. The sticker shock…" I mimed having my mind blown.

"I might get an apartment and see what kind of work I can find. Save up for a place of my own."

"Is Dad helping?" I asked.

"He wants to. It's just I don't want to ask him. He's done so much for me, and look how I repaid him."

I assumed he meant getting arrested, which led to the board ousting our dad from the company he'd founded. It wasn't Charles Petrie's greatest moment. Although, our dad didn't seem to hold it against Peter. Which says a lot about the man.

"I don't need a big place," Peter continued. "I want to be close to all of you and figure out what to do with my life now. You know. Easy things."

We all laughed, the tension easing from the room slightly.

Sarah had to go and ruin it by saying, "We want to tell Demi before Thanksgiving."

"That's in a few days," I whispered instead of employing a screech worthy of raising the dead.

"It's when her project is due," Sarah said as if this school assignment would determine her fate.

Which in a way, it would. Education could be terrible sometimes.

Peter nodded, but I could tell by the fear sloshing in his eyes he didn't like the idea.

As it turned out, Peter and I had a lot in common.

CHAPTER SIXTY-THREE

AFTER PETER HAD GONE TO OUR DAD'S HOUSE, I FELL back onto the couch in the library, tossing an arm over my face, not wanting to get up ever again.

Sarah entered the room. "How you hanging in?"

"Are you sure this is the right thing to do? For most of my life, I didn't know about my brothers Allen and Gabe. Neither did Peter. Look how we turned out."

Sarah rubbed her throat before saying, "Do I need to state the obvious?"

"Maybe." I'd rather she didn't because she had a way of bursting my Lizzie bubble with unappreciated pinpricks of reality.

"You missed out knowing you had two more brothers all of your childhood, and when you found out, it was a shock."

I massaged my forehead with my fingers. "I don't want Demi to hate us."

"We need to handle it just right so she won't."

"I'm not known for being delicate." Or honest. Although, I was constantly working on that. Was it in the Petrie DNA to deceive those we love?

Sarah took a seat next to me. "Don't you wish you'd known about Allen and Gabe earlier in your life?"

"Sometimes, but it would have been weird considering Dad was still married to my mother. Who vowed to ruin his life and everyone else's if he left her." I turned to Sarah. "Do you think Demi would do something like that? She's half Petrie, and Tiffany was a piece of work. Have you factored in the whole nature versus nurture aspect? Maybe we should read *Frankenstein* before we—"

Maddie and Willow burst into the library, Willow jumping up and down, squealing with happiness.

"What's up?" Sarah asked, laughing over Willow's antics.

"We bought a house!" Willow jumped into the air, clicking her heels together.

I marveled over this ability. If I tried something like that, a trip to the hospital would be the result.

"That's amazing!" Sarah got up, jumping up and down with Willow.

I'd known they'd been looking for a place, but given the cost of weddings, I didn't think they'd have the money for a down payment so soon after getting hitched. As much as I'd hated the thought of Willow moving in back in the day, now I couldn't imagine her not living in the basement.

Everything was changing. Way too fast. My vision blurred, and I had to force down some bile inching up my esophagus.

Sarah gave me a glare and a slight jerk of her head to indicate I needed to get up and join the celebration.

I forced a smile as I got to my feet. "That's very exciting for you two."

Willow tossed her arms around my neck. "I can't wait to show you the place. It has the perfect podcast room."

That relieved my mind some. She wasn't ditching me—rather, the podcast—completely. Unless of course, she'd go out on her own in the podcast world. That would doubly hurt.

"When do you move in?" Sarah asked.

"We close on the house right before Christmas." Maddie reached for Willow's hand.

"Wow. That's soon." I swallowed.

"I know. We only have four weeks to pack." Willow did another hop into the air. "I can't believe I'm going to wake up Christmas morning in my own house."

"It's a Christmas miracle." Maddie gave Willow a kiss on the cheek. "We need to start planning."

With that, they left the library.

"It's going to be okay," Sarah pulled me into an embrace, sensing my distress without me having to put it into words. "Change can be good."

I wiggled free, escaping her arms as a symbolic way of rejecting her absurd premise. Change was, and always would be, horrible. Only sometimes, it was also inevitable. "Speaking of change, I've been thinking about Peter's housing issue."

"Y-yes," Sarah dragged out the word.

"We have the apartment over the garage."

"We do." It seemed she was keeping her voice and facial expression neutral, as if unsure where I was going.

"Would you be opposed to Peter living in the apartment? It'd give him some space, but it might help having him close. For Demi. That is, if breaking the news to her goes well."

"You want Peter to move into the apartment you've been eyeing for yourself for weeks?"

"I don't know if *want* is the right word, but he can't afford a place. I can't stop thinking of Demi. What will be best for her?"

Once again, Sarah pulled me into a hug. This time, I didn't squirm. "You really are amazing, Lizzie Petrie."

"Because I'm offering my brother an apartment over the garage? I feel like an asshole for not buying him a place of his own."

"He doesn't want that. But if he lives in the apartment

while he saves up the money for a place of his own, it might be the best thing you could do for him."

"There's also the basement now, but that's part of the house. Dad said Peter wants his own space. Would the apartment offer him enough of that?"

Sarah shrugged. "I have no idea what Peter needs after his ordeal."

"That's a diplomatic way of putting it."

There was another shrug.

"Why do you think Demi will handle this news okay?"

"It's in her nature. She'll probably be confused, but to outright hate people for trying to make the best choices for her under extreme circumstances—I don't see that."

"Probably because you married into the Petrie family. We're not rational people. You have to keep that in mind."

"You have sparks of rationality." Her smile was soft and encouraging.

"When we agreed to this, Peter said he didn't want Demi to know."

"I'm aware, but did you notice he didn't really fight the idea? Sure, he's scared, but he didn't put his foot down. That tells me a lot."

I started to rebut this but replayed his words in my head. "He was more concerned about ripping her away from her home."

It wasn't the first time we'd spoken about telling Demi the truth, and there was a part of me, deep inside, that knew this was the right choice. Being on the correct path didn't necessarily equate to going the easy way. I often found choosing the best way forward was the hardest option on the table.

CHAPTER SIXTY-FOUR

"You're my dad?" Demi's bottom lip trembled as she sat on the couch in the library.

The uncertainty in her tone struck me directly through my chest.

Peter knelt down on one knee, his back to me. "I am."

"H-how?" Demi stuttered.

Peter looked to Sarah, who sat next to Demi, his eyes pleading for intervention.

"Are you asking why we adopted you?" Sarah motioned to where I stood behind Peter, and then back to herself.

"Yes." Demi's face twitched, and I feared tears were about to flow. "If I have a dad, why did you adopt me?"

I let out a silent whoosh of air. It was odd to feel relief in this moment, but I couldn't help it. At least we didn't have to start with the birds and bees. This conversation was hard enough without tackling that aspect of life.

Sarah shifted on the couch. "Do you remember us telling you Peter had to go to prison?"

Demi nodded, her eyes brimming with tears. I was pretty

sure it didn't have to do with the prison part but the fact we'd just turned her safe, little world upside down.

"He was maybe going to be gone for a long time, and he couldn't take you, so we adopted you." Sarah kept the facts to the most basic level, which I appreciated. I would like it noted I didn't want to do this at all.

"You aren't really my moms?" Her tiny voice squeezed my heart like a wet sponge.

"Of course, we are. We're your adoptive moms." Sarah kept a calm smile on her lips.

Mine, I feared was more of a horror-stricken smile. Hence why Sarah was sitting next to Demi, taking the lead. If I had to say a single word right now, I would fall apart.

Did I mention I didn't want to do this?

"Do I have another mom?" Demi directed this question to Peter, but her eyes returned to Sarah.

"Yes, but she's no longer with us," Sarah explained.

"Is she in prison, too?" Demi sucked her lips into her mouth, seeming to brace herself for the answer. Unfortunately, I knew nothing could prepare her for the truth.

"No, honey," Sarah said softly. "She died when you were a baby."

Demi blinked, causing the brimming tears to fall from her eyes. "My mom is dead?"

"Sadly, yes." Sarah wrapped her arm around Demi, pulling the girl close.

Demi didn't fight it. Was that a good sign? Or was she simply in shock? I was pretty sure I was in shock from this whole ordeal.

"Do I have to live with Uncle Peter in Colorado now?"

Before I could shout no, Sarah asked, "Is that what you would want to do?"

Demi looked to Peter, then me, and back to Sarah. "I-I like it here."

My knees almost buckled, and I collapsed on the couch opposite Sarah and Demi. Up until the words had come out of her mouth, I truly hadn't been sure what she would say. I'd hoped for this answer, but I had no way to know.

"This will always be your home." Sarah wiped away some of Demi's tears. "All of us will always be there for you."

"I will," Peter's voice was soft but firm.

Demi's brow knotted. "You live in Colorado."

"What if Peter moved to Massachusetts?" Sarah asked. "Would you like that?"

"He seems nice," Demi whispered to Sarah, avoiding looking at him.

Honestly, I didn't know how such a sweet person had come from Peter and Tiffany. Or any Petrie, really.

"I'd like to get to know you better." Peter now knelt on both of his knees, making himself as small as possible. "And your siblings. Do you like hiking?"

Hiking. Peter liked to hike? For some reason, this revelation was like finding out he spoke a foreign language I'd never known about.

Hiking used to be one of my favorite things to do before kids. How did I not know Peter was a hiker? Sure, we both grew up in Colorado, and it was a fantastic place for outdoor sports. But hiking and Peter? I'd never had a clue.

"I think I do," Demi answered. She turned to Sarah. "Do I like hiking?"

"We haven't done much, but we can all go and see if you like it."

Demi nodded, still looking shell-shocked. I wish I could wave a magic wand to remove all of her suffering. Studying the stiffness in Peter's shoulders, I was fairly certain he wished for the same. It seemed the two of us had more and more in common with each passing second. The revelation tipped the world on its side.

"I like ice cream," Demi spoke in a ragged whisper, her emotions all over the place.

"What's your favorite flavor?" I could hear the smile in Peter's voice.

"It depends." Demi tapped a finger on her chin, giving the question the attention it deserved. This was one of the many things I adored about children. Their honesty and earnestness, especially when it came to life's most important topics. What was a family tree compared to the much more urgent question of favorite ice cream flavor, after all?

Peter's shoulders softened.

"I really like cotton candy," Demi announced with a hint of melancholy. "But I can't have that now."

"Why not?" Peter asked.

"The local place is closed for the season," Sarah explained. "What about strawberry?"

"That's my second favorite." Demi nodded, and a faint smile appeared on her lips before it faded.

"We should get ice cream." Peter stood. "All of us."

"Right now?" Sarah asked.

"Yes, right this very minute. It always makes me feel better."

Demi smiled again, but it wavered. "Do we have to share why we're going with everyone else?"

"Do you want to?" Sarah tossed back, reminding me of all the times my therapist did that with me instead of outright telling me anything.

It drove me mad then, and it still did.

Demi shook her head. "I don't think so. Not right now."

"We'll do it when you're ready." Sarah brushed some hair out of Demi's eyes.

"Do I have to put it in my school project?"

"Not if you don't want to."

Demi gave Peter the once-over. "What's your favorite ice cream flavor?"

"Peanut butter and chocolate."

"That's mom's favorite." Demi pointed to me.

"Same with our dad, your grandfather." Peter turned to me. "Great minds."

My mind sputtered to a stop for a brief moment. All three of us liked the same ice cream flavor. What were the odds?

CHAPTER SIXTY-FIVE

Sarah stood at the end of the Thanksgiving table, wiping her brow with the back of her hand. "I think that's everything."

I eyed the feast before us. Turkey, stuffing, glazed carrots, parsnips, mashed potatoes, cranberry sauce, green bean casserole, and some other items I hadn't quite identified and more than likely would skip. "What? No cinnamon rolls? Just plain old bread?"

I crossed my arms, and she glared menacingly at me before breaking out into an evil grin. "If you don't behave, no pie for you."

Uncrossing my arms in an instant, I mimed zipping my mouth shut.

"Now, before we tuck in, we should go around the table and say what we're thankful for." Sarah took her seat. "I'll start. I'm thankful for all of you. I can't imagine my life without any of you." She glanced over her shoulder at the kids' table. "I'm truly blessed."

Willow went next. Then Maddie, Dad, Helen, and Allen. They all shared heartfelt messages of gratitude that I only vaguely caught because I was too busy thinking about what I should say when it came to me. I hated the pressure of this type of public declaration. No matter what I said, it would probably be wrong, at least according to someone at the table. Why couldn't we just eat? I'd be grateful for that.

Peter cleared his throat, catching my attention and pulling me out of my thoughts. I was intrigued enough to listen, wondering if he would mess it up, like I was bound to do, or knock it out of the park.

"Like Sarah," he said, "I'm thankful for my family. I didn't always appreciate or treat everyone that well, but when I needed all of you the most, each and every one of you stood by my side. I'll never be able to say thanks enough."

"That's what family is for," Sarah said.

I glanced at Demi, who stared at Peter as if trying to determine if she could trust him. I hoped she would get to that point, but it was going to take a lot of work on Peter's part. If he didn't put in the hard work, I was going to kick his ass. Might be time to join a gym. I gazed at the wall, picturing my workout routine. Would building muscle help me with my quest to lose a few more pounds? How hard would it be to work out enough to kick a grown man's ass, anyway?

By the time I checked back into what was going on around me, it was Rose's turn. I thought she'd say something along the lines of being grateful for covid tests given her recent avoidance of crowds and insistence all of us took a test. We were going to anyway, given the amount of family members under our roof. But her request got my hackles up. I still took the test, because I wasn't an asshat. But it irked me nonetheless.

"These past few years have been difficult for me." Rose stopped suddenly, and I wondered if that was all she planned to say. Kudos to her if she had nothing to be grateful for, I guess. Sarah would probably murder me right there at the table with the same carving knife she'd used on the turkey if I tried to pull a stunt like that. Troy, on the other hand, just gave Rose an encouraging nod.

I raised my water glass to my lips, partially because I was parched, but also in an attempt to mask my involuntary facial expressions that may or may not get me into trouble, depending on what Rose said next.

"But all of you have been patient with me, and I'm ready to rejoin the world." She punched the air with a lackluster effort. "I can't think of a better way to usher in this stage of my life than going on an Alaskan cruise with Sarah and Lizzie."

I nearly choked on my water, my eyes seeking out Sarah. Who flashed me her *not now* smile. Was this what Sarah had meant when she said she needed to talk about the cruise? That somehow her mother had been invited?

Hold the phone!

Did Sarah know what I'd done, and this was her way of getting back at me? It was brilliant in an evil way, and part of me admired it if that was the case.

This was my stupid luck biting me in the ass for not doing what I'd been told to do in the first place. All I had to do was donate a fancy meal at the French place. Better yet, I should have simply asked Sarah last Christmas what she wanted instead of coming up with the cruise coupon at the last minute. It hadn't gone over well then, and somehow, I was still paying the price for being a terrible gift giver.

It was my turn to state what I was thankful for, and at that moment, I had zero thanks to give. This was a disaster.

"What can I say?" I began. What I was silently wondering was whether it would be socially acceptable to demand Sarah explain how the cruise now included her mother. Was Troy also going? None of this had anything to do with thankfulness, but it was what was in my heart.

As the silence dragged on, Sarah gave me a look that said I'd better speak now or risk being deep fried later like the neighbor's turkey, which had been put into a large vat of oil in their driveway earlier while still partially frozen and caused a huge scene.

"I'm truly the luckiest person on the planet," I said. *Who also had rotten luck due to my own conniving*, I added silently. "A beautiful wife, amazing kids, and all of you to keep me on my toes."

That elicited laughter, but Sarah's seemed forced.

I finished with, "Now can I have pie?"

There was more laughter, and the kids were on my side one hundred percent.

Everyone tucked into their meals, the chatter blooming all around me. Sarah met my eyes, and I boosted my eyebrows.

She shrugged one of her shoulders.

I jerked my head toward the kitchen and then excused myself from the table.

Two minutes and twenty-five seconds later, Sarah joined me.

"Your mom hasn't left her house for months, and now all of a sudden she wants to go on a cruise with us?" This time I was the one who wasn't beating around the bush.

"It's a Thanksgiving miracle." Sarah's smile was too wide, like she couldn't believe what was happening either.

"Or a curse."

"Don't be that way. Mom used to cruise all the time until she started dating Troy."

I didn't need to remind her that Troy was the son of one of Rose's former cruise buddies who didn't approve of the relationship. She'd kind of lost her cruising privileges after the two of them had gotten together, and I couldn't really say I blamed Troy's mother one bit.

"She needs to do things again, and I know you got me the cruise for me to spend time all by myself, but that's not me. I want my loved ones around me." She studied me. "Isn't that a good thing?"

Honestly, I couldn't process any of her words, let alone a response. I was in deep trouble now, for sure. How was I going to tell Sarah what I'd done with the tickets?

"I'm going back in there. Don't be too long." She kissed my cheek.

I leaned against the counter, more to stay upright than anything else. My knees were on the verge of giving out.

My dad came into the kitchen. "We need more rolls—are you okay?"

I shook my head, unable to keep up the pretense.

"What's wrong?"

"Sarah's going to kill me."

"I need more information." He rested a hand on my shoulder, not really looking surprised. Then again, it was hardly the first time he'd seen me get myself into a situation where someone close to me wanted to commit homicide.

"It's possible I donated the Alaskan cruise tickets to the school charity, and I haven't told Sarah yet. And now her mother wants to go with us."

"I see."

To his credit, his eyes stayed kind and supportive.

"It was stupid. Ingrid was bragging about her big, expensive donation and—" I flicked a hand in the air.

"I see."

It was clear from his expression that he did, in fact, see. I raked a hand through my hair, wishing it was long enough that I could pull it all to the front and hide behind it. Would I ever stop being such a fool?

"It's a good donation," my father said, his tone far kinder than I deserved. "It'll help raise money."

"Sarah wanted to give a gift card to that French restaurant in town."

"That would've been nice, too. Helen loves that place."

"What am I going to do?" I hugged myself.

"It's not that big of a deal. Simply be honest."

"That's not something that comes naturally to me."

My father let out a sigh that surprised me. "You didn't have great role models on that front."

I started to speak, but he raised a hand. "We should get back to the table. Later on, we'll figure out the best way to tackle this problem. Just know Sarah loves you, no matter what."

I believed him but couldn't help wondering if there was a *Lizzie being an idiot* limit. If there was, I was pretty sure I was approaching it at light speed.

DECEMBER (AGAIN)

CHAPTER SIXTY-SIX

I skidded to a stop as I entered the bathroom.

Sarah, wearing a dress I'd never seen before, stood in front of the mirror, inserting an earring.

"Wowzers!" I blinked excessively. "That dress! It's so hot. Fucking hot."

"What? This old thing?" Sarah winked at me. "Love your suit."

"It's not old, but I did wear it to the wedding. Maddie and Willow's. Not ours. I wouldn't fit into that one anymore. I'm babbling. Your dress. Hot. Did I mention that yet?" I licked my lips as I imagined taking it off later. Or why not now and skip the whole evening? That sounded like a much better idea.

"You did, and you look great, too." She inserted her other earring. "I can't believe the gala's finally here."

"Me either." I swallowed, wondering if this was the time to tell her about the cruise tickets. Or perhaps I should wait until after plying her with a lot of booze. Yeah, that might be the best moment even if it'd be cruel the next morning if she woke with a doozy of a hangover. Did it count if she was so drunk when I confessed that when she woke the next day, she had zero memory of it? I was pretty sure it did, or at least one could hope, right? Idiots like me had to put a lot of faith into hope to get themselves out of jams.

"I gotta call Mom. Meet me outside in five. We don't want to be late, or we'll endure the wrath of Ingrid." She gave me an air-kiss, presumably so she wouldn't mess up her recently applied lipstick.

If I messed it up beyond repair, would that save me?

Sadly, before I knew what was happening, we were walking into the gala, Sarah and I holding hands.

Ingrid stood at the entrance of the old town dance hall, like a despot surveying her disappointing minions. "Sarah, you look lovely. What a dress. Lizzie."

The woman barely even looked me in the eyes as she gave me a curt head nod. Not even a mention of my suit. Granted, it wasn't as remarkable as Sarah's dress, but just because I was wearing trousers didn't mean I wouldn't have appreciated a compliment.

Sarah squeezed my hand as she gave Ingrid a *fuck you* smile.

It was hard not to burst into laughter because Ingrid acted like she and Sarah were besties. Of course, it was all for show on Ingrid's side. She wasn't the type to have true friendships. You couldn't be friendly when your sole purpose in life was to destroy others all the while hammering home the point you're even better than Jesus. Clearly, the woman knew nothing about the teachings of Christ.

I suspected Sarah tolerated Ingrid simply to make the kids' lives easier. The woman ran a lot of the events tied to the school, and she had no qualms about making a child a pariah in their peer group simply to get their parents in line.

That meant I also had to play nice with the bitch. It didn't mean I couldn't imagine spitting repeatedly in her champagne flute.

"Lizzie, do you think your donation will receive the most

money tonight?" Leonard, Ingrid's twin, stood off to the side, mostly hidden because why would Ingrid share the spotlight? He gave Sarah a kiss on the cheek. "You look fantastic."

"Err..." was all I could say in response to his question. Sure, I hoped it did considering I might end up divorced for having donated it. Having the best donation might ease the pain, but not really considering how much I adored Sarah. It was hard not to notice how many heads she was turning this evening. Trying to picture my life without—nope, I couldn't even entertain the thought.

Sarah started to speak, but my father and Helen arrived, garnering all of the attention.

"I hope you brought your checkbook," Ingrid teased my father.

He patted his breast pocket. "I've got my eye on a few things." He casually met my eyes and then shifted back to Helen. "Shall we get some drinks, dear?"

"Yes," Helen looked relieved to have an excuse to leave Ingrid's presence, and they'd only just arrived.

If even Helen didn't like Ingrid, that spoke volumes. Would it be wrong to actually spit in the woman's drink for real? Ingrid's drink, not my step-mom's. I weighed the pros and cons and decided, yes, it would be wrong. Not that the thought wasn't still tempting. Part of me kept blaming Ingrid for this jam I'd gotten myself into. I know that wasn't fair, even to someone like her. I did what I did and only I could be held responsible.

More people were arriving, diverting Ingrid's attention.

Sarah pulled me to the side. "What was that about our donation?"

"Just Leonard being Leonard. I think he truly wants everyone to succeed. How he's Ingrid's twin is baffling." I didn't look Sarah in the eye, pretending to take in the party.

"I've wanted to ask him if there was a mistake at the hospital. Like were they not the only twins born that day?"

"It would explain a lot." My eyes continued to scan the party. "I feel like we're crashing a party for the royals."

"Does the woman know this is for playground equipment? She's not raising money for cancer." Now Sarah looked like she wanted to spit in Ingrid's drink, and I couldn't be prouder.

Then a thought struck me.

What if the money was for something more noble? I wouldn't be so terrified of Sarah's reaction. Was it possible to divert the funds to children's cancer research? How could she get upset about that?

"We should take a spin. See what we want to bid on."

"N-nothing," I stuttered. "I've seen all the entries. Nothing we want or need." I made a definitive slash in the air as if that wouldn't raise Sarah's spidey sense.

"That's not the point, though. We're here to help raise money. Which means we have to open our wallets."

I was relieved her bullshit meter hadn't been activated.

"What if we just bid on our item? I'd be happy to do that while you chat with everyone."

"You hate French food."

"I like French toast." There was stupid, and then there was that statement.

Sarah slanted her head, scrutinizing every part of my face, and I sensed the BS meter activating. "You've been acting weird about this night for so long. Will you please tell me what you've done so we can get the punishment out of the way and enjoy the night?"

"W-why do you think—wrong. That I wrong... I mean, that I did something wrong?" Could someone just shoot me now?

She took a step back. "I was bluffing, but now I know you did something. Tell. Me. Now."

I froze in terror.

She glared at me with an expression that said if I didn't start confessing, she'd begin torturing me. Not the good kind. What I wouldn't give for some sexy-time torture. She was killing this dress and me.

"Lizzie."

"It's possible I changed our donation." My eyes dropped to my shoes, which needed a polish. Could I excuse myself for a shoe polish emergency?

"You didn't donate the gift certificate to the French restaurant like I told you to."

"No. So, good news. I can take you there for a fabulous date. Will you wear this dress? Because it really is spectacular."

This didn't seem to appease her at all.

"What did you donate?"

"Something I had laying around. I panicked and just did the only thing I could think of."

"Please tell me you didn't donate one of our kids or something."

"Geez, I'm not that much of an idiot." Given my past history, though, I really wouldn't be able to win that argument if she decided to push me on it.

"That remains to be seen." She crossed her arms.

"The cruise."

"What about it?"

"I gave the tickets to the gala."

"The Alaskan cruise tickets?"

I nodded.

"But my mom's going with us." Her voice was quiet, making me squirm even more.

"That wasn't a possibility when I did it."

Sarah's chest heaved up and then deflated while she let a whoosh of air out of her lungs. "I don't even know what to say right now."

"What if it was children's cancer research?" I blurted.

"Maybe we can get them to donate the money to that instead of playground equipment. That would be better, right?"

She glanced around the room. "I need a drink."

"I'll get you something."

"No. I will."

She stormed off toward the bar.

Moments later, my dad sidled up next to me. "I'm going out on a limb here, but you told her, didn't you?"

I moved my head in what I hope implied yes. My neck—no my whole body, was jelly-like, and my vision was all wobbly.

"Do you want me to talk to her?"

"I appreciate the offer, but there's no reason for you to put your head on the chopping block. I got myself into this mess. I need to fix it."

If only I knew what that would entail.

CHAPTER SIXTY-SEVEN

Considering I didn't know how to fix the situation, aside from building a time machine and going back to —geez, where would I even start? I'd fucked up so many times when it came to Sarah it was amazing she was still in my life. I feared even Sarah would tire of my Lizzie-ness eventually, and then I'd be screwed. It was possible that time had arrived.

Overwhelmed, I accepted a glass of wine from one of the waiters. I wasn't much of a wine person, and I hadn't partaken in alcohol in a long time. But fuck it. This was quickly morphing into a wine night.

I took a teensy sip, not enjoying it much. That didn't stop me from taking another.

"Interesting choice." Sarah approached me looking as if she wasn't sure she wanted to talk to me but more than likely, she also didn't want tongues to start wagging.

"Seemed like the best option given everything."

She took the wine glass from me to indulge in herself before handing it back to me. "Can you explain why you donated the cruise tickets?"

"Utter incompetence." I took another drink of wine.

"I'm going to need more than that, because I got to that particular conclusion on my own." I wished I could say there was a hint of a smile on her lips, but there wasn't.

"Ingrid was crowing about her week at her lake cabin. I… wanted to beat that."

"Looks like you did." Her facial expression was unnervingly neutral.

"I plan on bidding on the tickets to get them back."

Sarah sucked in a deep breath. "It'll be cheaper to buy a new pair."

"Is it that simple? Because I could do that." I handed her my wine glass. "Before you answer, have another drink. Should I get you a bottle or two?"

That earned me a tiny chuckle, before she said, "What am I going to do with you?"

"Love me because no one else will."

Her brow furrowed.

"Or not. I get it. I'm impossible, and you've already put up with so much. I wouldn't blame you for walking away right now."

She sighed, but not an angry one. More frustrated. "Why do you think you're so unlovable?"

"To start, I donated your Christmas gift to one-up a woman I don't really know all because said woman made me feel insignificant."

"That's just stupidity. It doesn't make you unlovable. You say that a lot. That I should leave you. Why?"

"Not really sure this is the place to dig deep into my psychological wounds."

She started to speak but stopped. "We're still going on the cruise with my mother."

"Absolutely." I added, "Is that punishment enough?"

She burst into laughter. "I need time to mull it over."

"Cool. Do you plan on listing reasons for why I should be

punished further? Like I don't do enough around the house. I work too much. I hide things from you."

"What are you hiding from me?"

"Uh—" I closed my eyes. "Nothing is coming to mind right this minute. But I am drinking after not having a lick of alcohol in a long time. Not sure my brain is fully functioning."

"How do I know if you're ever telling the truth?" She placed one hand on her hip.

I let out a puff of air, frustrated that I deserved that question and with my inability to give a suitable answer.

"I guess the better question is why don't you trust me?" She pressed a hand to her chest, drawing my attention to her killer dress. Not that I hadn't been ogling her the entire time.

"What do you mean?"

"As soon as you did it, why didn't you just tell me? I've done plenty of stupid stuff in life."

"True. You did marry me, after all."

She shook her head, but she also smiled for a fleeting second. "That's one of the best things I've done. I was talking about petty stuff. Last week, I hid all of Lucinda's French roast coffee pods in the break room. She's always gloating how she's super organized and comments on how I look disheveled every morning."

"Do you need me to have a talking to this Lucinda?" I balled a fist with one hand and mimed giving a knockout blow.

"Nope. I prefer petty acts that don't end up with arrests." Sarah looped her arm through mine. "Try believing in me more."

"I will, and while I appreciate your story, I'm not sure hiding coffee pods ranks the same as donating cruise tickets."

"No, you have a special knack for one-upping people. Which is exactly how you got into this mess."

"Maybe you shouldn't trust me as much. I know I'm supposed to trust you more, but clearly I can't handle simple tasks like attending a parent meeting." I took another sip, the buzz really kicking in now.

"Oh wow! Was that your master plan to forever get out of those meetings?" She was laughing, but I suspected she believed it.

"I appreciate you thinking I have that much foresight, but the sad fact is I only dream of being evil. My execution is severely lacking, and my imagination is not sufficient."

Sarah laughed even more. "For the sake of our family, do not try to become a villain. I'm exhausted enough from every day disasters. I can't handle much more."

"You really aren't going to kill me for this?"

"No."

"Hold a grudge?" Every muscle in my body tightened.

"Do you want me to?"

"What I want doesn't matter. It's what I deserve." I released an anguished sigh. "I don't know what's wrong with me sometimes."

"That's a loaded statement and not one I want to tackle in the middle of a party. Buck up, Lizzie. I'm pretty sure you've been living in fear of the moment when I did find out. And now I have. So that's one thing you can stop worrying about."

I nodded. "My dad told me to simply tell you."

She tilted her head to the side. "You told your dad?"

"On Thanksgiving when I found out your mom wanted to go on the cruise with us. I confessed that you were going to murder me." I took a step back to assess her. Fully. "Are you trying to put me at ease so I don't see it coming?"

"It?"

"Whatever punishment you're playing in your head?"

"Like driving my heel into your forehead or something?"

"New fear just dropped." I visibly shuddered as my eyes traveled down her body. "Might not be a bad way to go. My last vision will be of you in that dress."

"Keep talking like that and I may let you live."

"Pretty sure the thoughts flitting through my mind will get me in trouble in this setting."

"I'm proud of you." Her tone implied she was serious, though I wasn't sure why.

"For having—" I mouthed the word *sexy* before speaking, "thoughts?"

"No. For confiding in your father. That's a big step forward for you."

"Pinch me." I stuck my arm out.

"Why?"

"I must be dreaming, because in the real world, you wouldn't be praising me for going behind your back and making a big mess of everything like this."

"Why do you keep thinking I'm an awful person?"

"I don't, although you did threaten to brain me with your shoe. Fingers crossed that was a joke, but you'd be in the right. I'm an awful person. You're a saint for putting up with me."

"You are not a bad person."

"Yeah, right." I blew a raspberry.

"I love you, Lizzie. In good times and bad. Please get that through your thick skull."

"Or else I get the heel?" I rubbed my forehead.

Her laugh had a huskiness to it that made me think not only was divorce not on the horizon, but getting her out of that dress and into bed tonight could possibly still be in the cards for me. Who would've thought?

CHAPTER SIXTY-EIGHT

Ingrid stood at the microphone, announcing the top bids of the night. "And now for the second largest bid."

Leonard, who stood next to his evil twin, pretended to play the drums, which I assumed meant drumroll.

"Rose and Troy..." Ingrid squinted at the card in her hands. "Sorry, I can't quite make this out."

"That's us!" Troy called out, waving his hand proudly.

Sarah and I turned to them, applauding.

"Ah, Sarah Petrie's parents," Ingrid continued. " How delightful. They'll be staying at my lake house. I hope you have a lovely time, and thank you for supporting the children."

There was more applause, but I sensed many in the room simply wanted to go home. I knew I did. My feet were sore. If mine were, Sarah's had to be killing her.

A pained expression flashed across Ingrid's face, and at first, I thought she was having a heart attack. Sadly, I was wrong. Her eyes briefly met mine, and that was when I realized the only donation that hadn't been announced yet was the cruise tickets.

Sarah must have realized it as well, since she reached for my hand, giving it a hard and excited squeeze.

"Now for the biggest donation of the night," Ingrid barely got the words out, and I had to admit, despite how bad it'd been for me to donate the tickets, I cherished this moment with all my heart.

Leonard did his drumroll routine again, and it made laughter bubble out of me considering he seemed genuinely excited and Ingrid looked as if she wanted to crawl into a hole. Or shoot me.

I shouldn't have been feeling exuberant, but I was. I fucking beat the bitch. Could that go on my tombstone? It could apply to others, too. Like my mother. It was hard to pass up such a multi-purpose epitaph.

"Charles and Helen are going on an Alaskan cruise!" Ingrid mustered the energy to come across as enthused, but I saw a piece of her soul fall off, slipping through the cracks in this world and plummeting straight to hell.

"Isn't that lovely?" Rose commented, adding, "The six of us are going on this cruise."

Sarah shot me an amused look that screamed, "You so deserve this punishment."

"Actually," my father started to speak, but Sarah interrupted by clearing her throat.

"We can't wait, can we Lizzie?" She hooked her arm through mine. "Your parents and mine going on a trip of a lifetime with us."

"Do you know who donated the Alaskan cruise?" Rose asked, her facial expression not giving away if she knew the truth or not. "Most of the cards listed a name, but that one simply said anonymous."

"Is that right?" Sarah turned to me, her eyes questioning.

I shrugged one shoulder.

Sure, I wanted to beat Ingrid, but I didn't necessarily desire to take credit for what I knew should have been a good deed but really wasn't. That's why I didn't list my name on the donor spreadsheet. Ingrid knew it was me, of course. And that was all that mattered. Did that make me an asshole? Yes, but I didn't let myself go too crazy with it.

"Whoever did, I thank them. I can't think of a better way to go on my first cruise in years. Having all of you with us." Rose rested her head on Troy's shoulder.

"It's going to be fabulous." Helen gave me a supportive smile, letting me know she was in on the situation. It warmed my heart that my dad had shared my dilemma with her and that she wasn't holding it against me. I wanted to be a mom like that for the entirety of all my children's lives.

Once we were alone in our SUV, I slumped against the driver's seat, turning my head toward Sarah. "Did you tell your mom about the tickets? Is that how she jumped to the conclusion that we were all going on a cruise together?"

"Nope. I don't know how she got there. Maybe just because it's an Alaskan cruise. But now we both get a lot of time with our parents on a vacation. This is really turning out to be the best Christmas gift you've ever given me." She playfully batted her lashes at me.

"Speaking of, what do you want this year? Ya know, so it doesn't turn into a disaster like this one." My grip tightened on the steering wheel.

"Please don't get me anything."

"I can't do that."

"Why not?" She quirked one eyebrow.

"Won't that make me a jerk?"

"I don't need anything. All I want is to have a nice holiday. No drama. Please."

"If you don't want drama, you should have accepted the single cruise ticket with zero family members. I hate to break it to you, but our family is drama-prone, and now we're all going to be trapped together on a ship in the middle of the ocean." My chest constricted.

"Not to point out the obvious, dear, but you cause a lot of the drama. Which is funny because you're always saying you aren't dramatic." Her smirk had several layers to it.

"I'd like to defend myself, but something tells me this isn't the night to try."

"It really isn't." Sarah's shoulders shook with laughter. "I'm serious, Lizzie. What do I need that I don't already have?"

"A lake cabin?" I took a stab at it.

"That seems a bit much to fit under the tree, doncha think?"

"I guess so." Then added, "What about one of those tiny homes by a lake?"

"I don't know if you noticed, this dress doesn't cover much."

"I have, but I don't see how that connects to the tiny home." I dabbed the air twice, like I was trying to connect the dots.

"It's cold. Start the car. Get me home. A hot bath is calling my name."

I turned the key in the ignition and pulled out of the parking lot. "Do I get to join you in this bath?"

"Can you behave for the entire drive home?"

"I'll do my best." The light turned green, and the idiot before me didn't immediately press the gas, so I laid on the horn.

"Lizzie! Seriously!"

"What?" I briefly turned to her. "Oh, I guess that means no bath for me."

"You're impossible, you know that?"

"Since the day I was born."

CHAPTER SIXTY-NINE

We sat at the dinner table, and Sarah gave me a reassuring nod, which didn't reassure me even the tiniest bit, before saying, "Kids, we called this family dinner meeting—"

Calvin cut off Sarah by saying, "This isn't the whole family."

"True." Sarah didn't seem overly bothered by the interruption. I wondered if she had medicated herself, and by that I meant consumed a bottle of wine, before taking a seat at the table. "It's a meeting for those of us here, who live in this house."

"Where are Maddie and Willow?" Olivia asked in all probability not to be outdone by Calvin on the annoying front.

"As you know, they're moving out—"

"Why is Peter here?" Calvin crossed his arms, shooting Ollie a top-that sneer.

Maybe I should have imbibed before this. I hadn't since the night of the gala, and I was seriously starting to rethink not being a drinker.

"Thanks for the segue, Cal." Sarah rubbed the top of his head like he was an adorable puppy.

Calvin loved and hated it given the conflicting emotions flashing across his face.

"What's a segue?" Fred closed both eyes as if trying to flip through a dictionary in his mind, and I couldn't have been prouder of him. Was it too soon to buy him a super fancy one with a stand?

"It's a transition to a new topic," Sarah sounded so much like an English teacher, and I can't lie. It was kinda hot.

The kids settled down, and Peter watched with amusement dancing in his eyes.

"We have some exciting news," Sarah's smile was wide. "Peter is moving into the apartment over the garage."

"Is he our new au—" Fred's face reddened, indicating he'd forgotten the term au pair, and settled on, "Nanny?"

"Not exactly, although he will be helping with ferrying all of you to your activities." Sarah gave Peter a *thank you* smile.

"Looking forward to it." Peter gave the kids a cheerful grin, and I couldn't quite believe it, but it seemed genuine. He'd come a long way from the finance dude I couldn't stand so many years ago. "Especially ballet classes." His eyes landed on Demi, who gave him a shy, knowing smile in return.

"Tennis is better," Ollie announced. "It's hard."

Should I point out to Ollie that if Demi stuck to ballet, she'd be dancing on her toes? Just the thought of that made me cringe, and I didn't know how I was going to sit in the audience while she did that without shouting, "Don't hurt yourself!"

"All of your activities are fantastic," Sarah deflected, not wanting to get derailed for the bigger announcement. "On Friday nights, Demi will be staying with Peter in his apartment."

"Why not me? I do ballet." Calvin jerked a thumb at his chest, and I loved that he thought the reason was because of ballet. To be a kid again and to possess that kind of logic.

"Because…" Sarah started and faltered.

I knew this was going to be the portion of the dinner meeting that would go off the rails.

"He's my dad," Demi spoke to the dino nuggies on her plate more than her siblings.

"Well, he's my dad, too, then," Calvin protested, not willing to give up the chance of doing something one of his siblings did. He had such *baby in the family* energy.

I started calculating how much therapy this was going to cost us over the years.

"No, he's not. He's mine." It was hard to tell if Demi was being possessive or frustrated by Calvin.

Same, baby girl.

"Why can't he be my dad?" Calvin wasn't going to let it go.

Yep, therapy bills were going to go through the roof. So long *tiny home by the lake* dream.

"Because I'm adopted," Demi blurted, before smothering her mouth with both hands.

Calvin tilted his head, looking to Sarah. "Can I be adopted? I want to stay at Uncle Peter's. He's cool."

"Demi," Peter said softly. "Would you be opposed to Calvin also staying with us Friday nights?"

"What about me?" Ollie roared to life, shaking one of her dino nuggies in the air like she was about to crack some skulls.

"I want to be cool," Freddie added his two cents.

"All of you are the coolest," Peter reassured.

"Does everyone want to stay with my dad?" Demi met her siblings' gazes one by one.

They all nodded.

Demi seemed to take to the idea.

"Is that alright with you two?" Peter asked Sarah and me.

"You want all four kids to stay with you on Friday nights?" I couldn't quite believe the turn of events. I'd envisioned a lot of tears, mostly mine.

"We can camp out on the floor and make pillow forts. Would all of you like that?" Peter asked.

I gaped at my brother, trying to figure out if he'd always had this desire to tap into his inner child because I knew we hadn't been the pillow-fort family. Or maybe this was a product of becoming a father. Was it because he'd missed too many years of Demi's life?

"That sounds like so much fun!" Freddie bounced up and down on his chair.

"He loves building things," I explained.

"You really want them all?" It was the first time since the conversation started when Sarah sounded as if she was walking out onto the thinnest of ice in the dead-center of a pond, while that was how I felt basically every second of my life.

"Of course I do." He added, "You two can have Friday night dates."

I blinked, not sure I was believing what was happening. We were being offered a free night once a week. When was the last time that had been the norm? I knew the answer. Eight years ago.

"Every Friday?" Sarah asked in her *no take backs* tone.

"I would love it." His eyes landed on Demi.

She nodded enthusiastically.

I continued to stare dumbfounded.

Every Friday night, Sarah and I would have alone time.

"I don't know what to say, Peter. Thank you."

"It's the least I can do for you two after everything." His eyes glistened.

So did mine, if my blurry vision could be believed.

Sarah sucked her bottom lip into her mouth.

While we still had a lot of explaining to do for the kids, like what adoption actually meant, there was time for that. The kids excitedly talked about pillow forts, enjoying their nuggets.

For the first time in a long time, everything seemed like it was going to be okay. The Peter news had broken, and the kids were fine. Halle-fucking-lujah.

CHAPTER SEVENTY

Wrapping paper was strewn about the room, while the kids were on the floor playing with their new toys that Santa had brought them. Sarah and I sat on one of the couches, side by side, exhausted.

Rose came into the room with a cup of coffee. "When should we start planning the Alaskan cruise?"

If I had the energy, I would have cried.

"What cruise?" Freddie looked up from his LEGO set.

"Your mom and I, along with our parents, are going on an Alaskan cruise together next year." Sarah eyed Rose's coffee as if she was contemplating stealing it.

If I were a better spouse, I would have gotten up to fetch Sarah a fresh cup, but let's face it; I wasn't that spouse. Especially on a morning after less than three hours of sleep.

"Why aren't we going?" Freddie looked incredulous to be left out.

"It's a grown-up thing," Sarah said as delicately as possible.

"And it's expensive," I added, my eyes sweeping over the piles of gifts that cluttered the room as it occurred to me that I may have gone a little overboard and was in danger of completely spoiling the children as thoroughly as a bucket of rotting fruit.

"But—isn't Alaska disappearing?" Freddie countered, his face reddening. "I heard about it at school. Climate change is making the ice melt, and it's all going to be gone soon."

"It's not really," I argued, even though he was kind of right about this. "It's changing, but—"

"I want to see it before it goes away!" Freddie had never looked or sounded more earnest. "The polar bears are dying!"

If this had just been the outburst of a kid demanding more pie after dinner or a new gaming system from Santa, I would have brushed it off without a thought. But suddenly it struck me that the world was changing quickly and the future was very much unknown.

Shoot. Freddie had a point about the polar bears.

And now the other kids were staring at us like we were the worst parents on the planet, as though we were personally responsible for destroying polar bear habitats. Two of them were on the verge of shedding actual tears. So much for a drama-free holiday. Even worse, given this had all stemmed from discussing the Alaskan cruise, it was technically my fault.

This would be a really good time to get off my lazy ass and get Sarah a much-needed cup of coffee. And escape what I could already see was going to be a hurricane-strength storm.

But before I could slip into the kitchen, Ollie stood up and declared, "I want to see the polar bears."

She put her hands on her hips, as though making herself bigger would drive the point home. Or perhaps terrify Sarah so she'd give in. To be honest, it would have worked on me. The other three kids got to their feet.

Dad watched this mutiny with a bemused expression. Same with Troy and Peter.

"I'm sorry, kiddos, but it's very expensive to go on a cruise."

Sarah held her ground, which is why I was grateful the kids were focusing their energy on her and not me.

"Well, now," my dad piped up, using the tone of an indulgent grandfather, "I don't know if it's completely out of reach. My investment portfolio had a pretty good year."

"We couldn't possibly—" Sarah began, but Freddie quickly jumped in.

"It's disappearing!" Freddie was honestly close to melting down, which was something he rarely did. From the way he looked, I knew it wasn't a tantrum but genuine despair.

The panic in Sarah's eyes said she could see it, too. "We can talk about it—"

"Do you really want to go?" My dad asked the kids directly, leaving Sarah and I to exchange uneasy glances as what little power we had to control the situation slipped out of our grasp.

"I want to see it before I can't. The way it is now." Tears streamed out of Freddie's eyes, and I had to wonder if part of the reason for all this emotion stemmed from him waking us at four in the morning, even though we explained to the children that we wouldn't be opening any gifts before seven.

I decided to take one last stab at correcting this mess. "Cruises are boring, kids. It's just grown-up stuff."

"Unless you go on a family-friendly one," Helen chimed in. She quickly consulted the phone in her hand. "It looks like there's a Disney cruise to Alaska with themed pools, fireworks, character breakfasts, and a nightly stage show with songs from *Frozen*."

As far as I was concerned, she had just described a floating hell on earth. This opinion was confirmed as the children broke into a rousing rendition of "Let it Go," while clasping hands and spinning themselves in a circle so fast I was certain one of them would throw up.

Much to my horror, Sarah leaned closer to Helen, clearly intrigued. "Can the tickets we have be traded in for that one?"

"I can't think why not," my dad said, though I was able to think of several reasons why not, starting with being forced to eat breakfast in a room full of people in costumes and ending with the nightly *Frozen* review. "Technically, what we've got is vouchers for the travel agency, not tickets for a specific cruise. As long as they offer the Disney cruises—"

"Oh, they definitely do," Rose offered, sealing my doom.

"In that case," my dad said after a quick nod from Helen, "I think we should all go. Our treat. I mean, we can't take it with us, right?"

Had my father actually just said that? He was officially no longer the man I knew growing up at all. I was torn between being really proud of him and really wishing he wasn't handing out cruise tickets to my children like some kind of Santa Claus wannabe.

"Is Uncle Peter coming, too?" Calvin asked.

"No, buddy," Peter said, and I could spot the relief in his eyes a mile away. This was so not fair. Now that Peter had come out as Demi's father, it seemed only right that he should have to suffer through a Disney cruise like a real parent.

"I'm not going unless Peter goes." Calvin stepped closer to Peter, taking his hand.

"Me either," Demi held onto Peter's other hand.

"Goodness, it's a revolt." Rose tried to defuse the tension with this joke.

"As much as I'd love to go," Peter said (as I waited for his nose to grow twelve inches, the big liar), "your mom was right. It's very expensive. And I already spent so much money to move here."

"Grandpa will pay for your ticket," Ollie said matter-of-factly. "After all, Uncle Peter is our dad."

It was torture that they still didn't understand that Peter was only Demi's dad. Given that Peter was my brother… well, it was too disturbing to contemplate. And it was only a matter of time before we started getting even weirder looks from the other parents than we already did. Not that it was any of their damn business. That wouldn't deter the gossip hounds, though.

Was it wrong the whole situation kind of made me want to laugh?

"It's okay." Peter gave Demi's and Calvin's hands a squeeze. "This isn't about me."

"It's about the family," Freddie gave Sarah and me a steely-eyed stare, the whiteness stained with red streaks.

Sarah's shoulders softened. "What do you think, Lizzie?"

"I'm with the kids. If Peter doesn't get to go, I'm not going." I finally got off the couch and stood next to my brother, resting a hand on his shoulder in what I hoped would look more like solidarity than an act of revenge. But seriously, if I had to eat my morning cereal with Olaf and Elsa, so did Peter.

Peter sucked his bottom lip into his mouth, clearly overcome with emotion, though I wasn't sure which one. Was he touched by my support? Or furious at the way I'd just thrown him under the bus? Only time would tell how he'd chosen to interpret my actions.

My father's eyes became moist, however, confirming that at least one person in the room was taking my advocacy for my brother at face value. "Petrie family, we're going to Alaska!"

As everyone cheered and the children launched into one of the lesser-known *Frozen* melodies, Sarah whispered into my ear. "Look at that. The single ticket you promised me for alone time just morphed into a full-on Petrie family vacation."

If I had been in her shoes, I would have been furious, but I could hear the evil glee in my wife's words as clearly as if she'd been sitting there tapping her fingertips together like a cartoon villain.

"I hope Alaska knows what it's in for," I remarked.

"Would you get me a cup of coffee?" she asked sweetly, not that I was fooled.

"There's not enough coffee in the world," I grumbled, resting my head on the back of the sofa in defeat.

"What if I told you there are fresh cinnamon rolls to go with it?"

That perked me up, although I'd be making myself tea.

LATER THAT NIGHT, SARAH AND I SNUGGLED ON THE couch in front of the Christmas tree, the only light coming from the bubble lights. All the kiddos were sound asleep, and no wonder, given the ungodly hour they'd woken us up. It was the first time that whole day the house was quiet.

I nuzzled my face into the crook of Sarah's neck. "I could get used to this peace and quiet."

"I can actually hear my thoughts." She kissed the top of my head. "Did you like your gift?"

"I'm torn," I confessed.

"Why?"

"You said you weren't giving me a gift, and then you did."

"Handing over a key to the basement for you to disappear to didn't cost me a thing. Also, you had to give up a lot this year, like Gettysburg."

"Don't forget the reenactment."

"How could I?" There was a snort. "It was about time you got your way about something this year."

"It's the best gift anyone has given me."

"Now I don't know how to react. You and your need for privacy. It's like you don't like hanging out with us." Her tone was teasing, but there was a layer beneath it that didn't bode well for me.

"Of course, I do," I said quickly, "but I need a break. So do you. We can share the space."

"At the same time?" She teased, or at least I hoped she was teasing.

"Occasionally."

She laughed. "I had a feeling that would be your answer."

I wrapped my arm around her, getting as close as I could. "Did you have the Christmas you wanted?"

"I wasn't expecting Freddie's meltdown about Alaska. He knows too much about the world, especially about climate change, and that worries me."

"He's sensitive and smart. That's a dangerous combination and will probably lead to a lot of heartbreak."

"Or he could come up with a way to save humanity."

"That would be something, wouldn't it?" I mused.

We fell silent for a moment, watching the bubble lights.

"I'm almost afraid to ask, but did you have a good year? If I remember correctly, you proclaimed this year to be yours." Sarah shifted so she could stretch her legs onto the ottoman.

"It's been eventful. That's for sure. If you'd ask me what I thought was going to happen before the year started, never would I have come up with Calvin taking to ballet, adopting Snickers, going to Hershey, Maddie and Willow moving out, Peter moving in, and the biggest thing of all—telling Demi about her dad."

"It's been a lot, and you're forgetting the whole Alaskan cruise debacle."

"Blocking it out completely. Not my best moment. They don't have roller coasters on cruise ships, do they?"

"We can hope." She let out an evil laugh. "I don't know if your Alaska shenanigans were all that bad. I know it didn't turn out the way you wanted, and I have to admit that gives me some joy." She jabbed my side with her elbow. "It seems fitting.

To experience it all with everyone. Peter was really touched by you and the kids insisting he come along."

"Yes, well…" I was about to make a bogus statement about how I wanted to do something nice for my brother, but I could already tell Sarah was onto me. "You know I only did that because I thought it was unfair if he got to stay home in blissful silence while I suffered."

"I had a feeling. Do you regret it?"

"Not at all," I said with a laugh. "But not for the reasons I would have thought. I'm glad we get to spend time with him."

"Good. We're all family, doing our best to survive each day. As long as we have each other, life won't beat us."

"We'll need all the happiness we can get with everything that's coming next year."

"True. The world's probably going to end." There was a small chuckle but paired with a healthy dose of fear that was unusual for Sarah.

"Hey now." I pulled her closer, holding her tightly. "I'm supposed to be the dark one."

Sarah gave the top of my head another kiss. "Are you making any resolutions this year?"

"Not a one. I've learned my lesson. The best thing to do with this family is simply to get up each day and see what shit happens. It's never the same, so there's that."

"That's the Petrie spirit." She laughed, and I couldn't help but laugh right along.

"I'm lucky. To have all of you. Now—" I got to my feet, put my hand out, and hopefully waggled my brows seductively. "Let me show you how lucky." Sarah took my hand, a mischievous glint in her eye. "Oh? And how do you plan on doing that?"

I pulled her up from the couch, drawing her close. "Trust me, I have a few ideas."

"You always do," she replied before kissing me lightly on the lips. "You always do."

A HUGE THANK YOU!

Thanks so much for reading *Woman of the Year*!

This book was written in monthly installments as a benefit for TB and Miranda's Patreon subscribers in 2024. (While TB is listed as the author of this book for continuity with the rest of the A Woman Lost series, this project was co-written with Miranda.)

We couldn't have done this without the support of our generous Gold-level Patreon supporters, including: **Diva007, Jackie, Zaïna Adam, Patti B., Debster, Debbie, Georgia Becker Scheve, Kayla Bhadra, Marie Clifford, Julia, Rose H., Buzz, and Erin Wade.**

If you would like to get access to the duo's latest Patreon-exclusive projects, be sure to visit their Patreon group. There is plenty of weekly free content as well as paid member perks. Proceeds help to support TB and Miranda's joint venture I Heart SapphFic, a site dedicated to sapphic fiction.

You can find their Patreon group here: https://www.patreon.com/IHeartSapphFic

ABOUT THE AUTHOR

TB Markinson is an American who's recently returned to the US after a seven-year stint in the UK and Ireland. When she isn't writing, she's traveling the world, watching sports on the telly, visiting pubs in New England, or reading. Not necessarily in that order.

Along with writing partner Miranda MacLeod, TB co-owns *I Heart SapphFic*, a website for authors and readers of sapphic fiction to stay up-to-date on all the latest sapphic fiction news. The duo won Golden Crown Literary Awards for *The AM Show* in 2022 and for *Midlife is the Cat's Meow* in 2024.

Printed in Great Britain
by Amazon